Vena Cork is from Lancashire, but has lived in London all her adult life. She attended Homerton College, Cambridge, where she was a member of Cambridge Footlights. She is married to the art critic Richard Cork and lives in North West London. She is also the author of *Thorn*.

Praise for Vena Cork:

'There's more to this methodical psychological thriller than meets the eye. Look no further for a real sense of menace' *Mirror*

'Vena Cork skilfully builds a sinister feeling of menace surrounding her attractive heroine . . . an interesting and successful debut' *Telegraph*

'An outstanding debut' *Time Out*

'This is a compelling, if dark-hued, psychological thriller and first novel that eerily captures some of London's more sinister undercurrents and sense of menace' Maxim Jakubowski, *Guardian*

'One of those rare and energetic books you can't put down yet don't want to end' *The Times*

'You'll be gripped as this persuasive thriller races to its grisly conclusion' *Marie Claire*

'The reader is compelled to turn to the next page and then the next in a frantic attempt to discover who is perpetrating the chilling acts of evil' *Oxford Times*

'A tense pace combined with a tightly woven narrative makes this a surprisingly compelling debut'

D0210078

Also by Vena Cork

Thorn

THE ART OF DYING

Vena Cork

headline

First published in 2005
by HEADLINE BOOK PUBLISHING

First published in paperback in 2006
by HEADLINE BOOK PUBLISHING

A HEADLINE paperback

1

ISBN 0 7553 2397 1

Typeset in Electra by Palimpsest Book Production Limited,
Polmont, Stirlingshire

Printed and bound in Great Britain by
Clays Ltd, St Ives plc

HEADLINE BOOK PUBLISHING
A division of Hodder Headline
338 Euston Road
London NW1 3BH

www.headline.co.uk
www.hodderheadline.com

To Jean, with my love as always.

ACKNOWLEDGEMENTS

My gratitude and thanks to the following: Martin Fletcher and the many people at Headline whose excitement and enthusiasm are such a spur to action; my patient and invaluable agents, Lisa Moylett and Nathalie Sfakianos; and, of course, my friends and family whose love and support has, as always, been incalculable.

ONE

The past

The tip of the knife pricked his flesh, and as the longed-for liquid bloomed crimson across the expanse of naked belly, he gloried in the release.

But what seethed inside him was too powerful to be dissipated by one miserable cut. He was about to blow. The stream freed by the knife was a trickle compared to the white-hot magma flowing beneath his skin.

He paced the room, struggling to contain his rage. Catching sight of the Metallica poster over his bed he bellowed and charged at it, battering the wall with his head.

In the first term, when he heard the Lion spouting Heavy Metal mantras, all black leather and tangled mane, he'd revealed that he'd just bought the latest Metallica US import. Lion had ignored him. He was too busy bragging to his circle of adoring women. The Witch was the only one who'd responded. 'You a

Heavy Metal fan too?' she'd said. He'd nodded. She'd looked into his face. 'Heavy being the operative word,' she'd cackled in that harsh voice. Then, 'Lighten up, sunshine. It might never happen.' Everybody laughed and he'd slunk away as soon as he decently could.

That combination . . . teasing, or blanking. How often had he approached them in the bar only to find they were just leaving? 'See ya later.' The only time anyone ever seemed to register his existence was when he bought a round of drinks. Then it was, 'Cheers, mate,' before turning away and continuing their private conversations.

He heard moaning sounds, and realised they came from his own mouth. He made a couple more quick cuts. This time just above his belly button. Criss-crossing in a diamond pattern. His head hurt. Everything hurt.

Unendurable.

He collapsed onto his bed.

Three years of indifference and derision.

Three years of watching Her. Of living with the knowledge that she belonged to Warlord.

Three years of being the college joke: in amongst the mixed-media installations and abstract scrawlings, the moron who liked to paint properly. Even the tutors despised him.

Three years of people disrespecting him. Sneering and sniggering behind his back at the beautiful pictures he'd painted with such meticulous and photographic precision. Bastards who didn't know one end of a brush from another. Bastards who couldn't paint a proper picture if their lives depended on it. Trend-driven, bone-headed, trashy bastards.

THE ART OF DYING

What gave them the right to rubbish him?

He reckoned they took their lead from the Lion, the Witch and the Warlord, whose indifference had become a byword. People thought he didn't know. But he did.

Even She wasn't above it all. He'd seen her sly smile after one of the Witch's casually cruel cracks.

But he forgave Her. He'd forgive Her anything.

Even what She'd done this morning.

He'd spent weeks on the portrait, painting on thick paper with the miniature brushes that he'd bought specially. His eyes still felt strained from working on such a minute scale. But the end result was worth it. Perfection. The thought of parting with it was unbearable, but it had to be done. When She saw it she'd finally know how he felt.

He'd put it in her pigeon-hole and then waited. She'd come in with the Witch. Neither of them noticed him, hidden behind a revolving leaflet display. She looked briefly at a couple of circulars before discarding them and pulling out his painting. But her action coincided with the punchline of the Witch's story.

Hooting with laughter, she'd hardly glanced at the painting before chucking it in the bin with the rest of the rubbish.

'Anything interesting?' the Witch asked.

'Usual crap. Couple of flyers for clubs, and something that looks like amateur night at the local hair salon.'

'Not free hairdos? Never turn down a free hairdo. Let me at it.' The Witch had fished out his painting. 'It's not a flyer, you fool. It's a funny little painting. Looks like you.'

'Do me a favour,' She'd snorted, peering over the Witch's shoulder.

'Maybe it's a secret admirer.'

'Creepy.'

She scrumpled it up and threw it back into the bin.

Then they'd both left the office.

When it was safe he'd retrieved it and rushed back to his room. Where he'd been cutting and slicing ever since.

She'd hardened since the first year. Mixing with those other idiots, that's what it was. But what if she had known it was his gift? Even if she wasn't with Warlord she'd never go with him. No one would. What did he have to offer? Nothing. He was a worthless piece of shit who'd never amount to anything. Just like he'd always been told.

He started on his arms. Normally he avoided them, in case anybody clocked the scars. But today he didn't care. What was the point? His knife followed the delicate tracery of blood vessels under the skin on his wrists. Why not do it properly? Why not end the misery? Would anyone care? He remembered the huge palaver when Henry Moore died. And bloody Warhol. Both of them eulogised. Sanctified. Responsible as they were, like countless others in the last fifty years, for the death of real art. But him? No one would care about the passing of an unknown anachronism who loved painting things as they were. No one.

Why not finish it?

Why not?

Before he could change his mind, he plunged the blade deep into his arm. It hurt, but it was a good hurt. A good feeling. He lay back on the pillow and let the good feeling flow through him, waiting for oblivion.

As he watched the blood seeping out onto the sheet he did a final audit.

He listed off all the bad times.

The time when . . .

The time when . . .

The time when . . .

Dimly, he heard the sound of his room door bursting open and somebody saying, 'Oi, Wanka, got any grass?'

Then there was a silence followed by, 'Fuck!'

Then, finally, there was peace.

TWO

The present

I don't believe in ghosts. But last night I saw one anyway.

It was the ghost of my dead husband, Rob. He was on the outside looking in. Just like he saw himself in life.

The evening had been a triumph. Rob's triumph. Maybe that's what drew him back from the underworld.

When Larry L'Estrange, Rob's dealer – or 'gallerist', as I gather he likes to be called nowadays – had suggested mounting a memorial show, I was against the idea. Not because I didn't want the world to see the last paintings of my dead love. More that I couldn't bear to be parted from them.

They were all I had left – apart from Danny and Anna.

But Larry had persuaded me that exhibiting Rob's work didn't mean losing it. He said it was enough to simply show it, and that later – when I was ready – there would be a market for the work, made up of people who'd seen and loved the memorial exhibition. Since Larry was the most powerful dealer in London, I decided I'd be foolish not to take his advice.

Which was why last night found me standing in the white cathedral vastness of Larry's new gallery in Hoxton, viewing the London art world viewing each other and, occasionally, Rob's last canvases.

Rob would have been proud of the turnout. I'd like to think it was because of the brilliance of his work, but I know that a fair number had come because of the circumstances surrounding the last eighteen months of the Robin Thorn story: his tragic death caused by a hit and run driver, and the attempted murder of his wife and daughter – me and Anna. As I stood with my children in the corner of the huge space, I was aware that the furtive glances aimed in our direction almost exceeded the attention being afforded to my husband's paintings.

Which was a pity because I thought they looked stunning.

Larry's new gallery had been built in the 1890s as a canning factory, and the conversion by a fashionable architect had retained the original Art Nouveau ironwork. The most striking feature was the long rows of ornate wrought-iron columns that marched diagonally across the massive space. My comparison to a cathedral was not misplaced. The room was a sacred space dedicated to the new religion – money, posing seductively in its winsome guise of art.

The canvases hung round the edge of the room: monumental paintings, executed with painstaking veracity. Before his death, Rob's claim to fame had been that he only ever painted closed doors. Many articles had been written by various learned critics, surmising the reasons why the doors were closed.

They would have a field day with Rob's last show. For in these works, the doors were partially open.

Not a lot. Just a crack really, with nothing more than a tantalising glimpse of what lay behind. But open, nonetheless.

I decided not to mention the ghost to Danny and Anna. They thought I was batty enough as it was, without me bringing intimations of the supernatural into the equation. I contented myself with pointing out the various groups of glitterati who'd seen fit to grace Rob's show on this hot summer evening. Not that my children were easily impressed. The glimpse of the *capo di capi* of all the Tates chatting to media and property tycoon, David Borodino, meant nothing to them. The plentiful and delicious trays of canapés caused them far more excitement than the moment when Tracey Emin accidentally tipped her drink down Danny's shirt, and the only time I witnessed Anna becoming even slightly uncool was when she thought she spotted the lead singer of the latest hot boy band slinking into the Gents.

'Go after him, Danny.'

'And say what?'

'I don't know, do I? Whatever blokes say in loos.'

'Something like "Big dick you've got there, mate. Wanna swop?"'

'Don't be crude.'

At that moment Gillian Gerard materialised. Gillian is the art critic of the *Correspondent*, and she wrote the catalogue introduction to Rob's show. Over the past couple of months we've become good friends, and are now teetering on the edge of exchanging the major disclosures about our lives that would take the friendship up to the next level of intimacy.

As Anna and Danny wandered off in search of nibbles, she watched them elbow their way across the crowded room.

'Look at that woman staring at Danny. She wants to eat him up. When did you say he was going to be eighteen?'

'September. Three days after Anna's fifteenth.'

'He's been trying to explain to me the merits, demerits and differences between UK garage, hip-hop and rap. He was very patient. Even offered a demonstration if I'd care to come to tea at yours one day.'

'You're very honoured. He normally considers anyone over the age of twenty beyond redemption when it comes to musical taste. We must fix up a tea-party straight away.'

'God, Rosa, I hope you didn't think I was fishing for an invitation.' She laughed, but underneath the laughter I heard embarrassment. Our burgeoning friendship had been conducted in various coffee-shops and wine bars within walking distance of the gallery, and was a light-hearted affair based on our common wish to do Rob proud, and a shared sense of the absurd. A couple of times I'd nearly asked her over for supper, but somehow never quite got round to it. I wondered why. Was it because Gillian was a high-profile critic and I didn't want to appear pushy, or was it my feeling that behind her sociable exterior lurked an intensely private person only interested in a superficial work-based friendship?

Or maybe it was me who was signalling so far and no further. I was so keen to avoid people's pity and appear self-sufficient and on top of things – places to go, people to see – that perhaps she'd misinterpreted me as someone who wasn't into making serious new friends. If that was the case, I'd better put her straight. Since

Rob's death I'd come to value my friendships more than ever.

'Don't be daft – I've been meaning to ask you for ages.'

She smiled. I couldn't tell whether she believed me or not.

'You're on,' she said. 'Provided Danny promises to play his guitar.'

Gillian has a real rapport with youngsters. Her ability to tune into their experience is one of the reasons she's acquired a legendary reputation for identifying important and interesting new art, unlike many critics of her age who get stuck championing the art which was current during their prime.

She has no children of her own. I'm almost at the stage in our friendship when I could ask why, but if ever our conversation strays into that area I sense an avoidance that discourages probing. However, she's renowned for mothering young, inexperienced artists and writers still floundering in their attempts to swim in the murky pond of the London art world.

'Are you pleased with the show?'

'It's brilliant. Rob would have been thrilled. And he'd have loved your essay.'

'That stuff you told me, about leaving Trinidad, and being in care – the paintings make total sense when you know that. I wonder, if he'd lived, how wide those doors would have opened . . . What do you think?'

I'd kept my feelings under control until now. Felt quite detached, in fact. But under Gillian's sympathetic eye I felt the façade crumbling. Rob wasn't here. He'd never hear the great Gillian Gerard calling him one of the foremost painters of his generation. He'd never see Damien Hirst in heated debate with Rhona Peebles and Alan Blow over the nature of death, inspired by *Mortuary Door*, one of his last works. And he'd never know that Mike Mason, his best buddy at art school, and now one of the giants of contemporary painting, had made the trip from Los Angeles especially to see his show. I spotted Mike the moment he entered the gallery. He was very difficult to miss. At six foot five, with his thatch of blond hair, he was, in every sense, larger than life. I saw Anna rush over to him, and smiled as he swung her round, shouting with pleasure.

He looked so alive.

And Rob was so dead.

'Do you believe in ghosts?'

Gillian raised her eyebrows.

'What if I told you I'd seen Rob's ghost staring in through the gallery window. Would you think I was mad?'

In her compassionate blue eyes I saw deep pools of sadness.

'After Peter died I spotted him three times on the Northern line, twice in the V and A, once, fleetingly, in Selfridges Food Hall and on countless occasions walking down Lamb's Conduit Street into the butchers. Strange, since he was a lifelong vegetarian.'

Gillian's husband, a professor of psychology at University College London, had died unexpectedly of a massive stroke five years ago. He was sixty, a year older than Gillian, who was so bereft when it happened that she went to bed and didn't get up for three months. She didn't usually talk about him, so this quiet revelation was a big step forward.

'So my ghost is just wishful thinking?'

'Well, you do wish Rob was here, don't you?'

'More than anything.'

She gave my arm a gentle squeeze. 'There you go, then.'

'Hi, Gillian.' The voice came from way below.

Gillian grinned. 'Leni! I'm so glad you could make it. Rosa, this is Leni Dang. She does listings for the *Correspondent*, and she's recently launched her own column in *Dame* magazine. Impressive for one so young, don't you think?'

A wisp of a girl blinked up at us. Her plain face with its rather heavy jawline was redeemed by almond-shaped, velvet-black eyes, and immaculate if somewhat thick make-up. Her boyish figure was covered in something clingy and cutting-edge, and the street cred extended to her shoulder-length black bob which had a streak of magenta running through it.

'Leni, may I introduce Rosa Thorn, Rob's wife.'

'I love your husband's work.' Her voice was low and husky and at variance with her slight frame.

'Thanks.'

'Actually, Mrs Thorn, I have a favour to ask.' She gazed up imploringly. 'May I interview you about Robin for *Dame*?'

Dame was top dog at the moment. Its edgy mixture of fashion, style and comment made it Metro Woman's must-have magazine.

'I'd love to.'

'Fantastic!' But then her face fell. She turned to Gillian. 'I'm not treading on any toes here, am I? I'd hate you to think I was muscling in on your patch.'

'Leni, my sweet, I don't do interviews. Show me the work and I'll show you the person – that's my motto. In interviews those monstrous artistic egos get in the way.'

'Gee, thanks.'

'Not you, Rosa, you silly arse. In any case, Leni, since I've done the catalogue essay that'll be my lot. So go for it.'

Leni was ecstatic.

'Not that anything I write could ever match one of your columns.' She turned to me. 'If I could write one piece about art as good as any of hers, I'd die happy.'

Clearly one of Gillian's more eager protégées.

'Cool it,' I warned her. 'You'll make her head swell so much she won't be able to get out of the door.'

Gillian pouted. 'She's just jealous, Leni. Give me more – I love it.'

'You would, you vicious old hag.'

A man thrust himself towards Gillian. His eyes were bloodshot, his thick black hair unkempt, and facial hair beyond designer stubble yet not quite a proper beard lay like a disfigurement across his handsome face. He wore a dirty sweatshirt over torn jeans and his breath stank of spirits.

'What's it like having people always licking your fat arse?' he went on. 'Makes you think you can dump all over the rest of us, does it? Do you get off on rubbishing people's life's work?'

Suddenly I'd strayed into a different movie.

'You don't even know who I fucking am, do you?'

'I'm sorry, I—'

'Fucking ironic – she destroys my life and she doesn't know me from bleeding Adam.'

I thought he was going to hit her. During my recent spell as a schoolteacher we were always told by our unions not to intervene in fights in case we got thumped by the miscreant or sued by his parents, but the instinctive urge to restore order usually intervened. It did so now. I grabbed the man by his grubby shirt. 'Stop it!'

'Steve!'

It was Caroline Sanders, Larry's assistant. The sound of her voice had an immediate effect. The man backed away from Gillian.

Caroline took him by the arm. 'Come on.' As she led him towards the back office she turned and mouthed, 'Sorry.'

The incident only lasted for a few seconds. No one else had noticed. The convivial hum continued unabated.

'What,' I said eventually, 'was that all about?'

'Are you OK, Gillian?' Leni's husky voice trembled.

Gillian's face was pale. 'Steve Pyne,' she said.

The name was familiar.

'Isn't he a video artist?'

'Yes. I recently reviewed his show at the Ikon Gallery in Birmingham. I wasn't terribly complimentary.'

'So what? Does he think that being an artist means it's OK to behave like an angry toddler? I'm going to give him a piece of my mind!'

'Leave it, Rosa. He's as drunk as a skunk anyway. He'll be mortified when he sobers up – if he remembers, which is doubtful.'

Gillian was a lot more charitable than I'd have been under similar circumstances.

Just then, Caroline reappeared. She's a familiar stereotype: the upper-class gel who works in a gallery for peanuts, before marrying well and going to live in the country. But unlike other young women of her kind who are simply passing time until Mr Right appears, Caroline adores her job. She's a huge asset to Larry, adding not only brains and class to his outfit, but showing its human, caring face. She's also a necessary antidote to Julian, Larry's other assistant, whose waspish devotion to their boss often leads to extreme-crisis scenarios. For Caro it's not a job, it's a vocation. One day she wants to open her own gallery. Then watch out, Larry! She's the person I've worked with most closely in the run-up to the show, and I've developed a huge respect for her commonsense and good humour.

No humour now. 'Gillian, I am so, so sorry,' she said. 'Steve's just having a really hard time at the moment.'

'Not your fault, Caro,' Gillian sighed. 'It's my job to duck when angry artists don't like what I write. Goes with the territory. He's one of Larry's, isn't he?'

'Was. Larry dumped him last week.'

'Ah.'

'He thinks it's because of your piece, but that's not true.' Caroline hesitated. 'Steve's got an alcohol problem. He'd taken to drinking himself stupid in the Groucho then rolling up to our other space in Vigo Street and insulting everybody, including our major collectors. In the past, Larry's been Steve's staunchest defender, but last Tuesday the shit hit the fan. Someone told him that Steve was claiming he'd cheated him out of loads of money, whereas the truth is that Larry's actually lent Steve thousands of pounds to tide him over between shows. Anyway, Larry finally snapped and gave him the boot. I love Larry to bits, but he does bear grudges. One word from him and no other dealer will touch Steve.'

'Sounds like you're well rid of him,' I said.

'The gallery is. I'm not. He's my boyfriend.'

Whoops. Rosa Thorn's first *faux pas* of the evening, but probably not her last. I've always possessed the uncanny ability to put my foot right in it. But how was I to know that plain, staid Caro, with her county tweeds and alice bands, would ever go out with an exotic scruff like Steve Pyne?

Caroline noted my surprise. 'You're not the first to wonder why an old-fashioned girl like me's involved with a wild boy like him,' she said, 'but that's because you don't know the real Steve. Underneath all the aggro he's really sensitive and caring. Besides, I've always been turned on by talent, and Steve's got masses of that.'

'You never told me about you and him.'

Caroline gave me her gentle smile. 'You never asked.'

Then Julian pounced on her. 'Larry's doing the speech in about five minutes, so can you mingle – make sure everyone listens. We don't want a repeat of the Vigo Street débâcle.' He turned to me. 'Larry had to stand on the table to make himself heard. So undignified.'

He darted off, and we watched him meeting and greeting, his thin body in its glittering designer jacket working the crowd like a summer dragonfly skimming a lake. Caroline followed.

From across the room Mike Mason waved at me.

'I must say hello to Mike,' I told Gillian. 'Are you sure you're all right?'

Gillian laughed. 'It takes more than that to bother an old boiler like me. Besides, I want to pump Leni for all the inside goss on *Dame*.'

Mike was chatting to Jess Mackenzie, my oldest and dearest

friend. She and Mike knew each other from way back when we were all at college, Jess and I doing drama, and Rob and Mike in the art school.

'Wotcher, Rosy. Give us a kiss.'

Mike always had sackloads of charisma. Even when he was poor and struggling he could light up a room. But success and wealth had given him a polish and a gloss that was new. He'd acquired an American drawl with an upward inflexion at the end of sentences and, along with his tan, he displayed a West Coast confidence that was almost too much. Almost, but not quite.

'How long's it been, baby? Too long.' His face changed. 'I'm gutted I couldn't come over for the funeral. One of those things. They were naming a new wing of an art school in Nevada after me. The Michael Mason Wing. Cool, huh?'

'You're here now,' I said between gritted teeth. I'd forgotten how Mike's mixture of vanity and charm wound me up. But it was good to see him. Jess thought so too. I could see a sparkle in her eyes that certainly hadn't been there earlier.

'We aren't your little Yankee cheerleaders, Michael Mason. Rosa and I have known you since you and Rob only had one pair of shoes between you and had to take turns going to class.'

Mike sighed. 'A prophet is without honour blah blah . . .' Then he became serious. 'The show's a wow. This is Rob's best stuff ever. I can't believe—'

He couldn't carry on. I put my arms round him and Jess, and we all clung together: three middle-aged people remembering being twenty when there were four of us and life stretched ahead, excitingly unknowable.

Our group hug was interrupted by loud shouting. Unlike his

attack on Gillian, Steve Pyne's next attempt at ruining the evening was much more high-profile. The room fell silent as he launched into Larry L'Estrange.

'My work not good enough for you, fuck-face? Know what – I don't give a shit. I just want the dosh you still owe me, you parasitic crook.'

Caroline pulled him away, but he swung out, jabbing his elbow into her face.

'Enough!'

David Borodino.

Not that that cut any ice with Steve.

'The voice of the nation! How many suckers have to buy your stinking rag for you to make enough cash to buy a painting by one crap dead artist?' He gestured towards one of Rob's paintings. 'This is what I think of you, you filthy capitalist leech.'

He flung his glass of red wine over the millionaire.

A collective intake of breath rippled through the room. Borodino's drenched face was a mask of cold fury.

'Please, Steve.' Caroline attempted to restrain him, but he staggered towards the exit, people parting like the Red Sea at his approach.

Then he saw Leni Dang. He lurched forward, and grabbed her. Once again Caroline tried to intervene.

'Steve—'

'Fuck off. I've had it with your clinging and moaning. You're a dried-up old prune, way past your sell-by date. I fancy a bit of oriental pussy for a change. Give us a kiss, Tiger Lily.'

He clamped his mouth over Leni's and began kneading her breast. This broke the spell which had paralysed the room. A waiter, rushing forward, pulled him off Leni and punched him hard. Then Larry's security guard materialised and frog-marched him out into the street. Caroline, her face the colour of a particularly brilliant sunset, took Leni into the back room, while Larry spirited David Borodino away to his inner sanctum, and Julian in his most officious tones informed us all that everything was under control.

Crap dead artist?

Note to self: don't add Steve Pyne to the Christmas card list.

'Remind me to advise Caroline to get a new boyfriend,' I said to Jess.

'No one's going to forget Rob's last show in a hurry,' said Mike.

He was right. Some people were already outside on their mobiles, spreading the word. I could see them through the big window, pacing up and down as they laughed and gesticulated.

Would Rob's ghost take vengeance on Steve Pyne for insulting him and upstaging his evening? No. Rob would have found the whole thing hilarious – 'part of life's rich brew', to use one of his favourite phrases.

After a suitable interval, Larry reappeared and Julian ostentatiously tapped his glass. The room fell silent and Larry began speaking, his soft pedantic tones echoing round the vast space.

'We are so glad you could all join us tonight in celebrating the work of Robin Thorn. As you know, Rob was tragically killed in a road accident last year, and the world has thus been deprived of one of our greatest emerging talents. Who knows what he might have achieved, had he lived. However, it gives us enormous pleasure to share with you his last works, completed in the six months before he died. We think you will agree that these pictures change and deepen enormously our understanding of the man and his *oeuvre*. We're also very happy to welcome Rosa, Rob's wife, who is here tonight with his children, Daniel and Anna. Without Rosa's close collaboration and support this show would not have been possible. Thank you, Rosa. And now please raise your glasses to the memory of Robin Thorn.'

As the art world toasted my husband, I glanced through the window. There he stood, separated by only a sheet of glass and the grave, Rob's ghost, staring in at his party.

The time when . . .

. . . the tutor had finally lost it.

'What fucking century are you living in? If you love the past so much, at least use it in a contemporary context.'

Then the shit had flung a catalogue at him. The title said Of Mutability.

'Read this – Helen Chadwick's take on the Vanitas genre. But totally up to date. Totally now. Not this archaic crap you've been peddling for the last couple of years. I'm sick of it. Don't show your face in this studio till you've made something that's part of this century.'

For once he felt visible. Too visible. Everyone was looking at him. There was an uncomfortable silence. They were used to tantrums from their teachers, many of whom were frustrated artists, but not this one. He was usually sweet reason itself.

Then Warlord had come over. The sympathy in his eyes was far worse than his usual indifference.

'Give the fucker what he wants, Wanka. It's easier.'

He'd stayed in the studio after they'd all gone. Paralysed. Listening to the ringing in his ears. Eventually he'd picked up the catalogue. The work was a fucking installation. A room containing a pool with pillars round the side. In the pool were photocopied cut-outs of Chadwick and other things – animals, fruit, bits of jewellery. All the traditional Vanitas symbols of mortality and decay. She was using her own body as a symbol of mutability.

Something he would never do.

His body would never be an art object.

Certainly not a photocopied cut-out.

It was crap. Shallow art crap.

He'd thrown the catalogue to the floor. His eye had fallen on a jar of dirty paintwater. He'd picked it up and poured the sludgy contents over the tasteful cover.

'Now that's mutability.'

He'd looked at his latest painting, still wet and vulnerable on the easel. Then he stretched out his hand and smeared his fingers across the canvas.

'So's that,' he said before quitting the room.

'Give the fucker what he wants, Wanka. It's easier.'

Is that what you did, Warlord?

THREE

After the private view came the dinner. Larry had invited about twenty of us – my family plus Jess, Mike and Gillian, his two assistants, a couple of collectors, and assorted art world people including a curator from Tate Modern, a PR woman and a brace of critics. Leni Dang was a last-minute addition. Larry no doubt wanted to compensate her for the Steve Pyne incident.

The meal was at *Zizz*, a restaurant opposite the gallery. It's one of those fashionable places which have sprung up over the past decade to cater for the media crowds flocking East. Larry regards it as his personal dining room, and in fact it was staff from *Zizz* who'd waited on us at the private view.

I was placed next to him, and on my other side was a man I recognised without being able to put a name to him. He was around forty and expensively dressed, all in black. He could have been an ageing male model with his slim figure, thin sculpted face and smooth complexion which extended up into the polished dome of his shaved head. He had one of those pencil beards around the edge of the face, with a branch line diverting over the top lip. Lenin's better-looking capitalist cousin. I'd noticed him at the private view, weaving through the crowd in a cloud of goodwill. He seemed to be everybody's best friend.

'Zander Zinovieff,' he said. 'I run the gallery next door to Larry – *Nature Morte*.'

Everyone had heard of *Nature Morte*. No wonder I recognised him. He and his gallery featured regularly in the weekend Style magazines. Interviews with celebrities in their highly desirable homes invariably displayed one or more pictures from his gallery on their walls. *Nature Morte* was *the* place to acquire instant art chic. Art as wallpaper for the expensive apartments of the metropolitan elite. Commodity Art, that's what Gillian calls it. She's particularly scathing about *Nature Morte*.

'I specialise in the modern still-life,' he went on, 'photography and painting – although I recently decided to diversify. From now on I'm widening my remit to include other art forms.'

'Lovely,' I said hypocritically.

As I hunted desperately for a follow-up comment, Jess came to my rescue.

Or not.

I'd been really pleased to find her sitting opposite me. In this arcane gathering she represented normality, and I was looking forward to our post-show post-mortem. But now I wasn't so sure. She'd put back a fair number of drinks at the private view and Jess under the influence was highly volatile. Rob's thirtieth birthday and an incident concerning table dancing, black olives and a Spanish waiter came to mind. I crossed my fingers and banished the image.

She stared at Zander.

'You so remind me of someone,' she said, her voice over-loud. 'Have we met?'

Zander wore the guarded smile of one who recognises inebriated unpredictability and is doing a lightning calculation on how to deal with it.

'I don't think so. What great earrings. They go so well with the dress.'

Jess preened. 'I wanted a matching necklace, but there's a six-month waiting list.'

'Did you buy them from *Glotch*?'

Jess shrieked. 'How did you know?'

'I recognise the house-style. Do you know Selena?'

'Selena?'

'The owner. She's a friend. I could ask her about the necklace. I'm sure I could prise one out of her.'

'Fantastic.' Jess was ecstatic. She adores baubles. I call her my pet jackdaw. 'Are you *sure* we haven't met?' Then she laughed in recognition. 'I know – it's Lenin!' She turned to David Borodino next to her. 'Doesn't he look like Lenin?' She was burbling now, but Borodino listened to her with immaculate courtesy.

Zander gave me a self-deprecating smile. 'She probably saw the feature in the *Observer* last month. People remember the face but can't remember why. I was talking to Carol about it only the other day and she said total strangers often greet her as their oldest and dearest friend.'

'Carol?'

'Vorderman. Great mate of mine. Do you know her?'

'No.'

'You'd get on like a house on fire – I'll introduce you.'

After listening to several more tales involving Zander's intimate familiarity with celebrity, my attention drifted. I became aware that Jess was interrogating David Borodino.

'Taken over any good companies lately?'

She was forthright enough when she was sober. What she might say to Borodino after several drinks didn't bear thinking about. Her rampant socialist conscience wouldn't let her sit next to one of our foremost capitalists without delivering some sort of lefty harangue.

But Borodino was well-used to dealing with the Jesses of this world.

'I gather you're one of Rob Thorn's oldest friends,' he said, and proceeded to draw her out with a practised ease. Cynical Jess became simpering putty in the man's hands.

Then I noticed Caroline. Her face looked drawn as she got up and made for the Ladies. I followed. She was rinsing her face.

'Caro?'

'He didn't mean those things he said about Rob. Or about me.'

No?

'Course he didn't.'

'He ruined Rob's opening. I'm so sorry, Rosa.'

'Are you kidding? He made sure no one will ever forget it.'

'It was awful. You know it was.'

'I'm calling you a cab.'

'But Larry—'

'Leave Larry to me.'

Caroline struggled to smile. 'Now the show's opened, you won't be around much. I'll really miss you.'

'Me too.'

'Let's not lose touch.'

I felt suddenly sad. As an actor I'm used to working intimately with people for short periods, and then moving on. But this time I didn't want to swear the usual insincere theatrical vows of eternal friendship. Caroline, like Gillian, was someone I genuinely didn't want to lose.

'I'll call you very soon.'

I helped her find a cab, then slipped back into my seat next to Larry.

'Caroline has a stinking headache,' I murmured, 'so I've sent her home. I said you wouldn't want her sitting here suffering.'

'Poor love. If she'd spoken up, we'd have let her go hours ago.'

Yeah right, Larry.

Then he fixed me with a gimlet eye. 'We do hope you're happy with the show.'

'You know I am.'

'We think the paintings look magnificent. We're delighted to be inaugurating the new gallery with the work of such a superb artist.'

'And I can't thank you enough for making it all possible.'

'We strive to serve,' he said. 'Now, Rosa, I wanted to ask you something . . .'

Here we go.

'We agreed not to sell until you feel ready. Is that still the case?'

I'd let Larry mount the show on the understanding that the work wasn't for sale. After his death I couldn't look at Rob's paintings; they were too much *him*. But when finally I made the leap,

I found I couldn't bear the thought of ever losing them. I knew one day I'd have to sell – the Thorn finances were not great – but I wanted it to be at my own pace. So what was Larry going on about?

'Why should you imagine my feelings have changed?'

'It's our duty to tell you that a certain someone is most interested in purchasing several of the larger canvases. Someone who's willing to pay way over and above their current market value. Naturally, it's entirely your decision . . .'

'You promised I needn't sell.'

Larry's mouth tightened. 'Indeed. And I always honour my promises.'

'Who wants them, anyway?'

Why couldn't I keep my big mouth shut? Now Larry would think he was in with a chance. He inclined his head imperceptibly.

'David Borodino.'

So? I still wasn't selling. End of story.

Borodino had extricated himself from the Jessica Mackenzie life-story, and was now chatting to the person on his other side: Leni Dang. I could see that a flirtation had been initiated, which appeared to be giving great satisfaction to both parties.

He must have sensed my scrutiny, for he suddenly switched his attention from Leni to me. His dark eyes met mine and he smiled. Somehow he set up an intimacy between us before even opening his mouth.

'David Borodino,' he said.

As if I wouldn't know.

'Your husband was a very fine painter.'

'Yes.'

'You must miss him.'

'Yes.'

'I gather the work isn't for sale at the moment.'

'No.'

'If they were mine, I wouldn't want to part with them either.'

I felt strangely tongue-tied. I'm not generally impressed by fame and fortune, but Borodino was different. His rags to riches story was a legend. The son of dirt-poor immigrants from Turkey, he'd worked in a chicken factory day and night till he had enough money to put a deposit on a terraced house in a road scheduled for redevelopment. Eventually a big conglomerate, wanting to build a multiplex cinema and leisure centre, bought up the other houses in the terrace. Only Borodino was left. They gave him ten times the value of his original investment. With the profits, he started his own business that within fifteen years became the biggest property company in Britain. Then he diversified into the media with the purchase of the *Correspondent* and a couple of TV stations. He was notorious for his unorthodox and brilliant business methods, and his jet-setting, adventurous lifestyle.

And here he was, sitting opposite me.

I was intrigued to see mega-money up close. In Borodino's case, it manifested itself as a sleekness which extended from his coffee-coloured skin to his dark, thick, wavy hair and deepset eyes. He exuded an air of understated confidence. This man didn't have to shout or bluster. The merest arch of his eyebrows was enough to send people scurrying to gratify his every wish.

But not me.

'I may sell one or two eventually,' I said. 'But not any time soon.'

Borodino smiled. 'I can wait, Mrs Thorn.'

He turned back to Leni. 'Did you inherit those wonderful eyes from your mother . . . ?'

I felt quite bereft when his attention left me and had to restrain myself from saying something dazzling to get it back again. So this was charisma, I thought. The man had it in spades.

Later, Zander Zinovieff was telling me about the time David Bowie had nearly bought up an entire exhibition from him and then changed his mind at the last minute, when Jess interrupted.

'I know who you remind me of,' she said. 'A male Meryl Streep.'

I remembered this game of old. Mike would chip in at any moment. Right on cue, he called down the table, 'Not a male Meryl Streep. A thin Pavarotti.'

'No!' cried Jess. 'A young Santa Claus.'

Conversation ceased as everyone tuned into Jess and Mike.

Zander, an object of general scrutiny, clearly didn't know how to respond to the teasing. For someone who'd spent a considerable amount of time over the past hour dropping names and indicating how intimate he was with the great and the good, he seemed remarkably gauche now the spotlight was on him.

'It's a stupid game we played when we were students,' I said. 'It can be quite funny.'

My explanation sounded pretty lame, but Zander took the cue. He even tried to join in when Jess and Mike extended the game to others at the table, although his clumsy attempts at humour fell on stony ground when he compared David Borodino to a male Shirley Temple. An anger of such ferocity that it made me flinch flashed across the magnate's smooth features. It was gone in a split second, and I thought I'd imagined it until I became aware that Larry was muttering into my ear.

'Not a good idea to question David's manhood. These foreign chaps and their machismo. Female equals weak equals failure, and people like him have to win. Be advised, Rosa, if that man wants something, he usually gets it.'

'What do you mean?'

Larry toyed fastidiously with a discarded prawn. 'An observation, my dear. That's all.'

'Are you implying he'd do something dodgy in order to get his hands on Rob's paintings?'

'We're merely commenting that he can be very persuasive.'

'And I can be very obstinate,' I said. 'I'll sell Rob's work when I'm ready. Do David Bloody Borodino good not to get his own way for once.'

Larry shrugged. 'Your decision, my dear,' he said, and turned to the American collector with an observation about the latest show at the Gagosian Gallery, New York.

As the evening drew to a close I wondered what Rob would have made of it. I decided he'd have relished every minute. Rob loved to party. And seeing his paintings hung in Larry's new gallery, the toast of the town – he would have loved that too.

As I climbed into a cab with Danny, Anna and Jess, I took one last look at the paintings behind the huge window of *L'Estrange East*. It was then that I saw the ghost again.

A bolt of fear crashed through me.

I'd been here before.

* * *

Weak with exhaustion, Gillian Gerard kicked off her shoes and settled down with a hot cup of cocoa and a couple of Prozac. Once more she'd fooled everyone. Nice, funny Gillian – always game for a laugh – everyone's favourite aunty. Once more she'd tottered across the tightrope of her precarious moodswings and avoided plunging into the gulf of despair waiting to drag her down into its black depths.

This was the best bit – reviewing things from the safety of her cosy little haven. The evening had, in spite of her fears, gone jolly well. She'd had splendid feedback on her catalogue essay, and Rob Thorn's paintings looked very fine in Larry's spanking new gallery.

The Thorns . . . what a nice family they were. Rosa was the first person she'd met in ages whose friendship she'd wanted to pursue. Now the work that had brought them together was complete, it would be easy to do as she'd done with most people since Peter died – let things slide. But Rosa was different. Gillian really liked her. She didn't know whether it was her finely-honed sense of the absurd, her refreshing lack of respect for the fads and foibles of the art world, or the fact that they had widowhood in common. She'd ask Rosa out to lunch soon.

'So stop accusing me of being an old recluse,' she said to the photo of Peter which sat on the occasional table next to her.

She knew people would think this one-sided conversation with a dead man a bit strange, but she didn't care. When Peter was alive they'd always had a glass of wine before dinner and mulled over the events of the day. Talking to his photograph was her way of perpetuating that. Like a child's comforter. It kept her sane.

'As have you, my lovely.' She picked up the tattered reproduction next to Peter's photo: the only known image of Elena Dias, subject of Gillian's magnum opus – the book she'd begun to write in an attempt to lift herself out of the despair that had engulfed her after Peter's death. Started as a form of therapy, it had become utterly engrossing. Gillian spent every free moment researching and writing. She'd never been a raging feminist in the 1970s when many of her fellow female art historians set out to rehabilitate the women the world had forgotten, but now Elena's story touched her in ways that she couldn't quite fathom.

She contemplated the girl's haunting eyes, which dominated her thin face.

'Don't worry, my lovely,' she whispered. 'One day the world will understand the sacrifices you made. I'll make sure of that.'

Am I not The Man?

Mike Mason leaned back in the plush interior of his car and watched London flow smoothly past. Coming back for Rob's opening had been a toss-up. He'd known he ought to, for the sake of Auld Lang Syne and respect and all, but up till the last minute he hadn't committed. Always keep your options open. That way you didn't miss out if something better cropped up. But he'd made it. Nobody could accuse him of not supporting his friends. As a feel-good factor, the evening rated pretty highly. He experienced a righteous glow. Rosa was thrilled he'd made the effort. So was Jess. And although virtue was its own reward, it looked like he'd done some excellent business too. And made contact with the powerful Larry L'Estrange, which was no bad thing.

You are The Man.

33

He stretched out his long legs, luxuriating in the space. One of the perks of wealth meant never having to squeeze his giant frame into a shoebox when travelling.

The pleasure of being loaded.

The pleasure of feeling pleased with oneself. Pleased to gratify old friends. Pleased to be received by the London art world as the returning hero. Pleased to be alive when contemplating the alternative as illustrated by Rob, whose show, he had a sneaking suspicion, he'd slightly upstaged by his own towering presence.

He toyed with the idea of calling his favourite agency and asking them to send a girl to the hotel. But maybe not. Maybe it was time to turn over a new leaf. Go back to basics. After all, London was basics. It was where he'd started out. Unlike California, London was real, and it was no bad thing to court reality for a change. The past was another country that he had no urge to revisit . . . but the present could kill the past. Make things how they always should have been.

The room swirled round as the cut-glass voice drilled into his head. *'Sit up. Take your clothes off. Lie on the bed instead of the floor.'*

Why couldn't she leave him alone? She was always on at him. She wasn't his fucking mother, although nobody'd guess it, the way she carried on. She looked like his mother too. Fucking minger. Not like that other girl. He tried to pluck her image from his spinning brain, but he couldn't. Little. Dark. Oriental. Luscious. He wanted some. He wanted a fresh little chicken, not a stringy old hen in twinset and pearls. Then he found he was sobbing. Poor old Caro. She didn't deserve a shit like him. A washed-up has-been who'd destroyed every chance he was given. Dumped on everyone who'd ever tried to help him. He wanted to make her proud. Show her what he was capable of. He'd show them all. He'd get back on his feet again. He knew things about fucking L'Estrange that would make the guy fall over himself to welcome him back into the fold. Or maybe he'd get another dealer. Someone who'd understand him. Who'd support him. Who'd know that genius couldn't live on hot air. Maybe he'd go and see Zinovieff. He'd be thrilled to take him on. He'd give him a show. Wouldn't that be something? Right next door to fucking Larry. And everyone would come. Zinovieff's PR machine was legendary. He'd be a sensation. Bigger than bloody Robin Thorn. Bigger than any of them. Larry would beg him to come back. But no. 'Piss off,' he'd say. 'Piss off, faggot breath. After you've paid me what you owe me.'

Then the floor came up to meet him and he puked again.

He called for Caro. He called and called but she didn't come. She'd gone. Abandoned him. What if he choked on his own vomit? Then she'd be sorry. Selfish cow. Who needed her? He fucking didn't. He didn't need anyone. He'd manage. He wept as he contemplated struggling manfully through life all alone. The pathos of it. His head felt like a bowling ball – too heavy to hold up. If Madame Butterfly was here, she'd hold his head for him. She'd look after him. She wouldn't desert him. Fuck Caro. Fuck Larry. Fuck them all. He'd show them. He wasn't finished yet. Not by a long way.

FOUR

On this beautiful morning, shimmering with summer heat, thoughts of the supernatural seem absurd. Danny, Anna and I laid Rob's ghost months ago when we scattered his ashes over a clifftop in Wales. We've all begun to move on with our lives, and this summer, unlike the last agonised wasteland, beckons, full of promise. Anna's going to India for the holidays with the family of her friend Laxmi, and Danny, with his friends Delroy and Dwaine, is going with their band, 3D, to a music festival in Bulgaria. And my first role in a police drama series is soon to be aired on the BBC. As yet my agent hasn't been inundated with any more tempting offers, but we live in hope.

This bright July day had better fulfill its early promise, because I'm doing a barbecue for the family, Jess and her son, and Mike Mason. Anna and Danny both leave tomorrow, and I want to give them a proper send-off. It will be the first time I've been parted from both of them at the same time, for more than a few days, and it feels like a big deal.

Also, there's Mike. Now he's a West Coast Icon he likes his luxury, and is staying at the Lanesborough. However, he's kindly consented to slum it at our house in Consort Park today. I've warned him that the red carpet's in storage and that he'll have to help with the washing-up, and he says that just for once he'll relax his rule on being waited on hand and foot and pitch in with the rest of us. His last visit was five years ago, so we're all looking forward to having a big catch-up, and it will also be a good opportunity for him to bring himself up to date with Lozz, his godson.

I leave Anna and Danny sleeping and drive to the supermarket. The car park's full. I circle for five minutes before spotting a space. I notice that the blue Ford Fiesta with the smoked windows that's been behind me for most of my journey is heading for the same space. It's Singing Vic, my next-door neighbour. In a burst of acceleration I swing in first and suppress a juvenile desire to crow. But Vic's already found another space. He hates being bested by a woman and I look forward to teasing him. But when he emerges, although I only see him from the back, it clearly isn't Vic. Much too tall and thin, and wearing a hooded top – something Vic wouldn't be seen dead in. I squint at the car number-plate. Not his car at all. My mistake.

I hate the supermarket. It's too full of stuff. I become oppressed by superfluity, weighed down by abundance. It gives me indigestion. I feel bloated and full, even if I haven't eaten for hours.

Also, a speedy getaway is impossible because there are usually at least three Consort Park residents lurking behind the towers of toilet rolls or the baskets of baked beans. Today is no exception. Who should emerge from between the shampoo shelves but

Mary the Hologram, self-appointed Consort Park town-crier. It's her capacity for garnering gossip that's given her her nickname: so avid is she for juicy titbits that she often manages to be in two places at the same time in order to collect. Or so it seems to the folk of Consort Park.

'Sacred Heart, Rosa, just the person! Have ye heard the latest?'

Even if you already know what she's talking about, it saves time to plead ignorance. Mary will tell you anyway.

'No?' I say, surreptitiously glancing at my watch.

'Skinny Minnie's dead.'

This isn't a huge surprise. Skinny Minnie's a woman of such extreme decrepitude that she claims to remember Queen Victoria's Diamond Jubilee celebrations in Consort Park. Her skeletal physique, pushing a battered pram containing an ancient, hairless cocker spaniel and numerous assorted carrier bags, is an integral part of our neighbourhood landscape.

Mary hasn't finished. 'Some months ago, apparently,' she carols. 'And you'll never guess . . .'

'What?' I say, obediently on cue.

'She's left three and a half million pounds.'

'You have to be joking!'

This really is news. No one thought Skinny Minnie had more than two pennies to rub together. In fact, the whole neighbourhood was under the impression that our small acts of charity had been the only things between Minnie and total destitution.

'Three and a half million . . .' I repeat, amazed.

'Yes. Probate's just been granted.'

'Who's the lucky beneficiary?'

'That's why I wanted to speak to you.'

For one mad moment I imagine that Skinny Minnie, touched to the core by my gift of an old overcoat of Rob's the winter before last, had decided to leave the lot to me.

'Most of it goes to some kennels in Hertfordshire in return for them taking care of her dog.'

'Fair enough.' I stifle an unworthy pang of disappointment.

'But the rest – nearly half a million – is a donation to the Residents' Association for a sculpture to be erected in Consort Park flower garden, and at last night's meeting it was decided to approach you since you know about these things on account of your man Rob, God rest his soul, and ask you to find a fella who'd make it for us . . . What do you think, Rosa?'

Little did I imagine, when I woke this morning, that I'd be in charge of commissioning a sculpture for Consort Park. Rob would find it hysterical – his wife, a patron of the arts.

'I'd be delighted.'

At the checkout I'm about to unload my shopping when I notice something odd. My trolley contains more food than it should – two more packs each of chicken and sausages, extra bags of both salad and potatoes, a jar of Jamaican spices, some fresh tarragon and three tubs of ice cream.

Someone must have mistaken my trolley for theirs, when I was talking to Mary. But how come the added items are an exact extension of my barbecue menu? As if someone thought I'd be having extra guests? The cluttered emporium begins to close in and I break out into a sweat.

I look around. The rest of the queue is in comatose mode, waiting their turn to shell out, like obedient little consumers, but it doesn't stop me from experiencing the uncomfortable sensation that I'm being watched. It takes all my willpower not to abandon my trolley and leave. Eventually I pay and scuttle back to my car. All the way home I keep my eyes peeled for the blue Fiesta, but there's no sign of it. I curse my over-active imagination, which sees bogeymen behind every tree.

Then I curse the man who made me react in this way to anything vaguely inexplicable. The man who, for a few nightmare months, made our lives hell. The man whose sick obsession with Anna had resulted in him eventually trying to kill both her and me.

The episode has indelibly marked all of us. It's a daily struggle to ignore the horrors that lurk in each of our minds. It's only been a short time and I know that the worst things will fade, but for now, it doesn't take much to knock me off balance.

This morning, I feel utterly enraged that what he did still has the power to affect me so strongly. I won't let it happen! By sheer force of will I focus on the day ahead, and banish the image of the overloaded trolley.

Once home I rouse my children from their teenage torpor and get the show on the road. The heat intensifies, and our long, tangled garden, leading down to the railway line, looks wild but wonderful: the perfect setting for a barbecue. We arrange the garden chairs and sun umbrellas, and Danny's just lit the coals when Jess and Lozz arrive. Lozz rushes to help Danny, who is his hero. I remind my son to be careful: Lozz has Down's syndrome and has to be watched around fire even though he's sixteen.

Jess has brought a criminally creamy strawberry Pavlova.

'Since you're on a diet, you won't want any,' she jokes. 'I thought I'd have your share.'

Jess never tires of the comedy inherent in the difference between our respective sizes. I'm almost as skinny as Skinny Minnie, in spite of eating like a horse, while she's engaged in a war of attrition with her weight which can never be won because she only has to look at a chocolate biscuit to put on five pounds, and she adores food. She makes enormous comic capital of our differences, describing to people the long list of diets which she claims I've tried, and referring to me as her fat friend.

Actually, she looks fantastic. Her motto is, 'If you've got it, flaunt it', and she always makes the most of her assets. Today she's dressed in something long and flowing with a pink peony design, loose dark curls framing her vibrant face. On her surprisingly delicate wrists, several silver bracelets glint in the sunshine, and she's painted both finger- and toenails to match the dress.

'Gorgeous dress. New?'

'Ancient. Mike not here yet?'

'No.'

'Maybe he's had a better offer.'

'How could any offer be better than a day with my favourite girls?'

Mike's massive frame is blocking the garden doorway.

'Don't you ever answer your bell?' he goes on. 'I thought I'd got the wrong day until Anna took pity and let me in.'

'Stop whingeing, Mason, and do something with that bottle of fizz you're clutching, or are you too grand to open your own booze nowadays?'

Jess has segued straight into the playfully combative relationship that she and Mike have always enjoyed. Before too long I'll doubtless be fulfilling my usual role of referee.

'Lozz, tell your mum she's a bossy old trout, and then come and give me a hug, big man.'

Lozz beams and launches himself on Mike, covering him with kisses. 'Mikey Mikey Mikey,' he shouts. 'Fight fight fight.' Although he only sees Mike intermittently, Lozz never forgets him. They have a relationship based on affectionate rough and tumble, of which the fatherless Lozz can never get enough.

Old friends are like old shoes – comfortable and easy to slip on. Mike, Jess and I are able to convey several years of news in the friends' shorthand that's incomprehensible to outsiders who don't have the reference points, and also indulge ourselves with a massive trip down Memory Lane, raking up old legends from our misspent youth.

'We've heard these stories a million times,' moans Anna. 'What was so special about back then?'

'You won't understand till you've lived a bit, young lady,' says Mike. 'It didn't seem like it at the time, but those days were golden.'

'Pass the sick bag,' she says.

Mike ignores her. 'Golden days. Filmed in glorious Technicolor.'

'Glorious what?' says Danny.

'I remember the tiniest things,' says Jess. 'My clothes – I remember every detail of various outfits I had back then. Who said what to whom, and where . . .'

'The highs were high and boy, were the lows low.'

'And friends were everything,' I put in. 'More important than work, family. Everything.'

'Remember when Mike crashed our psychology seminar and

42

dragged me from under the nose of that terminally boring lecturer? He said my grandmother had died . . .' Jess is off, and the stories start again.

I look round at the circle of laughing faces, and marvel at the power of shared memory to forge a chain that can survive years of physical distance and frequent bouts of neglect. Even when Anna, pointing out that in my version of the story, it's me who was rescued by Mike, and not Jess, sparking a mock-acrimonious row, my gratitude for the capacity of memory to bind us all together is unshaken. What do the details matter? The important thing is this common history that helps us validate our past, by the telling of our joint stories.

After lunch, when Anna and Danny take Lozz off to the park, I fill Mike in with the more gory details of the family's recent experiences with maniac stalkers, and he give us a breakdown of his latest marital disaster. It's been his usual mismatch: Californian gold-digger half his age thinking she was on to a good thing hooking herself a famous fish, and then discovering that life as an artist's wife required a degree of self-sufficiency that someone barely out of the cradle couldn't be expected to possess.

'Where do I go wrong?' Mike moans. 'Why can't I meet someone like you two – beautiful, fun, and mature enough to understand the imperatives of my ridiculous life?'

'Less of the mature,' says Jess. 'Rosa and I aren't remotely mature. Forty's the new thirty nowadays. Course, she'd look younger if she lost some of that weight, but in general I reckon we're both wearing extremely well. At least we've got our own hair.'

'Excuse me?'

'Those Californian hair-weaving techniques are fab. You can hardly tell it from the real thing.'

As I watch my friend with her old sparring partner, a thought occurs. Maybe it's no accident that Jess looks so great today.

She is particularly animated.

And she doesn't normally paint her toenails . . .

I pay close attention after this, but decide, eventually, that I'm imagining things. Rosa the Drama Queen rides again.

Mike and Jess? That would be just too weird for words.

Later, Mike gives us a great piece of news.

'I'm staying in London for the summer. I met David Borodino at Rob's private view and he's commissioned me to paint a mural for his penthouse. I've rented a place in the East End and I'm moving in tomorrow.'

David Borodino again. He's popping up all over the place.

After this announcement, there's nothing for it but to open another bottle of fizz. We toast everything we can think of, open another bottle, then another, and end up completely bladdered.

Eventually I pack Jess and Lozz off in a cab, and wait with Mike for his car.

'Are you really all right, Rosy?'

His familiar face reminds me so much of those bright days of long ago, I want to cry and say, 'No, I'm not. I'll never be all right again.'

Instead I say, 'All the better for seeing you, you old fraud.'

'You know I'd do anything for you?'

'Course I do.'

He bends down and his lips brush my cheek.

'Good,' he says. 'See you, babe.'

He leaps into his car which has pulled up alongside us, and then he's gone.

I'm staring after him when, for the second time today, I experience a feeling of deep unease. I scan the road, but it's empty. In the park, dark shadows shift in the moonlight, and I resolutely ignore the spot where, on a winter night not too long ago, I'd found a dog fox feasting off the spilled guts of a freshly killed body skewered to the railings.

These things happened, Rosa. Face up to them. Recognise them for what they are and then banish them. Don't let them beat you.

Then there's a brief flash of light and the sound of footsteps running away, down the side road.

This is not my imagination.

The time when . . .

. . . the bitch biologist from the Science Faculty and her poncy boyfriend in the mascara and lipstick took the piss over the fact that his Megadeth T-shirt was covered in dandruff.

In front of the Lion, the Witch and the Warlord, who stood there like it didn't matter that he was dying inside.

Pain: merciless, unremitting. Chalk scraping down a blackboard. Fingernails torn away. Scabs ripped off exposing bleeding flesh beneath. The geography and meteorology of pain: whirlwind spiralling into vortex. Unending desert of enduring recognition. Black night of total loss.

Rage: tsunami of the soul, ferocious, remorseless. Devastation. Obliteration Wasteland.

Why, this is hell, nor am I out of it.

FIVE

I woke this morning with a feeling of deep dread.

It's nothing to do with last night, when I thought for one stupid moment that time had gone into reverse and I was back in the siege situation of last winter. No, this is common or garden maternal anxiety. Today Anna and Danny are off on their respective jaunts, and what has seemed for weeks like such a brilliant idea has suddenly become something I can't bear. What if Anna's plane is targeted by a terrorist bomb? What if the brakes fail on 3D's clapped-out old van and they drive off a cliff in a remote corner of Bulgaria, and their bodies are never found? What if Anna catches some dreadful disease in India? What if the boys, being black, are subjected to some awful Eastern-European, far-right racism and beaten senseless in a dark alley? I lie in bed stewing in my neurotic imaginings until, sick of myself, I leap up and assume my jolly it's-an-everyday-occurrence-that-my-children-go-off-for-weeks-on-end-to-foreign-parts-and-I'm-not-a-bit-concerned routine that I hope will fool everyone, myself included.

At breakfast Anna and Danny are manically cheerful in a way that suggests they are also secretly viewing their imminent departure with a certain amount of trepidation. It's not surprising. We've been a very tightly knit little trio since Rob's death, and our recent ordeal only served to bring us even closer. The family therapy we've had to help us deal with our various traumas has also made us look carefully at our relationship, and we all understand each other in a way that wasn't the case in the immediate aftermath of Rob's death. Now that closeness is being tested by absence. Quite right too. To prolong the siege mentality would be wrong and unhealthy. The children need to make their way in the world without me watching their backs, and I need to know that tragedy won't strike the minute they're out of my sight.

But I still feel like shit.

Danny's the first to go. Promptly at ten o'clock, a rickety old van thunders to a halt outside our house and Dwaine, Delroy and Delroy's cousin, Jackson, pile out. Jackson is the main driver, along with Delroy, who passed his test rather too recently for my liking. Jackson, twenty-two, six foot two and built like a battleship, has designated himself as the boys' minder. He stands on the doorstep, face immobile, cooler than cool in his braids and shades.

'Yo.'

'Hello, Jackson.'

Dwaine and Delroy are bouncing behind him like over-excited puppies, and I realise I'm very thankful for Jackson's all-round heavy qualities.

'Cuppa before you go?' Anything to put off the evil moment.

Delroy, always ready for sustenance, surges forward, but Danny is shouldering his way past me, rucksack and guitar already strapped to his back, and is exchanging, with Jackson that complicated handshake favoured by streetwise youth.

'Yo, blood. Scrap drinks, Mum, we gotta split.'

'But—'

Too late. The little posse heads towards the van.

'Bye, Rosa!' shout Dwaine and Delroy.

'Laters,' grunts Jackson.

'I'll email you,' calls Danny.

Within seconds they're driving away. Then there's the squeal of brakes, a door slamming and Danny's voice. 'So I forgot my passport. Wanna make something of it?'

Then he's giving me a bone-crushing hug. 'Wanted to say a proper goodbye,' he whispers.

I'm not going to cry.

'Be careful. Specially when the festival's over and you're off on your travels. Keep up your fruit intake, change your underwear regularly, and any problems, just call.'

'Mum, chill. Where's my stupid sister? Anna! Get your skinny ass down here! I'm off.'

Anna appears. 'Enjoy your little local trip, bruv. I'll let you know what real travelling's like when I'm back from the mystic East.'

'Cheeky tart.'

And then he's really gone. I have to take some very deep breaths. I don't want to disgrace myself in front of my daughter.

'Done all your packing?' I say briskly.

Anna's tone is equally matter-of-fact. 'I can't fit in the presents for Laxmi's grandparents.'

'Want some help?'

'OK.'

I suspect she's manufacturing a task to take both our minds off her imminent departure. Eventually we're finished. It's time to pick up the Vekarias and head for the airport.

As I drive towards the M4 everything I pass is indelibly printed on my brain in super-bright colours and hard, harsh outlines. It's even worse at Heathrow. The hotch-potch of people in the check-in area merge into a fast-moving blur, and yet odd things stand out in crazy relief: a group of Hassidic Jews in their wide black hats and overcoats carrying deckchairs and a sunshade; a hugely obese woman, gobbling her way through a bagful of doughnuts; a tiny Chinese cleaner pushing a trolley that's bigger than she is, full of brushes, buckets and bleaches. I note them all, as we shuffle forward in the queue, towards the check-in desk.

Then it's time to say goodbye. Anna will never forgive me if I blub in front of the Vekarias. 'You're the actor, you stupid woman,' I tell myself. 'So act.'

'Have a wonderful trip,' I trill. 'Heena, say a big thank you to your parents for inviting Anna.'

I'm hugging my girl, and neither of us is making eye-contact. She pulls away, and I watch them walk through the departure doors, Anna, at five foot nine, dwarfing the diminutive Vekarias.

Then they're gone.

The tears spill from my eyes, but I don't care who sees me now. The main thing is that she's not like Rob. She's not dead. She'll be back soon. I picture the arrivals hall, and Anna bounding through, full of travellers' tales.

I drive home, forcing myself to become deeply involved in a dreadful radio play about two old women sitting in a shelter on the sea-front at Hove, and by the time I reach Consort Park, I feel almost normal.

Then my heart thuds.

The side gate's open.

I always lock it when I'm away from the house.

I must have forgotten. Mustn't I?

I walk round the back to the garden. No signs of disturbance.

Except . . .

Something white . . . Caught on a rosebush . . .

Paper?

I pick it out of the foliage, and turn it over.

It's a blurred Polaroid.

Of my house.

Why would anyone be taking photographs of my house? Unless it's someone who's interested in buying it. I'm forever getting estate agents' letters telling me how desirable these houses are.

And the wind will have blown it into the back garden.

What wind?

I ignore the humid stillness and go inside.

The house is empty and silent: the kind of silence that hurts the eardrums. I wander into every room, ending up in my bedroom. I look out of the window at the spot where Rob was mown down. The bloodstain from his massive head trauma is still faintly visible, and occasionally I go and sit on the kerb and stare at it, wishing for the millionth time that I could turn back the clock to the moment on that bright winter's day when he rushed downstairs shouting to me that he was going to the park.

If only I'd stopped him. Three little words would have been enough to save his life. *Wait for me.*

Eighteen months later I'm still replaying that moment. I lie down on my bed, close my eyes and drift into sleep. From experience I know this is the only way to break the mood. When I awake it's half past ten at night. I've been asleep for hours. I'm ravenous.

In the kitchen I'm struck again by the unnatural stillness. It's as if I'm the last one alive on the planet. I haven't spent a night alone in ages. When was the last time? I trawl back through the years until an unbelievable thought occurs: I don't remember ever spending a night on my own. Since having the children, one or both of them has always been here, even if Rob was away. Before the children, Rob and I, in the early stages of our romance, were joined at the hip and never spent a night apart as far as I recall. At college, pre-Rob, I shared a room in a student hall of residence, and before that, I was a child, at home with my parents, who never went anywhere. It's crazy, but I suspect that somehow I've contrived to reach the age of forty without ever spending a night alone.

I feel deeply foolish. I've always considered myself pretty independent. This is humiliating. I glare at my reflection in the kitchen window. My face is paler than usual, throwing into stark relief my amber eyes and tangled red hair. I look a wreck, like one of the revolutionary hags in the West End production of *Les Mis*. The only thing missing is a couple of blacked-out front teeth.

'You're on your own. Get used to it,' I scowl.

Then I see something move in the garden. Heart pounding, I peer into the darkness.

Nothing.

Why am I so jumpy? I've been like this ever since Rob's private view – seeing ghosts, thinking I'm being watched, making up weird stories about stupid little things like the photograph.

All my imagination. The imagination of a pathetic woman who's never been alone at night.

'Grow up,' I tell myself. 'One day this is how it will always be. Danny and Anna will be adults and gone for good, and you'll be an old woman with only yourself to talk to. That's life. Face it.'

Because of my earlier nap, I can't sleep. I spend the dark hours before the summer dawn wandering round, trying to get a handle on solitude – testing it out for size.

I don't like it much.

At daybreak I go into the garden. The dew soaks my bare feet. Unlike the remorseless silence of the night hours, this morning stillness enchants me. It's full of promise: renewal. I feel a surge of strength. I'll be OK. I pick some flowers – pink roses, blue cornflowers, scarlet crocosmia.

I'm about to go indoors when I see the shed door is open. It's only recently been rebuilt after a fire, and it's still empty.

In the dust on the floor are footprints. Large ones.

They weren't there yesterday.

SIX

It's Wednesday and I'm meeting Leni Dang at *L'Estrange East* to do my interview for *Dame*.

I'm relieved to be going out. Although Anna phoned to say she'd arrived safely, there's been no word from Danny. His mobile's not working and the inbox on my PC remains defiantly empty. I've had BBC News 24 on permanently since Monday night, listening out for Bulgarian catastrophes, and I'll go mad if I don't hear from him soon.

Added to which, ever since I found the footprints in the shed, I've felt really scared and I can't shake the sensation that once again I'm being watched.

Walking through the park on my way to the tube earlier, I knew with total certainty that someone was following me. I tried to catch him at it, but each time I turned round, all I could see was Mary the Hologram chatting to an old woman, a gaggle of gossiping nannies wheeling their designer babies towards the sandpit in their highly expensive buggies, and various people lying on the grass enjoying the morning sun.

Then I spotted him. Distant, but gaining on me quite fast.

A tall man. With blond hair.

I started to shake. Where to go? What to do?

Then he veered off into the playground and held out his arms to a young girl who flew into them with cries of, 'Daddy!'

I told myself to get a grip. But I couldn't.

The feeling persisted all through the tube journey, and now, on the walk through fashionable East End dereliction towards *L'Estrange East*, I'm convinced I can hear footsteps. But whenever I stop, they stop too. And when I turn round, no one's there.

Logic says it would be too much of a coincidence if yet another stalker has attached himself to the Thorn family, and commonsense says that all the hysteria is probably misplaced maternal anxiety about my two globetrotters. But I'm so traumatised by last winter that logic and commonsense shoot out of the window at the least sign of anything remotely unusual.

It's all utterly absurd.

Larry's on the phone in his office.

'My dear Steve, do not take that tone with us. We don't appreciate being threatened . . . What an insulting insinuation! If mistakes have been made it's not of our doing. The accountant is investigating . . . Absolutely not an option . . . Not after what's been said . . . No . . . We're not prepared to discuss this further . . . No . . . Look, we're rather busy, so if you have anything else to say, we suggest you contact our lawyer.'

Phone hits base and then Larry's voice again, pettishly loud.

'Julian, we are no longer at home to Mr Pyne, telephonically or otherwise. We thought we made that clear.'

Overwrought, in an orange Oswald Boateng suit, Julian explodes from his own office into the main body of the gallery.

'*Mea culpa*, Larry. *Mea culpa*. It's just been too, too dreadful this morning. *Mein lieber Herr* from Frankfurt is seriously interested in the Peebles and Blow triptych but they, in their wisdom, are choosing not to return my calls. God save us all from temperamental bloody artists. They think they're so superior to us toiling gallerists. We're only the poor saps responsible for selling their wretched offerings — Oh! Rosa! I didn't see you lurking behind that column. Fab top.'

He scoops me into his office with fulsome offers of coffee and pastries. 'Who's doing the interview?'

'Leni Dang. For her column in *Dame*.'

'*Vraiment? Quelle* busy little beaver.'

'What do you mean?'

'Seems only yesterday she was scribbling listings for various lowly organs, and now she's got her own by-line in *Dame*. Nice going.'

'I'd never heard of her before Rob's opening.'

'Sprung fully formed from nowhere, darling. Venus rising from the waves.' Julian's eyes gleam and his tone becomes increasingly arch. 'A lady who puts herself about, it would seem. Has her dainty little finger in lashings of pies all of a sudden. Wherever one turns, *voila*! There she is!'

'Good luck to her. It's a hard world out there if you're a freelance.'

'Harder for some than others.'

Julian wants me to ask what he means.

'What do you mean?'

He leans towards me, voice low and confidential. 'Have you read any of her stuff?'

'No.'

'Not one of God's born scribes.'

Bull's eye, Rosa! Your first interview promoting Rob is with someone who can't write.

'*Dame* would hardly have given her a column if she couldn't write.'

Julian sniggers. 'I don't think her writing skills entered into the transaction.'

Once more I feed him his cue: 'What do you mean?'

'I gather the Editor's particularly susceptible to the odd morsel of Eastern Promise.' His words drip with innuendo.

'Have *you* read her column?'

Julian's anorexic frame twitches shiftily. 'Not as such.'

Misogyny and racism is alive and well and currently located in *L'Estrange East*.

'Well then—'

'But I know people who have. Word is, she doesn't know her Richard Longs from her Rachel Whitereads.'

'I thought she was very nice and I'm sure she'll do a great interview.'

'Anyway, there's no such thing as bad publicity. It'll be good for the show whatever old rubbish La Dung churns out . . . Leni, darling! Wonderful to see you. Come and have some scrumptious strudel.'

It says a lot for Larry and Caroline that the gallery is so highly regarded, with Julian's interpersonal skills in the equation. But if Leni heard his bitching, she gives no sign of it. She's breathing raggedly, her pasty skin flushed and blotchy.

'I'm so sorry I'm late. I had to wait half an hour for a bus, and then the whole of City Road was completely snarled up. In the end I just jumped off and ran.'

The poor girl's in such a state that even the waspish Julian takes pity on her, fluttering around with coffee, cakes, iced water and comforting platitudes. Once she's calmed down I look pointedly at him.

'I'll leave you to it, then,' he says. 'Can't wait to read your little *aperçus* about poor dear Rob, Leni. Simply panting with anticipation.'

Leni gives him a sweet smile. 'Isn't he lovely,' she says when he's gone. 'So warm and caring.'

Is she for real?

Then we spend a couple of hours talking about my favourite subject: Rob. One thing Leni persistently returns to is whether he saw himself as a *black* artist, or just an artist.

'I think he was more preoccupied with the dislocation that comes from moving countries than with his colour. That, and losing his family. He never knew his father, his mother abandoned him and his grandmother brought him to England from Trinidad. When she died he was completely alone. That affected him much more than being black.'

'So race didn't enter into his thinking at all?'

I have a flash of insight: this particular line of enquiry has nothing to do with Rob.

'Where do *your* family originate?' I ask.

'Vietnam.'

'When did you leave?'

'My brother and I were born here. My parents came over after the fall of Saigon.'

'Then they'd understand something of what Rob went through.'

'Yes.'

She doesn't elaborate and from this point on, the dynamic of the interview changes. Our previous easy exchanges tail off, and there are several awkward silences. Eventually I ask her if she's got enough material. She seems relieved that I want to finish.

'Thanks for giving so much of your time.'

'Thank *you*. When's it coming out?'

'Later in the week, I hope. Would you thank Larry for letting me use the gallery for the interview.'

I stare after her tiny figure as it trudges down Navarre Street. A bit of an enigma, our Leni. Julian's jibes about her lack of talent seem misplaced: she asked all the right questions. But was it sensible of me to grant an interview to such an inexperienced writer? Gillian seemed to think so, but then she's fiercely protective of her young protégées. Still, I'll give her a ring – find out what makes Ms Dang tick.

I knock on Larry's door.

'Enter.'

He's writing a letter. No word processors for Larry. All his correspondence is written in exquisite italic script with a highly expensive fountain pen on thick paper, the colour of clotted cream.

'Can I have a word?'

'Certainly.' His tone is cool. He still hasn't forgiven me for turning down David Borodino. However, he cheers up a bit when I reveal my new role as patron of the arts on behalf of Consort Park.

He cheers up a lot when I reveal the sum of money involved.

'My dear Rosa, how splendid. There are several sculptors on our books who would be ideal. Come and have supper at the house tonight, then we can talk some more. You don't mind taking pot luck, do you? Flavia would love to meet you. I'll send the car.'

Flavia, Larry's rich wife, is something of a recluse, and rarely seen around the art world.

'Shall we say eightish?'

I'm pleased to have secured an evening away from my grave-quiet house, and curious to see the inside of Larry's. He must be very keen to get my custom: not many people are known to have penetrated his hallowed Belgravia portals. I once went there with Rob to deliver some drawings, but we didn't get further than the hall. I remember seeing a painting of a very beautiful woman, asking Larry who it was, and being surprised at the love in his voice as he replied that it was his wife. I hadn't associated Larry with such strong feeling. So, being a nosy cow, I'm delighted to be meeting this paragon in the flesh.

As I pass *Nature Morte*, I bump into Caroline.

'Thanks for the other night,' she says. 'You were an absolute angel. I don't know how I'd have got through the rest of the dinner.'

'Was Larry OK about it?'

She laughs. 'You know Larry.'

'I don't know how you put up with him.'

'Me neither. If he weren't quite so brilliant at what he does I'd be off like a shot. But I'm learning so much from him about running a gallery that it more than makes up for all his infuriating Larryness. Besides, underneath the posturing he's really a bit of an old sweetie.'

'I'll take your word for it. How's Steve?'

'Spent two days weeping down my cleavage and begging for forgiveness.'

'Good.'

'When he'd sobered up, he was gutted.'

'I'll bet.'

We look at each other and burst out laughing.

'Remember David Borodino's face?'

'And Julian reeling around like a robot saying "everything's under control" like some kind of demented mantra?'

'Steve could pretend it was a piece of Performance Art.'

'He's really devastated about what he said to me – sent me a darling bouquet of flowers which he couldn't afford, particularly since he doesn't have a dealer any more. Anyway, I'm going to persuade Larry to take him back. Steve's a jolly fine artist when he isn't sloshed, and Larry knows it.'

I don't mention the phone conversation I overheard earlier. Caroline's chances of persuading Larry to take Steve back are less than mine of bringing Rob back from the dead.

Instead I tell her about my forthcoming dinner at Larry's. She's amazed.

'He never invites people home. He must badly want something from you.'

I'm telling her about the Consort Park sculpture project when I hear tapping. A face peers through the window of *Nature Morte*.

'Golly gosh, it's Zander,' whispers Caroline. 'I'm off. He's such a gossip, I'll be here all morning. *Ciao*, Rosa. Let's do lunch soon.'

But before she can make her escape, Zander emerges waving a couple of tickets.

'Caro, wait!' He presses the tickets into her hand.

Her face lights up. *'The Producers*! Zander, you darling! Front stalls too. How did you swing that? They're like gold dust.'

'Mate of mine works in the box office.' He gives her a peck on the cheek. 'Enjoy, lovely lady.'

Caro turns to me. 'This man's a miracle worker.' Then she glances at her watch. 'Gosh, Larry'll kill me. Thanks again, Zander.' She shoots towards *L'Estrange East*, stuffing the precious tickets in her bag.

Zander's beaming at me. 'You've come to see the show. Great.'

There's no way I can escape without being very rude.

'I don't have much time,' I mutter ineffectually as he steers me into the gallery.

He doesn't seem to hear. Maybe he thinks I'm a rich widow. A potential buyer. Think again, Zander.

Nature Morte is part of the same building that houses *L'Estrange East*, but the two spaces couldn't be more different. Whereas Larry's architect has retained the echoing grandeur of the nineteenth-century temple to industry, Zander has opted for intimacy. His space is all alcoves, sofas and vases of white lilies, placed strategically on stone pedestals, which flood the gallery with their sickly-sweet smell.

The walls are covered in photographs of kitsch objects – the kind you see in seaside giftshops – all displayed on garishly bright, patterned-cloth backgrounds. They are uniformly hideous.

I hate looking at art with people breathing down my neck, expecting me to have an opinion. Rob could spin something out of nothing, and extract gold from any amount of dross. I'd always hidden behind his consummate verbals. Now I have to conjure up something appreciative but honest about these ghastly pictures all by myself.

My mind remains resolutely blank.

'Who's the artist?' I'm playing for time here.

I've committed my first blunder: I should know who the artist is, particularly as the name's written on the window – a fact I spot as I'm halfway through the sentence.

'Daisy Fortuna,' says Zander in surprise. 'Mega-talented lady. Great niece of William Bathurst.'

'William who?'

'Bathurst. Do you know him? Owns half of Lincolnshire. Lovely guy.'

'Nice colours,' I venture.

'Absolutely. The choice, and juxtaposition of the objects in the pictures says so much about the value we place on ephemera in today's world, don't you think?'

I look at a particularly depressing photograph of a cheap imitation Chinese vase containing a sprig of artificial bougainvillaea, set alongside a small gilt model of Blackpool Tower.

'Absolutely.'

As we wander round, Zander keeps up a continuous patter. 'Cherie wanted to buy a couple of Fortunas, but I wouldn't let her. I said, "It won't go with the Downing Street ambience. I'll give Larry L'Estrange a bell. He's got just the thing".' He smiles. 'You may think that's crazy – doing myself out of such a high-profile sale, pimping for the competition – but that's the way I am. She was so chuffed she sent several of her mates to the gallery, and they all bought work. As she said last week, when I was having dinner with her, "It's trust, isn't it, Zander? Trust is everything. And I trust you".' He leans forward confidingly. 'Old Larry was a bit surprised, but I said, "Good neighbours, mate. You scratch my back et cetera". I think he took my point.' He fixes me with an impassioned gaze. 'I won't sell anything just for the cash, you see. The work must fit the client.'

I try my best to care.

I fail.

His mobile suddenly chirrups out the theme tune from *The Godfather*. 'Elton! How ya doing, mate? How's David? Great, great . . . So what can I do you for my son?'

I use this final diversion to assert myself. I head for the door, mouthing goodbyes. Zander holds up his hand to detain me. 'Listen, mate, can I call you back? Great.'

I'm at the door of the gallery when he catches me up.

'Zander, it's been fascinating but I must go – my daughter's expecting me . . .'

'I thought she was in India.'

'. . . expecting me to call her. Mustn't be late – time differences and all that.'

He follows me into the street. Is he planning to come home with me or something? He enfolds my hands in both of his and

64

looks meaningful. Is this the moment when I'm supposed to make an offer for a Fortuna?

'Pop in again, now you know where we are. We've a great show opening soon. You probably know the work of Ronnie Spiller. He does bone-china wall mosaics of animal entrails – very visceral . . .'

Zander, I'd rather sit in an ice-cold bath for three hours.

'Super.'

Zander Zinovieff watched Rosa Thorn's willowy body sway down the street, sunlight bouncing off her chestnut curls. She hadn't had much to say for herself. Fancy not knowing Daisy Fortuna. You'd think being the wife of an artist for all those years she'd be a bit more clued up. He'd tried his best, but he could tell not much had gone in. She quite clearly couldn't wait to make her escape, never mind how rudely it came across.

She'd stopped. Maybe she'd changed her mind and was coming back for more. No. She was tying her shoelace. Zander saw a movement behind her: a man ducking into a doorway. When she started to move again, so did the man. Intrigued, Zander watched. Was she being followed? Ought he to leap to her rescue? As she crossed the road, so did her pursuer. As he glanced backwards to check for cars, Zander caught sight of his face.

What he saw knocked the breath out of him.

'No,' he muttered. 'That's impossible.'

'What's impossible?'

A dishevelled figure had lurched around the corner from the back of the gallery.

Steve Pyne.
'Can I have a word?'
Still reeling from what he'd seen, Zander invited him in.

> *From:* dannythorn@bplondon.org
> *To:* rosathorn@hotmail.com
> *Subject:* 3D World domination
>
> Yo! xx

SEVEN

One little word is enough. He's alive – that's all I need to know.

I celebrate by catching up on some weeding. I also stand in the shed for a long time, looking at the footprints. There's a reasonable explanation – I just haven't thought of it yet.

The afternoon is sticky and humid, and after a cold shower, I choose my outfit for a simple supper in Belgravia. This takes longer than I think. I try on several unsuitable garments, standing in front of the mirror experiencing my usual dissatisfaction with my tall, angular body and unruly hair. Then I realise that unless I rush, Larry's driver will be ringing on the doorbell while I'm still in my underwear.

I'm right: no sooner have I flung on a cotton dress from Monsoon, than I hear Larry's Merc purring outside the house.

Larry lives in Chester Square. The door is opened by a small woman dressed in a starched blue and white uniform who speaks very little English. She shows me up to the first-floor drawing room. Heavy damask drapes in old gold provide a sumptuous backdrop to the Louis Quinze furnishings arranged tastefully on the pale pink and apple-green Aubusson carpet. The evening light is fading fast, and the ornate Venetian glass chandelier is supplemented by various silk-covered lamps that glow discreetly on fragile occasional tables. On one wall is a painting which looks suspiciously like a Boucher.

I'm astonished.

This is not the room of a man who makes his living at the cutting edge of contemporary art.

I'm also severely under-dressed.

For this pot-luck 'simple' supper, Flavia's wearing a 'simple' dress in pewter-grey silk that must have left little change from a grand, and a 'simple' diamond choker that could probably pay off the national debt of a small African state.

Then I see the gnarled and twisted fingers of the hand that is raised to greet me, and register that she's seated, not on a spindly antique, but in a twenty-first-century state-of-the-art wheelchair.

Rheumatoid arthritis.

No wonder she isn't often seen around the art world.

'Do excuse me for not getting up.' The light musical voice is at variance with the ravaged hands. 'This ghastly disease has its ups and downs, and today's very definitely one of the downs. I'm so pleased to meet you, my dear. Larry's given me a private view of your husband's work. You must be very proud of him.'

She's a good ten years older than Larry – in her mid-sixties, I'd say. Once she would have been a great beauty. Actually, she still is. Her face has more lines criss-crossing it than Willesden Junction, but they can't hide the finely sculpted bones that set off eyes of a deep turquoise blue. Young eyes. Beautiful. Her hair is a soft, snowy white, untouched by tint or dye, and is tied at the nape of her neck with a grey velvet ribbon.

And she's incredibly nice.

Larry is clearly besotted with her. He's never been my favourite person. I appreciate his expertise, his business acumen and the care he lavishes on his artists, but I find his foibles and idiosyncrasies a bit irritating. It's difficult to be patient with his elaborately fastidious posturings, and I've always felt there was a cold core at the centre of his smooth charm. But with Flavia, he's a different man. He's immensely protective and constantly concerned for her well-being. And – wonder of wonders – when addressing her, he actually reverts to the singular.

His feelings are obviously reciprocated. As Larry glides about the room, refreshing drinks, offering olives from a Lalique bowl, her eyes follow him with a look of such tenderness that I feel I'm intruding into something deeply private and personal.

'What a lovely house,' I say.

'Yes. It's been in the family since it was built. I can't imagine life without it.' She smiles. 'Everything here means something, you see. Every object conjures a memory – not just of my life, but of the family through the years – through the centuries.' She sighs. 'My brother and I are the only ones left now.'

This explains the lack of Larry in the place. Even he would find it an uphill task to change nearly two hundred years of family history.

'Your brother lives here too?'

'He has a set of rooms on the top two floors. When I married Larry, Theo said he wasn't playing gooseberry to Love's Young

Dream, and even though we begged him to stay down here with us, he moved everything upstairs.'

'He couldn't wait,' said Larry. 'For the first time in his life he was able to escape his bossy big sister.'

Larry? Teasing? This has to be a dream. But no, Flavia is laughing and stroking his arm with her poor misshapen fingers.

Our 'simple' four-course supper is served by the woman who answered the door. The food is exquisitely arranged on French porcelain and tastes divine.

'Tell Constanza she's excelled herself, would you, Dolores, and ask Mr Grey to join us for coffee.'

'Very good, Mrs L'Estrange.'

What must it be like to have servants? On the plus side – no more slaving over a hot Hoover. On the minus – no more privacy.

Give me the minus side any day. Having Dolores breathing down my neck, awaiting my orders and judging my chaotic life, would soon drive me completely potty. Not to mention coping with my lefty liberal guilt about Western exploitation of the immigrant underclass.

Our talk turns to the Consort Park sculpture. Larry mentions several suitable candidates. I describe Consort Park flower garden and we discuss the kind of work that would be appropriate.

'Maybe I should choose a short list and then ask the people of Consort Park to vote on it.'

Larry shudders. 'If you do that, you'll end up with some frightful naturalistic bronze of your local bigwig.'

'Not if it's not on my short list.'

'Once the general public thinks it's been given leave to speak, it starts throwing its philistine weight around and your short list won't mean a damn. If you want good art in your park, Rosa, you must play the autocrat. You must do the choosing. Give them a *fait accompli*. With a little help from your friends, of course.' He smiles meaningfully.

Larry's right. If the views of Mary the Hologram or Singing Vic are anything to go by, I'll be caught between a statue of Princess Diana, and a group piece depicting the heroic fire-watching activities of the burghers of Consort Park during World War Two. I've no choice. I'll have to set myself up as Consort's lone guardian of culture. Apart from anything else, Rob really will come back to haunt me if I'm responsible for erecting a monstrosity in his precious park.

Larry's wrong, however, if he thinks I'm gullible enough to put all my eggs in the L'Estrange basket. He's not the only dealer in town.

'Larry, you've been so helpful. Obviously your artists won't be the only ones I look at – that would be unfair – but I know I'll be able to rely on your impartial advice when push comes to shove.'

Not part of Larry's plan.

'Push comes to shove. What a delightful expression.' His voice drips bitter lemon. 'Must be one of those Northern gems of yours that dear Rob used to find so amusing.'

I need to keep him on side. Time for a diversionary tactic.

'Wasn't Steve Pyne a sculptor before he got into Video Art?'

Diversionary tactic?

Please.

More like a suicide bomb.

I've conjured up the one person that Larry wants to forget.

71

His pebble eyes glare.

Then Flavia chips in.

'I knew there was something I had to tell you, darling. Steve Pyne came here this morning—'

I didn't think Larry was physiologically capable of losing his strange pallor, but his cheeks have turned a liverish purple.

'What did he do, the miserable little oik?'

'Darling, calm down. He didn't do anything. He just wanted me to plead his case with you.'

'Plead his case? Plead his case? The man's a foul-mouthed, lying drunk. How dare he come here and pester you!'

'He was very contrite. He says he's stopped drinking . . .'

'I'd be a very rich man if I'd bet on how many times he's promised that.'

'But—'

'If I find out he's attempted anything like this again, I shan't be responsible for my actions. Excuse me – I have to make a call.' He storms out.

I take an inordinate interest in the exotic bird patterns on Flavia's plates.

'You must excuse him,' she says quietly. 'He's rather over-protective sometimes.'

Flavia and I take a mirror-and-gilt lift back up to the drawing room where an unbelievably skinny man with wire-wool hair and Flavia's bone structure unfolds himself from a chair.

'Good Lord, Floss, Larry's just passed me with a face like thunder. What's up?'

'Larry doing a Larry, that's all. Rosa, this is my brother, Theo Grey. Theo, this is Rosa Thorn.'

His fingers are parchment-dry and his eyes are identical to his sister's.

'Robin Thorn's wife. How nice to meet you. Shocked when I heard of his death. Modern art's not my bag, but all the same – a tragic waste.'

'Theo's stuck in the Middle Ages,' Flavia says. 'Illuminated manuscripts, to be precise. Anything painted after about 1480 is a no-no as far as he's concerned. Piero's *Flagellation*'s about the outer limit, isn't it, Theo?'

'My sister thinks that just because she's married to Mr Brit Art, she can make fun of old fuddy-duddies like me, who know what real painting is.'

'Are you a dealer too?'

'Good Lord no. I'm in the death business.'

'Sorry?'

'I'm a funeral director. The manuscripts are my little hobby. But in a moment of rebellion a very long time ago, I nearly broke my father's heart by going to art school for a while, so I'm not completely ignorant of what's what in this benighted century of ours.'

The penny drops. *Grey & Son*, Funeral Directors to the rich and titled. Discreet, exclusive – anyone who's anyone is buried by *Grey & Son*. Rumour has it they made their original money by devising a secret magic formula to deal with the tricky cosmetic details of re-attaching severed heads to bodies for aristocratic families during the French Revolution.

Undertaker? That's like calling Chippendale a chippy. More like a national institution. A funeral by *Grey & Son* is a work of art.

I don't really want to talk about death, if indeed Theo Grey were willing to give me any choice details about the funerals of the famous, which I doubt, so instead I quiz him about his self-confessed passion. He's a shy man, but gradually, as he sees my genuine interest, he opens up. He's immensely knowledgeable on his subject, and the more interest I show, the more animated he becomes.

Eventually, Flavia intervenes. 'Rosa doesn't want to spend all evening listening to you droning on about dusty old bits of parchment.'

Theo blushes, self-conscious all of a sudden. 'So sorry. I get a bit carried away. Hope I haven't bored you to death.'

'Certainly not. You make it all come alive—'

'Really?'

'Absolutely.'

A big grin suddenly illuminates his cadaverous face.

Flavia chips in, 'He keeps his collection at the office. I'm sure he'd love to show it to you one day.'

Theo looks embarrassed. 'Only if you're interested.'

'I'd love to.'

I'm not lying. I've always been fascinated by the rich colours and intricate detail in illuminated manuscripts. Normally in museums these things are behind glass. To handle one myself would be a genuine thrill. And I like Theo. Although he's at least fifty, his boyish enthusiasm makes him appear much younger.

Eventually I take my leave. As I bowl through Knightsbridge towards Kensington and Consort Park beyond, I sink back into the plush leather seats of Larry's car. I could get used to this.

Back home in suburban North London, reality once more

bites. Someone has stuck an empty Coke can and two crisp packets in the hedge.

'Dolores,' I call. 'Clean up this mess, would you.'

But Dolores is several miles away in Chester Square, doing the washing up. I fish out the litter and deposit it in the bin, smiling at two passing dog walkers who are staring at me rather strangely.

My house is comfortingly familiar in the darkness. It doesn't have any airs and graces, but it's mine, and I love it. As I unlock the front door I catch a heady whiff of night-scented stock. I remember the day I planted the seeds in the spring, and my excitement when the first shoots emerged. I've kept it alive through the blazing summer heat and have an emotional investment in it, probably unknown to the folk of Belgravia who no doubt employ contract firms to deal with such trivial matters as garden maintenance.

Who needs staff?

I go to the kitchen for a drink.

It's while I'm opening the fridge door that I see a movement in my peripheral vision.

Infinitesimal.

Outside the window.

Must have been a cat on the sill.

I reach into the fridge.

There it is again.

Not a cat.

Larger.

I turn.

Nothing.

Heart thundering, I switch off the kitchen light and leave the room. Then I extinguish the hall light. Now the house is in darkness. I creep back into the kitchen.

I've been through worse than this. Much worse.

Larger than a cat.

Probably a fox.

I approach the window. At first the blackness outside is impenetrable, but as my eye adjusts, various shapes loom up: the big sycamore tree by the railway line at the end of the garden; the bulk of the shed halfway down. Then I see movement. I press my face against the glass, and see a cat weaving between the bushes. The window feels cool against my forehead, and my speeding heart is quietening when suddenly it happens.

A face rears up next to mine.

Only the thin pane of glass separates us.

It's Rob.

EIGHT

My legs lose all strength. His face fuzzes over like a faulty TV, and the sound of my screaming comes from miles away.

So this is what it's like to have a full-blown hallucination. No wonder it freaks people out. It's so real. Through the shock and the fear, I'm conscious of bitter disappointment. I thought I'd accepted Rob's death, and started to move on. And now this: the product of a disordered mind still locked in grief.

Hallucinating, for God's sake!

Please!

Indignation at my own weakness brings a kind of strength. I will not give in to this foolishness. I will be the rational creature I've always considered myself to be. The fuzziness recedes. Hopefully the face will too.

But no. It's still millimetres away from me. I can see every pore. I can see his molasses eyes gazing into mine. I can see through his parted lips the slightly protruding front teeth, with the ugly metal train tracks running across them.

Wait.

Rob didn't have braces. Surely the afterlife doesn't come inclusive of dental treatment? That has to be one of the perks of being dead: no more dental appointments.

His hair is worn in tight braids next to his scalp. Rob never wore braids.

Then there's the fear.

His fear.

Why should he be frightened? He's the one doing the haunting.

Inescapable conclusion: no ghost.

So who is this doppelgänger presently turning tail?

He'll be gone in seconds.

After what I've been through, everything in me screams that chasing after a Peeping Tom is insane. What I should do is phone the fuzz and lock all the doors.

I do the one, but not the other. While making the 999 call, I grab my carving knife.

Someone *was* following me. I'm not just a wimp with a neurotic imagination. A burst of insane energy surges through my body. I will not be terrorised in my own house.

Not again.

Not ever.

And I have to find out why he looks so like Rob. He could be Rob. Maybe he *is* Rob, in spite of the braids and the braces. Maybe Rob's death and everything that's happened since was some ghastly dream and I've just woken up. Woken up to see my darling inexplicably running away from me. Why would he do that? Rob would never run away from me or his house – he loved this house, his security blanket after all the Children's Homes. A million thoughts whip through my head in a nanosecond. I'm dimly aware that I'm straying into the realms of fantasy and hysteria but I can't help it. *It is Rob.* Back from the dead. Miraculously restored to me, but now fast disappearing – and I'm letting him go. I have to stop him! I have to get to Rob!

Flinging open the back door, I hurtle down the garden and catch him as he's climbing the end fence. I grab his leg. He tries to shake me off, but I hold on tight. No phantom menace here: too, too solid flesh.

'Get down!'

The laws of physics and my adrenaline rush are on my side. I hang on like grim death. No way is he leaving me again. I've suddenly acquired super-strength. Eventually he drops to the ground. I shove my knife towards his face.

He's not Rob.

I can see that clearly now – even in the moonlight. He's thinner, and younger. Still in his twenties.

Sanity seeps back, and with it a searing grief. A limitless yearning.

And a rampant urge to reach out and touch his face.

To pretend for a few more seconds.

I struggle to regain control over myself, and him, scrabbling around for the rudiments of classroom authority that I picked up during my shortlived spell as a teacher.

'Who are you?'

He remains silent.

'Who are you?'

Still nothing.

'Why do you look like my husband?'

'I'm sorry.'

'Sorry doesn't begin to cover it.'

We eyeball each other.

'The police are on their way.'

I hear the approaching siren. So does he. His hand goes towards his pocket. I brandish my knife. 'Don't move!'

'I'm Robin's brother.'

My heart slams into my ribcage. Whatever I was expecting, it wasn't this.

Liar.

My mouth is dry, but I force the words out. 'You'll have to do better than that. My husband was an only child.'

Then I hear shouting.

'Police!'

'Move,' I say. 'Up to the side entrance.'

He obeys, eyes fixed on my knife. Once there, I open the gate. Two wonderfully large policemen shine their torches on to us.

'Are you all right, madam?'

'I'm fine.'

'Is this the intruder?'

'He was looking through my window. And I think he's been following me.'

'Name, please, sir?'

He remains mute.

'Sir?'

When he speaks, his voice is low but defiant. 'Joshua Gayle.'

'Are you aware that you're trespassing, Mr Gayle?'

'I'm her brother-in-law.'

That again.

'I don't have a brother-in-law,' I snap.

'Let me explain.'

All of a sudden my legs buckle. I'm shaking uncontrollably. 'Get him away from me,' I say.

'You've had a shock,' says Plod I. 'I'm going to take Mr Gayle down to the station and hear what he's got to say for himself. My colleague will make you a cup of tea.'

I watch as Rob's double is led away.

'What'll happen to him?' I say hoarsely.

'Do you want to press charges? We can get him for trespass.'

'I don't know. I just . . . I don't understand why he looks so like my husband.'

'We'll check out his story. Don't worry.' Plod II hesitates, looking uncomfortable. 'I'm new to Consort Park nick, but I heard what happened to you and your family. This is the last thing you need.'

For a second I relive the unbearable fear I'd experienced in this very house the night Anna disappeared. 'I can't have him hanging around. I can't go through that again.' To my horror I burst into tears.

'You shouldn't have gone after him.' His voice is gentle.

'I know. It's just that for a moment I thought he was . . . I thought . . .'

'Hopefully he won't try again, but if he does, leave it to us, will you?'

Later, when Plod II's leaving, I say, 'I need to know who he is.'

'We'll be in touch tomorrow.'

I double-lock both doors, check all the windows and switch on every light in the house.

I don't fall asleep until way after the birds start singing.

NINE

'I'm Robin's brother.'

The words reverberate round my brain all night. They're still with me this morning. What kind of sick joke is this?

Rob didn't have a brother. Rob would have given his eye-teeth for a brother, but he had no family at all.

He was born in Trinidad to a young girl who wilfully neglected him. Eventually his grandmother, on a visit from Brixton, brought him back to England. When she died a couple of years later, social services tried to contact his mother in Port of Spain. They failed, and Rob spent the rest of his childhood in care. Once, not long after we'd had Danny, he tried to trace her, but without success. He'd always assumed she'd died of drink or drugs.

Was it possible that she'd lived? Produced another child?

No.

Because she'd have tried to find Rob. She must have heard about her own mother's death, and even she, with her flaky parenting skills, would surely not have left her child to the tender mercies of an unknown state on the other side of the world.

Conclusion: Joshua Gayle is playing some dark game of his own.

At least I know I was right about being followed. That's good. Now I can put a face to my fear even if, unbelievably, that face is Rob's. That's all good, isn't it? It's not like last time. Apart from anything else, the police won't make the same mistakes. When Anna disappeared they didn't want to know. This time they'll listen. They have already. Those officers were round last night in double-quick time.

It'll all be all right.

I do such a good job of convincing myself, that when the door-bell rings in the late afternoon, I'm absorbed in emailing Anna and the shrill noise shocks me. It's Plod II from last night.

'Come in,' I say.

'Sorry we haven't contacted you before now, Mrs Thorn,' he says, 'but we've been waiting on information that's only just come through.'

'And?'

'Mr Gayle is the second son of Tani Gayle, formerly Tani Thorn. He is who he says he is: your late husband's half-brother.'

For a moment the world tips on its axis.

'Are you sure?'

'We've been very thorough. We've spoken to our colleagues in Port of Spain, who did the research for us, and all the legal documentation's been faxed through this afternoon. I've brought the printouts for you.'

I stare at copies of various certificates, plus a couple of letters from respectable citizens of Trinidad who've known Joshua Gayle since birth, and a reference from his ex-employer, a hotel manager.

Can this be happening?

'The lad's very anxious to talk to you, Mrs Thorn, but he does realise that he's gone about things the wrong way, and he understands if you want him charged with trespass and don't wish to see him.'

It's all too much.

'Do you want us to charge him?' asks Plod II.

'I don't know. No.'

'Are you sure?'

'Yes. But I don't know what to do – whether to see him. It's such a shock . . .'

'You could speak to him at the station, if you're still feeling nervous. It's up to you.'

'I don't know . . .'

'The thing is, as soon as I tell my guv that you're not pressing charges, we'll have to let him go.'

'I'll come.'

Twenty minutes later I'm sitting opposite Joshua Gayle in a bleak little room at Consort Park Police Station.

'Do you believe me now?'

The lilt is Rob's. Trinidadian. But whereas Rob retained only a vestigial echo from childhood, the voice of this young man is straight from the island – melodic and sun rich. And very correct. He sounds more English than any Englishman.

'The documents say you're Rob's brother.'

'My name is Joshua Gayle and I swear on my mother's grave that I am telling you the truth. I am your brother-in-law.'

'Rob thought his mother was dead. Otherwise why did she abandon him after his grandmother's death? What sort of a mother would do that?'

Joshua Gayle's eyes flash. 'A good mother. *My* mother. She did what she had to do.'

'You're much younger than Rob. We thought that with her history of drug abuse she'd have died long ago.'

'Not till three months ago.'

When you've been married to someone for a long time, even if they're dead and no longer with you, you feel their emotions as if they are your own. And hearing that Rob's mother had lived on all these years without trying to find him, an intense pain shoots through me.

'Why didn't she come for Rob?'

It's quite a story.

Rob's mother knew she was a bad parent, but she still loved her boy and wanted the best for him. England and Miss Pearl were the best, so she let them go. Then she sank into despair and degradation, and would have died, if she hadn't been rescued by Solomon Gayle, minister of God. After he married her, he said she was to forget her previous existence. He burned the paper containing Rob's address in England, and whenever she mentioned her son, he would close his eyes and chant the 23rd Psalm.

All went according to Solomon's plan except for one thing: no pregnancies, in spite of Reverend Gayle's twice-weekly servicings. He blamed Tani, the sperm of Solomon Gayle being unquestionably potent, and became nastier with every passing year.

Eventually she secretly consulted a gynaecologist who told her that the problem lay with God's shepherd. Tani despaired. She couldn't tell the Reverend that he was shooting blanks. The gynaecologist suggested a radical solution. He offered his services as a stud. For a small fee.

She fled from the hospital, horrified. But the idea took hold. If she could give the Reverend a son, her life might become tolerable, and another child might fill the place in her heart vacated by her little lost boy. She returned to the gynaecologist and said simply, 'Do what you have to do.'

Ten months later, Joshua was born. Gayle poured all his energy into educating his son in the ways of the Lord. This involved much chastisement, physical and mental, but as the Reverend repeatedly told Tani, you can't make an omelette without breaking eggs.

As Joshua grew into a man, so Tani retreated into herself, dwindling almost to vanishing point. Then four months ago, the Reverend Gayle was haranguing sinners outside his church, when the nails holding Our Saviour prisoner on the Cross above the church door, finally rusted through. Jesus crashed down onto the Reverend's head, killing him outright. A month later Tani succumbed to pneumonia and followed him to the grave.

'It was the freedom, you see,' Joshua explains. 'She couldn't take it. The cage door was open but she'd forgotten how to fly. She died of fright.'

'So how did you find out about Rob?'

'One day, just before she died, my mother told me to fetch a wooden box she'd hidden in a space underneath the house. In it were some papers.'

He rummages in his pocket and produces a pitiful collection

of objects: a birth certificate in the name of Robin Thorn, a dog-eared black and white photo showing a young woman clutching a beaming toddler, and a newspaper cutting dated from last year announcing the death of Trinidadian-born artist, Robin Thorn, in a car crash.

'That's the other thing that killed her – finding her boy was dead.'

I pick up one of the photos. 'You?'

'Robin. My mother said she was frightened of looking at this picture too much in case it wore away. It was the only one she had, you see. She said it was taken on the last occasion she remembers feeling happy. The following day she met someone and fell in love. That's when she started to neglect Rob. She told me that she used to have an irrational belief that if she stared hard enough at the photograph, relived the memory hard enough, somehow she'd be able to go back in time to that moment, and change the future.'

Rob snuggles into his mother's shoulder, his chubby fingers clutching her hair. They both look happy, and my heart feels close to breaking.

'Why had she never told you about your brother?'

'She said she was too ashamed.'

'Ashamed?'

'Of her sinful past, and of not standing up to my father and searching for Robin. I said I wished he were not my father. So she told me about the gynaecologist.'

'That must have been a shock.'

'Solomon Gayle was a cruel, vindictive bully. Knowing his blood didn't flow through my veins was a great relief. I no longer felt unnatural for loathing my own father. Then my mother died. She'd had one month of happiness. One month of freedom. I thought about her wasted life, and realised I didn't want to waste any more of mine. I could do whatever I liked, and what I most wanted was to come back to England and find out about my brother. He was dead, but if I could find his family, I could somehow make him come alive for me.'

'Come *back* to England?'

'I was at art school in Brighton for a while about eight years ago.'

'You're an artist too?'

A complex series of emotions passes across his features. 'It didn't work out for me, so I went home and got a job in the hotel business.'

'You never heard of Rob when you were over here?'

'No. Back then I didn't even know I had a brother.'

And eight years ago Rob was a struggling unknown.

Who would have been overjoyed to find he had a brother.

'When I found the gallery mentioned in the article there was a poster in the window advertising my brother's exhibition. It said it was at their new gallery in the East End, opening that very day. But when I arrived I didn't have an invitation, so I hung around outside. The door was open, and I could hear the speech about Robin. The man mentioned Robin's family and everyone looked at you, so I knew that you were my brother's wife.'

'Why all the sneaking around?'

'I planned to introduce myself, but when I saw all the rich people at the party I felt too shy. You were part of a different world, and you and your children seemed like a closed circle with no room for me. But I so wanted to find out what it would be like to be part of my brother's family, so I followed you home, and then I started watching you. And once I started I couldn't stop.'

'I *knew* I was being followed! I thought I was going mad.'

'I stayed hidden because I didn't want you to feel threatened in any way.'

'What you didn't know was that I'd had a very bad experience recently involving a stalker.'

'Oh.' His face is a picture of dawning horror.

'Where are you staying?'

'I hired a car for a few days, and slept in that, but then I had to take it back.'

'A blue Ford Fiesta?'

'Yes.'

'Ah.'

'So . . .' He can't quite get it out.

'Yes?'

'. . . I've been sleeping in your shed.'

He looks so forlorn. I see Anna and Danny in his face as well as Rob, and I imagine them all alone in the world with no home and no one to care for them.

'Why did you think I'd turn you away?'

'Even if you believed who I was, my mother had abandoned your husband. You might have hated me. Then I'd have had to leave. And I wasn't ready for that.'

I know what I must do. The documentation's clear, and the letters of reference talk of a decent, respectable person – the son of a preacherman, for God's sake.

He is Rob's brother. Rob's flesh. Danny and Anna's flesh.

And I trust him.

Why? Because he looks like Rob? No, not just because of that.

I want to keep him here, if only to pretend for a while. He's not Rob, but he's the nearest thing to him that I've seen since that fatal autumn day.

I want to be with him.

I *have* to be with him.

What if I am taking a risk? Life's a risk. I know that, more than anybody. I can't cower in the corner, opting out of all risk-taking, just because I've encountered one maniac.

And anyway, I've had my quota of madmen. It's hardly likely that lightning would strike twice in the same place. Plus it's my own safety I'm gambling with. No one else's. The children aren't here.

The events of last January clamour to be heard, leaving me breathless and trembling with the memory, but the urge to talk to this wonderfully familiar stranger is even stronger.

'You must stay with me,' I hear myself say.

A look of elation illuminates his face for a split second. But then he says, 'I could not possibly impose on you.'

'And I couldn't let Rob's brother live on the streets.'

'I'm not a beggar. I still have a little money.'

I've offended his pride.

'I just wanted to spend time near my brother's house.'

'Then stay.'

His eyes search my face to see if I mean it.

'I could do with the company,' I go on. 'Danny and Anna are away and the house feels very empty.'

It's not an outright lie. And as I say it I realise that even if I am being stupid, I don't care. I can't bear to part with Rob's brother.

Not yet.

'You are very kind.'

'That's settled then.'

In the subterranean twilight, Theo Grey gazed at the remains of Sir Simon Gilbert, banker and bully.

'Perfection.'

Sir Simon lay naked on the slab, his bony body awaiting the Savile Row suit in which he was to be clothed for all eternity. Theo's eye travelled lovingly over the angles and planes of the emaciated frame. 'Holbein's *Dead Christ in the Tomb*,' he murmured. 'Exquisite.'

The embalmer had done an excellent job. Being a perfectionist, Theo liked to check all aspects of what went on in *Grey & Son*, but the employees he watched most closely were the embalmers. He knew his staff whispered among themselves about his constant presence in the embalming rooms. He knew they thought it odd that he frequently slept down here. He didn't care. He was the boss: he could do as he pleased. Occasionally, as a treat, he'd take over a job himself, glorying in all the rituals and routines. One of his great sorrows was that, with all his other responsibilities, he couldn't do it more often.

Down here was his favourite place. Down among the dead.

The dead were so perfect. At ease in their flesh. Completed. Finished. Like art. You knew where you were with art and death.

No messy uncertainties. No painful misunderstandings and uncomfortable negotiations.

The dead were his friends. They spoke to him. He could fathom their contradictions. Understand their stories. Whatever end they'd made, however ugly, the finality of death made them beautiful. Made sense of their lives.

The living were something else. Them he couldn't cope with – or understand. They said one thing but meant another. Gave out contradictory and conflicting signals. Encouraged you to enter, then shut the door in your face. Rosa Thorn, for example. Said she'd like to see his collection. Did he believe her, or not? Judging from past experience, was it not better to leave well alone?

He ran a hand over Sir Simon's frozen flesh, his fingertips lingering intimately in all the humps and hollows.

'What should I do?' he asked the dead knight. 'Ask her or not?' He pulled up a chair and settled down for a cosy chat. It was late. Nobody would disturb them.

TEN

Joshua and I drop off the radar for a while. We have a lot to talk about, and there's a depth of feeling on both our parts that won't brook interruption from any outside source. On his side, he needs to climb inside his brother's life and explore every nook and cranny, and on mine I have to search out and experience the Rob in him before I share him with the rest of the world. I know that the resemblance will fascinate all who meet him, and I can't yet bear the emotions we're both going through to be modified and dissipated through the prism of other people's reactions. I haven't even told my children. The discovery of their father's brother is an event of such magnitude that its revelation has to be a face-to-face thing. Fortunately, Anna's emails from Delhi are so focused on the wonderful time she's having and the wonderful people she's meeting that I could write out the alphabet ad infinitum without her noticing, and as Danny's communications are, as ever, super-minimal, I take a leaf out of his book and mimic this style in my replies.

But eventually the heightened emotional temperature drops, and the extraordinary becomes ordinary. I stop doing double-takes every time I round a corner to be confronted by my husband's back view, I've heard every last thing about Rob's mother, and Joshua has pored over every photograph in every album, read all Rob's press cuttings, and pillaged my memory for the minute details of all major events in Rob's life and a fair number of the minor ones as well. We reach a point where we are no longer talismanic figures; the veil is torn away and we are revealed to each other as mere mortals like everyone else. It's time to face the world.

Step one is to deal with the messages on the answerphone: Gillian, Leni, Caroline. Several from Jess and Mike, a couple from Larry about the sculpture project, one from David Borodino's snotty PA trying to fix up lunch, and a rambling aria from Pru Gibb, chair of the Consort Park Residents' Association. This one I have to replay several times to extract the main burden.

'Pru Gibb here, Rosa. I want to get moving asap with this Consort Park sculpture whatsit so the work can be inaugurated on Consort Park Day in September. Do run your short list by me before any definitive decision's made. Bit of a tip – don't go for anything too avant-garde – people won't like it. I've always admired the work of Dick Pinker, but don't feel you have to take my wishes into account. Oh – another tip – don't listen to anything that Greg Holden has to say. He doesn't know what he's—'

My answerphone cuts out at this point. Even machines can't cope with Pru Gibb in full flood. Being chair of the Consort Park

Residents' Association is just one of Pru's myriad voluntary activities. She's known as PG Tips, in recognition of her favourite phrase and the fact that she's a walking advice bureau to some people, and a bloody know-all to others. I'd forgotten that dealing with Skinny Minnie's legacy would bring me into contact with Pru Gibb.

I decide that she's not top priority at this point.

Jess is.

She's my best friend. She has to be the first to meet Joshua. I give her a ring and ask if she can pop round.

'Yes, miss, no, miss, three fucking bags full, miss. Suddenly, having ignored me all week, La Thorn wants to play.'

'Shut your face and get your fat ass round here pronto. It's worth your while. Promise.'

Ten minutes later she's on my doorstep with Lozz.

'What's so important that I have to be dragged away from my sodding sixth-form coursework marking? You know how I love it.' Her face fizzes with impatient curiosity.

I take them through to the kitchen.

'Close your eyes.'

Jess grumbles, good-naturedly, but does as she's told. Lozz is bouncing with excitement, fingers fixed tightly over his eyes. I fetch Joshua.

'Open.'

I'm not prepared for what happens next.

Jess's face loses all colour and Lozz dives under the table.

'Robbie dead, Robbie dead,' he whimpers.

Jess drags her eyes away from Josh and puts a comforting hand on Lozz's head.

'It's OK, my lovely.'

'Lozz don't like no spookies.'

Jess glares at me. 'Frightening Down's children's your new hobby, is it?'

I've blanked on how shocked I was when I first saw Joshua. I could kick myself. I know how frightened Lozz is by situations that he doesn't understand. It shows how self-absorbed I've become over the past few days, going over every detail of my life with Rob for Joshua's benefit.

'This is Joshua, Lozz. He's not a spooky and he isn't Robbie, although you're right – he looks just like him. Don't be scared.'

'I'll go . . .' Joshua glances towards the door.

'Wait. Lozz, you once told me that you'd like a brother . . .'

From under the table comes a sniff.

'Robbie always wanted a brother too.'

'Yeah?'

'And now it turns out he had one all the time. But his mum didn't know Robbie's address so she couldn't tell him. Joshua is Robbie's little brother. He found out where we lived and came right across the world to see us.'

Lozz slowly emerges.

'Hey, Lozz, pleased to meet you.'

Lozz stretches out a tentative hand and feels Joshua's face.

'Not Robbie,' he says eventually. 'Robbie's brother.'

'That's right.'

'Has Lozz got a lost brother too?'

Jess snorts. 'Now see what you've started,' she says to me. 'Afraid not, my lovely. You'll just have to make do with your dear old mum.' Then she turns to me. 'So let's have it.'

'Tell her, Joshua.'

Second time round I'm aware of how theatrical he is – how skilled at painting the circumstances of poor Tani Thorn's hapless life.

Jess's shrewd grey eyes continually flick from me to him, and I swear I can hear the cogs in her brain whirring.

Finally he finishes.

'That's quite a tale,' says Jess. 'You must tell it to my Year Elevens. It'll do wonders for their creative-writing skills.'

Creative writing?

'I'm sorry?' Joshua's puzzled

'She's teasing,' I say.

'Can I play outside?' Lozz has had enough.

'What about a game of football?' Joshua grabs his chance to escape Jess's beady eye.

Lozz regards him, eyes huge and solemn. 'All right,' he says eventually, and slowly follows him into the garden.

'Well,' says Jess.

'Well what?'

'It's remarkable.'

'I know. You'd think he was Rob's identical twin.'

'Not his looks.'

'Then what?'

'It's remarkable that he should turn up now.'

'What do you mean?'

'Just when Rob's getting maximum publicity, as a dead icon who's worth a bob or two.'

'And your point is?'

'You know what my point is.'

'What?' I pretend ignorance.

'Isn't it just too fucking convenient?'

'The police checked his story. He is Rob's brother – I've seen the documentation. And he's a very sweet bloke.'

'So was Ted Bundy . . .'

'Ha ha.'

'I can't believe you're letting him stay. It's madness, Rosy. You of all people should know that.'

Outside, Lozz and Joshua kick the ball around in a desultory fashion.

'Lozz likes him.'

Lozz is our bullshit detector. He has an uncanny instinct for it. If Lozz hangs back – beware.

'Lozz isn't infallible.'

'Look at him. He's fine.'

'My son may not be your normal Norman, but he knows his manners. Joshua's your guest. Lozz is being a polite host.'

'Jessie, I know you mean well, but you mustn't worry. Joshua's OK.'

'You're fucking insane. After everything that's happened . . .'

'I know. It's just that . . .'

Her eyes are full of a sudden understanding. 'It's just that you can look at him and pretend the last year and a half hasn't happened.'

I'm not going to cry.

Her voice is soft. 'But it has, babe, and taking a complete stranger into your house isn't going to change anything.'

'Leave it, Jess.'

'At least find him a B and B.'

'He can't afford a B and B.'

'Not when he can scrounge off you.'

'You're starting to seriously piss me off.'

'What does he do for a living when he's not on a freeloading holiday bender?'

'Why should I tell you? You'll only carp and sneer.'

She looks at me and then shrugs. 'Suit yourself. I'd better go. Marking beckons.' She rises and bangs on the window to Lozz.

'He's a photographer.'

'What kind of photographer? Documentary, fashion, catalogue – what?'

'Beach.'

'Didn't quite catch that. For one moment I thought you said beach. As in beach bum.'

'For an unreconstructed lefty, you sure are bigoted sometimes. He was in the hotel trade but he's really keen on photography. He gave up an assistant hotel manager's job in order to concentrate on it.'

'Concentrate on taking happy snaps of boozed-up tourists on package Caribbean holidays? Great career move.'

'It's a way of earning a few bob until he establishes himself.'

'He's established himself here quite nicely. The boy done good.'

'Jess . . .'

'There's something about all this that stinks to high heaven. But I can see I'm wasting my breath. I'm off. Just be careful – that's all I'm saying.' She bangs on the window again and shouts, 'Lozz, I'm counting to three and then I'm going. Get your big fat bum in here right now, or you can forget about chocolate-chip ice cream for tea.'

Lozz and Joshua come inside.

'I'll be seeing you again, I expect, Joshua,' says Jess. 'I'm always in and out. Rosa's my dearest friend. We look out for each other, don't we, Rosy?'

She's very subtle, my friend.

'That's good, Jess,' says Joshua. 'It's good that Rosa has such a wonderful friend. And it's good that now she also has me.' There's a challenge in his face.

'Whatever,' Jess says eventually, making no pretence of good manners.

After she's gone, Joshua says, 'I don't think she likes me.'

'It's just Jess. She's been super-protective since Rob died.'

'You are fortunate to have such a friend.' There's a brittle quality to his voice that I haven't heard before.

'Yes, I am,' I say. 'Now tell me about this hotel you used to work in. You're very brave, chucking in a good job for freelance beach photography.'

The National Gallery was packed. Gillian cursed herself for not arriving before the bulk of the tourists. She wouldn't mind if she felt that people were enjoying themselves, but most of them trailed morosely from room to room, barely glancing at the treasures arrayed along the walls. An image appeared unbidden in her mind: herself, mowing down the press of bodies with a Kalashnikov in order to get a clear view of her painting. Good God! Had she taken her pills this morning? Perhaps the dosage needed adjusting. Or perhaps it was the pills themselves. She really ought to phase them out, get back to normal.

Whatever that was.

Her usual bench was occupied by two children who were thumping each other. Gillian waited. Eventually their mother dragged them away and she was able to view her painting: *Broken Lute* by Salvator Vera (*b.* Toledo 1623 – *d.* Seville 1670).

In the foreground a table, covered in a dark red velvet cloth of Moorish design. On it a half-spent candle in a brass candlestick, a lute with a broken string, and a skull. Behind the table, emerging from deep shadow, a young child with merry brown eyes, scarcely tall enough to peer over the table at the objects arranged so carefully before her, blowing bubbles from a clay pipe. The largest bubble, at the moment before bursting, hovers over her, its iridescent colours caught by the candlelight.

The painting never failed to work its magic. The National Gallery possessed only one Salvator Vera, and Gillian was grateful that it was *Broken Lute*. Unlike most of Vera's work, which was unremittingly dark and gloomy, this painting, in spite of all the *mementi mori*, had a kind of strange life-force. It emanated from the child with her radiant smile.

'Hello, Gillian.' The husky voice made her jump.

Leni Dang.

Gillian's heart lifted. 'Leni! I see you're taking a leaf out of my book. The only way to learn about art is to look. And the National Gallery's one of the best places to do it.'

'Actually, *Dame* sent me. They want a piece on the restored Titian.'

'Oh, wonderful! I do so love late Titian. All those effulgent colours.'

Leni looked blank and stuffed something into her bag – the

Gallery audio-guide. She blushed when she saw that Gillian had noticed, and indicated *Broken Lute*.

'That's dark,' she commented.

'Often the point of these Vanitas jobbies.'

'Excuse me?'

'Meant to encourage us to have a bit of a ponder.'

Leni clearly didn't know what she was on about.

'Very popular in the seventeenth century. Done to remind us of the transience of existence – you know: "Vanity of vanities, saith the preacher, vanity of vanities; all is vanity". Ecclesiastes.'

Leni's incomprehension deepened.

'The paintings depict symbols of mortality and the fragility of earthly delights. The skull and the guttering candle represent death, the lute with the broken string, the futility of art and ambition, and, of course, there's the bubble. *Homo Bulla* – Man as a bubble – vanishing like the ephemeral products of a child's play.'

'Goodness, Gillian, you know so much.'

'The seventeenth century's my period – Still Life in particular. I've told you about my book.'

'You did mention it.'

Gillian caught the flash of panic in her eyes.

The self-absorption of the young.

She'd met Leni at White Cube. The girl was crying in the loo. She'd been commissioned to write about the Sam Taylor Wood show, but she didn't have a clue what it was on about. Gillian had plied her with wine and told her what to write. Since then, Leni had called her on a regular basis for advice and Gillian had spent many hours trying to beef up her shaky knowledge of all things artistic.

Mentoring such an eager young acolyte gave Gillian a satisfyingly warm glow, but occasionally she felt it would have been nice if the relationship were a little more reciprocal – that her own activities were not completely marginal as far as Leni was concerned.

'My book about Salvator Vera.' She indicated *Broken Lute*.

'I remember now. Fascinating artist – you told me all about him.'

'Her.'

'Sorry?'

'Salvator Vera was a woman.'

Leni's blush deepened. 'Yes, of course.'

'Her real name was Elena Dias. The only way she could be an artist in seventeenth-century Spain was to pass herself off as a man.'

Gillian felt like crying whenever she contemplated the alias Elena had chosen: Salvator Vera. What made a young girl give up everything, even her sex, in order to pursue her wish to paint? The answer lay in her choice of name: by becoming male she had found truth and salvation.

'Oh.' Leni was still covered in confusion.

Gillian decided the kindest thing to do would be to ignore the *faux pas*.

'Her deception was only discovered after her death. It ruined her reputation and she fell into almost total obscurity until about twenty years ago. I became interested when I was researching something else and discovered a diary of hers.'

'You do so much, Gillian – not only the weekly column, and all the other things, but writing a book as well. And you still have time for me. I've learned masses in the last few months. I'm so grateful.'

One of the imperatives of Gillian's job was to take with a pinch of salt the flummery of those who tried to flatter and cajole, but somehow she believed Leni's naive compliments to be sincere. She allowed herself a daydream in which, in extreme old age, all passion spent, she'd hand on the sacred flame to Leni, by then, under her tutelage, the most brilliant critic of her generation . . .

Though she couldn't help but wonder if Leni was the obvious candidate for this noble scheme, since however much Gillian passed on, she still seemed woefully ignorant of even the most basic art history.

What was it about this particular girl that so strongly brought out her maternal instincts? Leni wasn't by any means the first youngster she'd helped. But she'd never felt this protective tenderness and exasperation before. Maybe it was the vulnerability, coupled with the touching determination to succeed. Or the dogged perseverance that kept her going despite her apparent inability to retain any of the pearls of wisdom that Gillian was so happy to share. Or was it her aura of loneliness? The girl exuded a quality of solitary defensiveness that spoke to Gillian rather in the same way as Elena Dias did.

'Oh dear, I'm going to be late filing my copy. It always takes me so long to write.'

'It should, if it's going to be worth reading.'

'Do you think so?'

'I know so.'

Leni frowned. 'You just said something fantastic about late Titian.'

'Did I? His colours, I expect. How they shimmer on the canvas.'

'What was the word you used? Began with e . . .'

'Word? Oh, you mean effulgent.'

Leni smiled. 'That's the one,' she beamed. 'Effulgent. Bye, Gill. Lovely talking to you.'

'Bye,' said Gillian, and watched the small figure totter away on her absurdly high heels. Goodness, she thought, I must let her into the secret of the successful art critic: take care of the feet before the feet take care of you.

She turned back to the painting. It had been painted in 1648, soon after Elena Dias, having been the secret mistress of the painter Francisco de Zurbaran for three years and having given him three stillborn infants, cast away her femininity for ever, joining the studio of Juan de Valdes Leal as Salvator Vera, one of his male assistants.

Gillian loved the child's face. There was a tenderness in the brush-strokes that spoke of deep affection and attachment, and Gillian, no stranger to the pain and longing of an empty womb, acknowledged again the thing that drew her to this long-dead tormented young painter.

No one could accuse him of giving up, thought Steve Pyne as he ordered flowers for Larry's bitch-hag wife. That'd get the bastard on side again since he was so rapt over the old crow. Make him think that Steve bore no grudges. That he was a reasonable man who didn't want to rock the boat unless Larry forced him to. *L'Estrange* was still the best gallery in town and he fully intended to be reinstated. When Larry took on board the implications of what Steve had told him, Steve calculated that re-instating him would be the least of Larry's concerns.

Meanwhile, there was *Nature Morte*.

Suddenly the world was full of opportunity. Difficult to know what to go for first. *Nature Morte*, probably. Because, even though Larry was in a different league from Zinovieff, the amount of immediately available money involved didn't compare. 'Follow the money,' his dad had always said. He'd ignored the advice up until now, but not any more. He'd had enough. Making great art didn't mean Jackshit if you were skint.

He'd played it perfectly. Let slip he knew about Zinovieff's diversification plans, and suggesting himself as a valuable addition to the gallery in view of said plans. At first Zinovieff hadn't wanted to know, but he soon changed his mind when he saw Steve's latest video project.

All in all Steve felt very pleased with himself. His first few days of sobriety had revealed a functioning brain underneath the alcoholic haze. Sharp as a tack, like he used to be. He'd still got a roof over his head, having grovelled to good old Caro, and he'd even coaxed the phone number of Luscious Leni out of a dim secretary at *Dame*.

Life was on the up.

ELEVEN

The next day dawns blazing hot. Joshua and I go to *L'Estrange East*. He wants to see his brother's show, and I have to talk to Larry about the Consort Park sculpture project.

As we turn into Navarre Street, a gangling black crow in his long undertaker's overcoat cannonades into me.

Theo Grey.

'I do apologise,' he says. 'How very clumsy of me.'

'Hello, Theo.'

Recognition dawns.

'Rosa! I'm so sorry. I was miles away. What brings you to these parts?'

'The gallery.'

'What?'

'Your brother-in-law's gallery.'

'Of course.'

'May I introduce *my* brother-in-law, Joshua Gayle. Joshua, this is Theo Grey.' It's the first time I've used the phrase *my brother-in-law*. It feels good.

'Delighted to meet you, Joshua.'

Theo doesn't comment on the resemblance between Rob and Joshua. Good. I already feel mightily oppressed by the buzz that the Joshua phenomenon is bound to provoke.

We conduct a halting conversation for a couple of minutes. Theo is shyer than ever. Then just as we're about to move on, he blurts out, 'Were you serious about coming to see my collection?'

There's an eager vulnerability about him as he hovers over me in his thick, unseasonable overcoat. I can't say no. Anyway, I wasn't lying when I said I was fascinated by the intricacy and beauty of medieval illumination.

'I'd love to.'

'Splendid,' he says. 'I'll be in touch.' He glances at his watch. 'Must dash. Rather tricky funeral today. One of our more exuberant captains of industry. Nightmare seating-plan with all the ex-wives and mistresses – not to mention the various little bastards.'

He zigzags off, coat flapping like giant batwings, narrowly missing a street-lamp in his preoccupied progress.

As we pass *Nature Morte*, Joshua says, 'I wouldn't mind popping in there.'

The last thing I want is another session staring at Daisy Fortuna's virulently-coloured creations with Zander Zinovieff breathing down my neck. 'Maybe later.'

The first person we see in *L'Estrange East* is Caroline. She registers Joshua with a gasp. The gasp is followed by a shriek from Julian and a severe intake of breath from Larry. Explanations take some time. Finally I leave Joshua to see the show, and follow

Larry to his office. Caro whispers that she needs to ask me something later.

Larry has prepared his pitch. Several files of photographs are spread across his desk. As I look through them Larry contributes a running commentary.

'Ah, we do so love Tim Lovat's things, the way he uses those divine blues . . . Raymond Banks – what a carver . . . so committed to an intimate relationship between sculpture and site . . . Ailsa Wallace – remember the steel and concrete womb piece at the Venice Biennale? Brilliant! Here's a particular favourite – Marion Fleming. Her stuff's rather on the large side, but isn't it stunning? We do admire the monumental in outdoor sculpture. Small things can so easily disappear into the landscape . . .'

And so on.

Eventually he sits back, a small blue vein throbbing at his temple.

'So . . . what do we think?'

My head is crammed with images of stone, wood, steel, concrete. I can't dredge up one intelligent comment.

'We can arrange studios visits, of course.'

I take a deep breath. 'I'll see that, that, that and that.'

Larry smiles wolfishly. 'Consider it done.'

The phone rings. 'My precious. What can I do for you? . . . Lilies? No, Flavia, I wish I had, since they're giving you such pleasure, but regrettably I didn't. Is there a card? . . . Dolores says what? . . . On the floor – there you are. Mystery solved. Tell your madly jealous husband who exactly has been sending you floral tributes . . .'

Then the fond smile is replaced by a fearsome scowl.

'Miserable little arse-licker! Apology for pestering you! What's sending you flowers except another form of pestering? I won't tolerate it.'

No prizes for guessing the target of Larry's rage.

I slip away.

Joshua's in front of Rob's last painting. It's the back door of our house, seen from the inside. Every whorl and mark in the wood has been painstakingly rendered, as has the patterning on the opaque glass panelling through which indistinct shapes can be seen. Unlike earlier versions, the door's ajar. Through the small slit there's a tantalising glimpse of the garden, hot colours blazing. The urge to push the door open and see the full glory of summer is overwhelming. This painting was still wet on the day he died. No one knows whether he'd finished, but for me it's his most complete statement ever, and whenever I look at the massive canvas I'm torn apart. All that life squandered by a stupid joy-rider who was never even caught.

Joshua is mesmerised. 'It's tropical. Like home.'

'Yes.'

'My brother was a great artist.'

'I think so.'

'One day maybe people will say that about me.' He's defensive and determined at one and the same time.

'Why is your preferred medium photography? Why not painting?'

'It's just the way it is for me.'

'You said art college didn't work out for you?'

His face blanks over. 'No, it didn't.'

I wait for him to say more, but he doesn't. Then after a

moment he says, 'How much would a painting like this sell for?'

Money.

Cash.

Moolah.

I hear Jess's voice. *'Brotherly love? Don't make me laugh.'*

'Nothing's for sale,' I say. 'Let's go.'

Is my friend right? *Is* it money that drives Joshua? Does he see his brother's widow as an easy mark? I look sideways at him, only to find he's looking at me.

'I feel I know Robin much better now,' he says.

The sweetness of his smile makes me curse Jess and her stupid suspicions. All he's done is ask an innocent question about the value of Rob's work.

And asking questions is what Joshua does.

All the time.

It's quite wearing.

We leave the gallery, but before we reach the end of the street I hear my name being called. It's Caroline.

'Caro! I'm so sorry,' I say. 'Larry was in a rage about your boyfriend sending flowers to Flavia. I needed a quick exit.'

'Steve's sent flowers to Flavia? I told him that Larry hates people bothering her. Why won't he ever listen?'

'What can I do for you?' I ask, in a bid to change the subject.

Caroline's looking fierce. 'To ask you a huge favour.'

'Fire away.'

'Steve was a sculptor before he turned to video art . . .'

'So I gather.' I know what's coming next.

'He still has a few unsold pieces. Would you look at them? For Consort Park?'

I need a working relationship with Steve Pyne like I need a pet porcupine, and making a mortal enemy of Rob's dealer isn't exactly part of my game plan. However, this obviously means a lot to Caro. I don't have a choice.

But my face has betrayed me.

'You don't want to offend Larry. I understand.' She's trembling even though the midday heat engulfs us as it rises from the dusty pavement.

I make a decision. I'm not going to be bullied or dictated to by Larry L'Estrange. If I want to buy Steve Pyne's work for Consort Park, then that's my prerogative.

'Fix up a visit, Caro,' I say, 'but don't get too excited. I shan't pick Steve's work unless it's right for the space. Warn him I'm seeing lots of stuff.'

Caroline's eyes are sparkling now. 'I'll call him right now. Cheers, Rosa.' She dashes back into L'Estrange East.

Where's Joshua? I look through the window of Nature Morte.

There he is, examining a still life of whelks and a Chianti bottle. I bang on the window. He's oblivious. Damn. I'm poking my head round the door and hissing his name, when there's an earsplitting crash. Zander Zinovieff has appeared. A huge vase of flowers has slipped from his hands and shattered into tiny fragments. Blood drips from his finger onto the glittering shards of glass covering the floor.

He sways. Joshua and I rush forward to catch him. 'Sit down and put your head between your knees,' I advise him.

'What?' He looks at his finger. 'Oh, yes. Just for a moment . . .

Went over on my ankle – stupid.' He collapses against the wall and slides down to the floor. 'It's the sight of blood.' He stares at Joshua.

'This is my brother-in-law, Joshua Gayle,' I say. 'Joshua, meet Zander Zinovieff. *Nature Morte* is Zander's gallery.'

Joshua smiles. 'I like your show. Great images.'

He sounds sincere. Does he mean it? If he thinks Daisy Fortuna has what it takes, I don't hold out much hope for him as an artist. Or maybe he's a first-class bullshitter.

That's what Jess would say.

'Joshua's an artist too. He works with photographs.'

Zander sounds more animated and the colour's returning to his face. 'An artist – like your brother. You look so like him, it's amazing.' He stands up unsteadily, holding his arm out and wrapping a handkerchief around his wound.

'My brother was a genius. I'm just beginning.'

'I didn't know Rob even had a brother.'

'It's a long story.'

Now Zander's OK, I'm anxious to leave. What I don't need is for Joshua to embark on his life-story. 'Perhaps another time. Will you be all right, Zander? Is there someone here to dress that hand for you?'

'Emil!'

A huge bearded man with long greasy hair full of dandruff appears.

'What you done now?' He grabs Zander's hand. 'This deep cut. Maybe need stitches.'

'Don't fuss. Meet Robin Thorn's brother. And wife.' He turns to us. 'My assistant, Emil Barbu.'

114

Barbu stares at Joshua. Then he gives a curt nod before turning back to Zander.

'You get gangrene don't blame me. I find first-aid box.' He lumbers away.

Zander grins at Joshua. 'Salt of the earth, but a bit lacking in the social skills department. Tell me about your work.'

No way. We'll be here all day.

'We really do have to go.'

Why is Joshua looking so stricken? Of course – a prominent dealer's asking about his work. He doesn't realise Zander's just making polite chit-chat. He must think I'm deliberately sabotaging his brilliant career.

'Why don't you stay,' I suggest. 'I'll catch up with you later.'

Zander's nodding. 'Good plan. I'd love to hear about your work, Joshua. I like to keep up with new young artists. As I always say, they are our lifeblood.'

I slink out into the blinding city heat, aware of a sensation that I can't identify. Then I get it: I feel free. It's the first time since Joshua arrived that I've been alone.

So? What's the big deal?

I force myself to admit something: *Joshua can be quite heavy-going.*

Example: humour.

One of the things I loved about Rob was his scurrilous wit. He made me laugh more than anyone I've ever known. But not Joshua. He's completely lacking in the irony department, taking every lightweight, throwaway remark of mine at face value.

And he's always asking questions. What do people in London do for fun? What's the in thing to wear? Who's hot on the scene?

How much do things cost? And multiple variations on these themes.

But the majority of his questions are about my life – my life with Rob, my life with the children, my career as an actress et cetera, et cetera. I feel like a rabbit caught in the headlights of his insatiable curiosity. It reminds me of when my children were little and first discovered the word 'why'.

Except Joshua isn't little. He's twenty-five years old.

But I suppose twenty-five isn't that old.

Be nice, Rosa.

Standing on the sunlit pavement I feel as I used to when I'd packed Danny and Anna off to school: giddy with the prospect of pleasing myself and no one else.

What to do? Shopping? Or a film? Or I could call on my agent and pressure her into fixing up some castings for me. That would be the sensible thing to do.

Then my mobile rings.

'Shame on you, loitering on street corners wearing that revealing summer frock.'

Mike Mason.

'Don't squint. You'll ruin your eyes.'

'Where are you?'

'Up here.'

Opposite *L'Estrange East* is a warehouse transformed into loft apartments. It has an expensive entrance complete with uniformed concierge.

Mike leans out of an upper window. 'Sixth floor,' he shouts.

And very nice it is too. Ultra-minimal. There's a mezzanine floor for sleeping which hangs over the large main living area.

One end is a working studio space. The other has three squishy sofas, a coffee-table and a vast home cinema system.

'You didn't say your place was opposite the gallery.'

'You didn't ask. Just like you didn't come to the movies with me and Jess last week, and you didn't respond to my dinner invitation, you bad girl. It was Larry who put me on to this place, at Rob's opening. I wanted a decent short-term let, and he suggested this.'

'It's very cool.'

'Almost as cool as your cold shoulder. I'm not here for that long, you know. You've gotta make the most of me.'

'Sorry. You wouldn't believe what a week it's been.'

'Try me.'

'It turns out that Rob's mother only died three months ago, and that Rob's got a half-brother.'

I've never seen a jaw literally drop. 'You're kidding me!'

'His brother's staying with me.'

I tell him all about Joshua. Mike is as devastated as I am to find that Rob's mother was alive during all the years Rob spent in Children's Homes.

'She never tried to find him?'

'Joshua says she couldn't.'

Mike grunts. 'Hell, Rosa – Rob would have given his painting arm to know his mom was still around.'

'Not his painting arm. Any other part of his body, bar the obvious, but not his painting arm.' I'm struggling for a light-hearted tone.

Mike puts an arm round me. 'Hey, it's OK.'

'It's been a bit of a shock.'

'I'll say. So what's this guy like?'

'A young twenty-five. Physically, he's Rob as he used to be twenty years ago. But his personality's very different. Eager to please. Anxious to fit in. A bit earnest sometimes. Massively inquisitive. A quick learner. Obviously enterprising – coming halfway across the world to find us. Sometimes a charmer. Sometimes not. Fancies himself as an artist. Takes photographs. Knocked out by Rob's stuff.'

'But?'

'What?'

'There's a but – I can hear it in your voice. It's me you're talking to, Rosy. I may be on the other side of the pond nowadays, but I still know you better than most.'

'Jess thinks he's a fortune-hunter out to bleed me dry.'

'Why?'

'No real reason. Just a feeling.'

'But you don't?'

'No . . .'

'Then trust your own judgement. Don't forget, Jess likes a good drama even more than you.'

'Drama? *Moi?*'

Mike's right. Suddenly I feel incredibly glad to have my old friend back in my life for a while. 'It's so good that you're back. Even if it's only for the summer.'

'So let's make it a summer to remember – lots of fun, no hassles. When can I meet my best buddy's brother?'

'Now, if you like. He's over the road in *Nature Morte*.'

'Ah.' Mike frowns. 'Pass. I keep bumping into that Zinovieff guy in the street and he's always on about who represents me in the States and do I have a UK gallery, and dropping the names of his other artists. Who is he anyway?'

'You've been away too long. He's flavour of the month. Darling of all the celebs. But absolutely not someone you'd want to show with. His artists are a bit . . . I dunno how to describe them.'

'"Rubbish", from what I've seen through the window of his gallery. I'd rather meet Joshua over dinner or something.' He smiles. 'Talking of food, how about I take you out to lunch?'

When did I ever pass up a free lunch? My agent can wait.

We find a curry-house in Brick Lane that's highly recommended by the *Observer*'s restaurant critic.

'Remember when we were students, that place in New Cross?'

'I remember the effect it had on my digestion. It was *the* place to go for instantaneous weight loss. I've never been quite so ill as I once was after one of their vindaloos.'

Mike's excellent company. He makes me laugh till I cry with his wicked stories about the American art scene. After one particularly scandalous tale I'm wiping my eyes when I become aware that he's staring at me.

'I've missed that laugh, Rosy.' His voice is soft.

'You're drunk.'

'Only a little.'

'Don't go all soppy on me. Doesn't suit you.'

'That's something else I miss. The cut-the-crap-don't-give-me-any-bullshit-routine. Did I tell you about the time Julia Roberts ate my lunch by mistake?'

His satirical patter keeps me so well entertained that I'm shocked when I find it's the end of the afternoon.

'Look at the time! I must dash!' I shriek.

'Always on the move, Rosy Posy. Streak lightning. Did Rob ever tell you about the first time we saw you?'

'In the Union Bar at college?'

'No, it was before then. In the main drag. You were rushing around like a blue-arsed fly sticking posters on walls for *Death of a Salesman*.'

'Now there was a production to forget.'

'Did he ever mention our arrangement?'

'What arrangement?'

'We both fancied the pants off you, so we decided to toss a coin over who should have first pull, on the understanding that if it didn't work out, the other one was free to make a move.'

'Rob never told me that.'

Mike laughs. 'I'll bet he didn't. There you go, you've learned something today. Maybe I should make my move now. Better late than never.'

'You wish.'

'You can't blame a guy for trying.'

Now it's my turn to laugh. 'You must be pretty desperate, Mason – coming on to me.'

He winks. 'Just practising.'

'I bet you've already got a couple of hot prospects lined up.'

'Oh shoot, woman, you know me too well. I'm seeing a sweet little art student tonight, and a very bottled blonde is taking me go-karting tomorrow.'

'You're incorrigible.'

'I know.' He grins. 'Let's fix up dinner soon so I can meet Joshua.'

'I'll give you a bell.'

*   *   *

Back at his flat Mike Mason looked through his window and revisited the moment when he'd spotted Rosy dreaming on the pavement. From his aerial vantage-point she'd looked exactly like the young girl he'd first met twenty years ago.

Uncanny.

He was swamped by memory. What times . . .

The time when he and Rob had made their fateful bargain . . .

What a true gent he'd been. Today if he wanted something, he took it. No stepping aside for anyone. But back then, he wouldn't have dared break his promise. Rob was wild. Orphan-boy wild. In the Children's Homes he'd had nothing and then he'd won the prize. Rosa belonged to him. Fuck anyone who disputed that. Mike remembered more than one incident involving fans of Rosa coming into contact with Rob's fists.

All that passion extinguished for ever.

He felt the warm sun pouring in through the window and the warm blood flowing through his veins.

The coming weeks beckoned.

New lands to conquer.

Old lands to revisit.

TWELVE

The tube was crowded and smelly. Gillian felt very sick, but it wasn't the armpit presently giving houseroom to her nose that was causing the nausea. She tried to focus on what had just taken place at the offices of the *Correspondent*, but there was a high-pitched whining in her head, and all she could see were the thin purple lips set in the bony face of the arts editor, Lulu Slater. 'So unfortunately, Gill, we're just going to have to let you go.'

Let you go.

As if she were an eager little terrier straining at some metaphorical leash, and they had regretfully decided to grant her wish and set her free.

After all those years this was all it took: a few insipid valedictory phrases from the editor's lackey.

Her legs turned to jelly. It took all her self-control not to fall down. As the train drew into Holborn, tightly clutching her carrier bags – the result of a productive hour in a bookshop before the fateful meeting – she fought her way to the doors through the unyielding forest of backs. When they opened, her path was blocked by a young man in an anorak. The bile rose in her throat. She was going to spew all over him.

'Get out of the way,' she cried.

His face contorted and he pushed her so violently that she almost fell between the platform and the train.

'Mind the Gap,' intoned a recorded voice. 'Mind the Gap. Mind the Gap.'

'Mad cunt,' snarled the angry young man.

He was still mouthing it through the glass, like some inverse Buddhist mantra, as the train pulled away, leaving her on the grimy platform. She groped her way towards the wall. Once her hands made contact with something solid, she sank down and lay, cheek on the dirty ground, unable to move, great waves of sweat engulfing her. Then for a while there was blissful nothingness, until she became aware of voices.

'Should we call someone? She might be ill.'

'She's just some old bag lady. This is probably her regular dossing spot.'

Gillian thought of Peter and how he would feel if he saw his beloved wife lying on the platform of the Piccadilly Line at Holborn, being mistaken for a tramp. She felt so sorry for him, and so conscious of the pain he would have suffered on her behalf, that she had a little weep. After a while, a tube official came and told her to bugger off. Ever obliging, Gillian said she would go immediately. She pulled herself to her feet, staggered up the escalators and then made her way back to Lamb's Conduit Street. Safe inside her flat over the hat shop, she made herself a cup of tea and then did what she always did in times of crisis: she went to bed for a few days.

Jess is still on my case.

We're at White City Leisure Pool watching Lozz having a swimming lesson when she kicks off.

'How's the fucking lookalike?'

'An asset to the family.'

'Pinched the silver yet?'

'No, he hasn't, you cynical old mare.'

Jess gives Lozz an encouraging wave. 'Seriously, I wish you'd find him somewhere else to stay. Whatever you think, you don't know a bloody thing about him. Not really.'

'Mike says I should trust my own judgement.'

'Mike? What's he got to do with anything?'

'That's what he said the other day when I was checking out his swish flat.'

'Aren't you the lucky one. Why hasn't he asked me round?'

'It's in Navarre Street opposite Larry's gallery. He saw me in the street the day I took Joshua to Rob's show, and invited me up.'

'That's all right then. For a moment I thought he was playing favourites.'

Is she serious? It's hard to tell with Jess. Although we're really close there's sometimes a brittle edge to her teasing that verges on the hostile. Usually when she's worried about Lozz, or in the middle of messing up yet another relationship with yet another highly unsuitable man.

But as far as I know she's man-free at the moment, and Lozz, presently showing off his newly acquired skill at breast-stroke, is coming on in leaps and bounds. There's even talk of him taking a couple of courses at the local FE college, which Jess is really thrilled about. One of her major worries in life is thinking about Lozz's future, and how he'll cope when she dies.

'Why are you being so awful about Joshua? Why can't you just be happy for me?'

'Because I'm worried.' She shouts to Lozz. 'Attaboy, Lozzie, go for it!'

'That boy will surprise us all one day.'

'Just be careful, Rosy. There's something about him I don't trust.'

'What do you mean?'

'I don't know. Nothing I can put my finger on.'

'Try.'

'Something leech-like . . . clinging. A clinging vine.'

'Rubbish. And anyway, if there is any clinging, it's reciprocal. You don't seem to realise what a big deal it is – for both of us.'

'I do. It's just that you've had to cope with a fucking night-mare recently and I'm not even talking about Rob's death. Don't think you have to show how tough you are by doing the exact thing most calculated to freak you out.'

'Which is?'

'Having a stranger live in your house.'

'He's not a stranger, he's Rob's brother. How could I turn him away? You're so wrong about this. Listen, Mike's going to take us both out to dinner. Why don't you come too? Once you get to know Joshua, you'll see that he's fine.'

'Maybe,' says my sceptical friend. And when she drops me

off later, she says, 'Keep your mobile by your bed. Call me any time.'

'Go home, Jess,' I say. 'Lozz wants his tea.'

'Lozz does want his tea,' affirms Lozz from the back seat.

I wave them off and go into the house. The weather's still unbearably humid. Time for a shower. I go up to my bedroom.

Where I find Joshua. On the floor.

'Looking for something?'

He jumps up. 'Hi.'

'What are you doing?'

'Taking photos.'

Yeah, right.

'Of my carpet?'

'Of the park.'

'Don't you have the same view from your own room?'

He looks so guilty.

'Same view, different angle. Sorry. I didn't mean to intrude.'

'OK.'

'I've finished now, anyway. I'll just . . .' He slips away.

I look around. The drawer of my dressing-table is open. Did I leave it like that? I check my jewellery box. Nothing's missing, but was it really in such a mess?

I'm a cow. I condemn Jess for her scepticism and here I am, leaping to sinister conclusions on the basis of nothing.

Nothing?

He was in my bedroom.

Because he was taking photographs of the park.

Or so he says.

I find him in the kitchen and I'm extra nice to make up for

my horrid suspicions. But he doesn't respond. He's nursing a mug of tea, looking grim. After my umpteenth attempt to jolly him along, I give up.

'Are you going to sulk all day because I was funny about you being in my room?'

'It's not that.'

'Then what is it?'

'Nothing.'

'Tell me.'

He sighs. 'Remember what Zinovieff said the other day?'

I'm hardly likely to forget. Joshua arrived home dancing on air because Zander Zinovieff had asked to see his work, and implied he might take him on if he liked it. I'd played it down, not wanting him to be disappointed. I'd reminded him that people often said things they didn't mean, and that it would be unheard-of for a top gallery like *Nature Morte* to take on a complete unknown.

'He was probably just being polite. I get the feeling he's the sort of person who likes making promises to people. I don't know him well enough to know if he delivers on them.'

'He phoned earlier. He does want to see my stuff.'

I'm astonished. 'So why are you so fed up?' I ask.

'I only brought a few small things with me, and even if I take more pictures, I've nowhere to develop them. I need a darkroom.'

'Aren't darkrooms obsolete nowadays? I thought everything was digital.'

'I work in black and white with an SLR, and a Polaroid which I use like a sketchpad. I've had a great idea – a series of studies of Consort Park – London park life. But I need to buy things and rent a darkroom.'

'Sounds like quite a mission.'

'Yeah – Mission Impossible, financially. My mother's legacy hasn't come through yet. I had enough for my fare over here plus a couple of weeks' subsistence, and that was about it. I planned to get a temporary job, then I met you and somehow all that went out the window.'

'You can still do that.'

'But I have to strike now. I've got to show him what I can do.' His words echo round the kitchen before fading into a profound silence.

Oh God. Why is Jess always right?

'You'll just have to save up, and hope Zander stays interested. Maybe your mum's money will come through sooner than you think.'

'You don't get it. Zinovieff says he's unexpectedly had a hitch with his next show. He has a couple of empty weeks to fill and if he likes my stuff he's willing to consider showing it.'

And pigs might fly, Joshua.

'I don't want to be a wet blanket, but high-profile dealers like Zinovieff just don't show complete beginners. Particularly when they haven't even seen the work.'

'Not normally, no. But he said he'd been thinking about having a yearly slot where he shows the work of young artists just starting out, and that this delay with his next show was the kick-start he needed to put the idea into practice. And he loved my London park idea.'

'But he must have loads of young artists beating a path to his door. Why choose you?'

'It wouldn't be just me. It's going to be a mixed show. That's another reason why I've got to make more work. I'll be in competition for a place.'

'How much money would you need?'

'Well, there's film, photographic paper, chemicals, technical equipment . . . A thousand pounds would probably cover it.'

The best scams are the big ones. I feel like someone's punched me in the gut.

'That's a lot.'

'I can't pass up this chance. Apart from finding Rob's family, getting a dealer's the other reason I came over here. You know that.'

During our days in purdah, he'd told me that ever since his mother had given him a camera for his tenth birthday, he'd been crazy about photography. For him it was a way of experiencing and reflecting a different reality to Soloman Gayle's hellfire and damnation. Taking photographs was his way of making sense of the world.

'I knew if I wanted to be taken seriously, I'd have to come to England. I thought it would take months to build up a body of new work and find a dealer, but it's happened too soon. I'm not ready . . .'

Yet again, I'm reminded of my children. I think of Danny in his stamp-collecting phase, and the fever of want engendered by the thought of a particularly desired stamp. Or Anna with My Little Pony. She'd have sold her grandmother for the My Little Pony special stable set.

But Joshua isn't a child. He's twenty-five years old. Making photographs is his life's ambition, not a passing phase. At least that's what he tells me. I haven't yet seen as much as one snapshot.

'It's not going to happen, is it?' He rushes out and up to his bedroom.

After a decent interval I knock on his door. He's lying on his bed.

'I didn't realise you had any work over here,' I said. 'Can I see it?'

'It's not my best stuff,' he says. 'I threw it in at the last minute.'

'I'd still like to see.'

Reluctantly he opens the drawer in his bedside table and takes out a folder. He extracts some photographs which he passes over.

Portraits. Of street vendors in Port of Spain. They're good. Not brilliant, but they definitely have something.

'What's wrong with showing these to Zander?'

'They're too ordinary. Anyone could have done them. Zinovieff will be seeing much better stuff from other people. If I submit this, I won't have any chance of being accepted.'

He's right. The portraits don't have that special quality that would set them apart.

'Well, I like them,' I say.

He turns to face the wall. 'I want to be on my own for a bit, if you don't mind.'

I go back downstairs, where I sit in the kitchen and think for a very long time. Without coming to any conclusions. Normally I'd phone Jess. That's what I always do when I have a problem. Not this time.

No prizes for guessing what she'd say. Her face swims in front of me. She's mouthing the words, 'Don't be a fucking idiot, Rosa.'

But how can she judge Joshua? She's spent less than an hour

in his company. I'm the one who should know whether he's trying to pull a fast one.

The money from the BBC series won't last for ever, even with residuals, and my agent hasn't exactly been putting me up for many castings. And I certainly don't intend to go back to teaching.

So why am I even contemplating lending my mystery brother-in-law money?

Money, incidentally, that he hasn't yet asked me for.

Supposing I did, where exactly would it come from?

At least I know the answer to that one.

I could sell one of Rob's paintings.

From what Larry tells me, it would fetch enough money for us to live on for a while.

With some to spare. To share with Rob's little brother.

I could sell one of Rob's paintings . . .

But I can't. Not yet.

Those paintings are all I have left of him. I can't part with them. I know I'll have to one day, unless I land the lead role in a Hollywood blockbuster, which is hardly likely at the ripe old age of forty. But not yet. Not till the time's right.

'And is the time not right, now?'

It's Rob's voice – the deep dark voice that I adored, and it's speaking loud and clear inside my head.

'I never knew my baby brother – never even knew he existed. I never had the chance to play with him, to watch him grow. I would have loved him well, Rosa, you know I would. I would have taken such good care of him. So if selling one of my paintings might give him the chance in life that I would have wished for him,

*please don't stand in the way. One painting, Rosa, that's all. Surely
you can spare just one.'*

You don't know what you're asking, Rob.

'Yes, I do.'

But what if he's just exploiting me?

'Is that what you really think?'

I don't know. It's possible.

*'Trust, Rosa. It's all we have. Trust him. If he's my brother, he
should have something of mine. It's only money, after all.'*

I sit for a while longer and then I call Mike.

'What would you do?' I ask.

'I'm Mr Miser where my money's concerned. You're talking
to the wrong person.'

'Then tell me what you think Rob would do.'

'You know the answer to that one. Rob would give his last
penny to a destitute stranger. To his own brother . . . ?'

'Would you think me a gullible fool?'

'You're going into this with your eyes open. You know it might
be a con, but you're willing to take the chance because he's Rob's
brother.'

'Yes.'

'You're sure that he *is* Rob's brother?'

'One hundred per cent.'

'Then on that basis alone, surely he's entitled to something,
morally speaking. Even if he fritters it all away on booze and
horses. If Rob had known about him, he'd have remembered him
in his will, wouldn't he?'

Mike's right.

Joshua's still lying on the bed looking bleak.

132

'What were you going to do when all your money ran out, before I took you in?' I ask.

He looks surprised. 'I told you – get a job.'

'Where were you planning to live?'

'Not in your shed, if that's what you're thinking. I've told you – I was only hanging round here because of Rob.'

'But where were you planning to live?'

'I thought I might try an old mate from college. Or the YMCA or something.'

'Right.'

'Why?'

Good question, Rosa. Why indeed?

'I'll give you the money.'

He stares at me.

'Call it an indefinite loan. Pay me back whenever.'

He's still staring.

'Say something.'

Eventually he speaks. 'I can't do that.'

'Yes, you can.'

'Taking money from you wouldn't feel right.'

'You're Rob's brother. It's what he'd want. If he were here he'd help you all he could. Really. Take it, Joshua. If not from me, from Rob.'

I watch my words slowly sink in.

'Are you sure?'

'Here.' I hold out a cheque. There's a long moment where nothing happens. Nothing at all.

Leave it, Joshua. Find another way. Prove Jess wrong.

Very slowly he reaches out and takes it.

Oh well.

'I've also had an idea about a darkroom,' I go on. 'Why don't you use our shed? Rob was converting it into a studio before he died. It would really thrill him to know his brother was making art there.'

Joshua's leaping off the bed and crushing me in a massive embrace.

'Thank you, Rosa. Thank you so much. I will never forget this. I'll make you so proud of me. You'll never regret it.'

'Don't suffocate me before the cheque clears.'

Then his face falls. 'I don't have a bank account over here.'

Without missing a beat I hear myself saying, 'No problem. I'll give you cash instead. I'll withdraw it first thing tomorrow.'

Then I leave him and phone David Borodino's PA to fix up a lunch before I change my mind.

Now it starts, thought Joshua Gayle. As if all the other stuff had been obliterated. Time to unpick the past and begin again.

THIRTEEN

Today I read Leni Dang's interview in *Dame*. Gillian reckons Leni could become a good writer. I think her judgement's somewhat skewed when it comes to Leni. To me the piece comes across like a schoolgirl's essay – *My Greatest Hero* – that kind of thing. Still, she's very enthusiastic about Rob's work and contrives to make me appear comparatively normal and not the traditional mad widow fiercely guarding the flame so often portrayed by the media when writing about dead artists. So I can't complain.

I phone to thank her, but before I can say more than a couple of words, I find myself being outdone by her gratitude over my gratitude. Her husky voice bubbles down the phone-line in a torrent of breathless pleasure.

'I'm so glad you like it. I was terrified that I couldn't do justice to him – that I wouldn't be able to capture his amazing spirit. But thanks to your generosity with your time and your wonderful memories, the whole experience was a total joy.'

Steady. It was a couple of hours of pretty superficial chit-chat. Let's not get carried away here.

By the end of our conversation, I feel as if I've escaped near-drowning in a vat of syrup.

I'm becoming a cynical old bag. As bad as Jess. Not content with finding Joshua's naive simplicity a bit trying, I'm now wincing at the sweet eagerness of Leni Dang. What's the matter with me?

Leni's call has made me late for a meeting with Caro and Steve Pyne. Steve's studio apparently needs sorting out before it's fit to be seen, but Caro says he'd like to have a chat and show me some photographs. I can't say I'm looking forward to this encounter. I'm doing it for Caro, pure and simple. She's taking time off work so she can be there too. Thank goodness. She can control Steve if he gets out of hand. For some reason she's chosen Tate Modern as the venue for this happy occasion.

I leave Joshua happily blacking out the windows of the shed. Since pocketing my cash he's been a thing possessed, returning home from trips to photographic supply shops with sackfuls of stuff and haunting Consort Park with his camera at all hours of the day and night. I've told him the park's a no go area after dark, but he just smiles and vaults over the railings into the darkness anyway.

The Turbine Hall at Tate Modern is full of fairies.

They dive and swoop through the vast space, iridescent wings glittering as they catch the sun, occasionally settling on the bridge over the middle of the concourse, or dive-bombing the crowds of visitors who gaze up in wonder.

The fairies are part of the latest and most spectacular in a line of Turbine Hall installations. People flock in their thousands to see the weird and wonderful holographic work.

It's my first viewing. Although I'm late, I stop, mesmerised by the myriad delicate creatures spinning and wheeling above me. One pearly-pink wraith swoops right down and hovers above my head. I put my hand up to grasp it, but my fingers clutch empty air. Gradually I become aware that there's a sound component to the work, too – a twittering chattering crescendo and diminuendo that doesn't intrude, but is there waiting to be tuned into. And when you do, it's like eavesdropping on a different plane of existence – something secret and feral.

Eventually I tear myself away and run up the long escalators to the café. Caro and Steve sit by the window staring out over Millennium Bridge. Steve's scowling.

No change there, then.

I'd much rather fly away with the fairies in the Turbine Hall, but Caroline's waving at me.

'Sorry I'm late. The fairies stole me away.'

Pyne snorts. 'Fucking kitsch rubbish.'

'Don't you like it?'

'Moody's a circus showman, not an artist.'

I nearly say, 'I'll get my coat then, shall I?' But I don't because Caro's eyes beg me to stay.

Pyne seems to realise that he's not exactly endearing himself. He attempts a smile. 'Thanks for coming. Much appreciated.'

He's had a radical haircut and shaved off the stubble, revealing a distinctive face – high cheekbones, a firm chin with a cleft in the middle and sensuous lips, curving up at the corners. But the eyes have it: clear grey. The eyes of someone who looks for a living.

At present they're looking at me. So disconcertingly that I say, more abruptly than I mean, 'Let's see the photos, then.'

He produces several prints. They're rubbish – so dark that the sculpture can barely be seen.

'Sorry they're so dim. It's fucking irritating – one of the great things about these pieces is the colour of the stone and the way it catches the light.'

Have I come all the way from Consort Park on a stifling tube train to see a bunch of over-exposed photographs?

'This is useless. I can't make anything out at all.'

His eyes crackle with temper, which he tries unsuccessfully to mask.

'I've seen one of this series at Sir Montague Smallwood's house in Gloucestershire. It looks divine.'

Loyal Caro, pitching in for her lover. Steve's hand rests loosely on her back. Like a ventriloquist and his dummy. He's got her exactly where he wants her. I can't believe my lovely friend is in love with such a jerk.

I curb my irritation. 'Tell me about the work.'

When he speaks I begin to see why Caro's in thrall. All the combative hostility disappears. He sculpts the air in front of him with sensuous movements of his slim, strong fingers, and there's a tenderness in his voice which makes compelling listening. Eventually he subsides. I swallow hard, freeing myself from the spell he's woven.

'Will your studio be ready in the next week or so?'

'You'll come then?'

'Yes.'

Caro is ecstatic. 'Rosa, I love you. It would mean so much to us, wouldn't it, Steve?'

'Sure.'

A tic of annoyance beats at the side of his top lip. He's finding Caro's abject gratitude on his behalf hard to take. She'd better cool it, or he'll sling her over the balcony into the Thames.

When I leave, Steve shakes my hand, holding on to it for a fraction too long.

'At Rob's opening I said some fucking stupid things, including shit about him being a bad painter. It's not true. He was a bloody good painter – one of the best. I shouldn't have dissed him. Sorry.'

Steve Pyne isn't used to grovelling. It's reluctantly torn out of him, like a bad birth. Is he apologising in order to get into my good books, or does he mean it?

'Rob was the best,' I say. 'Apology accepted.'

The phone had been ringing intermittently all day. She scarcely noticed, being too deeply sunk in misery. But the pitch of its insistent tone had eventually set off her tinnitus, and the double whammy – ringing inside her ear as well as outside, was finally too much. Wrapping her tatty angora bedjacket round her, she picked it up.

'Gillian Gerard.'

Her vocal cords were thick from misery and lack of use. She knew she sounded terrible, but she didn't care. Let the world think what it liked. Here she lay, an old woman too beaten by life to stir from her smelly sheets. So what?

The voice on the other end oozed remorse. 'I'm so, so sorry, Gillian.'

She'd felt for days that she was caught in a waking nightmare. The voice proved it. Leni. Her doe-eyed deceiver.

'You must believe me, I knew nothing. I had an email from Lulu Slater saying the editor wanted me to take over the art column. I assumed you'd decided to retire. I had such a shock this morning when I heard that . . .'

Here the voice broke off. A long silence settled over the airwaves.

'That I'd been given the chop?'

The bald statement provoked a small but tragic sob. It reverberated round Gillian's already jangling inner ear. She waited.

'I just don't know what to say . . .'

Gillian didn't feel like helping her out. Another silence ensued.

'Is there anything else?'

The response was a deeply distressed squeak. Followed by more silence.

'I am rather busy, so if that's all . . .'

'You hate me, don't you? I don't blame you – I'd hate me too in your position. But it wasn't my fault. I did nothing – I swear on my mother's grave. Can you forgive me?'

'I *can* forgive you. Whether I *will* is another matter entirely.'

The pedant in her strangely satisfied by this parting grammatical shot, Gillian replaced the phone carefully on its base and lay back on her pillows.

A moment later she was overtaken by a bout of crying so violent that she felt her lungs would burst free from their imprisoning cage of ribs, and detonate over Holborn with a huge bang. She'd cried a lot over the past few days. But not like this. Those tears had been tears of stunned shock at the blow which had come upon her out of a clear sky. These tears were entirely of another order: they spoke of rage and betrayal – violent, explosive and untrammelled – that threatened to blow her apart in their ferocity.

She was not familiar with such feelings. By nature she was easygoing and tolerant. Live and let live was a motto which had served her well. Peter always said she was a soft touch. He was right, but it didn't bother her. Conscious of her general good fortune, she'd easily tolerated the foibles of others. Truth be told, apart from Peter, it was art that held the central position in her life and aroused her strongest feelings. Even the help and advice she so willingly gave to young artists and writers was everything to do with her passion for art.

Until Leni. The girl had split her defences wide open. Drawn forth the mother so carefully hidden away behind her redundant womb. How had she done it? Was it her fierce wish to succeed in the face of demonstrably mediocre talent? Was it her childlike vulnerability and the blind trust she placed in Gillian? Or was it the blatant hero-worship by which even worldly Gillian found herself shamefully beguiled? Gillian didn't know. She only knew that Leni's betrayal hurt more than she could ever have imagined. She felt storm-tossed in uncharted waters. Throughout her life, art's consoling absolutes had succoured and supported her. Where were those absolutes now when she most needed them?

She scrabbled through the pile of detritus on her bedside table till her fingers closed around the well-thumbed self-portrait of Salvator Vera.

'Come on, Elena. It's pay-back time. Help me. Be my consolation.'

The solemn face stared out at her. 'Get real. Life's shit. Deal with it.'

Get real?

Gillian felt the beginnings of a white-hot fury stirring inside her. Was that all Elena Dias could come up with? This woman who'd occupied the central place in her existence for so long? The person she had striven to understand, whose movements and motivations she had meticulously followed, documented and dissected? She looked at the sombre image for a moment longer and then closed her hand around it, squeezing hard until it was nothing but a crumpled ball of paper which she threw across the room.

'Get real? Well, pardon me for mentioning it, my darling Salvator, but real is exactly what you never were, even in life. And now you're just a heap of dust in a Spanish cemetery. How real is that? I'm not going to waste any more of my time on you. I could have made you live again, but as you say, sweetheart, life's shit. Welcome to eternal obscurity.'

This anger was a new sensation. With forensic detachment she observed it flashing through her, reconfiguring sixty-five years of attitude and belief. And then, as it cooled she witnessed a new person emerge from the gutted shell of her former self.

That person would not lie down and die. That person was going to find out why the career of Gillian Gerard had been so carelessly destroyed.

And then do something about it.

*　　*　　*

Fuck! Thanks to Rosa bloody Thorn he was going to be late. And for what? OK, so his photos had been shit. She needn't have been quite so dismissive. It had taken every ounce of willpower to be nice, especially when it came to apologising for dissing her husband. She'd never know much it had cost him to praise the fucker. He'd done it for Caro's sake. He owed her that much, she was so thrilled at fixing up the meeting. And he had to admit, it would be great to offload one of his old sculptures. Particularly for such a mega-bundle of cash.

More good luck coming his way. He was on a roll.

Caro was speaking. *Yada yada yada.* He forced himself to zone in.

'I've got to get back to work soon, angel, but I thought we could have a walk along the river first . . . Steve?'

'What? Oh. No, sorry, babes – gotta get on with sorting the studio ready for the royal visit.'

'You can spare half an hour, surely. It's such a beautiful day.'

'Have you seen the state of the place? If I want to show the pieces off properly I'll have to work twenty-four seven to get it halfway presentable.'

He knew he ought to feel guilty, but he didn't. Just impatient. 'Fuck off,' he wanted to say. 'Fuck off and let me get on with my life.'

But she was rallying – doing her plucky little soldier routine.

'You're right,' she was saying. 'I'm just being selfish. This is a huge chance. You can't afford to mess it up. Go. I'll pitch in after work, if you like.'

'No!' Disaster loomed. 'I'm better on my own. I know where I want everything to go . . .'

'Are you sure?'

Why did she always look like a hurt puppy when he pushed her away?

'We'll go out for a meal tomorrow,' he said, and winced at the pure pleasure on her face.

After seeing her to the tube he made two calls.

'Any decisions? I need a definite answer in the next few days. Don't take too long. I do have other options.'

The second call was even more brief. 'I'm on my way.'

FOURTEEN

I spend the next few days looking at art. The task is simplified by the fact that most established sculptors like their work to be site specific, and the timescale, with Pru Gibb's Consort Park Day deadline, means it would be impossible for any of them to make a work at such short notice.

By the end of the week I've had it. Aside from Larry's artists, I've spoken to several other dealers, spent every day looking at work, and I'm still no further forward than I was the day I started. I need help.

Gillian.

It would be fun working on the project with her, and would give us the perfect excuse to see more of each other. I give her a ring, but there's no reply, not even an answerphone message. I try again later. The same. This is strange. I know that if she's out, she always leaves the answerphone on.

I'll try her again tomorrow. Now I have to get ready for a night on the town: Mike's dinner for Joshua. Jess is coming too. We're going to *Sketch* in Conduit Street.

Joshua's in a state. He says he's got nothing to wear. It's true. He only brought a couple of changes of clothes, and nothing suitable for tonight.

'I can't let you down by wearing this old T-shirt. You'll have to go without me.'

I'm discovering that Joshua can be a bit intense. To put it mildly.

'If Rob were here he'd think I was far too scruffy to meet someone like Mike Mason. What would he have worn for an evening like this? Something really smart, I expect.'

I take a deep breath. 'There's a cupboard full of his clothes in your room. You're his size – why don't you see if you can find something there?'

For the first time I'm glad I haven't been able to part with Rob's stuff, although it does very funny things to my heart when Joshua emerges in my husband's navy linen suit and a soft white shirt. He's very excited now, striking attitudes and parading in front of me as if he's on a Parisian catwalk.

'How do I look?'

Tears spring to my eyes.

'What's wrong?'

For a second I wish he didn't exist. I was moving forward. Now this constant reminder of things dead and gone is dragging me back into misery.

I pull myself together. I'm not going to spoil a rare chance to gobble posh nosh.

'Not a thing,' I say. 'You're the cat's pyjamas.'

When we arrive at *Sketch*, Jess is buzzing. Her cheeks are flushed, her eyes sparkling. I haven't seen her looking this happy for ages. Not since her last disastrous fling with a market-gardener from Spalding who turned out to be a bigamist. She's even nice to Joshua, greeting him with a peck on the cheek and a smile.

Mike has turned pale under his Californian tan. Even though I've warned him about the resemblance between Rob and Joshua, nothing can prepare him for the actuality of it. He grasps Joshua's hand and pumps it up and down. 'Oh man,' he keeps repeating. 'Oh man.'

After that, the evening goes with a swing. Joshua, goaded on by Mike, allows a kind of laddish humour to emerge as he recounts some steamy tales about his time as assistant manager at a tourist hotel in Tobago. And he's his usual inquisitive self when it comes to *Sketch*. Exclaiming over the décor, the prices in the menu and the cross-section of media London who fill all available tables. There's only one sticky moment: when I accidentally let it drop that I'm subsidising his portfolio. Joshua looks embarrassed and Jess's face goes blank. She kicks Mike and I kick myself, for not being more careful. But then I think, Hey, why should I be secretive? I'm not ashamed of giving Rob's baby brother financial help. Quite the contrary. I'm proud to do it. It's what Rob would want. I pray that Jess doesn't interrogate Joshua about his repayment plan. I can see she's itching to, but my intimidating glare keeps her quiet.

Or maybe her mind isn't fully on Joshua's case tonight. It's clear as the evening progresses that Jess's main preoccupation is Mike.

There's no mistaking it.

And him?

He'll flirt with anything that moves. But he's also a teaser. And he and Jess have a long history of winding each other up. Is that what's happening tonight?

The sparks are flying. But what kind of sparks?

Jess has had such a roller-coaster ride with romance over the years. More than anyone I know, she deserves a break. And Mike's run the gamut with mindless bimbos on either side of the Atlantic. Maybe, finally, he wants to settle down.

With Jess?

What am I thinking?

Mike and Jess? Would that be so bad? At least their relationship would be based on a long and loving friendship. What better recipe for success?

How would I feel? I don't know. It would take a lot to convince me that Mike Mason was ready to abandon his alley-cat ways.

As I look round the room, shocked by my speculations about Jess and Mike, my eye is caught by a couple at a corner table. The woman's face, as she talks, is vividly expressive. Her companion, whose profile I can just make out, listens with tolerant indulgence. At one point, he leans forward and kisses her on the lips. Afterwards she looks around the room and her eyes meet mine. I smile. But she doesn't reciprocate. Then she turns so I can't see her so clearly.

Leni Dang.

With David Borodino.

Cutting me dead.

'Wake up, Rosy. I've promised Joshua a night-ride round tourist London. Are you up for it?'

'You bet,' I say.

THE ART OF DYING

Later, when we head for home, I notice that Mike insists Joshua and I are dropped off first.

Well, well.

The time when . . .

. . . he'd found a silver brooch lying on the pavement. It was dirty and dull but he could see that with a bit of a polish it would be beautiful. Just the thing for Her birthday. He'd gone to the bar and was sitting at a corner table, quietly polishing it when the Witch appeared.

'What the fuck are you doing?' she'd bellowed across the room and everybody stopped and stared. 'Wanking under the table? Gross or what!'

The whole place had erupted.

'Willie Wanka,' someone had called, and soon the name was on everyone's lips. Willy Wanka. Willy Wanka.

Even now the thought of it made him want to vomit.

FIFTEEN

I call Gillian again this morning. Still no reply. I try her mobile.

'The number you are calling is unavailable.'

Even if she were away, she'd keep her mobile on. She told me as much once. 'We never close,' she'd joked.

I'm worried. And I really do need her help. So in the spirit of concerned self-interest I decide to pay her a visit.

Joshua's in the shed. The red light's on above the door. Bob Marley's blasting out at top volume.

Rob's favourite singer.

The track still playing on his mp3 player as he lay dead in the road.

'I'm off out.'

'Wait!' The music stops. 'Can't open up, or I'll spoil the pictures. I just wanted to ask . . .'

Pause.

'What?'

'The problem is, it's all costing more than I thought, so . . .' He tails off again.

'So?'

'I was wondering if . . .'

'Spit it out, I haven't got all day.' *Cool it, Rosa, he's a guest, not one of your kids.* But I'm fed up. I know what he's angling for.

First time round, I offered. Him asking is something else. Does he imagine I'm a bottomless pit of cash? That's so far from the truth it's laughable. I'm now running an overdraft. And I haven't yet fixed up lunch with David Borodino. His PA said he was unavailable and she'd call me when he had a window. Rich men are notoriously capricious. What if he's not interested in Rob's work any more?

Meanwhile Joshua's stuttering and stammering in the shed.

I must stick to my original decision. As Rob's brother, he's entitled to my support.

'How much?'

His relief is palpable. I can feel it through the thick wooden door.

'A couple of hundred.'

Could be worse.

'I'll see what I can do.'

'Rosa, I can't tell you what this means to me.'

'But it'll be the last time, I'm afraid. Until I sell one of your brother's paintings, I'm flat broke.'

Shocked silence from inside the shed, apart from Bob's warbling.

'Joshua?'

'Please . . . Forget I ever asked.'

I feel deeply ashamed. Rob would never have lent his brother money and then thrown the gesture back in his face, pleading poverty. It would have been a matter of honour to him that Joshua remained sublimely oblivious of any hardship the loan had caused.

'Sorry, Joshua. I must have been wearing my Scrooge nightcap when I got out of bed on the wrong side this morning. Two hundred's really not a problem. I'll give it to you later, OK?'

'But—'

'I'm really looking forward to seeing what you've done.'

'Rosa—'

'You'll take it and that's that.'

'Thank you. Thank you so, so much. I'll make it up to you somehow. You'll see.'

I've redeemed myself.

Not that Joshua took much persuading.

Did he?

'So when can I see the results of all this hard labour?'

'Soon.'

I need to see those photographs, I think as I stride across the park to the tube.

When I ring Gillian's bell there's no response. I shout through the letterbox. I scream up at the window. Nothing.

A woman emerges from the hat shop below her flat.

'Can I be of any assistance?' she enquires.

'I'm a friend of Gillian Gerard. Do you know her?'

'Yes.'

I wait for elaboration, but that's it.

'Do you know if she's away?'

'No.'

'No she isn't away, or no you don't know?'

'No I don't know. And I'd be most grateful if you could desist from shouting in front of my shop. It's deterring the customers.'

'I don't suppose you keep a spare key?'

'Well yes, but I can't give it to a complete stranger.'

'She may be ill. She could be dying in there and no one would know. Do you want to take responsibility for that?'

This rattles her.

I press on. 'Why don't you go and see if she's OK?'

'I can't leave my shop.'

'I'll keep an eye on it. It'll only take a minute. I'll tell any customers to hang on till you get back.'

'How do I know you won't steal one of my hats?'

'Do I look like a criminal?'

The woman looks me up and down and sniffs. 'I suppose, in the circumstances . . .'

She's still dithering when Gillian herself walks round the corner, clutching a copy of the *Correspondent* and a bottle of whisky. Her curly hair is matted and dirty. She's wearing a shapeless food-stained dress, laddered tights and odd shoes, one of which is a slipper. Her face is grey and haggard and she's lost weight.

At first I think she doesn't even recognise me. But then she says, 'Hello Rosa.'

'Any chance of a coffee?' I say brightly.

'Sorry. I'm rather busy.'

The hat-shop woman, relieved of the guilt trip I've been trying to lay on her cashmere shoulders, is now avidly curious. Her bright little eyes take in the scene, and her tongue darts back and forth across her thin lips, ready to flick up and devour any juicy gobbets of gossip which might fly her way.

'Thanks for your help,' I say to her insincerely. Reluctantly she retreats into her shop.

Gillian unlocks the front door and I nip in behind her.

'Didn't you hear me? I can't see you now.'

I disregard this and follow her up the stairs into a living room of indescribable chaos. Books piled everywhere, dirty plates and glasses littering every surface including the floor, and a layer of dusty neglect over the whole thing.

'What's up, Gill?'

'Just go.'

'Not until I know what's happened.'

'What right do you have to come barging in here?'

'The right, as a friend, to be concerned. You're not answering the phone, or your mobile. Are you ill?'

'I've had flu. I'm better now. So you can go.'

'OK, but first let me help you tidy up a bit. Flu leaves you with no energy for anything, let alone housework.'

She's still clutching the whisky, and she keeps shooting furtive glances at it.

She wants a drink. Badly. It's only ten-thirty in the morning. This isn't flu.

I go to her tiny kitchen, wash up a dirty glass, and take it back to the living room. I prise the bottle out of her hand and pour her a large slug of alcohol. She swallows it in one gulp, seizes the bottle and pours herself another. Then she sinks down into a saggy-baggy old armchair and looks at me properly for the first time.

'You haven't heard, have you?'

'What?'

'Read that.'

She hands me the *Correspondent*. In the middle of the front page under the headline *Star in Fatal Car Smash* is a large picture of Haz Kem, one of our most famous rap imports.

'Oh no,' I say. 'Danny'll be devastated. Haz Kem's one of his idols.'

'Not that,' snaps Gillian. 'Arts section. Page thirty-two.'

It's a double spread on the latest exhibition at Tate Britain. Underneath a handsome colour reproduction of a beautiful Gainsborough duchess is another, tiny photograph.

Leni Dang.

'But . . .' I'm puzzled.

'"But this is your space, Gillian?" Is that what you're trying to say?'

'Leni does listings for the *Correspondent*. Not reviews.'

'As of last week, butter-wouldn't-bloody-melt little Leni has taken over as art critic of the *Correspondent*.'

'*What?*'

'Got my marching orders, haven't I? Yesterday's woman. Not young, hip or pretty enough to inform the nation about art any more.'

I'm so shocked I don't know what to say. 'Leni Dang's hardly God's gift,' I finally manage.

'Well, she's certainly got something that's helped her nick my job.'

I can't take it in. Gillian Gerard, one of the most gifted and respected critics in the country, kicked out in favour of . . . of what, exactly? Leni Dang's prose style seems more in the Peter and Jane, Ladybird Book style of writing. Adequate – just. Pedestrian – certainly. In Gillian's league? Not a chance.

'The sick thing is, I thought she was my friend.'

This is unbelievable.

'What will you do? What about money?'

'Money's not a problem. I inherited a whacking great pension from Peter. But . . .'

She trails off. Her face is devastatingly sad.

'What?'

'Writing that column's been my life. My way of externalising all the excitement and joy I feel about art. What will I do without it?'

'You'll get another column.'

'At my age? I don't think so.'

I stare into Gillian's future with her, and find it unbearably bleak.

'I still don't understand. Leni Dang's come from nowhere. How could anyone, let alone the editor of a respected broadsheet, possibly dump you in favour of her?'

As I speak, an image, startling in its clarity, springs up before me. Last night at *Sketch*. Leni Dang and David Borodino. David Borodino, the proprietor of a certain national newspaper – the *Correspondent*.

Then I remember something Julian said.

'I gather the editor of *Dame* is particularly susceptible to the odd morsel of Eastern Promise.'

Gillian's still talking. 'She had the nerve to call me and apologise. Said it was as much of a shock to her as it was to me.'

Do I tell Gill what I saw? I look at her poor tortured face. The answer has to be yes. This is a woman trying to make sense of a nightmare. Wondering what she did wrong.

Which is precisely nothing. Except to be elderly, plain and clever.

I tell her what I've seen. 'Don't have to be Hercule Poirot to work it out, do you?' I finish.

Gill shakes her head in disbelief. 'It can't be – she only met him at Rob's opening. Oh God! I was the one who suggested to Larry that he might like to invite her to the dinner, to make up for Steve Pyne's ghastly slobberings.'

I remember. Leni next to Borodino, eyes lowered, a demure smile on her face.

'She's only just got her own by-line at *Dame* – and now she's moving on to the *Correspondent*?'

Fast worker, our Leni.

'I really thought I meant something to her, Rosa, not just as a walking art-history primer. I thought she and I had a connection. I don't understand. What have I ever done to her except try to help?'

I'm deeply shocked. That wide-eyed innocence certainly had me fooled. It's hard to believe that the gentle little person with the soft, hesitant questions about Rob's work could ride roughshod over Gill's life in such a self-serving, destructive way.

'Why did she do it?' Gill sounds utterly bewildered.

'Don't forget it takes two to tango. She was offered your job. She didn't nick it all by herself.'

Borodino.

What a bastard. Like so many men he's led by his cock. Unlike most men, though, he can do whatever he likes to gratify its seedy little urges. He's fully prepared to see the paper he owns produce pap, overruling his editor in the process, if it pleases his latest squeeze. And if it means ruining Gillian's career in the process – well, tough. Nothing personal.

'She could have turned it down.' Gillian's swigging whisky as if Prohibition re-starts tomorrow.

'It's none of my business, Gill, but booze isn't the answer.'

'You're right. It is none of your business.' She looks round at the chaos. 'God, this place is a major disaster zone.'

'I'll help you clear up. It'll make you feel better.'

'OK. Let's do it.'

She jumps up suddenly and goes into manic overdrive, clearing away piles of books, washing plates, dusting. It's an astonishing transformation. I was right to tell her what I saw. The truth may hurt, but in the long run it's easier than wrestling with shadows. Knowing why she's been ousted, and knowing it's nothing to do with her, may just help her stop beating herself up.

When we've finally restored some kind of order, I remember my other reason for coming here today: to ask for Gill's help with Skinny Minnie's legacy.

But now we've finished she's slumped onto the sofa, eyes closed. Nonetheless, I tell her about my onerous task. In a washed-out way, she finds it quite amusing.

'What you know about modern sculpture could be fitted onto a pinhead, Rosa Thorn.'

'Excuse me! I may not be a world authority, but I have picked up a fair bit over the years. What do you think of Raymond Banks?'

'You have to be joking.'

'What's wrong with his stuff?'

'Don't get me started.'

Her eyes have opened. Do I spy a gleam in their desolate depths?

'I've also seen a rather good Marion Fleming.'

Gillian groans. It's the groan of a person engaging with the world, not opting out of it. Maybe advising me is just what she needs.

'Actually Dick Pinker's front runner at the moment,' I lie. I know she loathes Pinker's work.

Gillian sits bolt upright. 'Are you insane?'

'No, but I'd really appreciate a little help from my friend?'

I swear she's about to say yes. But then an indefinable expression passes across her face.

'Sorry, love. Normally I'd do it like a shot – you're obviously going to make a pig's ear out of the whole thing – but I can't spare the time.'

'You've just lost your job. You've bags of time.'

Why don't I ever think before I speak? I see the pain in Gillian's eyes and I could kick myself.

But her voice is gentle. 'I'd love to help. But I really have got stuff to do.'

What stuff? I try again, but she steers me firmly to the door.

'Thanks for coming. Much appreciated. I'll give you a ring when I'm a bit more sorted.'

Before I know it I'm outside. I look up at Gill's window. She waves.

At the corner of the street I turn round. The curtains are drawn.

I ring her number.

'Go home, Rosa. I'm fine.'

Back in Consort Park, I open the front door to the sound of hoovering.

Joshua's in Danny's room. He's cleaned, tidied, polished, and done a major rearrangement of the furniture.

Danny will go berserk.

Joshua beams. 'I thought it needed a bit of a springclean. Then I had some great ideas about reorganising the space. What do you think? Will he like it?'

Danny and Anna's rooms are no-go areas, forbidden to prying adults. The cleaning and tidying is their responsibility.

'I'll do Anna's room too. Moving the bed against the far wall would open it up a lot. What do you think?'

'No!'

I've startled him.

'Anna prefers to do that kind of thing herself. She's very possessive about her room. It's her private space.'

His brown eyes – Rob's eyes – stare mournfully into mine and I see the implication of my words slowly sinking in. 'I wanted to do something for them.'

'Joshua . . .'

'I've messed up, haven't I?' He looks incredibly woebegone. 'You said Rob liked surprising his children.'

'The room looks great – a hundred times better. It's just the privacy thing with teenagers. It's very important.'

'I'll put it back how it was.'

'No – leave it. I'll explain. Danny'll understand.'

'Will he?'

'Of course.'

'I need to know more about them. I need to know about all the years I've missed.'

All of a sudden I feel crowded. Like it's not just Danny's space that's been invaded, but mine too.

Not physical space.

Head space.

Their rooms were terrible – untidy, disorganised. A disgrace. Those children needed guidance. A father's hand. Joshua knew enough about bad fathers to know how to be a good one. They'd be grateful for his input. His take on things. If only Rosa could be made to realise it.

Theo loved Flavia very much. She was the nearest approxima-tion to a proper relationship that he had with anyone. Dearest sister. Best friend. He didn't know how he'd negotiate life without her. But even Flavia was unaware how disconnected he really was. Not from his manuscripts or his work. Art in the evenings and Death in the day were the twin pillars of his existence. But he saw the rest of the world through a grey gauze. It never felt quite real to him. He could never quite connect.

It made for a solitary life, which didn't bother him.

Unfortunately, it bothered Flavia. For years it had been her mission in life to push any suitable women his way. The fact that she was always unsuccessful never deterred her. Women found him shy and awkward; he found them tedious and unrewarding. But Flavia never gave up. Her latest venture was Rosa Thorn. She kept on nagging him to show Rosa his collection. On and on. Finally, in order to shut her up, he'd issued an invitation. To his surprise Rosa had accepted. To his even greater surprise, he found that he was pleased. She'd seemed genuinely interested in medieval illumination that night at dinner. He'd enjoyed talking to her. He was, therefore, anticipating her visit with uncharacteristic pleasure.

Apart from anything else, it would help him momentarily forget the other thing. The stain seeping across the grey gauze of his days and turning it into permanent black night.

SIXTEEN

I call Gillian regularly over the next few days with no success. Eventually I ring the hat shop and speak to Madame. To my great relief the woman says Gillian's in and out all the time. Whatever she's up to, it doesn't sound like she's going to bump herself off. Nevertheless I'll go and see her again soon.

Today Theo Grey has invited me to call at his office and check out his manuscripts, and later on I'm meeting Caroline and Steve Pyne at his studio.

As I'm dashing out of the house in my retro-1970s peacock-blue shirt, it hits me that I may be dressed totally inappropriately for a visit to a funeral parlour. For it's only just properly occurred to me that this is what Theo's 'office' is. I suspect I haven't wanted to dwell on the fact that my little cultural sortie is to a place full of dead people.

Grey & Son isn't a shop on a High Street like most undertakers. It's a grand house in St John's Wood. There's no indication of its function, not even a discreet brass plaque. It looks like someone's hideously posh pad. Do the neighbours realise that they're living next door to the new dead? They must, with all those hearses and mortuary vans coming and going. Grim. Rather them than me.

Theo meets me at the front door. I'm relieved to see he's dressed in cavalry twills and a green cashmere sweater. Off duty. Corpses must be thin on the ground today.

He ushers me across a thickly carpeted central hallway, I glance through an open door into what would have originally been someone's elegant drawing room, but now, with lowered blinds and a raised dais at one end, is obviously a viewing room. On the dais I see a coffin and the figure of a woman, hunched over it.

There are other doors opening off the main hall with dark-clothed figures gliding in and out. Theo's staff. He pauses only to tell one lugubrious young man that he's not to be disturbed, before taking me to a large, airy room at the back of the house. His own private space. Two walls of the vast room are lined with bookshelves crammed with hundreds of books. The other two walls are floor-to-ceiling glass-fronted cabinets in which various ancient volumes and pieces of parchment are displayed.

Theo's collection.

But I'm immediately drawn to the tall French windows which open on to a tranquil and beautiful garden. Gravel pathways wind in and out of secluded arbours and niches. Two small fountains are playing, and the planting is in various shades of green with low box hedges and lavender bushes.

'I designed it myself,' Theo tells me, noting my interest. 'I wanted a peaceful place where the bereaved could sit and think about their loved ones.'

He then launches into a staggering performance of bumbling ineptitude over a coffee percolator, which he finds almost impossible to operate, and a packet of biscuits, which prove almost impossible to open. I get the impression of someone who finds the everyday practicalities of life very difficult to negotiate. More at ease with the rituals of death than with those of living, perhaps.

As his skeletal frame lurches about the room, he makes a valiant attempt at small talk. He's not very good at it, and his awkwardness spreads like a virus to me. I'm so mesmerised by his stumbling forays into conversation that I feel my own words slowing down and eventually I grind to a halt. There's a silence which lasts for a beat too long.

Then he tries again. 'Where are my manners? Here am I, asking you to take time out of your busy day to view my collection, and then keeping you waiting in the most monstrous way. I don't know how much you know about Italian Renaissance illuminated manuscripts . . .'

He opens the glass cabinets and proceeds to show me the most exquisite objects that I've ever seen. And his own transformation is astonishing. All the awkwardness drops away as he brings to life the great Italian patrons of the Renaissance: the Medicis of Florence, the d'Estes in Ferrara, Federico da Montefeltro, Duke of Urbino, the Malatestas in Rimini and many others. My favourite thing is a beautifully decorated page from a choir book – one of a set made for the Cathedral in Siena, illuminated by Girolamo da Cremona with musical notes,

Latin words, an intricate border of leaves and flowers, and a huge decorated capital O with a miniature annunciation painted inside it.

'Apart from the cathedral, which still has twenty-one of these books, it's mostly odd pages here and there that survive in museums and private collections. It's my dream to discover one of these choir books intact.'

'Surely they're all accounted for?'

'You'd be surprised what pops up if you keep your ear to the ground. In fact, there's word that something may have surfaced – I'm hoping to hear more very soon.' He shoots me a pleading glance. 'Don't tell Flavia. She doesn't approve of my collection, says it keeps me from real life – whatever that is.'

Then, as if the bond between brother and sister is so close that merely saying her name will conjure her, the door bursts open and Flavia wheels herself in.

'Surprise!'

Theo's thin face flushes. 'Hello, old thing.'

'I had Faisel drive me to St John's Wood High Street to that divine cheese shop – you should pay it a visit, Rosa, there's nowhere like it in the whole of London – and I thought that since I was in the area, it would be foolish not to pop in.'

Theo regards her with a mixture of affection and exasperation.

'You should have phoned me,' he says. 'I would have brought home whatever you needed.'

'I needed an outing – and you mentioned Rosa was coming today, so I thought I'd stick my head round the door and say hello.' She beams at me. 'Have you two had an interesting morning?'

She's very eager for me to say yes. All of a sudden I've had my fill of medieval magic.

'It's a great collection. But actually, Theo, it's time I was on my way . . .'

I'm confronted by two identical pairs of crestfallen turquoise eyes.

'So soon? But I haven't shown you my book of Petrarchian sonnets.'

'It's been fantastic, but I really do have another appointment.'

'I quite understand. I hope I haven't bored you to death.'

'On the contrary. It's been wonderful.'

'Well, it's a delight to chat to someone who takes such a lively interest.' He glances at Flavia. 'Unlike some people not a million miles from here, who think art's only worth looking at if it was thrown together yesterday.'

Flavia giggles. 'Pipe down, you reactionary old windbag. Maybe you can take Rosa out to lunch one day and show her the rest of your collection.'

I stand. 'Thanks again, Theo – it's been an unforgettable morning. Please don't get up, I'll see myself out. Good to see you, Flavia.'

'Goodbye, my dear. We so enjoyed your company at dinner the other week You must come again very soon. I'll telephone.'

As I close Theo's door behind me I can't help overhearing what Flavia is saying.

'I want you to talk to Larry about Steve Pyne. He's becoming obsessed. He won't rest till he's destroyed the poor man – and all for such silly reasons. He won't listen to me so I was hoping you might be able to persuade him to lay off.'

Just as well I didn't reveal that Steve Pyne is my next port of call. The coward in me hopes that I'll hate his work. Larry will go into orbit if I choose it for Consort Park.

When I arrive at the railway arches in Stockwell where Steve has his studio, Caroline's pacing up and down in front of a padlocked door.

'I'm so sorry,' she says, seeing me. 'He isn't here yet.'

'Oh.'

'He's probably popped out on an errand.'

'How long have you been waiting?'

'Not long.'

'How long?' No answer. 'How long, Caro?'

She can't look at me. 'An hour.'

'An hour?'

'I thought I'd come early and spend some time with him.'

Make sure he was sober, more like. It's all too obvious what's happened. Steve's fallen off the wagon and is rat-arsed in some dismal South London gutter.

'If you've been here for an hour, that's that then. No sense standing around here. He won't come now. Let's go.'

'No!' Caro is desperate. 'Wait, Rosa. Please. He'll be here, I promise.'

'I hate to say it, Caro, but he's probably pissed. In which case I won't stay. I've seen him drunk and I don't like it.'

'He hasn't touched a drop since Rob's opening. Why start on the day he finally has a chance to sell some work?'

'Alcoholics don't operate according to reason and logic.'

'I spoke to him first thing, and he was completely sober. He'll have a good reason for being late. You'll see.'

The afternoon sun beats down on my head. There's no shade, nowhere to sit, and I'm not one of nature's stoics.

'I can't stand out here much longer. The heat's intolerable.' If I go now, I won't come back. Caro sees it in my face.

'I suppose *I* could show you the work.'

'How? The place is like Fort Knox.'

'I have keys.'

I must be mishearing. 'Caro, if you have keys, why've you been standing out here in the blazing sun for the best part of an hour?'

Caroline's eyes beseech me not to sneer or laugh.

'He doesn't like me to go into his studio without permission. It's like the inside of his head. He prefers it to be private. Invitation only.'

He'd rather see her with heat-stroke than risk her getting inside his arrogant head? I want to tell her to get up off the pavement so he can't walk all over her any more, but I don't because I can't bear her hangdog expression.

'But since he's not here,' she goes on, 'I wonder whether he'd mind us going in. He is desperate for you to see the work.'

She finally unlocks the door and in we go. Most of the place is covered with the trappings of video art: a huge plasma-screen TV takes up one section of wall, a flashy video camera rests on the table and there are lots of technical bits and bobs lying around as well as arcane objects which probably feature in his films. But at the far end of the studio, with its high barrel roof, are four towering objects shrouded by tarpaulins. Caro pulls the sheets away from three of them, and opens the back doors so that daylight floods through the arched space.

I'm astonished. Steve's work is simple, elegant and harks back to the mid-twentieth century – Barbara Hepworth, Henry Moore – even Brancusi. The works are carved, and abstract. Two of them are made from a heavily veined dull pink marble – undulating forms that could be a human figure, or just as easily a form from a landscape. The third piece, much harsher and more angular, is in forbidding granite: an angry, jagged splinter of a work reaching upwards as if trying to break its ties with earth.

'What's under there?' I indicate the fourth tarpaulin.

Caroline smiles. 'That's not for sale.'

'Why not?'

'It's mine – a present from Steve. He's storing it for me till I buy a house with a garden.'

'Can I see it?'

Caroline pulls off the tarpaulin.

I have found my sculpture.

Carved from a white marble so dazzling that it makes my eyes ache, it's a girl struggling to escape from the rock out of which she is formed. The abstract shape of the rock blends seamlessly into the outline of the girl. I recognise the face. It's Caro.

'Did you model for it?'

'I even chose the rock. It's Carrara marble. We found it in Pietra Santa, a village in the hills near Pisa. Michelangelo used stone from there too, so Steve felt he was in good company.'

'It's stunning.'

'He calls it *Andromeda*.'

'But it's not for sale?'

'Steve made it for me as a memento of that trip. It's my most precious possession. What do you think about the other pieces?'

I like them much more than anything I've yet seen, and if I

hadn't fallen for *Andromeda*, I'd be very keen on one of the pink marble works.

'I love that one.' I point to the larger of the two.

'*Marble One*?' Her eyes are bright with hope.

'Obviously I'll need to talk to Steve . . .'

'But you like it?'

'If I can't have your beautiful *Andromeda*, it's definitely the best thing I've seen so far.'

'Brilliant!'

'I haven't finished looking, remember. Nothing's settled yet.'

She's calling his mobile. 'He's still not answering. Bother.'

'I must go.'

She looks at me. 'You're a good friend, Rosa – thank you.'

'I haven't said I'll take it.'

'I know. I'm saying thank you because you're trying to help.' She pauses. 'Even though you don't like Steve. I really appreciate it. I just want you to know that.'

'What are friends for? Listen, I really do have to go. Are you coming?'

'I think I'll hang on here.'

'Make sure you wait inside. I shan't buy anything from him if I find he's responsible for you getting sunstroke.'

I leave her standing in front of *Marble One*.

Patience on a Monument, waiting for the elusive Mr Pyne.

Nothing like outdoor shagging. Especially the kinky sort. Not that he'd ever done anything as kinky as this. What a revelation. How to settle for anything less – that would be the problem. He found himself singing a song about being addicted to love. Then he

was drifting into sleep. He knew he was supposed to be somewhere, but he couldn't remember where. He had a feeling it was
important, but he couldn't give a fuck. The booze had kicked
in. He had to sleep now.

The bushes rustled around him. Good. After all this heat, a
cooling breeze was just what he needed. Or maybe it wasn't wind
that he was hearing. Maybe it was her. Maybe she'd come back
for more. He grinned. That was probably it. She couldn't stay
away. She was begging for it.

SEVENTEEN

Today I'm lunching with David Borodino. I'm not happy about it – in fact, I feel disgustingly guilty. I'm about to do a deal with the man who's callously cut short Gillian's career to suit his own sexual gratification. It feels like betrayal.

Let's face it: it is betrayal. But I don't have a choice.

I've been dithering about whether to cancel – give Borodino the metaphorical finger. This morning I'd all but decided that somehow I'd manage without his input. Then my bank statement arrived. Even more in the red than I thought. Reeling from this unwelcome revelation, I checked my emails and found one from Anna. She's been invited to a very grand Indian wedding, and needs money for several outfits. Several? The celebrations, apparently, last for at least three days. She also needs cash to buy a decent wedding present – none of your rubbish, she informed me.

In a moment of foolish hope, I called Boo Hardy, my agent, who did her usual 'things are very slack at the moment' line, and promised insincerely to get on my case. How did I feel about Management Training Videos? she enquired. Ecstatic, I said. Bring 'em on!

'That's the spirit,' she trilled. 'Don't worry, darling. Things'll pick up in September, you'll see.'

Which is what she always says. There's always a mythical month set conveniently in the near future, in which things will pick up. Trouble is, it never arrives.

After this triple whammy, I faced facts: I had to sell a painting. But why did it have to be to Gillian's destroyer? He wasn't the only one interested in Rob's work.

I called Larry and told him I needed to sell something really quickly. Like yesterday. To his eternal credit, apart from a startled dramatic pause that reverberated down the line, potent with unspoken meaning, he refrained from commenting on my change of heart, and immediately started babbling about Borodino. I asked whether there was anyone else who'd be interested in making a quick purchase.

'As we've told you, Rob's paintings will all achieve a substantial sum, but very few potential buyers can lay their hands on that amount of money quite so quickly.'

This was rubbish. Larry sells to some of the richest people on the planet. The kind of money we'd be asking for one of Rob's paintings is pocket change to them. I said as much to him.

He let out a small sigh. 'We're full of admiration for your many talents, Rosa, but feel that perhaps when it comes to the intricacies of selling pictures, it may be a wise move to lean on our professional expertise. Believe me, David is your best hope for an instant sale.'

'But he's really not my favourite person at the moment. Not after what he's done to Gillian.'

'The Gillian Gerard affair is unfortunate, but we can't let sentiment interfere with business.'

Heaven forbid, Larry.

His message is loud and clear: Borodino or nothing. He's determined to keep on the right side of the tycoon. Nothing I say will affect his devious plans and hidden agendas.

So, feeling like the biggest hypocrite in the universe, I'm now preparing for lunch at *The Ivy* with the arch-villain. I decide to skip my daily attempt to contact Gillian. It would be just my luck if today she finally picks up, and then what would I say? 'Can't talk for long, Gill. Just off to lunch with the bloke who sacked you. Chin up. Speak to you soon.'

I don't think so.

I'm not pleased with myself, and it's affecting my appearance. I can't seem to strike the right note for my lunch-date. I'm scowling at myself in the bedroom mirror, wishing I wasn't so tall and stick-like, and berating myself for caring what David Borodino might or might not think about my outfit, when the phone rings. It's Jess. Sounding particularly perky.

'Wassup?' I ask. 'Won the lottery or something?'

'In a manner of speaking.'

'Go on.'

'Promise not to laugh?'

'Laugh – me? I'm Ms Supportive Best Friend.'

Knowing what I was about to do to Gillian, this kind of sticks in my throat. But Jess really is my best friend – has been for twenty years, whereas I've only known Gill for a few months.

And she doesn't want me around anyway.

And is therefore not as entitled to your loyalty? Give me a break, Rosa.

Jess is in full swing.

'I've fucking fallen in love.'

'Again?'

Jess's love affairs are legion, always end messily, and guess who has to pick up the pieces?

'Don't be like that, Misery Guts. This time it's for real.'

They always are.

'And this time it's different.'

It always is.

'Where have I heard that before?'

'When I tell you, you'll have to admit I'm right.'

'Go on then, surprise me.'

'It's Mike.'

I don't know how to react. Or how I feel. Even though I'd noticed something that night at *Sketch*, I'd dismissed it as drunken speculation on my part.

I ought to be pleased for her. But I'm not.

It's not as if I fancy him myself – he's more like a brother. Maybe that's the problem. That I see Mike as Jess's brother too. Or is it that he's an irredeemable womaniser and I don't trust him with my precious Jess who, beneath that tough exterior, is a vulnerable woman teetering on the edge of middle age, and desperate to be in love and settled for life. Ripe for being very badly hurt.

'Weird, huh?' she says now, and I can hear how anxious she is for me to say the right thing.

'Weird, yes,' I agree.

'Why? Why is it weird?'

'Because he's . . . he's Mike. He's like a brother.' Talk about treading on eggshells.

'*Your* brother, maybe.'

'You know what I mean.'

'Yeah, of course I do.'

'And if you get past that, why would you be any different to any of the other squillion women he's loved and left?'

'I know. I know. But he's different with me. I couldn't believe what was happening at first, either. But . . .'

'But?'

'But I've changed, and so's he. It'll work, Rosy – I know it will. What are you thinking? And don't bullshit me.'

I'm feeling my way with this one. 'Weird, but possibly wonderful?' I'm not fibbing. Not really. I may well think it wonderful. When I've got my head around it. 'Does he feel the same way?'

'I think so.'

'You think so?'

'He hasn't said he loves me in so many words, but I can tell. You can, can't you, when it's the real thing?'

How many times have you said that, Jess? There was the actor from the RSC who turned out to be gay; the geeky computer programmer with the bad teeth; the nightclub bouncer whose fists were never off-duty. Et cetera.

Jess chatters on, oblivious. 'We've spent nearly all our time together in the last week or so. I'd be with him now, but he's having lunch with his dealer. And he's fantastic with Lozz –

always has been, you know that. The perfect godfather. And Lozz adores him.'

Lozz is one of the major reasons for Jess's chequered love-life. He comes first, before anything and anyone. If her boyfriends have a problem with Lozz then they're dumped, however much she likes them.

And that's meant a lot of dumping over the years.

But Jess travels hopefully. Somehow the worldly streak which tells her that men willing to take on a teenager with Down's syndrome are few and far between, doesn't get in the way of her capacity to plunge headfirst into amatory adventures.

But Mike?

There's a quality in her voice I haven't heard before: a softness. The satirical tone with which she usually presents her new relationships is absent. She seems wide open. A sitting target for love's poison arrows.

She wants more from me.

'Wow, Jessie, I'm really happy for you.'

'I do know how fucking strange it is, with our history and all.'

'Yeah, it's strange. But . . . I think it's great.'

'You don't sound it.'

'I do. It's really great. Honestly.' I put all my effort into convincing her.

And myself.

'Just don't go off and live in America, that's all. I need you here.'

She laughs. I can hear the relief in her voice. 'Let's not get ahead of ourselves. It's early days yet.'

Another difference – Jess being cautious in a longterm kind of way.

I'm out of my depth with this one. I listen to five more minutes of love-struck burbling. Why can't I feel unadulterated happiness for my friends?

I know why: Mike can't be trusted around women. I love him dearly, but I'm pretty clear-eyed on that one. The other day in his flat, he'd even started vaguely flirting with me. Not because he particularly wanted to, just because I was female and there. It's like a compulsion. Jess says he's changed. If he has, it's happened in a suspiciously short time. Mike finally monogamous? The jury's out on that one.

I change the subject and tell her about my imminent lunch with Borodino. I don't mention the Gillian complication.

Why not?

Because I'm ashamed. Jess puts a high price on loyalty. She'd be horrified if she knew that I was lunching with the man who'd thrown away Gillian's career like so much trash.

'You know what, Rosy? I'm fucking glad you've decided to start selling Rob's stuff. Not just for the money, but because I think it's all part and parcel of moving on. Rob wouldn't want you to make him into some sort of martyr. He'd hate his pictures turned into an everlasting shrine for you to worship at. And he'd certainly hate to see you struggling to make ends meet, when his sodding paintings are hanging in *L'Estrange East*, with pound signs dripping off them. You're doing exactly the right thing.'

I've said what she wants to hear about Mike. She's done the same for me about Borodino. What a team.

'And as regards lunch with the millionaire – don't wear black next to your face. Wear cream – it reflects the light off your ageing skin.'

'Cheeky mare.' I ring off, promising to give her a full breakdown of *The Ivy*.

When I'm finally ready, having taken Jess's advice and put on a cream linen dress, I shout goodbye to Joshua. No answer. He's not in the house. I check the shed. Not there either. I'm very tempted to take a sneak preview of his photographs, but I don't.

Firstly because it would be dishonest. Secondly because I can't.

He's fitted a lock.

To protect all the expensive equipment?

Or to keep me out?

I still haven't had a single sighting of any photograph.

Nor have I had a single sighting of Joshua recently.

Not since I gave him the extra two hundred smackers.

When I handed the cash over, I made some jocular enquiry about seeing the fruits of my investment. I remember his face momentarily blanking over. Then he muttered something about buying mounts, and left the house in double-quick time.

I stare at the locked shed. Why does it fill me with such discomfort? In an effort to make sense of my feelings I walk down the garden and sit on the bench in Anna's pet cemetery. This is the spot where she's always buried her dead pets. A series of little crosses made by Rob marks their final resting-places.

And now there's an addition.

By the fence, in a specially cleared area, stands another cross, larger than the rest, beautifully carved and varnished. In the centre is a photograph, protected by a little circle of glass.

Rob.

The time when . . .

. . . Warlord's feeble portrait of Her won best painting in the Diploma Show and someone did a mock ceremony in the bar afterwards, presenting the Fabulous Willie Wanka with an empty beer bottle for The Dullest Work of Art in the Entire Universe.

Eat your heart out, folks. Who's cutting edge now?

When the time's right, the world will be falling over itself to see. Not yet.

When the time's right.

And nobody will stand in the way. Or mock.

Nobody.

EIGHTEEN

I'm fashionably late. *The Ivy* is full. At a glance I identify two theatrical Dames, a trendy furniture designer, three ageing rockers and a Cabinet Minister. But I can't see Borodino anywhere. Maybe he got tired of waiting and thinks I've stood him up. The maître d' is approaching.

'Mrs Thorn? Lovely to see you.'

I'm wondering how he knows who I am, when I see something that leaves me speechless.

Mike. Deep in conversation with Leni Dang.

It's like a rerun of *Sketch*. But much worse in view of Jess's revelation earlier this morning.

Leni catches my eye and waves.

Brass nerve.

Mike turns. When he sees me, he too waves. I'm too far away to see the expression on his face.

'If you'd care to follow me, Mr Borodino is waiting for you in our private dining room upstairs.'

I can't deal with this, and I'm keeping my host waiting, so I gesture feebly to Mike, and then follow the maître d' up the narrow stairs to the elegant panelled room where David Borodino is sitting in solitary splendour and glowing with the patina of extreme wealth.

He's charm personified. Brushing aside my apologies he pours me a glass of champagne. I can't look him in the eye. The weight of what he's done to Gillian is pressing down on my chest. My breath feels constricted and I can hardly talk.

'I've taken the liberty of ordering,' he tells me. 'Some things they prepare especially for me when I come here. The main course is particularly fine – sea bass in a sauce. I'm not sure what they put in it, but it's a rare and beautiful thing.'

Controlling bastard. Can't even let me order my own lunch.

He picks up my hostility – not difficult since, I realise, I'm scowling.

'If you'd prefer to see the *à la carte*?'

I order myself to behave. I have to sell my painting and I must do so graciously. I don't want to frighten him off. My betrayal of Gillian remains whether I'm nice to him or not. I force myself to be pleasant. It's hard.

'Sounds perfect.'

After that we talk about this and that and eat our way through a delicious first course, followed by the sea bass, which is everything Borodino had promised. I let him do most of the talking, but endeavour to smile in the right places, and ask the right questions. In spite of everything I find myself thawing. What is it about him? I try to hold on to the image of Gillian, huddled in her old armchair, steeped in despair, but the image fades as the lunch proceeds.

We're tucking into a melt-in-the-mouth fruit concoction before he raises the reason for this whole shebang.

'I'm so thrilled you've reconsidered selling the paintings.'

'Painting.'

'Sorry?'

'Painting. In the singular. I'm only selling one.'

A flicker of annoyance passes over his smooth features and for a split second I see the ruthless deal-maker, the man who always gets his way.

'One it is then, and in the light of that, I consider myself extremely fortunate that you've chosen me to be the recipient. Top of my shopping list is *Garden Door Open*, if you're agreeable. It's sublime.'

Like a heat-seeking missile he's locked on to the one picture I'll never sell.

Rob's last painting. The one he finished minutes before he was blasted into oblivion.

'That's not for sale.'

Again, that lightning surge of anger, quickly disguised.

'Larry gave me to understand that all the works were available.'

'Larry was mistaken.'

'I can't persuade you to change your mind?'

'I'll never sell that one.'

I see him assessing how far to push me, and then, like the good businessman that he is, he shrugs his shoulders and lets it go.

'In that case, it has to be *Shed Door Outside*.'

How come this man goes straight for my favourites? *Shed Door*

Outside is unique because, as its title suggests, instead of the door being an interior one, keeping the world out, like all his other pictures, this is an exterior door, with bindweed and campanula creeping round the frame. It's opened the merest crack, giving us a tantalising glimpse of the cool darkness inside the womb-like shed.

I would really like to hang on to it.

I read in Borodino's face that if I don't comply this time, he'll forget the whole thing. Not a man to be messed around. Nevertheless, knowing I'm pushing it, I still try to point him in another direction.

'What about *Pool Door*? Everyone loves that one. It's a real crowd-pleaser. All that hot steam drifting out, and those deep turquoise blues . . .'

'I'm not a person who runs with the crowd.'

Long pause.

'In that case, what can I say. *Shed Door* it is.'

Borodino is voraciously pleased. His hand tightens round his wine glass and his eyes gleam. I see the greed of the fanatical collector capering behind the civilised veneer.

'I plan to send the picture to my house in the country,' he says. 'I have the perfect place to hang it.'

He leans forward. His deepset eyes brim with compassion.

'I know how difficult this must be for you. I'm deeply grateful that you should trust me to take care of what clearly means so much. After the painting is hung, what I'd like to do, if I may, is invite you down to *Cedars*, so you can view it *in situ*. Then you'll always be able to picture it. It won't have disappeared down some black hole.'

He's very perceptive. The prospect of being able to see *Shed Door*'s new home does make me feel better.

Over coffee we talk of other things. In spite of myself I'm having a good time. He's a great raconteur, who also has the knack of making one feel included rather than a cardboard cut-out conveniently placed to be talked at.

I'm increasingly bewildered that this man could do such a horrible thing to Gillian, and the more I like him, the harder it feels to keep silent about it.

I'm not comfortable keeping things from people I like. It makes me feel dishonest. My situation has changed during the course of the lunch. I still feel I'm betraying Gillian by consorting with her executioner, but now I also feel bad for harbouring nasty notions about Borodino's character, while laughing at his jokes and enjoying his company.

Eventually I crack.

'I was surprised to see that Leni Dang's taken over Gillian Gerard's job on the *Correspondent*.'

His eyes widen. 'That was a bit of a jump,' he says. 'One minute we're swapping old Monty Python sketches, the next you're questioning my staff appointments. I sense you don't approve.'

'It just seems a strange decision, to replace one of our leading critics with, well, with Leni Who?'

He regards me steadily. 'You would find it strange since you don't know the circumstances.'

I wait for him to elaborate. But he doesn't. So I stumble on. I've blown it now anyway.

'Leni isn't exactly experienced.'

'I couldn't agree more. However, she does have other qualities.'

It flashes out before I can stop myself. 'I bet she does.'

He gives a full-throated laugh. Then he says, 'Leni's energetic, enthusiastic and diligent. What she doesn't know she'll learn on the job. We all had to start somewhere.'

'And what about finishing? How's Gillian meant to feel, suddenly being chucked in favour of an ignorant amateur?'

This time he's not amused. 'You don't know what you're talking about.'

'She's destroyed.'

He leans forward. 'Believe me, Rosa, neither I nor Leni Dang has destroyed Gillian Gerard. She's done that all by herself.'

'What do you mean?'

'I don't make a habit of discussing employees or ex-employees with anyone other than those immediately concerned.'

'I am concerned. You've just made a very damaging insinuation about Gillian Gerard, who happens to be a good friend of mine. The least you can do is finish what you started.'

His full lips tighten. He wants to give me a tongue-lashing.

He also wants *Shed Door Outside*.

He stares at me for a long time, then runs a hand through his dark hair.

'If I tell you, it has to be on the understanding that it goes no further. Is that understood?'

'Of course.'

He sighs. 'I'm sorry to say this, since she's a friend of yours, but whatever Gillian may have led you to believe, the fact of the matter is, she's an alcoholic.'

What?

'Has been for years. Until recently she's hidden it very well, but in the last few months, it's really interfered with her work. She's been missing deadlines, not filing copy. Rory Whittacker, my editor at the *Correspondent*, has been at his wits' end. Gillian's a longstanding colleague and he couldn't bring himself to hurt her. So as proprietor, I stepped in and made the decision for him.'

'No consultation? No explanation? No second chance?'

'Rory Whittacker gave her more second chances than you'll ever know.'

'But Leni of all people . . . Did you know she was a protégée of Gillian's?'

His eyes register genuine surprise. 'No, I didn't.'

'Would it have made any difference?'

I'm pushing it again. His expression's a cross between irritation, resignation and weary amusement.

'You're very fond of your friend, aren't you?'

'Yes. I think what's happened to her is appalling. Please tell me, would it have made a difference if you'd known how close Gillian was to Leni?'

He smiles. 'On the contrary, it would have reinforced my decision. Anyone Gillian takes under her wing is bound to have talent. And that's what I'm interested in – talent. Even if it's still at a rather raw stage.'

'Gill has more talent in her little finger than Leni Dang has in her whole body.'

'The newspaper business is a cut-throat world. I do what's best for my paper. When I met Leni at the dinner for your husband,

I was very impressed by her genuine enthusiasm for art. I know she doesn't have Gillian's scholarly authority, but that doesn't matter. People don't want scholars any more. Leni will go down very well with our readers. The fact that she doesn't know much more than they do will get them on her side. She's got the popular touch and that's what people want nowadays. Besides, Gillian's addiction is at such an advanced stage that she wouldn't have been able to keep going for much longer without making some terrible blunder. She had to be replaced, Rosa. For her own sake. None of us would want to witness the public humiliation of that great talent.'

He makes it all sound so plausible. Do I believe him?

I remember Gillian clutching her bottle of whisky, desperate for a drink. I'd assumed it was a temporary response to losing her job. Now he's saying it's the main reason she lost it in the first place.

'I've seen a lot of Gillian recently. She's never seemed even remotely tiddly.'

'That's the mistake we all made. For a long time. She's very clever at hiding it. We think it started after her husband died. None of us realised that she just wasn't coping. That's partly why I've held off getting rid of her. We should have picked up on it earlier. We let her down.'

He seems genuinely upset. He leans forward. 'I know how you must feel, but don't blame Leni. She happened to be in the right place at the right time. If it hadn't been her, it would have been somebody else.'

'Yes?'

'Yes. Well now, can I tempt you to a brandy?'

He's drawing a line. I'm grateful. I need to mull it over on my own. We both talk trivialities, until the maître d' appears and whispers discreetly to Borodino that his driver's arrived.

'Can I drop you somewhere?' he asks.

'No, thanks.'

I want to be alone to digest not only my meal, and the fact that I've agreed to sell one of Rob's irreplaceable paintings, but also the unpalatable contents of Borodino's disclosures about Gillian. Not forgetting the implications of Leni Dang lunching with Mike who, according to Jess, is supposed to be with his dealer. I wonder if they're still there? I hope not. I don't want to face either of them.

To my great relief, they've gone.

I go to the Ladies. There, retouching her elaborate maquillage, is Leni. Her face lights up.

'It *was* you earlier,' she says.

I remember Gillian's unspeakable pain and bewilderment, I remember Jess's ecstatic babble about Mike, and then I remember Leni pawing Borodino in *Sketch*. I look into her smiling face, and I turn tail and run.

Gillian watched the comings and goings with a keen eye. She thanked the Lord that Leni's lunch destination had turned out to be *The Ivy*. Gillian was an old friend of the maître d' who always found her a table, however full the place was. Today at her request, he'd put her in an out-of-the-way corner that allowed her to observe everything without anyone taking the slightest notice of her. Although, she mused sadly, she would have been invisible wherever she'd sat. Sixty-five-year-old women were. No wonder some of them took to shoplifting: it was one way of getting attention.

It had been easy procuring Leni's address: she just told the secretary on the arts desk that she had to forward post to her successor.

The flat was a shock. Gillian had been led to believe from various casual conversations that Leni lived in a loft in fashionable Clerkenwell.

Not so.

It was on the first floor of a broken-down building in the middle of a crumbling council estate. It had one of those mock Georgian doors with a fanlight that opened on to a depressing balcony running the length of the block. Not an image Leni would care to share with the art world, Gillian surmised. Leni had always implied she came from a wealthy, highly cultured, old Vietnamese family. This notion was reinforced by the clothes she wore: definitely more Bond than Berwick Street.

For Gillian's purposes, it was ideal: not that far from Lamb's Conduit Street and, by pulling a dilapidated old bench under cover of a walkway, she was able to remain concealed and yet observe in comparative comfort. Her funny turn in the tube had given her the idea for her disguise: if people could mistake her for a bag lady, then that's what she would be. No one takes any notice of mad old women with plastic bags. And so it had proved. After the first day she'd brought her flask, and a book, and was quite content, reading a new biography of Bernard Berenson and waiting for developments. She felt energised by her plan. Vindicated. As the days went by she found that her resolve, far from weakening, became increasingly strong.

She'd followed Leni hither and yon, all over London. She went to private views, where she would jettison her plastic bags and dirty mac, and become Gillian Gerard, respected art critic whom everyone, especially Leni herself, was trying to avoid, on account of her current misfortune. She'd accompanied her several times to a fashionable hair salon where she'd lurked outside at a bus stop until Leni emerged, freshly trimmed and disgustingly glowing. Once she'd tracked her round a major show at the V and A, noting with interest that yet again, Leni was relying on the audio guide. Gillian had toyed with the idea of grassing her up to Rory Whittacker – 'You do know that your new art critic's so ignorant she has to rely on the audio guide to see her round all the major shows' – but she thought it might seem a tad petty.

All the while she noted down the quality of Leni's sugary interactions, not only with artists, dealers and art-world regulars, but with shopkeepers, bar staff and folk she bumped into in the street. This was a woman who badly needed to be loved, and Gillian documented every coy laugh, every winsome flutter of her long spidery eyelashes.

Gillian had once suggested going to Leni's flat to help her with her first commission for *Dame*. Now she knew why Leni had so forcefully steered her away from the idea. It wasn't just the ramshackle location of the flat itself. It was that, unlike the impression she'd given Gillian, she was not all alone in the world. She had a boyfriend: a young man who kept odd hours and who was very protective. Gillian had watched them walk down the street arm-in-arm, chattering away, completely absorbed in each other. Once someone had jostled her, and the man had turned on that person and shouted aggressively. Leni had to pull him away.

As she sat at her table in *The Ivy*, Gillian wondered if he knew what Leni got up to when he wasn't around. She watched the girl making eyes at Mike Mason. She noted down every shy smile, every piece of come-hither body language. She noted Mason's response, too: laughably predictable. He clearly wanted to gobble up every morsel of her firm young body.

But they didn't leave together. What was one to make of that? And what was one to make of the earlier matter?

First David Borodino had swept in and been ushered upstairs to the private dining room, to be followed some minutes later by Rosa Thorn. Why would Rosa be lunching with Borodino? She knew what the bastard had done.

Unless . . .

Surely the dear old thing wasn't trying to persuade him to reinstate her as art critic of the *Correspondent*? Gillian was deeply touched despite her knowledge that Rosa would fail in her attempt. People like Borodino never went back on their decisions. It smacked of weakness.

She watched Leni go into the loo and then, moments later, Rosa, who emerged almost immediately with a face like a sour lemon.

Gillian's heart swelled with affection for her loyal friend. She pulled herself to her feet, waited until she could follow a tearful Leni from the restaurant and vowed to return Rosa's next call.

NINETEEN

All the way home I brood.

Do I believe David Borodino's claim that Leni's a blameless innocent and Gillian's a drunk? Or do I believe he's a heartless destroyer of lives and Leni's a Machiavellian manipulator of staggering proportions?

Does it matter what I believe? It won't get Gill her job back. It won't stop me selling Rob's painting to the man who took that job from her.

If she is an alcoholic, she needs my support even more than when I believed her problem was a temporary blip brought on by losing her job to a scheming Jezebel.

The question is, do I want to get involved?

I like Gillian a lot, but I had an uncle who was an alcoholic. He died when I was a child. I still remember how his antics wrecked not just his life, but his whole family's. I remember him coming round to our house where my aunt and my cousin had taken refuge from his drunken blunderings. I remember gagging on his beery breath as he begged them to return, swearing on his life that he'd never touch another drop. Five years and umpteen broken promises later, he died of cirrhosis of the liver, aged forty-two. That's why I don't believe Steve Pyne's empty declarations to Caro.

Alcoholics are impossible to deal with. You have to be inextricably attached in one way or another to put up with the lying and deceit, the drunken scenes, endless recriminations and betrayals. If it were Jess, there'd be no contest. Our lives are bound together by twenty years of shared life experience. Surely, by the same token, Gillian will have other closer and more intimate friends than me to help her through this.

If she needs help.

If I believe Borodino.

Until I've asked Gillian point blank about the drinking, the jury's still out.

Back home I ring her. No reply. I try her mobile. She picks up straight away, sounding as perky as a puppy on speed.

'It's Rosa. I was wondering how you were feeling?'

'How kind. I'm fine – more than fine, fantastic. I'm so sorry about the other day. You caught me at my lowest ebb. Everything's so much better now.'

'You're OK?'

'Better than OK. After you left I had a long think. I realised that for the first time in years, I was free – the column was quite restricting, you know. I decided it was time to enjoy myself. So that's what I've been doing.'

She doesn't seem drunk.

'Enjoy yourself?' I prompt.

'Oh, you know, visiting friends, treating myself to expensive lunches just for the hell of it . . .' There's a slight question mark at the end of her sentence.

'Expensive lunches? How nice.'

'Yes, at *The Ivy*, today. Actually, I thought I caught a glimpse of you there.'

Caught red-handed.

'Oh.'

'You were coming downstairs – you seemed in rather a rush.'

She's waiting for me to elaborate.

'Yes.'

'Nice meal?'

'Lovely.'

There's a long pause. She couldn't have seen me with Borodino, could she? If she had, she wouldn't be sounding quite so friendly. I can't bring myself to come clean, so I try to deflect her attention.

'Gill, you would tell me if you were still feeling bad? You wouldn't pretend?'

'It's very sweet of you to be so concerned, but I've told you – I'm hunky dory. Couldn't be better. You look to your own life.'

What does she mean? I struggle to pull myself together and ask the big question: *are you an alcoholic?*

But it's too late. 'I'm sorry, Rosa, but I have to go. Thanks for phoning. Speak to you soon. Bye.'

End of little chat. That was a bit abrupt.

She sounds pretty sane and sober to me.

She saw me at The Ivy.

What exactly did she see?

I have to phone her back and tell her the truth. Both about Borodino's identity and also about what he claims is his reason for sacking her.

Then Joshua appears and other concerns disappear. He's cut off his braids. His hair is cropped close to his skull.

Like Rob.

He's wearing a grey tracksuit.

Like Rob's.

There's a paint smear on the left sleeve.

It *is* Rob's.

Who said he could wear Rob's clothes?

Why shouldn't he? Danny won't touch them. They've been waiting for me to take them to the charity shop. Why shouldn't Joshua get some use out of them? I let him borrow Rob's suit for our dinner at *Sketch*. Maybe he misunderstood and thought I was inviting him to make free with all Rob's things.

I want to tear the clothes away from him. I know if I refer to them at all, I'll scream in his face.

'Hi, Rosa.'

'Long time no see.'

'Yeah. I've been very busy – checking stuff out an' all.'

He even sounds more like Rob. The mellow Trinidadian tones are fading and the ultra-correct English gentleman delivery is becoming more London street. Like Danny's.

Like Rob's.

Drama queen alert, Rosa. Stop embroidering the situation. It's just Joshua, with a new haircut, borrowing his brother's tracksuit. What's the big deal?

Borrowing his brother's voice?

'How's the work coming along?' I ask.

'Great.'

'When can I see it?'

'Soon.'

'How soon?'

'I'm mounting them at the moment.'

'It feels good having an artist in the house again.'

'Nobody's called me that for a while.'

'Well, it's what you are.'

'Yeah?'

'If you're making art, you're an artist. I don't know whether you're a good artist. I'll have to see your stuff before I make my mind up on that one. Soon, you say?'

'What was my brother like when he was in the middle of an important painting?'

'Moody, unpredictable, impossible. Up and down like a yoyo. Just as well I'm a saint – no one else would have put up with him.'

'He wasn't like that all the time, though?'

'No. He was funny and loving and caring.'

'Funny?'

'Yeah. He had a great sense of humour.'

Joshua nods slowly. 'A great sense of humour is very important. It took a while for his talent to be recognised, you said.'

'Most of his life up until the last couple of years.'

'How did he cope? Painting away and nobody interested?'

'Self-belief. He knew he was good. So did I. We were certain it was only a matter of time.'

'He was well lucky to have you.'

'I was lucky to have him. I just wish he could have lived to see his dreams . . . to see his show . . .'

My throat aches. Joshua puts his hand on my shoulder.

'You don't have to worry about anything any more,' he says. 'I'm here now.'

His hand feels hot against my skin.

'Why didn't you tell me you'd put that cross in the garden?'

He snatches his hand away. 'You've seen it?'

'Yes.'

'Do you like it?'

'I—'

'I carved it myself.'

'What for?'

'It's a memorial. Do you like it?'

'It's . . .' It's creepy, that's what it is. 'It's beautifully done. Thank you.'

He looks at me long and hard, as if assessing something. Then he says, 'Gotta go. I only checked in for some stuff.'

He runs upstairs and I hear him moving round his room. Five minutes later he's disappeared and I'm left standing, in a state of confused incoherence.

In my mind I see his arm reaching towards me, gold watch glinting on thin wrist. A gold watch identical to the one I gave Rob for his thirtieth birthday.

Wearing his brother's clothes is one thing. Stealing from my jewellery box is quite another.

I run upstairs and open the box. Rob's watch gleams up at me. I turn it over. Rob's initials and mine, intertwined, and the inscription *Love Always* are on the back.

Whatever Joshua's wearing on his wrist, it isn't Rob's. But it is identical.

How did Joshua know that, unless he's been through my things? And why would he want the same watch as Rob? It must have set him back a few quid.

Around two hundred quid, to be more precise.

The time when . . .

. . . Indifference stopped and they showed their true colours.

The day it all ended.

'We all know what Willie Wanka wants. Push off, perv.'

Vengeance is mine, saith the Lord. I will repay. A man that studieth revenge keeps his own wounds green. Green shoots mean life. Revenge is a dish best eaten cold or let's make medicine of our great revenge, to cure this deadly grief. Grief. Don't get mad, don't get mad, get even. Revenge is wild justice. Revenge triumphs over death. If you wrong us, shall we not revenge? Spur my dull revenge. My unconquerable will, and study of revenge, immortal hate. Hate. Hate. Murder's out of tune, and sweet revenge grows harsh. My bloody thoughts, with violent pace, shall ne'er look back, ne'er ebb to humble love, till that a capable and wide revenge swallow them up. Soon. Soon. Soon the whirligig of time brings in his revenge. I will have such revenge on you that all the world shall – I will do such things – I will do such things – I will do such things . . . they shall be the terrors of the earth. Terrors of the earth. I'll be revenged on the whole pack of you. I'll be revenged on the whole pack of you. The whole pack of you . . . I will do such things . . .

TWENTY

I can't get my head around anything that's happened today. It's time to do something practical. I phone Larry to give him the good news about my lunch with Borodino.

But it's not Larry who answers. It's Caroline.

'Hi, Caro. Larry said you weren't in today.'

'I wasn't this morning.'

'Are you OK?'

Silence.

'What's wrong?'

'It's Steve.'

He's fallen off the wagon. I knew it when he didn't turn up the other day.

'I'm so sorry, Caro.'

'He's disappeared. And he's not answering his mobile.'

'What?'

'No one's seen him for three days.'

'Do you think he's gone on a bender?'

'That's what everyone says, but you're all wrong. Steve's definitely stopped drinking. And he wouldn't have blown that opportunity to show you his work.'

'When did you last see him?'

'The day before your studio visit. In my lunch-hour. He said he wanted to stay at the studio overnight to finish off some things. I called later that evening and he was fine. And then I spoke to him the following morning. Remember – I told you.'

'How did he sound?'

'Jolly pleased at the prospect of selling some work. Certainly not drunk.'

True, or just Caro's wishful thinking?

'The chap who runs the garage a couple of doors away from the studio says he saw Steve around eleven that day, talking on his mobile.'

'To you?'

'No. Kevin says that after the phone call Steve charged off in a frightful hurry.' There's a catch in her voice. She's on the verge of tears. 'I should have been with him that night. I knew he was in a bit of a state. I shouldn't have listened to him. I should have just turned up.'

'Stop blaming yourself. Whatever's happened, it's not your fault.'

'I pulled a sickie this morning and went looking. No one's seen him. When I came into work I made the mistake of telling Larry. Do you know what he said? "Good riddance to bad rubbish!" If I wanted to find him, he said, I was to do it on my own time, and that as far as he was concerned, a disappeared Steve Pyne was the best kind. Would you believe he could be so callous? I honestly don't know how much longer I can go on working for him if he's going to be so foul about Steve.'

I've never heard Caro slagging off Larry. She really must be worried.

'There'll be a perfectly reasonable explanation. You just haven't thought of it yet. If Danny and Anna are late I always imagine the worst, and it's usually something blindingly obvious that I haven't taken into account.'

Except for that one time with Anna. But I don't tell Caro about that.

'If you really think something's wrong,' I go on, 'maybe you should tell the police.'

'I already have. They say he's over eighteen and free to come and go as he chooses. Until I have concrete evidence that something's happened, there's nothing they can do.'

'What about family?'

'He's an only child and his parents are dead. He doesn't have any family. Only me.'

I want to say something comforting but I can't. She's placing too much faith in the new, alcohol-free Steve. Leopards don't often change their spots, but Caro doesn't want to hear that.

'I'm sure he's OK,' I say feebly.

'I've let him down.'

'You never let people down, Caro. That's why we all love you.'

'Larry's calling. I must get back to work, Rosa. I'll let you know when I have some news.'

Larry. I'd almost forgotten why I called the gallery in the first place. I ask her to put me through to him.

'I've agreed to sell *Shed Door Outside* to David Borodino.'

Larry laughs. 'Old news, my dear. He's been on to us already. Doesn't let the grass grow under his feet, our David. Secret of his success, I dare say. He wants the painting straight away and although it's against gallery policy to let something go before the end of the show, in this case we thought it politic to agree.'

'Straight away?'

'Absolutely.'

'But I thought buyers couldn't do that!'

'This is a special case.'

'Why?'

'David Borodino. When he wants something, he has to have it immediately.'

'That's true of a lot of people. Doesn't mean to say they get their way, though.'

'It does if it's Borodino. With him one gives in graciously or loses the sale. He has no concept of delayed gratification. The painting's going to his place in the country.'

'When?'

'Tonight.'

'You're joking.'

'We never joke, Rosa.'

Things are moving far too quickly. I thought I'd have the full duration of the show to psych myself into parting with *Shed Door Outside*. Not the fag end of an afternoon.

'I'm on my way.'

'My dear, panic not. Nothing's happening until after the gallery closes.'

Larry thinks I'm over-reacting. Maybe I am. So what?

In no time at all I'm approaching *L'Estrange East*. As I pass
Nature Morte I glimpse a familiar figure inside.

Joshua.

He must be handing in his portfolio.

How come Zander Zinovieff gets to see his work before me?
I try not to feel hurt. I toy with going in and embarrassing him,
but I'm desperate to get to Rob's painting.

At *L'Estrange East* I sit down in front of *Shed Door Outside*
and try to memorise every little detail. The problem is, that for
me, the paintings are like the eponymous wardrobe in the C.S.
Lewis classic: a conduit to another world – my past. Each of
them contains moments of my life with Rob. Looking at the
delicate, pear-shaped blue-purple campanula creeping up the
doorframe, I remember teasing him because even though he'd
painted it so beautifully, he didn't have a clue what it was called.
Seeing the dark velvety interior of the shed I recall his frustration as he tried to mix the perfect colour to convey soft dark
space, and me threatening to throw acid over the canvas if he
didn't shut up and put up. And how our mock fight ended most
wonderfully on the studio floor. This isn't just a painting. It's me
and Rob.

A state of affairs that no longer exists.

I've wallowed enough. I say a quick hello to Larry, ask for a
photo of the painting to be sent to me, and then look for Caro.
Julian says she's popped out for a minute.

'Have some coffee while you're waiting,' he says. I can tell by
the gleam in his eye that he's gagging for a gossip.

'Frightful news about poor Gillian. Have you spoken to her?'
Is he talking about the job loss or the alcoholism? Or both?

It's immaterial because there's no way I'm prepared to discuss Gillian's business with the biggest gob in London.

'What did I tell you about the Dung creature? Madam on the make or what?'

I remember how I'd refused to believe Julian's bitchy assessment of her.

'You were right, Julian.'

He preens. 'I always am, darling. I've got this knack of intuiting people's real agenda. It's either a gift or a curse, I can't decide which.'

Through his open door I see Caro. She goes into her office. Her eyes are red and puffy. She looks dreadful. Julian follows my gaze.

'I've told her she'll ruin her looks if she carries on like this. "At your age," I said, "it doesn't do to make a habit of blubbing. Plays havoc with that whole eye area".' He leans forward. '*Entre nous*, it's not too good for the old career either. We all know how Larry feels about our Mr Pyne. Caro's doing herself no favours trailing round like the proverbial wailing widow. Oh fuck, I'm so frightfully sorry, Rosa. I didn't mean . . .'

I enjoy the novel sensation of accepting Julian's grovelling apologies then go off to talk to Caroline. She's leafing through her address book.

'Where would he go to get away from me?' She's frantic.

'Away from you?'

'I think you're right. He's started drinking again and he's too ashamed to tell me. But then where is he? No one will admit to taking him in, which they would do normally. Usually they're desperate to get rid of him if he's been crashing on their floor, puking all over the place and insulting them.'

'I thought you said this was the first time he's gone awol?'

'I lied.'

'Why?'

'Because I didn't want to believe he'd broken his promises yet again. And I didn't want you to think he was unreliable in case it put you off buying his work.'

I give her a cuddle, like I do to Anna if she's upset. I experience a sudden overwhelming desire to see my daughter.

'You've got to stop upsetting yourself like this. Now you've accepted that it's more of the same, leave it. He'll surface when he's ready to face you. Personally, I'd give him the elbow. He's not worth all this grief.'

'But he's never gone missing for this long. Usually it's no more than twenty-four hours.'

'Remember after Rob's opening, how sorry he was?'

'Not this time. He obviously couldn't give a damn about how I feel.'

'I bet the first thing he thought about when he sobered up was you. But what if he's so ashamed of himself that he can't face you at all? I reckon he'd still want to be close to you. Is there anywhere he'd go – somewhere that's special for the two of you?'

Caroline has an instant answer. 'Hampstead Heath. Our secret place. We take picnics up there sometimes. It's a fantastic view. We love it. We've even stayed there overnight.' She blushes. 'It's where we first – you know.'

'What are we waiting for?'

'He won't be there.'

'It can't do any harm to check. And if he isn't there, no probs. It'll do you good to have some fresh air.'

'Larry won't give me the time off.'

'I'll say I'm upset about *Shed Door* going, which is true, and that I've asked you to come for a walk to cheer me up. He wants to sell more of Rob's paintings, so he needs to keep me sweet. Anyway, it's the end of the day – you'd be going home soon anyway.'

Within minutes we're in a cab, heading for the Heath.

TWENTY-ONE

Caro asks the cabbie to drop us at the main gate of Kenwood House. We walk down the winding drive past dark, overhanging rhododendron bushes, through a tunnel of honeysuckle to the back of the dazzling white Robert Adam mansion with its majestic green sweep down to the lake.

As we walk out onto the Heath I'm aware of how high up we are. London lies below, hazy in the late-afternoon sun. Caro leads me across a steeply sloping field dotted with wild flowers, down to a muddy ditch forded by a couple of planks of wood, where memories lie in wait to ambush me. It's the Troll Bridge. When the children were small we'd bring them to the Heath to play, and on this very spot Rob would pretend to be the wicked Troll luring the Billy Goats Gruff to a terrible death.

Don't go there, Rosa.

Sometimes the happiest memories are the ones you can't revisit. Not without those who made the joy. The pain's too much.

Once over the bridge we walk up into another meadow of

uncut grass, a metre high in places, surrounded by deep woods. Young children play hide and seek in the tall vegetation, watched over by their mothers, who lounge on rugs and gossip lazily in the sunshine. As we skirt the field, I notice several lone men sitting on logs, lying down sunbathing or walking aimlessly through the trees. Once, on a long-ago family walk, we saw the husband of a good friend of mine wandering lonely as a cloud around this very field in a pair of dangerously skimpy shorts and no top. As he passed us he broke into a run, mumbled something about Sunday jogging and made a beeline for the nearest gate.

Caro points to a clump of bushes.

'Through there,' she says, plunging into seemingly impenetrable undergrowth. I follow her, fighting my way past bush and bramble until the tangled mass opens out into a small space that's perfectly hidden, but which has a spectacular view of the hayfield and the city beyond. It's a green and secret cave of foliage with a spongy floor of moss, ideal for picnicking or canoodling or whatever.

Someone's sitting in it now.

Steve.

He sits against the trunk of a small tree. His eyes are open and unblinking. His mouth is open too. Encrusted vomit trails down from it onto his shirt. Flies crawl over the exposed parts of his flesh – his face, and his hands, one of which clutches an empty rum bottle. There is a gut-wrenching smell.

'Steve?' Caro moves forward, but I stop her.

'Caro . . .'

Her face is the colour of porridge.

'He's ill.' She wrenches herself free. 'I'm here, Steve.'

But she doesn't touch him.

Whatever she's saying, she knows as well as I do that he's dead.

We stand, frozen, in Caro's special place for what could be several seconds or several minutes.

Eventually I say, 'I'll call the police.'

She sinks to her knees. I don't think she hears me.

I make my call.

'Caro, the police won't be able to find us in here. We should wait at the edge of the wood.'

'I'm staying with Steve.'

I can't persuade her to move.

'I'll only be a few yards away,' I say eventually. 'Call if you need me.'

In the hayfield the children are still playing, their mothers still chatting. On the edge of the path running alongside the field, a billiard-bald, middle-aged man sits on the grass rhythmically rubbing sun cream into his tanned and bulging pecs.

Life goes on.

Oh for the recuperative power of youth, thought Gillian as she settled herself on the bus, three seats behind Leni. Trailing her back from *The Ivy*, she'd been struck by how exhausted the girl looked. She could barely drag herself up the rubbish-strewn stairs to her flat.

But what a transformation! The person who'd danced back down those very same stairs two hours later was a different person. Even from a distance Gillian could see the animation in her face, and the energy crackling from every pore as she flew along the road to the bus stop. The make-up was plastered on even more carefully than usual, the hair elaborately coiled into a French pleat, and the exotic dress was clearly, even to Gillian who didn't concern herself with fashion, a Vivienne Westwood. She felt even sorrier for Leni's nice young boyfriend. How unfair. Wasn't it always the innocent who got hurt?

The bus took a circuitous route, giving Gillian time to ponder the strange conversation she'd had earlier with Rosa. Why hadn't her friend admitted lunching with Borodino? Was she mistaken in thinking Rosa was putting in a word for her with the bastard? Could she trust Rosa? What was the woman playing at? Her thoughts travelled in circles until they were interrupted at Park Lane, where Leni made a swift exit, Gillian puffing surreptitiously behind. Mayfair, eh, she thought as they beetled down a side street into Shepherd's Market. A deeply appropriate place, considering the girl's tendency to sell herself to the highest bidder. Looking round, Gillian remembered an elderly friend who, after the death of his wife, regularly availed himself of the services of a girl who operated from a room in Shepherd's Market. Cheaper and less wearing on the nerves than taking another wife, he'd told her.

But Leni wasn't making for one of the tiny terraced doors with the interesting name-plates. Instead she walked through the Market into Curzon Street and entered an imposing mansion block. The doors were glass so Gillian, lurking behind a lamp-post, was able to see her chattering animatedly with the concierge behind the desk. Why waste all that dazzle on a lowly-paid man in uniform who wouldn't advance her career one jot? Gillian smiled to herself. The interpretation of such behaviour was what made the whole enterprise so compelling – brought her that much nearer to her goal.

She was pondering how, with considerably fewer assets on the charm front, she could persuade the concierge to let her follow Leni into the building, when she saw a Porsche Boxster pull up. A familiar figure jumped out.

David Borodino.

As he opened the passenger door, Leni emerged from the building, ran down the steps and slid into the sleek leather interior. Then, with a few high-octane revs, they roared off, leaving Gillian slumped against her lamp-post, brain whirring.

'Well well,' she said aloud, absentmindedly accepting fifty pence from a passing stranger intent on doing his good deed for the day, by providing the less fortunate with the wherewithal for half a cup of tea. 'Nearly time for the main event.'

TWENTY-TWO

It's late by the time I arrive home. Dealing with the police took hours, and after that I accompanied Caroline back to her flat. I wanted her to spend the night at my place, but she refused.

'I need to be alone, Rosa. Don't worry, I won't do anything stupid.'

'Promise you'll call if you need me, any time – even the middle of the night.'

'Promise.'

I hope she'll be all right. She's taken on the whole burden of responsibility for Steve's death.

'If only I could take back all those frightful messages I left on his mobile, when I thought he was avoiding me. I said it was the end of the relationship. That's why he chose our special place to kill himself. To hurt me.'

'I think he went there to feel close to you.'

'Go home, Rosa.'

I leave her sitting blank-faced and bolt upright, staring into the pit of her own despair.

When I call Larry to tell him that Caroline won't be in to work for a few days, because Steve's committed suicide, there's a long silence.

'Larry? Are you still there?'

'Suicide, definitely? That's what the police think?'

'There'll be a post-mortem, but they didn't find anything suspicious. Looks like a straightforward overdose – booze and pills.'

'How is poor dear Caro?'

'Blaming herself.'

'Ridiculous! The man was a walking disaster zone. She's well rid of him.'

'Larry! He was obviously in one hell of a state to do what he did.'

'He's no loss to anyone.'

'Just make sure you keep your opinions to yourself when Caro's around.'

'As you well know, Rosa, we're the soul of discretion.'

It's late. I should go to bed, but my nerves are so sensitised by the events of the day that I'm beyond tiredness. I check my emails, make a hot drink and switch on a rubbish TV programme.

Joshua's out late. It's not like him.

But then who am I to say what he's like or not like? What do I really know about him? Precious little. And recently, it seems, the more I see him, the less I know.

The less comfortable I feel.

Not that I feel comfortable about anything tonight. It's Steve's death. It's made me jumpy again. So jumpy that when the front door opens I nearly leap out of my skin. I rush out into the hall. It's Joshua. Something about him jangles my already frayed nerves.

It's his feet.

What's wrong with his feet?

Nothing. It's not his feet. It's what he's wearing on them.

He's wearing Rob's Doc Marten boots. I know they're Rob's because he personalised the toecaps by painting green stars on them.

'Dead men's shoes.'

The words shoot out before I can stop them. I see Joshua's eyes widen and then, unable to cope any more, I run upstairs to my bedroom. I know I ought to go and apologise, but I can't. Those boots, more than any of his clothes, conjure Rob up so clearly.

So clearly.

I go to bed and close my eyes in an attempt to banish the image of the big black boots on Joshua's feet, but then all I see is Steve Pyne, propped up against the tree, staring over a city that's lost to him for ever, and poor Caro kneeling beside him, drenched in grief.

The next thing I know the sun's streaming in and for a moment I think yesterday was a bad dream. Only for a moment, though.

When I stagger into the kitchen, Joshua's already up. He's singing along to one of Rob's favourite CDs. I remember one of his recent interrogations: what music did Rob like? Did he go to the movies? What kind of films did he like? What did he think about sport? Was he a football fan? And so on.

Singing is not the only thing he's doing.

Ten years ago, when we redecorated our kitchen, Rob prepared a rectangle of wet plaster above the worktop, and the four of us made handprints.

Happy families.

Now Joshua is singing Rob's reggae tunes with his hand fitting perfectly into the indentation made all those years ago by his brother. He stands rigid and still in spite of the rhythmic music.

When he sees me he snatches the hand away and switches off the music.

I don't refer to my strange behaviour of the previous evening, nor do I ask him what the hell he thinks he's doing pawing my wall. I can't face it.

Instead I tell him about Steve. He's very shocked. Afterwards we eat our breakfast more or less in silence.

I'm about to go back upstairs when he says, 'This man was an artist?'

'Yes.'

'Who was having problems with his work?'

'Yes.'

'Then that's why he killed himself. You should tell Caroline. Men don't kill themselves for love, whatever women think.'

There's passion in his voice. Is he talking about himself?

'That's a sweeping statement.'

He's wearing a pale-blue sweatshirt that I bought for Rob three Christmases ago. It suits him. As do Rob's khaki cargo pants.

'It's true.'

'You're talking from personal experience, aren't you?'

'What do you mean?'

'Zander's turned you down, hasn't he? I did warn you. I'm so sorry.'

'No, he hasn't.'

'You mean he's taking you on? That's fantastic.'

'No.'

'I don't understand. What did he say about your portfolio?'

'He hasn't seen it yet.'

'But I saw you in *Nature Morte* yesterday.'

'Not me.'

'Yes, it was.'

'You must be mistaken.'

'Are you sure?'

'I should know.'

'Then Rob must have another brother kicking around, because whoever I saw was the spitting image of you.'

Our eyes lock.

'All black men look alike to white people.'

'I beg your pardon?'

'All black men look alike to white people.'

'Whoa! Stop right there, Joshua. Are you saying I'm racist?'

We eyeball each other.

He cracks first. 'Sorry.'

'So . . . when can I see your work?'

Joshua slams his coffee mug onto the table. 'What up wid you, woman? No wonder my bruv walk under a car. You probably drove he to it wid you naggin' an' naggin'.' With that untypical lapse into West Indian vernacular, he storms out.

What was all that about? Why would he lie about being at *Nature Morte*? And why is he so angry all of a sudden?

I feel very shaken. Shaken by his rage, shaken by his lie and shaken by the sight of his hand fitting so exactly into Rob's plaster print.

And by the boots.

I tell myself to get a grip. I'm making something out of nothing. OK, so I feel funny about Joshua wearing Rob's clothes. My problem, not his. OK, so I feel stifled and crowded and slightly threatened by his interminable questions. My problem, not his. And rather than accuse him of lying about being in *Nature Morte* yesterday, why don't I accept the fact that I must have been mistaken. If I'm feeling jittery it's not about Joshua. It's about finding Steve Pyne's body. Yet more death to deal with.

I'm staring through the kitchen window at Anna's pet cemetery. From my position I can't see Joshua's cross, but somehow I can feel a vibration from it pulsating up the garden.

Rosa, you are losing it.

Five minutes later, Mike phones.

'How do you fancy a visit to David Borodino's penthouse this morning? I have to take some measurements for the mural and I thought you might enjoy a bit of a sniff around. I know how much you like contemporary architecture. I also know what a nosy cow you are. So I thought it'd be just up your street. Borodino won't be there. He's left instructions for me to be admitted.'

'I'm not in the mood, Mike.'

I tell him about Steve. He can't believe it.

'Didn't seem the self-harm type to me. Too aggressive and egotistical. Just goes to show, you never can tell. Poor sod. And poor you, being the one to find him. How are you holding up?'

'Not so good.'

'All the more reason to come with me. It'll take your mind off things.'

Maybe he's right. I don't want to stay here looking at my four walls, thinking about the dead and decaying Steve Pyne or about Joshua and his funny little ways.

And as Mike burbles on, I realise something else: this is the ideal opportunity for me to get his side of the burgeoning romance between him and Jess.

And to find out what the hell he was doing with Leni Dang when he'd told Jess he was with his dealer.

Of course I could ask him these things over the phone rather than schlepping all the way to Borodino Inc., but I'd rather see his face when he comes up with his answers.

And if I'm honest, I'd love to see Borodino's famous apartment. It's at the top of the spectacular thirty-storey building that contains the offices of the *Correspondent* and all Borodino's other businesses. It's designed by Jonathan James Friedmann, Britain's most innovative architect, and has been hailed as the ultimate in luxury living space for the new millennium.

'Mike, you're on.'

'Great. I'll meet you at Borodino Inc. in an hour.'

Before I leave, I phone Caro. Her mother answers and says that she's sleeping. I'm very relieved that she's not alone. I am, however, surprised. Caro once told me that she and her mother hadn't spoken since Steve accused Frances Sanders of being a neurotic bloodsucking old bat who was draining Caro's life away. She'd given Caro an ultimatum – Steve or her. No prizes for guessing Caro's choice.

I take a bus over Tower Bridge into the hinterland of new

developments which overlook the wide stretch of the Thames where it meanders down towards Greenwich. The sunshine glints off the glass and steel structure of Borodino Inc. on the south bank of the river. With its curves and sweeps, it's the seductive yin to Canary Wharf's phallic yang.

Mike's waiting outside. We enter a vast atrium full of self-important bustle, and make for reception, where an immaculate blonde directs us to a lift, manned by a blank-faced security guard, which takes us straight up into the penthouse.

The apartment has the largest living room I have ever seen. It must be the length of half a football pitch. The front wall is an unbroken sheet of glass through which the wide river glitters way below us. The ceiling is also glass, a vast dome with a complex set of blinds which can be adjusted to let light and air in or keep it out. Dotted around the room are various islands of furniture – leather sofas, glass tables and very little else – the ultimate mini-malist chic. At the far end a door leads through to other rooms.

Mike turns his attention to the back wall, where his mural is to go. I leave him to it, and wander round this glorious space. Having drunk my fill of the view, I explore the other rooms. The place isn't as extensive as the main room would suggest. Just two bedrooms, and a stainless steel kitchen, which seems to be a food-free zone. I peek into the industrial-size American fridge and am confronted by six bottles of Krug and a carton of orange juice. Borodino's clearly a supernatural being who doesn't need earthly sustenance like the rest of us.

The master bedroom has the same magnificent view over the river as the main room. The focal point is the bed. Eight foot square and suspended from the ceiling on barely visible steel cables, it hovers in the air like a prop from a twenty-first century *Bedknobs and Broomsticks*.

Mike appears. 'Some bed, huh?'

'Shame I left my wings at home.'

'Hey presto!'

He presses a switch and the bed sinks to the ground. The inviting softness of its billowing white duvet and plump pillows is irresistible. I collapse onto it.

Mike flops down beside me and presses another switch on the bedhead.

'Come fly with me!'

The bed rises into the air, transparent, protective sides emerging from its base.

It's like revisiting childhood – all the excitement of hiding in a secret den. I stare out over the river. Now's as good a time as any to confront Mike.

'What were you doing with Leni Dang yesterday?'

'What?'

'You told Jess you were lunching with your agent, but I saw you in *The Ivy* with Leni Dang.'

'Leni's doing an interview with me for the *Correspondent*. Not that it's any of your business.'

'So why pretend you were seeing your dealer?'

'I did. Before lunch.'

'Oh.'

The Thames glitters below. Silence seeps into the four corners of the room.

'I must have got the wrong end of the stick.'

But I saw the way he was looking at her. I return to the

offensive. 'Anyway, I think it's excellent news about you and Jess.'

'There is no me and Jess.'

'That's not what she says.'

He massages the bridge of his nose. I know this gesture. It means he's playing for time.

Eventually he speaks. 'It's true we've seen a lot of each other recently. But as friends, that's all.'

'Friends?'

'Come on, Rosy, me and Jess? We were practically in the cradle together.'

'So how come she says you're an item?'

Mike shifts. The bed sways. The movement makes me feel sick.

'You know how she is with guys . . . She gets crushes.'

I can't deny it. The cynical, worldly Jess with her biting, satirical wit, has always had one major blind spot: unsuitable men.

'Yes, she gets crushes, but usually on strangers.'

Mike sighs. 'It's been great hanging out with her, like I was twenty again. But I didn't mean this to happen. There is no Big Relationship.'

'You're saying she's imagining it?'

He doesn't answer.

'Mike?'

'A kiss and cuddle, maybe. Affectionate canoodling. That's what I'd call it. Yeah – affectionate canoodling. Nothing serious.'

'Affectionate canoodling?'

'Jessie's just dramatising. It's what she does.'

Talk about two conflicting stories.

'Are you sure you're not in denial? I mean, we've always been like family to each other. Developing sexual feelings for Jess is a bit like incest. Maybe you can't hack that.'

He frowns. 'Incest?'

'You're not related to her, but the friendship's always been a very sibling thing.'

He grins. 'Rosy Posy, you kinky little devil.'

'What you say and what she says doesn't match. I want the truth.'

He's suddenly serious. 'I know one thing: I'm fucking jaded with the endless parade of Identikit women trooping through my life, only interested in the celebrity stuff. At least Jess knows the real me.'

'So there is something?'

'No!'

'Excuse me but yes!'

'We've had a few laughs, a few cuddles. It's not my fault she's misinterpreted it.'

'You have to set her straight.'

Mike groans. 'Can't I just cool it and hope she gets the message?'

Selfish, cowardly git.

'Don't even think of treating her so casually. If you won't then I will.'

'Mind your own business, Meddling Mary.'

'Jess is my business.'

He sees that I'm deadly serious. 'You win. I'll tell her that the last thing I want is a deep and meaningful.'

'And don't hurt her more than you have to. She's crazy about you for some bizarre reason. Let her down gently or you'll have me to answer to, Mike Mason.'

Below us, I hear a discreet cough.

'Fun bed, isn't it? I had it imported from Italy. Designed by a very talented young furniture-maker – Emilio Sartori. Remember the name – you'll be hearing much more of him.'

David Borodino leans against the doorframe gazing up at us.

I am beyond embarrassment.

Not only must he be wondering what the hell I'm doing in his house, since he certainly didn't invite me, he must also think Mike and I have been at it on his precious floating bed. In his position I'd be furious. My bed's my own. Anyone using it without my permission, I'd regard as completely violating my privacy. But Borodino's black eyes are crackling with . . . with what? Amusement? Excitement? Titillation? Impossible to say. I suppose if you're that rich you have so many beds in different parts of the world that you don't have the same primitive attachment to any of them. I suppose too that if you're that rich you despise possessive bourgeois notions of bed as private personal space. To say nothing of your attitude towards women as disposable playthings.

I want to die. To cease to be.

Mike presses the switch and we sink to floor level.

'All right, Mike?'

The two men smile at each other. A smile of male complicity that excludes me.

'All sorted. Got my measurements. Had another butcher's at the wall. Great space. Should be able to install the final thing very soon. Just showing Rosa round your lovely home. Hope you don't mind.'

'Be my guest.' Borodino turns to me. 'Drink, Rosa?'

I can't hack this. 'No, thanks. I'm in a bit of a rush. I've just remembered something I have to do.'

I babble my farewells and make a dash for freedom. It isn't till I'm recrossing Tower Bridge that the heat from my burning cheeks subsides.

Always sticking her nose in where it wasn't wanted. She didn't get it. Things were different for a man in his position. The ordinary rules didn't apply. Who the fuck did she think she was, telling him what to do? They weren't students any more. Interfering cow with her small-time life. She didn't have the first clue. One day that big mouth would get her into big trouble.

He was damned if he'd let her dictate to him. One way or another it would have to stop.

Theo told his staff that he'd prepare Steve Pyne himself. The task had, as always, put him in the zone. He took a deeply sensuous delight in performing his rituals and exercising all the skill and artifice at his command to make the young man beautiful again. As he assessed his completed handiwork he experienced a glow of pure pleasure. Steve Pyne was restored to a perfection he'd never achieved during his short life. Thanks to Theo's artistry there was no inkling of the horrid depredations caused by the manner of his unfortunate death.

Theo smiled to himself. All that pain and trauma he'd suffered during the art-school débâcle. All that wasted grief over his apparent ineptitude, when all the time the secret lay back in the place he'd been so keen to leave. He remembered, fondly, the bewildered joy of the prodigal's return, and the realisation of where his true talents lay: not in the painting of canvas, but in the painting of flesh.

He ran his long fingers down Steve Pyne's cheek.

> *'Dear, beauteous death! the jewel of the just,*
> *Shining nowhere but in the dark . . .*
> *What mysteries do lie beyond thy dust . . . ?'*

As his words echoed around the silent chamber, he gently stroked the young man's forehead. 'Do you peep into glory, Steve Pyne?' he asked. 'Can you tell me what you see?'

The dead face was enigmatic in its response.

Theo didn't mind. It was what he expected. It didn't diminish his joy in a job well done.

But his satisfaction was short-lived.

The phone call put paid to that.

TWENTY-THREE

It's the day of Steve Pyne's funeral. I'm standing on a grassy mound in Kensal Green Cemetery, overlooking the Grand Union Canal, staring down at his coffin. As always at burials, I'm astonished at the depth of the grave.

We cremated Rob. I couldn't bear to think of his beloved body rotting under all that London clay.

I'm filled with sorrow. Not only for a young man who should still be living his life, but also for the pitifully few people who've turned out to say goodbye: Caro, me, the man who runs the garage next to Steve's studio and, unbelievably, Larry and Flavia.

'Flavia insisted on coming,' Larry muttered in my ear on our way to the burial plot, as he negotiated her wheelchair over the uneven ground. 'She feels we bear some responsibility for what happened. Pure nonsense, of course. As if losing his dealer would drive him to commit suicide. But my wife is an angel who takes the miseries of the world unto herself, and if she wants to be here, then so be it.'

Much as he loves Flavia, I'm still astonished to see Larry at the funeral of his current pet hate.

'The police are still certain it was suicide?' he asks.

'Yes.'

The shabby vicar is impersonal and impatient.

'Man that is born of woman hath but a short time to live . . .'

The age-old words never fail to move me, even when spoken at speed, in a Brummie accent. I try not to think of Rob. Caro is trembling, even in the midday heat. I slip my hand into hers, which is icy cold.

'He cometh up and is cut down like a flower . . .'

She makes no effort to wipe away the tears.

'In the midst of life we are in death . . .'

I'm struck by the aptness of the phrase on this bright day. For life burgeons and blossoms all around the ancient cemetery: the variegated ivy creeping up the crumbling mausoleums; a Red Admiral butterfly fluttering round the purple buddleia which springs out of every cranny; a blackbird perched on the head of a Victorian angel, orange beak open wide, dispatching its deliriously joyful song into the fragrant summer air.

I look more closely at the angel. Someone is standing, half-hidden behind its great stone wings. It's Leni Dang, dressed in an elegant black suit with a cute little arrangement of black feathers perched on her immaculate bob. She's dabbing her eyes with a tissue.

Our eyes meet. She steps back reflexively and then, evidently deciding there's no point in remaining hidden, comes forward and stands on the edge of our sparse little group.

What is she doing at the funeral of a man who only weeks

ago subjected her to very public embarrassment and humiliation?

'Earth to earth; ashes to ashes; dust to dust . . .'

Finally it's over, and we leave Steve with the gravediggers who wait, incuriously, to one side, leaning on their spades and eating sandwiches.

Leni catches me up. 'I just wanted to—'

'I didn't know you were a friend of Steve's.'

'I wanted to pay my respects. I was so sorry to hear about his death. Such a waste. I thought there'd be more people here and that I'd be able to blend in.'

She seems genuinely upset. But then she seemed genuinely respectful and admiring of Gillian two weeks before she pinched her job.

'So it's definitely suicide?'

Seems to be the hot question today.

'Clearly. Otherwise we wouldn't be here. The police would be holding the body pending enquiries.'

I want to curtail this conversation, so I turn to the others and offer them lunch at my house, which is nearby. I don't ask Leni. I can't have her in the house.

Kevin from the garage says he has a car to deliver, and Larry and Flavia's driver is waiting to take them home. So it's just me and Caro — as it was a couple of days ago when I accompanied Caro to St John's Wood to view the body. Theo, I suspect at Flavia's request, had offered to deal with everything for Caro, although when we arrived at *Grey & Son* he was nowhere to be seen. One of his minions showed us to the door of a small room. As he melted into the shadows, Caro stared at the closed door.

'I can't do it.'

I put my arm round her.

'I keep remembering how he was. That day.'

'He'll look like himself again now. These places are experts . . .'

Caro's teeth were chattering, her face grey and clammy.

'You don't have to do it, Caro. We can leave right now.'

'I've never seen a dead body before, apart from . . .'

'Let me take you home.'

'No!' She pulled away from me. 'I have to say a proper goodbye.' She staggered. 'I need some air.'

I steered her out into the peaceful garden that I'd admired on my previous visit, and we sat in an arbour of sweet-smelling honeysuckle. I talked about everything and nothing until her colour returned to normal.

'I'm better now. Let's do it,' she said.

We were about to go back into the house when suddenly the air was filled with what I can only describe as ululation. A bizarre group of individuals swayed down the path. The person around whom everyone else revolved was a woman, dressed from head to toe in scarlet trimmed with jet. Her hair was styled into long braids into which more pieces of jet had been woven. They glittered viciously as she moved her head. She was the one making most of the noise. Her voice rippled up and down the vocal register in a mixture of chanting, shrieking and moaning, and as we watched, she fell to her knees and shook her fists at the sky. Several other women dressed equally theatrically, taking their cue from her, also fell down, vying with each other to emit the wildest expression of grief. Flanking them and muttering into walkietalkies, were men in dark overcoats and even darker glasses. As the group, in motion once more, snaked past us, one of the men glared at me and Caro as if we were international terrorists about to commit an unspeakable atrocity against their client.

'I recognise her,' I said, as they reached the end of the garden.

Caro smiled for the first time that day. 'It's Shamila.'

Shamila – four number one hits in a row. Winner of two Mobo awards this year alone.

'She's Haz Kem's wife. The one who was recently killed in a car crash. Poor thing.'

She started to cry again, but her tears, drowned by the noise from the other end of the garden, turned to shaky laughter.

'I can't compete with that.' She stood up. 'Let's go and see Steve.'

This time she didn't hesitate. She opened the door and marched straight in.

Steve looked more peaceful in death than he ever had in life. Caro stared down at him. Then she leaned into the coffin and kissed his cheek.

'So cold. I didn't know he'd feel so cold.' She turned to me. 'I need to be alone with him.'

'Sure.'

I was returning to the garden, when I heard my name. It was Theo, peering anxiously round the door of his room. 'How is she?'

'Not so good. Thanks for taking care of everything, Theo.'

'Least I could do.' His face brightened. 'If you can spare a moment, I'd love to show you my latest acquisition.'

He ushered me into his office, and from a safe hidden behind his desk, he produced something cocooned in silk: a very old and battered book. He put on a pair of cotton gloves and turned the fragile pages to reveal the most exquisite illuminated illustration: delicately complex borders of fruit and flowers and animals, surrounding intricately painted and gilded musical notation.

'A complete Sienese choir book,' he breathed.

'It's wonderful.'

'Isn't it just.'

'Didn't you say these choir books are like gold dust?'

'Absolutely.'

'How on earth did you find it?'

He gave a sly smile. 'I told you something was in the offing. This was it. I can't believe it's actually mine.'

He was almost vibrating with excitement. The rich of London must be dying in droves in order to finance Theo's little hobby. This will have cost him a small fortune.

As I contemplated the heartbreakingly beautiful work with its vision of a bygone age, I lost all sense of time until, returning to the present with a jolt, I realised that Caro would be wondering where I'd gone. I left Theo poring over his treasure.

She was still beside Steve's coffin.

'Caro?'

'Let's go.'

I wanted to tell her that she'd get through it, that eventually the worst of the pain would subside, but I couldn't. When Rob died, that was the last thing I wanted to hear. Losing the pain meant losing him.

As we walked past the main room I saw an open casket on a wooden dais. Inside it lay a familiar figure: Haz Kem.

No more rapping for him.

* * *

Today, when we arrive home from the funeral, Joshua's in the kitchen. To my relief he's wearing his glasses. Eyesight is one major area where he differs from Rob. Rob had twenty-twenty vision: Joshua's as blind as a bat. Lately he's taken to wearing his contact lenses nearly all the time. I prefer the glasses – they make him look less like my husband.

The day after his outburst he drowned me in apologies.

'I'm so sorry. I'll make it up to you, Rosa, I swear.'

And that's what he's been doing ever since – hoovering, dusting, cleaning windows, gardening, making me cups of tea. His capacity for doing chores seems endless.

But I wish he didn't do everything with Rob as his yardstick. Did Rob do the ironing? Was he any good as a handyman? Did he come shopping with me? Could he cook? Everywhere I turn there he is, staring at me with big eyes and yet more questions.

'Joshua,' I said the other day after he'd cleaned out all the kitchen cupboards single-handed and unasked, 'you're a guest. You don't have to do this.'

'A guest?' I couldn't fathom the expression on his face.

His intensity is very hard to cope with. I feel crowded. Stifled. Sometimes, in the house, aware of his constant presence, I find it hard to breathe.

And here he is again today, looking like Rob and polishing the work surfaces in my already spotless kitchen. He expresses his condolences to Caroline, gives me a mournful glance and goes off to his room. She stares after him.

'It's uncanny,' she says. 'Even with the specs.'

'What do you mean?' I pretend ignorance in order to get her

talking, take her out of herself. These are the first words she's spoken today that haven't been about Steve Pyne. If commenting on Joshua's resemblance to Rob diverts her, I'm willing to go along with the conversation, even though the whole Rob thing's starting to spook me. Take the other night. Joshua was watching TV in his room. After a while I became aware that there was something odd about the sound. The same sentence was being replayed. A very familiar sentence. Later I remembered where it came from: a home video of me, Rob and the children in the garden.

What was that all about?

And this morning, I noticed a newly framed photo on his bedside table.

Taken from my family album.

Me and the kids on the beach in Spain.

No sign of Rob.

Surely the face of his eternally absent brother was the one he'd want to see on waking? Not me and the kids.

Caro's still talking.

'When you brought him to the gallery I had quite a shock before I realised the resemblance was only superficial. But now it really is like looking at Rob. Not just his looks – it's his manner, his walk, his clothes, even his speech patterns – everything. He's Rob's clone. Doesn't it freak you out, Rosa?'

What to say?

'He's not remotely like Rob. Not really.'

I want to tell her how I really feel but she has enough on her plate at the moment. She doesn't need me unloading onto her. Anyway, Rob always preferred to keep family business in the family. If he were here, he'd say it was no one's concern but ours.

But he's not here. I'm the one who has to deal with it.

Just then the doorbell rings. It's Leni Dang, bold as brass. She holds out a black glove.

'You dropped this,' she said, 'so I followed you. I've been in the park trying to summon up the courage to—'

'Thanks.'

Is she waiting to be invited in? Hell will freeze over first, Leni.

'I know you think I stole Gillian's job . . .'

I really don't need this.

'You have no idea what I think, Leni,' I say. 'Thanks for the glove.' I start to close the door.

'But—'

Then Joshua appears. His glasses have gone. The contacts are back.

'I have to go out for a bit, Rosa,' he says, 'but I won't be long.' He sees Leni. 'Hello.' He waits for me to introduce him, but I don't oblige.

She peeps up at him through lowered lashes. He's looking very handsome in oatmeal-coloured linen trousers and a sky-blue open-neck shirt.

Courtesy of Rob.

'Leni's just leaving,' I say.

She's still looking at Joshua. 'Where is the nearest tube?'

'I'm going there myself. I'll show you,' he says.

'Would you?' She gives him a mega-watt smile. 'Thank you so much.' She swivels her almond eyes in my direction again. 'Give Caroline my condolences. And tell Gillian I really am sorry. For everything.'

Yeah right.

I watch the two of them as they walk into the park.

I don't want her hanging round Joshua.

Caro's comments have really unsettled me. Until now I could pretend that his transformation was in my head, but I can't do that any more. It's out there, independently observed. It's official.

Joshua is turning into Rob.

Consort Park was really rather special, thought Gillian as she trotted along at a safe distance behind Leni and Rosa's new brother-in-law. If she weren't so wedded to her flat, this would be a good place to live. She had a little daydream – buying the house next door to Rosa, chatting over the garden fence, popping in and out for cups of coffee . . . Then she came back to earth with a bump, as she remembered the events of the last hour or two.

Leni had emerged from her flat that morning dressed in black. Gillian should have guessed straight away where she was heading, but it wasn't until she was in the cemetery, lurking behind an obelisk, that she realised whose funeral it was.

She'd had an extremely nasty shock.

What was Leni Dang doing here? How come she was chummy enough with Caro to be one of the tiny number of mourners attending Steve Pyne's meagre obsequies? And, even worse, how come she was chummy enough with Rosa to chat intimately with her at the end of the burial?

A double blow.

Gillian had leaned against the mildewed stone and abandoned herself to the shuddering feelings of betrayal washing over her.

Whatever Rosa had been doing at *The Ivy* with Borodino, it certainly wasn't putting in a word on her behalf. There was quite clearly a new clique in the making. One that had no place for her.

She'd told herself not to be paranoid. The Rosa she'd grown to like so much would never pal up with Leni Dang. But then, what did she really know about Rosa? What did any of us really know about the inside of other people's heads? She'd thought Rosa wanted to be her friend – the first proper friend she'd made since Peter died. But it was just cupboard love.

She laughed mirthlessly, causing two passing toddlers to burst into tears and rush to their mothers babbling about the nasty witch lady.

Live next door to Rosa, in harmonious friendship?

Rosa couldn't give a toss. Gillian had just been a means to an end – the end being the catalogue essay for her husband's show.

But what about the many phone calls, the anxious visit, and the seeming concern?

Keeping me sweet for the next show.

Leni and friend were nearly out of the park. She'd lose them if she wasn't careful. She must forget Rosa. Concentrate on the project. This was the second time today she'd nearly blown it. In the cemetery she'd been so upset, she'd only registered at the last minute that everyone was dispersing. She'd caught up with Leni walking down the Harrow Road. The shock of finding her ringing a doorbell that turned out to be Rosa's had almost winded her. Leni obviously knew the place well. She herself had never been invited there.

Still, it made her plans easier to carry out.

No more so-called friends to poke and pry with their feigned concern. She remembered the passage from Elena's diary when she decided to become a man. *Above all, I mourned the loss of female friendship. Until I remembered the worm of betrayal lurking in the bud of each soft, tender confidence.*

And once the Leni project was completed she could turn her attention to Rosa, whose betrayal, although not on the same scale, was still fairly unforgivable.

On the tube, installed in the next compartment to Leni but with an excellent view of proceedings, Gillian was fascinated to watch the girl go to work on Rosa's brother-in-law. It was a salutary exercise. Leni's main asset was her soulful eyes. The rest of her heavy face verged on the ugly. No wonder she was always plastered in make-up. What was it the French called it? *Jolie-laide.* But the eyes had it. They drew people in, made them feel like alpha and omega. Thorn Minor was clearly captivated.

Gillian jotted down her observations in the notebook. Things were starting to gel. She could see her way forward to implementing the next stage of the project.

TWENTY-FOUR

Later I take Caroline for a walk round Consort Park, hoping fresh air and exercise will do her good. The heatwave shows no sign of abating and the park's full of people enjoying the sunshine. Pink and brown bodies in brightly coloured clothes stretch out on the grass. Games of cricket and rounders are in full swing, and the shrieks and splashes from the paddling pool and children's playground compete with the satisfying plop of ball on racket coming from the tennis courts.

'Where are you going to put the sculpture?'

I hadn't planned to show her the proposed site of the new Consort Park sculpture, in case it reminded her of Steve. However, now she's asked, I take her into the secluded flower garden and point out the spot.

'Perfect,' she says wistfully. 'Steve would have loved one of his pieces to have a home here.'

I suddenly know what I must do. I say, 'It still could.'

Caroline scans my face. 'What do you mean? You want Steve's work?'

'Yes,' I said.

For the first time in days Caro looks herself again.

'That's wonderful,' she says. 'Wonderful. I know it's a memorial for the woman who donated the money, but it would be Steve's memorial too, wouldn't it.'

'Definitely.'

Joy blazes from her face.

'Which piece are you interested in?'

Andromeda, of course, but Caro's even less likely to part with that one now. I won't even ask.

'*Marble One.*'

Though not in the same league as *Andromeda,* the undulating pink form will look very good in its niche surrounded by clematis and roses.

'Ah, just the person I need to see. Don't whine, Fergus, or Mummy will have to renegotiate our bedtime agreement.'

A Valkyrie strides towards us, in Birkenstock sandals, wearing a long flowing orange garment which matches her long flowing orange hair. The sun has caught her large nose which is peeling profusely.

PG Tips.

She's surrounded by a tribe of ginger children with faces smeared in snot and dirt, who squabble and shout and roll around on the grass, punching each other.

Not a person to meet if you're feeling fragile.

'About the short list,' she says. 'September's coming up fast, and the Committee's anxious to know that everything's on track. We've asked Ken Livingstone to inaugurate it but he hasn't responded. Not to worry – I know several celebs who'd love to do it.'

'Actually, Pru, there is no short list.'

'No short list? But I distinctly said I wanted to see the main contenders.'

'There was only one. Steve Pyne.'

'Who?'

'Steve Pyne.'

'Look, Rosa, we don't want some local yokel that no one's heard of. We want to put Consort Park on the cultural map.'

'In fact, Pru, Steve Pyne was one of the country's most talented young artists. I say "was" because he died last week. Consort Park's very fortunate to be acquiring one of his last works. Of course, if you'd rather I went for someone else . . .'

'No!' Pru's eyes popped with excitement. 'He sounds just the job. Nothing like a tragedy to attract publicity.'

I can't help myself. 'Did I mention that Caroline was Steve's fiancée?'

For once in her life Pru is speechless.

'We buried Steve this morning,' I go on. 'I was just showing her the site for his work.'

Pru stares aghast at Caro. 'Do accept my most sincere condolences, my dear. And my heartfelt apologies. I don't think before I speak sometimes. I look forward to seeing your fiancé's work installed in our little park. Now if you'll excuse me . . .' She sails out of the flower garden, accompanied by her bickering brood.

'Rosa, you're a wicked woman. Fancy embarrassing poor Prudence like that.'

'Pru Gibb doesn't know the meaning of the word embarrassment.'

'Can we sit down for a minute? There's something I'd like to run past you. It's been really bothering me . . .'

'Go on.'

'When we found Steve, he had a bottle of rum in his hand.'

'Yes?'

'But he detested rum. He once drank two bottles on the trot when he was seventeen and was hospitalised with alcohol poisoning. Ever since then even the smell of it made him heave. Why would he choose to kill himself with a drink he couldn't stomach?'

'Maybe he was so full of self-loathing that he wanted to make his death as unpleasant as possible.'

'Not Steve. I keep going over and over it, and it doesn't make sense.'

Poor Caro. I know too well the pitfalls of obsessing over things you can't change.

Three little words . . . 'Wait for me.'

'I think you should forget about the last weeks of his life, and concentrate on the good times.'

'I can't stop thinking about it.'

'You must, or you'll never have any peace. Anyway, if there was anything dodgy about his death, surely the police would have found it.'

'Something isn't right.'

'Something else, apart from the rum bottle?'

'Nothing concrete. It's Steve. He wasn't the type to commit suicide, however bad he was feeling.'

'But you were convinced he'd done exactly that, because you chucked him.'

'Not now I've had time to think. It just doesn't feel right. Much as I loved him, I was never blind. Steve was far too egotistical to kill himself.'

'Have you told the police?'

'They don't want to know. As far as they're concerned it's an open and shut suicide. An hysterical girlfriend's gut feelings are the last thing they're prepared to listen to.'

The police are right to be sceptical. Caro's first reaction apart from grief was guilt. She blamed herself. Maybe thinking that Steve was killed is one way for her subconscious to get her off the hook.

And why would anyone want to kill him? Granted, he was a nasty little shit. But being nasty's not reason enough for someone to bump him off.

'You don't believe me, do you?'

'Caro . . .'

'Well, I don't care. I'm going to find out exactly what he was doing in the days before he died.'

My heart bleeds for her. 'I think that's a very good idea. Then hopefully whatever you discover will set your mind at rest.'

Later I ask her if she wants to stay the night, but she says her mother's expecting her.

'She really wanted to come today, but she loathed Steve with such a passion that she couldn't face it, poor lamb. Thanks for everything, Rosa. I don't know how I'd have got through it without you.'

'I'm just glad I was around to help.'

When she's gone I stand in my memory-filled house and think about all the issues that remain forever unresolved and all the questions that remain forever unanswered when someone you love dies, and I hope that Caroline's futile quest will bring her some peace.

Talking of unresolved things, I still haven't decided when and how to tell the children about their new uncle. Time is passing. They'll both be home soon. I don't really want to do it by email or over the phone. On the other hand, if I wait till their return, they'll have no chance to assimilate the enormity of the news before being confronted by the actuality of it. And anyway at the moment my feelings about Joshua are so confused that I don't trust myself to say anything to them.

I go upstairs, pondering the problem. Out of longstanding habit I wander into what used to be Rob's studio, and is now Joshua's room. I see the photo on his bedside table. What's all that about? Why am I not touched that he's so thrilled with his new family that he wants their images to be the first thing he claps eyes on when he awakes?

The drawer of the bedside table is open. Inside I see a leather-bound notebook.

I don't pry. I've never, like some mothers I know, made a habit of rifling through my children's drawers to keep an eye on what's going on.

But this book . . .

It sits in the drawer, begging to be opened.

After all, as Jess has pointed out more than once, Joshua may be Rob's brother, but he's still a stranger. And his behaviour's starting to worry me. I owe it to myself, to Rob, to the family, to find out more about him. It could be said that I'd be doing him a favour, because if reading this notebook reassures me, then my

behaviour towards him will improve, and I'll be able to introduce him to his niece and nephew with wholehearted affection.

The phone rings, putting off the moment of decision. It's Jess.
I haven't called her since my showdown with Mike. I knew if I
talked to her before he did, I'd spill the beans. I wouldn't be able
to keep quiet if she was still burbling on about her blissful new
love affair.

'Hey, Jess. How's tricks?'

Her voice has lost its sparkle. Mike must have done the deed.
Although I hate to hear her sounding so low, I'm relieved it's all
over.

'How was the funeral?'

I babble on about Caro, and the bare-faced effrontery of Leni
Dang, but eventually I dry up. I've exhausted the subject. I take
a deep breath.

'What's up?' I ask.

'Wish I fucking knew. It's Mike.'

'What about him?'

'I told you how things were. We were seeing each other every
day – he'd practically moved into my house . . .'

'Yes?'

'Now all of a sudden, he's the Invisible fucking Man. He said
he had to be out of town for a couple of days, which was fine,
but he hasn't called me, and his phone's always on message. I
don't understand what's happening.'

Bastard.

He hasn't done it. Instead he's taken classic evasive action.

Out of town? Yeah right.

Why are men such cowards?

What do I do now? Mike told me to butt out. Well, that would have suited me fine if he'd done the honourable thing, but I can't let Jess continue in this state of miserable ignorance.

'Have you heard from him, Rosa?'

A warning voice in my head tells me to shut up. I ignore it.

'Jessie, are you sure you're not reading more into this relationship than there is?'

'What do you mean?'

'Are you sure you're not confusing close platonic friendship with love?'

Jess gives an incredulous snort. 'Close platonic friendship? You are joking! You don't fuck the brains out of your close platonic friends every night for days on end . . . Rosa, do you know something I don't?'

I feel an incandescent anger against Mike. *Affectionate canoodling? Jess is suffering from a delusional crush?* He's been screwing her senseless and then having the nerve to tell me she's reading things into the situation. What a conniving, gutless wonder.

'Rosa, come on.'

'You need to talk to him.'

'You've seen him, haven't you?'

How to put it without hurting her?

'Spit it out.'

Here goes.

'He said that a relationship was wishful thinking on your part.'

Silence.

'Jess? Are you still there?'

When she finally speaks, her voice is thick and she stumbles over her words. 'Why are you doing this?'

'He's using you, Jess.'

'Why were you having this conversation in the first place? Why would Mike be telling you about private stuff between him and me?'

'I said how happy I was for you both, and he came out with this bilge about you taking it all too seriously.'

There's such a long silence that I think we've been cut off.

'Jess?'

'Some things never change, do they?'

'Listen—'

'You saw the way things were going and you had to muscle in.'

'Sorry?'

'It was just the same at college.'

'Excuse me?'

'You were never satisfied till all the blokes were running after you. Even when you'd settled for Rob, you still had to keep your talons in the rest of your fucking band of merry men. Make sure they all still followed you around slavering at the mouth. I remember wanting to shake them all. Tell them to get a life and stop being so pathetic and undignified.'

Where did all this come from?

'Jess—'

'You've had your fucking eye on Mike ever since he came back, and you're trying to split us up so you can have him for yourself.'

'What utter rubbish. You know I'd never do that.'

'Do I?' says Jess, and slams the phone down.

It's like I've been punched in the face. I call her back, but she's left the phone off the hook. Fine, I think. Two can play at that game. I switch on the answering machine.

After this I can't settle to anything. Part of me wants to call Mike and give him hell, but most of me doesn't want any contact at all with the slimy deceitful creep. I've always closed my eyes to Mike's faults: his vanity, his monstrous ambition, the way he shamelessly uses his abundant charm to get his way, his endless skirt-chasing. They've always been cancelled out by his generosity, his huge sense of fun and our shared youth. After all, who's perfect? But what he's done to Jess, that's a step too far. And to cap it all, he's done what no one else has ever managed to do: make trouble between her and me.

The phone rings. Jess, phoning to apologise.

'Speak to the machine 'cos the friend ain't listening,' I say.

It isn't her. It's David Borodino. He knows it's terribly last minute, but would I care to come down to *Cedars* tomorrow for the weekend and see Rob's painting. He leaves a number for me to call.

All of a sudden a weekend away seems like a great idea. I've had it with Consort Park, and I'm thrilled by the prospect of seeing *Shed Door Outside* again. Borodino was right. To see the painting in its new home would reassure me that it hadn't somehow ceased to exist. OK, so I still haven't found out whether his reason for sacking Gillian was valid, but the urge to see Rob's last painting and also escape from Jess's accusations, Mike's treachery and Joshua's odd behaviour for a couple of days is very strong.

I phone Borodino and say I'd be delighted. He offers to send a car, but I tell him I'd prefer to drive myself.

After this I try to sleep, but it's impossible. First it's Jess's tirade going round and round in my head. Then I spend some time giving Mike a piece of my mind in the fluent and eloquent language which never emerges in real confrontations. Finally, I move on to Joshua. I think about the book in his bedside table. After a while I get out of bed and go to his room.

The book lies quietly in the drawer.

Waiting for me.

I take it out. Underneath is the folder he brought from Trinidad containing samples of his work. I take that out too.

TWENTY-FIVE

I open the folder first. Under the pictures of street vendors are more photographs. At least a hundred.

They are shot from countless different angles and at different times of the day and night

All of the same subject.

Powerful studies of an elderly man. He wears a black suit and round his neck is a clerical collar. In every single shot his eyes are closed.

In every single shot he is lying in his coffin.

No doubt who it is.

Tani Thorn's tormentor. The Reverend Solomon Gayle.

My hand trembles as I replace the photographs and open the book.

It's a diary.

Of sorts.

THE ART OF DYING

October
Took the stabilisers off Danny's bike. We went out to the park, and with a lot of encouragement from yours truly, he managed to ride on two wheels for the first time. Rosa smothered him with kisses when we told her and even little Anna looked impressed. A truly memorable day.

January
Darling Rosa's birthday. Went ice skating with the family. Fell over and bruised my bottom. Family teased me unmercifully. After kids went to bed I did a charcoal drawing of Rosa. She gets more beautiful every year. I can't believe she's mine.

August
I love Italy. When I'm rich, I'll buy a house here and we'll spend as much time as we can in the sunshine, drinking wine and eating pasta. The heat reminds me of Trinidad, although it's so long since I was there that the memories are very faint now.

Christmas Day
A perfect day with my perfect family. After we'd opened our presents we went for a long walk on the Heath. I wore the woolly hat that the children gave me, and Rosa looked wonderful in the new red coat which was my present to her.

July
A barbecue with friends. Great to see my mate Mike after so many years. Old friends are the best friends. Find it

very touching to see how kind and gentle the children are with Lozz.

July
Jess, Rosa and me enjoying the high life at Sketch. Photo taken with Mike's flash new digital camera, straight from California. Food superb, company exhilarating.

The handwriting is upright, neat. Rob's writing.

Almost, but not quite. There's a cramped quality to it which is alien to my husband's free-flowing scribble.

Below each entry is a photograph with a caption written beneath it.

In Rob's new, neat writing.

The photos are familiar.

They should be.

With the exception of the last one, they are all culled from my albums of snapshots. Each picture is a variation on a theme: the Thorn family and friends. Each picture has one thing that differs from the originals: in place of Rob, there is Joshua. Joshua in the park with little Danny; Joshua falling over on the skating rink; Joshua knocking back a glass of wine on a sun-kissed Italian terrace; Joshua in a bright red woollen hat, smiling broadly as he strides out across the Heath, surrounded by laughing family.

And the last two images.

No need for him to replace Rob here. Rob was already dead when these shots were taken.

But there he is, anyway, or rather there is his alter ego, inserted in one shot behind Jess's chair in the sunlit garden, on the occasion of our recent barbecue, and standing between us, a hand on each shoulder as we linger over our after-dinner coffee in *Sketch* in the other.

I feel sick.

Then I hear the front door open.

Joshua.

I shove the book back into the drawer, straighten the bed and rush back to my bedroom.

Footsteps mount the stairs.

'Rosa, are you awake?'

I lean against the door, praying he doesn't try to open it. He must be able to hear my heart, so near to him through the thin layer of wood: its beating is deafening me. I wait until the footsteps retreat. Then I ram a chair under the door knob before crossing to my bed. I don't dare undress, but lie on top of the duvet, ears straining for any sound.

What to do? Confront him and ask for an explanation? Break Rob's rule about keeping family business in the family, and call the police? And tell them what? That I've found a make-believe diary while snooping in my brother-in-law's room? That he does too much housework and looks like my husband? That he takes pictures of old men in coffins? I want to ring Jess, but she isn't speaking to me. I ring her anyway, but her line's still engaged. I could ring Caro. She thinks Joshua's appropriation of Rob is creepy. But it's late, Caro's had the worst day of her life, and I'd hate to risk waking her. She deserves oblivion tonight.

I try to assimilate the implications of this extraordinary discovery, get it into some sort of proportion, but I can't formulate any coherent thought.

He's coming upstairs. He's outside my door, whispering my name. I see the door handle move. I breathe heavily, trying to simulate sleep. Eventually he pads into his room, closing his door behind him.

I'm still awake at dawn when the birds start their ridiculously loud twittering. I get up, pack, write a note to Joshua saying I'm away for the weekend without going into any details, and by six o'clock I'm tip-toeing out of the house.

Gillian slept under the stars. The heatwave showed no signs of breaking, and it had been a long day following Leni hither and yon. Unable to face the trek back to Lamb's Conduit Street, she'd dozed off on her bench opposite Leni's flat. When she awoke, it was the fag end of the night. Far from feeling frightened, unprotected as she was in the rundown, graffiti-covered complex, Gillian had a sudden rush of exhilaration. She stared up at the fading night and experienced a surge of freedom – she could do anything, be anything. It was a feeling she dimly remembered from her youth before the years had intervened to dull that vibrant, unrealistic glow. Was this how Elena felt when she ran away from Alonso and Beatriz Dias and made her way to Seville to join Pacheco's Painting Academy?

But she was no longer interested in what Elena Dias thought. She had other fish to fry. It was almost time. She looked around. On the far side of the complex was a block of shabby little shops – mini-mart, newsagent's, laundrette, bookies – that kind of thing. She still had to check them out: Leni's local profile was the one thing still missing.

She must have drifted off to sleep again. When she awoke it

was morning proper and someone was leaving the flat. The boyfriend. He walked across to the mini-mart.

Fully alert now, Gillian took her morning dose of pills, washed down with a little something from her flask and followed him into the shop. He had his back to her and was putting a carton of milk into his basket. She strolled up to him, stretching, ostensibly to grab some biscuits, and then stumbled into him, keeping her head down so that he didn't see her face. She didn't want to draw too much attention to herself.

'Oh dear, I am so, so sorry,' she twittered.

'Clumsy cunt,' he snarled.

Gillian scuttled out of the shop, head averted.

Back under the walkway, she felt quite shaken up. Not a nice young man at all. She watched him leave the shop and go back to the flat. She'd been concerned that the note she'd slipped into his pocket, although necessary, would cause him undue pain. Not any more. He could take it, she thought, swallowing an extra pill.

Forty-five minutes later the flat door opened again. This time Leni emerged, dressed up to the nines and clutching a small Louis Vuitton holdall. She was her usual serene self. The boyfriend obviously hadn't found the note yet. Still stiff from her night on the bench, Gillian set off in pursuit. The journey followed a familiar pattern: a bus to Park Lane, and then the ducking and diving through Shepherd's Market until once again Gillian found herself observing the mansion block which appeared to serve as a fake address for Leni as far as David Borodino was concerned. This time the girl waited on the steps. Eventually a gold Mercedes pulled up. A uniformed driver emerged. Leni handed him her bag and slid into the back seat.

Gillian watched the car pull away. Cinderella's golden coach, she thought. In spite of everything, a small part of her admired Leni. The girl certainly knew how to capitalise on her assets, like women throughout history – utilising their bodies to get what they wanted. Look at Elena, mistress of Francisco de Zurbaran for three years after her rejection from Pacheco's just because she was female. But it wasn't enough in the end, was it? All those dead babies, and watching him do the thing she wanted to do more than anything, while she was supposed to sit and sew . . .

Gillian knew she should go home and get some proper sleep, but she wanted to see the boyfriend's reaction to her note, so she caught a bus back to Paul Robeson Buildings. To her surprise, someone was at Leni's door. An old woman, so elephantine it made Gillian feel like Twiggy, was talking to the boyfriend. By the look of things he was giving her short shrift. As Gillian watched, she turned away and, puffing and blowing, heaved her way down the staircase. Gillian followed her to the mini-mart and watched her buy three Cadbury's creme eggs which she demolished in quick succession on her way to a heat-frazzled patch of grass with a climbing frame, some swings and a couple of benches. She collapsed onto one of these benches, her face streaming with sweat. Gillian chose another. She wanted to initiate a conversation, but something about the expression on the woman's face stopped her. She sensed that in order to prise this particular shell open, she'd have to use a bit of low cunning.

It didn't matter. She had all the time in the world.

TWENTY-SIX

Cedars, David Borodino's country retreat, is in the heart of the Cotswolds. I'm expected for lunch, but since I left at such an ungodly hour I find myself within striking distance by breakfasttime, so I stop off in Chipping Campden, marvelling at the beauty of the ancient honey-coloured houses in the High Street, and wondering why I live in London when there are places like this around.

I find a café that serves breakfast, and as I eat I try to focus on last night's bizarre discovery. But there are too many diversions – people going about their Saturday-morning business, earlybird tourists reading aloud to each other from their guides, local characters popping in for a gossip with the proprietor. I can't concentrate. Then I remember Broadway Tower. Rob and I visited it on a weekend break not long before he died. It's an eighteenth-century folly perched on the second highest point in the Cotswolds. The view is unbelievable. I need to get on top of things – literally – and this is just the spot.

I only get lost a couple of times. I know I'm on the right track when the road begins to climb steeply, winding round and round, and I have to keep the car in first gear. Fish Hill. At the top I park the car and walk to the folly. The turreted tower dominates the skyline, and the view is everything I remember. The day is clear and bright and I can see for miles across the valley to the Welsh Hills. I find a secluded hollow and settle down. Although it's still early, the midsummer sun bathes me in its warmth as I stretch out and attempt to get my head around the night's events.

But my brain still shies away from constructive thought. The beauty of the scene sends me into a fugue state, and time passes unheeded as I stare at the green fields and little villages lying below, with the River Avon a glittering ribbon snaking through the landscape and in the far distance, the tower of Tewkesbury Abbey.

Eventually I force myself to concentrate. First: my Brother-in-law, The Borrower.

Things he has borrowed:

1. Large amounts of my money.
2. Rob's clothes.
3. Rob's voice.
4. Rob's mannerisms.
5. Rob's walk.
6. Rob's hairstyle.

And now there's this weird diary.
He has stolen our past.

Is he mad? Or bad? Or something else that I haven't thought of?

And what do I do about it? Confront him? Kick him out? Send him to a good shrink?

Jess would say, 'I told you so.' So it's just as well she isn't speaking to me.

Jess, my oldest and closest friend, thinks I'm some scheming, conniving Dung-type hussy, hellbent on stealing her man. Jess, it seems, has harboured dark thoughts about me for years. Ever since the beginning of our friendship. And I never knew.

One thing I do know: nothing will ever be quite the same. What she said cannot be unsaid. And if Jess thinks for one second that I'd steal Mike from her, then she doesn't know me at all. I don't know her either.

Eventually I realise that instead of being early, I'm going to be hideously late. I decide to put my problems out of my conscious mind for the weekend, in the hope that my subconscious will take over and dredge up some answers by the time I return to London.

I'm very surprised when I finally find *Cedars*. After seeing the penthouse. I'd somehow imagined an equally modern extravaganza. I couldn't have been more wrong. It's a late-eighteenth-century mansion built in the same mellow stone as everything else round here. Small enough to be a home, but large enough to qualify as grand, it is set in grounds of exquisite beauty at the head of a lush valley, next to a magnificent group of cedar trees.

Borodino's Stepford housekeeper shows me to my room. 'After you've settled in, Mr Borodino would be grateful if you'd join him on the terrace for a drink before lunch,' she says.

My bedroom, with private bathroom attached, has a stunning view down the valley of sheep and horses grazing on green, rolling slopes. The room is furnished eclectically. Everything is well-used and on the edge of shabby, without being neglected. There's a pile of inviting books on the bedside table, and a cornucopia of expensive oils and lotions in the bathroom alongside a pile of white fluffy towels.

This house has the look of a place that's been cherished by one family for generations. But not David Borodino's family. Thirty years ago he lived in an inner-city slum. Now his wealth has bought him a history. I wonder whose.

After unpacking I make my way down the wide staircase and through the comfortably worn drawing room onto the terrace.

Borodino leaps up. 'My dear Rosa! So glad you could make it.'

When I look around, I'm not in the least glad.

For with the exception of Flavia, in her wheelchair, looking exquisite in a large floppy hat, and a wispy woman whom I don't recognise, the rest of Borodino's weekend guests constitute Rosa Thorn's House Party from Hell. There's Larry, sitting next to Flavia, and across from him Zander Zinovieff in a pair of flash shades. And that's just for starters. For the main event, I stare straight into the treacherous eyes of Mike Mason, while noting at the same time the unsuitably short dress worn by Leni Dang.

'I think you know everybody, except perhaps Sylvia, Zander's wife.'

Asked to pick Zander Zinovieff's wife from a line-up, I'd have chosen some designer dolly, all style and no substance. A trophy wife, glossily appropriate for one of London's most fashionable gallerists. Sylvia Zinovieff is a revelation. Her clothes are dowdy and ill-fitting, and her mousey hair frames a face whose features, devoid of make-up, blend into each other in a fuzzy, indeterminate blur. If asked to describe her from memory, I wouldn't have a clue.

She regards me with eyes that could be brown, or grey, or muddy green. 'Pleased to meet you,' she mutters.

Her voice is accented. Eastern European? Russian? I can't tell. What I can tell is that she's taken an instant dislike to me. I feel an electrical charge of hostility zipping through the air between us. Then I chide myself for being paranoid.

I try unsuccessfully to draw her out, but her eyes constantly flick towards her husband, who's talking fashionable florists to Flavia. The only time she comes to life is when he speaks to her. Then her thin face is transformed, and she responds with vivid animation. When he turns away it's like someone turned the lights off. She slumps back in her seat and responds monosyllabically to everything I say.

Perhaps I'll plead a headache and go to my room, but the housekeeper is announcing lunch. Too late.

We're led to another, larger terrace, where a selection of delicious salads is laid out on a table shaded by a vast canopy.

Over lunch Borodino takes centre stage, recounting a string of highly indiscreet tales concerning the great and the good, and also telling us tales about his many daredevil exploits. For not only does he have the Midas touch, but the uses to which he puts his pot of gold add enormously to the gaiety of the nation. He's a compulsive thrill-seeker who makes Richard Branson look like Timmy Timid in his endless quest for adventure. His last undertaking was a solo cycle across Africa from coast to coast, raising money for charity. During this he lost his bearings and disappeared for ten days. A nationwide cheer went up when he was eventually found, exhausted, severely dehydrated, but otherwise fine.

'Aren't you brave,' coos Leni. She snuggles up to Borodino, gazing into his eyes. Every now and again she feeds him a forkful of food, making him beg before she puts it into his mouth. He loves it. From where I'm sitting I can see his hand on her thigh. At one point his eyes meet mine, and between us flashes the knowledge of our conversation at *The Ivy*, when he claimed it was Leni's enthusiasm for art which had landed her Gillian's job. I meet his challenging stare. He's daring me to say something. I don't have the guts to do it here and now, in front of everybody. He gives me a small smile and I experience a stab of pure dislike.

At the end of lunch he looks round at us all, excitement flickering in his dark eyes – the same primitive excitement I detected on the day he caught me on his bed with Mike.

'Anyone care to sample my lake?'

He doesn't wait for the communal muttered refusal. He strides down to the ornamental lake in front of the terrace, grabbing Leni and removing his clothes as he goes. By the time he reaches the water, he's naked. Leni shrieks as he dives in.

'Come on,' he calls to her. After a small hesitation she peels off her skimpy summer dress to reveal a pair of French knickers with matching bra in virginal white lace. There's a collective intake of male breath as she walks slowly into the water.

'It's wonderful,' she calls to the rest of us.

Larry's face is a study in fastidious distaste.

'Time for your afternoon nap, my darling,' he says to Flavia, before turning to the rest of us. 'Would you excuse us. We'll see you all at tea-time.'

I'm left with the Zinovieffs and Mike. I want to go to my room, but if I do, Mike might follow and I'm not yet ready to face him. I'm utterly enraged by the way he's treated Jess and I know what I'm like when I'm this angry. I could say something that would escalate the whole situation. I don't want to burn my bridges with Mike. There's too much affection and history between us for that. I just need to find the right words to make him understand that he can't play silly buggers with Jess's feelings in this hurtful and disgusting way.

But I can't hack it quite yet.

Zander's describing the plot of the latest Al Pacino film to Mike, together with an account of how he befriended Al at an exclusive beach hotel in the Maldives a couple of years ago. Time for another sparkling chat with Sylvia Zinovieff.

'Is that a Russian accent?'

'Romanian.'

'Is Zander originally Romanian too?'

Zander must be half-listening to our conversation. He answers for her. 'My parents fled here from Russia in the thirties. At that time Zinovieff was not a good name to have.'

He waits expectantly for my reaction, but my knowledge of Russian politics is hazy and mainly based on my children's experience of school history lessons, in which instead of learning the bare bones of Britain's past they are experts on the rest of the world – the farther away the better – and given essays with such titles as: *The Russian Revolution: Mistake or Miracle? Empathise with the Tsar.*

'Grigori Zinoviev? Executed by Stalin in 1936? He was a distant cousin of ours. My parents got out as soon as they could.'

'It must be dreadful, leaving your country, knowing you can't ever go back.'

'They never recovered. Their hearts remained in Russia till the day they both died.' Then he turns back to Mike.

I ask Sylvia how she met Zander.

'In Bucharest – in a gallery. Zander had come over to look at the work of one of our Romanian artists. I was sheltering from the rain.'

'How romantic.'

For the first time she smiles. 'It was love at first sight. By the time he left we were engaged.'

'Do you miss Romania?'

'My life is here now.'

'Do you still have family over there?'

'No.'

'Are you in the art world too?'

'I keep house for my husband. That is all.'

'Oh. What did you do in Romania?'

'I was industrial chemist.'

I can't think of anything to ask about industrial chemistry.

Zander butts into our scintillating exchange.

'Don't go on about Romania,' he says. 'You'll bore Rosa to death.' He turns to me. 'She's such a little chatterbox, aren't you, sweetheart?'

Chatterbox?

'Have you seen Rob's painting yet?' Zander's tone is proprietorial. As if he, not Borodino, owns *Cedars*.

'No.'

'It's in the new gallery. What a building! Great improvement, don't you think?'

'I don't know. I haven't been here before.'

'Really?' Zander's eyes widen in astonishment.

He's playing that familiar game of one-upmanship. The one where people tell you things they know you won't know, but make it sound like they thought you would, and pretend to be astonished when you don't. Thus proving that *they* are infinitely more intimate with something than *you* are.

Zander rattles on. 'The hang's perfect. I'll show you if you like.'

'Lead on,' I say.

Mike's trying to catch my eye. Tough. After a moment, he gives a brittle laugh. 'I might as well join the bathing party. See you later, guys.'

He walks down to the lake, emulating his host by stripping off all his clothes. I watch the muscled torso, tanned from the Californian sun, plunge into the lake. No wonder women fall for him in such numbers. That combination of looks, talent and fame – lethal.

Personally I wouldn't touch him with a seven-foot bargepole. He's become spoiled and selfish. All the glory's gone to his head. The old Mike would never have done this to Jess. He needs pulling down about ten pegs, and it looks like I'm the woman who's got to do it. And since I'm never going to find the perfect words, there's no sense in putting it off for much longer. The sooner the better.

Zander's muttering to Sylvia. 'Why don't you go home, sweetie. I'll see you later.'

I put my hand on her arm. 'You're very welcome to come with us.'

'I have some things to do.' She stomps off across the garden.

Zander seems blithely unaware of her rudeness. 'Come,' he beams. 'Let me show you *Shed Door Outside*. I don't think you'll be disappointed.'

We walk round the house to the gallery.

'You seem to know David very well,' I say.

Zander smiles. 'Yes.'

'He's clearly a fascinating man.'

'He's been very good to me.'

'Oh?'

'Apart from anything else, he lets us have the use of a house on the estate for a peppercorn rate. Sylvia spends a lot of time here. She loves the country – much prefers it to London.'

'How did you meet him?'

'I used to work for a picture restoration business in Hampstead. We did a lot of work for David. Not long after I married, I happened to mention that Sylvia's asthma was giving her problems and David, bless him, said the country air would do her good and offered us the house.'

This is the man who threw away Gillian's career like a used tissue?

'He was also instrumental in my setting up *Nature Morte*. He knew I wanted to open a gallery devoted to modern still-life, and so when he bought the factory in Navarre Street a couple of years ago he gave me first option on renting half of it.'

'So which Hampstead gallery did you used to work for?'

'*Goldman*. It's where I started out as a picture-restorer. Leon Goldman was like a father to me, to the extent that he even left me the gallery in his will. The things he sold were very traditional – not remotely like *Nature Morte*. But major collectors used to take their stuff to him for restoration and I got to know them all, so when I started *Nature Morte* I had a first-class client list.' He beams. 'Lucky man, or what?' Then he stops and gestures. 'Here we are!'

David's new hanging space is a long, light-filled building. It blends in beautifully with the existing house. Rob's painting is the only work on display and it looks stunning. The soft, golden daylight enhances the colours of the flowers and adds an even bigger mystery to the velvet interior of the shed. I'm choked.

'Like it?'

David Borodino has come up behind me, Leni hanging on his arm. They're both wearing white towelling dressing-gowns, with *B* monogrammed on the breast pockets.

'It's perfect.'

'I told you so.'

Leni interrupts. 'I'm off for a shower. I'm covered in pond slime.'

I stop myself from saying, 'You are pond slime.'

Borodino watches her undulate away. There's a greediness in his eyes which he doesn't bother to disguise. It makes me feel like a grubby voyeur.

He turns to me. 'Feel free to come down and visit the painting at any time. If I'm not here my housekeeper has been told to admit you.'

Why is he being so nice?

Don't be naive, Rosa, You have something he wants: Robin Thorn paintings. He believes that by cultivating you, he'll be in with a bigger chance than anyone else.

'Rosa – make yourself at home. Tea will be served in the library at four and we'll meet again for drinks on the terrace around six. Zander – a word.'

I'm being dismissed, in the nicest possible way.

I have a horrible feeling that I can't avoid it any more. The moment has come to tackle Mike. And right on cue, as I climb the intricately carved oak staircase and turn the corner onto the landing, there he is, in front of me.

'Mike,' I say. 'We need to talk.'

After a while Gillian made her move. She crossed the scrubby patch of grass and sat down on the other end of the old woman's bench.

'Sorry to intrude,' she said, 'but the sun's in my eyes over there.'

The old woman grunted. Close up, she was hideous. Her features had all but disappeared between the folds of fat on her face, and several wiry black hairs sprouted out of a huge mole above her top lip. And she smelled. Of age and decrepitude. Gillian wondered if she, too, smelled like that, then decided she didn't care if she did.

'Lovely day.'

Not the most original opening gambit. The old woman thought so too. She glanced at Gillian with rabbit-pellet eyes but didn't respond. Gillian switched to Plan B. She rummaged in one of her plastic bags and produced a giant-sized bar of Galaxy. She broke off a large chunk and popped it into her mouth with a pleasurable sigh. She was aware of stirrings at the other end of the bench, and felt the old woman's eyes on her.

'Pity the council doesn't take proper care of this place,' said Gillian gesturing around her, the block of chocolate clutched in her hand. 'Re-do the grass, put in a couple of flowerbeds . . . it'd be so much better.' She bit off another chunk of chocolate. 'Still, I suppose it's nice for the kiddies – swings and suchlike.'

For a moment she thought Plan B was a dead duck too, but then the old woman's mouth opened to reveal a set of yellowing broken teeth with several missing. 'Yes,' she said.

It's a start, thought Gillian.

'I might just bring my grandchildren when they next come to see me,' she said, devouring another piece of chocolate. 'Do you have grandchildren?'

'No.'

'I have three,' said Gillian sunnily. 'Emma, Suzy and baby Oliver – such a dear little chap. Here, have some chocolate.'

She broke off a small piece and held it out. The old woman pounced greedily. Gillian extemporised for a while about her beautiful grandchildren. She felt herself becoming quite attached to these fictional little paragons, and had to remind herself that there was a job to be done.

'I'm . . .' She thought for a moment. 'I'm Beatriz. It's a Spanish name – my grandmother.'

'Pleased to meet you.' The old woman. She paused, and then, as if making a momentous decision, said, 'Mrs Prewitt – Ethel.'

Gillian rewarded her with another piece of chocolate.

'Course, my son wouldn't think this place was good enough

273

for his kids. Very particular he is about where they go and what they do. He gives me what for, I can tell you. Children, eh – you bring them into the world and what thanks do you get! Just a whole load of grief. Do you have children, Mrs Prewitt?'

Something extraordinary happened. Ethel Prewitt smiled.

'Seventy-two,' she said.

'Goodness!' exclaimed Gillian. 'I wouldn't have put you a day above sixty-five.'

'I mean I've got seventy-two children,' cackled the woman.

'Have some more chocolate,' said Gillian faintly.

After more munching and much glee, Ethel Prewitt revealed that the figure represented the seventy-two children she'd fostered over the years.

'How brave,' said Gillian. 'Taking on society's cast-offs. Well done, Mrs Prewitt.'

The chocolate fest had finally loosened Ethel's tongue and it took very little prompting for her to reveal that Leni Dang was one of the seventy-two children – indeed, the one she'd remained closest to.

'She's very good to me, my Leni. Not like some I could mention.'

'Oh?'

'Don't ask.'

'What's her history?'

Leni's parents had come to England to escape the war in Vietnam. They set up home and eventually had children, first Lien and a couple of years later Khan. But London had not been kind, and within a few years the family was torn apart. Leni's father, violent, disturbed and probably suffering from post-traumatic stress syndrome, killed Leni's mother in a fit of depressive rage, and then, overcome with remorse, killed himself. The children had witnessed everything. They were put into care, and Ethel Prewitt eventually became their longterm foster mother.

'It was me what give them their English names,' she said proudly. 'Them foreign ones weren't no good for school an' that, so I told everybody they was Leni and Kenny, and that's who they've bin ever since.'

There was a time, not too long ago, when Gillian would have been moved to tears by the story of poor little Leni's tragic childhood, but now she didn't feel a thing. She observed the change in herself with detached curiosity.

'My Leni done good an' all, in spite of everything,' said Ethel, accepting another square of chocolate. 'She's got a very good position, see, working for a newspaper. Writin' and whatnot. She's very ambitious, is Leni.'

'Don't we know it,' murmured Gillian.

'Pardon?'

'You were saying?'

'But she never forgets me – always makes sure I'm doin' all right.' She sniffs. 'Not like 'im.'

'Who?'

'Her brother, that's who. Right little sod. Always was, always will be. He couldn't give a monkey's whether I live or die. Leni'd have me move in with her if it weren't for him. As it is I can only visit occasionally or he gets mad and tells me to bugger off. He's a right little bastard.'

'He lives with her?'

'Too right he does.'

'She doesn't have a boyfriend then?'

'You must be joking! Kenny'd beat up any fella who came sniffing round 'er.'

The note has gone, not to a boyfriend, but to a brother.

A possessive, over-protective brother.

'Finish it off,' said Gillian, pressing the remains of the chocolate bar into the eager paws of Ethel Prewitt.

TWENTY-SEVEN

Mike follows me into my bedroom.

'Nice room,' he comments. 'Much better than mine.'

'What the hell are you playing at?'

'Rosy Posy! Have you become such a prude in your old age that skinny-dipping offends your delicate sensibilities?'

'I'm talking about Jess.'

'Can we forget Jess, just for one moment? It's great you're here. I was feeling mega-trapped till you turned up. These weekend house-parties so aren't my thing. Don't know why I accepted the invitation really. Curiosity, I suppose.'

It's as if the whole Jess thing hasn't happened. He shows no signs of shame, no remorse. Quite the opposite. He clearly thinks it's absolutely fine to lead her on, lie to me about what he's done, and then break his promise to level with her. Either that, or he's so disgusted with himself that he's blanked it all out.

'If I'd known you were here I wouldn't have come within five miles of the place.'

He laughs uneasily. 'Whoa! Where did that come from?'

'You know exactly where. You told me it was just a flirtation – that you weren't sleeping with her.'

'I—'

'You lied. Then you promised me you'd straighten things out. You lied again.'

'Now just hold on there—'

'No, *you* hold on. You promised to tell her the truth. Instead you just leave her dangling, saying you're leaving town, not calling her, not answering her messages. What's going on?'

'You've spoken to her?'

'Of course I have.'

'What did you tell her?'

'What do you think?'

'That was my call.'

'And when, precisely, were you planning to make it?'

'In my own time and my own way. You had no right—'

'I had every right.'

'How did she take it?'

'Three guesses.'

'Shit.'

'And now she's not speaking to me either.'

'Why not?'

'She thinks I've set out to split you up because I want you for myself.'

Mike bursts out laughing.

'It's not funny. She genuinely thinks there's something going on between us. She was saying some really odd things too – about her and me at college.'

278

'I told you not to mess with it.'

'Don't give me that. You may be prepared to let her stew, but I'm not.'

'You should learn to butt out.'

'You're behaving like a spoiled child. For God's sake, have the guts to take responsibility for your own actions.'

'Same self-righteous old Rosy. Listen to yourself. Always in there, telling other people what to do. One good thing about Rob dying – he'll have some peace now you're not on his back any more.'

A step too far, Mike Mason.

'Get out!'

'You can dish it out but you can't take it, Little Miss Bossy Boots.'

'Get out of my room right now, you dishonest, gutless bastard!'

'Sanctimonious bitch, always sticking your oar in.'

I've had enough.

'All right, if you won't go, then I will.'

I storm out. Down the stairs and out of the house, hell-bent on putting as much distance between us as possible.

I notice a small gate leading into a wood. Perfect. Just the place to calm down, out of sight and on my own.

This is all so unreal. What's happened? Within the space of twenty-four hours my two oldest friendships have been shaken up and re-formed into something I don't recognise. Something alien and horrible. We've bickered and squabbled through the years, but not like this. Not saying things to each other that really hurt.

The wood is dense enough to provide cover yet I can still see the cloudless sky through the trees. I re-run the scene with Mike. Both he and Jess think I'm an interfering old cow. It's so unfair. I just wanted to protect her, and this is what I get in return: a whole heap of shit shovelled over my head. Well, good riddance to both of them. From now on, I'll stay away. If they want me, they'll have to whistle.

My indignation has led me deeper into the woods. I'm surrounded by brambles and nettles and I can't see the sky any more.

I'm lost. I try to get my bearings. It's ridiculous – I've only been here for a few minutes. I sit on a log and look around.

It's then that the rustling starts in the undergrowth behind me. Probably a squirrel, or a bird.

I stand up.

The rustling stops.

I listen.

Nothing.

I move, and it starts again.

I choose the path I think might lead me out and walk as fast as I can. The rustling follows me.

I stop.

Silence.

I start. So does the noise.

Woods are full of noises. Dead silence would be much more sinister.

Here we go again.

It's me that's the problem, not the woods. Anything even slightly odd threatens to rip off the scabs of last winter and expose the bleeding flesh beneath.

Paranoid imaginings.

This assessment of my mental state calms me down for the two seconds it takes for my brain to remind me that paranoia hadn't entered into it a few weeks ago. I really *was* being followed.

By Joshua.

Perhaps my experiences have sharpened my defence reflexes so that they're super-tuned. To legitimate danger.

The fight or flight mechanism kicks in. I break into a run, careless of branches whipping across my face and nettles stinging my legs, desperate to reach the edge of the wood. But I'm going deeper and deeper. The brambles are higher now, and they scratch me as I push them away. And always there is the noise – behind, in front, to the side. I can't locate exactly where it's coming from.

Then suddenly I'm in open country. Facing me across a field is a farmhouse. Next to the house is an ancient barn, and from it a woman and a dog emerge.

The relief is absolute.

The woman is Sylvia Zinovieff. The dog is a large German Shepherd, with a low, menacing growl, displaying a lot of saliva and the most horrific set of white teeth with which it's preparing to rip out my throat.

'Marcel. Sit.'

The dog falls silent and sinks to the ground beside Sylvia. There's no welcome in her face. Quite the opposite. I struggle to regain my equilibrium. It goes against the grain to expose my fear in the face of such hostility. But I'm desperate to get inside, away from the woods.

'Hi, Sylvia. I'm lost. Stupid or what?'

She doesn't answer.

A huge man appears from the house, clutching what looks like an electrical circuit-board.

'Sylvie—' He breaks off when he sees me.

Sylvia's stillness cracks. 'May I introduce my brother, Emil Barbu. Emil, this is Rosa Thorn, one of David's guests.'

It's Zander's assistant from *Nature Morte*. His beard is even bushier now, and I'm reminded of the Edward Lear limerick about larks, hens, doves and wrens nesting in an old man's beard. Emil Barbu could have a whole aviary hidden in his facial foliage without anyone noticing.

'You will take tea with us, Mrs Thorn?' Emil's smile reveals a mouthful of gold teeth.

Judging by the expression on her face, that's the last thing Sylvia wants. Too bad. A cup of tea with two other people, one of them very large, seems to me a brilliant suggestion. I could do without the dog, but hey – beggars can't be choosers.

'I'd love to,' I say, ruthlessly avoiding her eye.

'Come.' Barbu leads me inside. Sylvia's face is like granite as she locks up the barn and follows us. To my great relief the dog slinks into a kennel near the back door.

The house is as cheerless as Sylvia. The furnishings are sparse and worn. No attempt has been made to brighten the place up. The walls are bare and there are none of the knick-knacks that people usually accumulate. It would be understandable if they merely used the place for the odd weekend, but according to Zander, Sylvia spends a lot of time down here.

If rooms are an outward manifestation of their owner's personality, I'd hate to see the inside of Sylvia's head.

Silently she makes tea in a cracked brown teapot, and after much tight-lipped banging about, she hands me a steaming mug. The hot, strong liquid immediately steadies me.

'So,' I say to Emil. 'You work with Zander. That's nice – keeping it in the family.'

Sylvia snorts. Or maybe it was a cough.

I press on. 'Did you work for a gallery in Romania?'

Emil scowls. 'No.'

'Oh?'

'Was top dog electronics engineer. Qualifications not recognised here.'

'That must be hard for you.'

'I am adaptable man. I have many ideas. England is good for inventors.'

'If you have face that fits.' That's Sylvia, the supportive sister.

'That man who invent wind-up radio – Baylis. He come from nowhere and he make it big. Why not me? Maybe one day I go back home with many pounds sterling, and build fine house in country near Bucharest.'

This time it's definite. Sylvia *is* snorting.

'If you imagine they will ever let you back in, you are more of a fool than I thought.'

I sense an old and well-worn argument is about to break out, but then Emil shrugs. 'If you will excuse me, Mrs Thorn, I have things to do.' He executes a funny little movement which is almost a bow, and hurries out.

Sylvia's muddy eyes move from her brother to me. Her thoughts are written across her face in large-print format for those with impaired vision. She wants me gone.

But I can't face those woods again. Not yet. So I soldier on, creating dialogue out of monologue, undaunted by Sylvia's curt responses. It becomes a kind of grim challenge: to see how long I can hold on before she snaps and boots me out. Then I crack it: Zander. Her specialist subject. Ask the smallest thing about him, and in spite of her blatant hostility, she can't resist answering. In triplicate. I learn all about his favourite foods, and how he likes Sylvia to cook them, his passion for 1940s films, grand opera and the great classics of literature, his insistence on wearing handmade shoes and bespoke suits, the great respect in which he's held by everybody in the known universe, and above all, what a fantastic husband he is to Sylvia. How he fought the immigration authorities to bring not only her, but also her brother over from Romania, how he single-handedly taught her to speak English, and how every Friday without fail, he sends her a bunch of red roses. At the end of an hour listening to her paean of praise, and privately marvelling at how well Zander has concealed all these cultural and emotional depths, the terrors of the woods increasingly seem the better option. I'm about to jack it in when the door opens. It's the paragon himself.

'Rosa! What are you doing here?'

He seems uncomfortable. It's not surprising. This place is hardly the image he's created for himself in the Great Metropolis. I'd bet money on my being their first and only guest. Somehow I can't see Zander inviting his friend Elton John down here for a fun weekend.

I tell him about my experience. He's most indignant.

'We turn a blind eye to the odd poacher, but following people and scaring them – that's not on. I'll inform the gamekeeper – he'll sort it. Thank God you found us. I hope Sylvia's been taking good care of you?'

With the appearance of Zander, she's clammed up again. She clearly doesn't like him talking to other women. I give her my sweetest smile. 'She's looked after me beautifully. Lovely cup of tea – sparkling conversation. What more could a lost traveller want?'

We stagger on for a few more minutes, but even Zander's endless capacity to chat shit peters out in the bleakness now emanating from Sylvia.

'Is there a way back that doesn't involve the woods?'

Zander jumps up. 'I'll take you.'

'No need,' Sylvia barks. 'Follow the edge of the wood, and you'll soon come to *Cedars*. It only takes five minutes.'

Thanks, Sylvia. Wild horses wouldn't drag me anywhere near those woods on my own, plus I need an escort past Marcel the Magnificent, currently lurking in his kennel and waiting to tear me limb from limb.

'Cheers, Zander,' I say, ignoring Sylvia. 'My sense of direction's non-existent. I'd be so embarrassed if David had to send out a search-party.'

'Let's go then.'

With a face like thunder, Sylvia follows us out of the house.

'Are you off?' Emil pops his head around the barn door.

'Afraid so. Thanks for the tea.'

'I hate to hurry you, Rosa,' says Zander, 'but David's a stickler for punctuality. Puts him in a real strop if people are late for dinner.'

'We can't have that, can we?' I murmur, and bid Sylvia a gushingly insincere farewell.

As we skirt the edge of the wood, Zander clears his throat portentously. 'As a matter of fact, I'm pleased to have the opportunity of a quiet word,' he says. 'It's about Joshua.'

'Oh?'

'I'm so sorry that I had to reject his work.'

'You've seen the portfolio?'

'Why, yes . . . Didn't he tell you?'

'No, he didn't.'

Quite the opposite. Joshua was adamant that he hadn't yet submitted the damn thing.

'When was this?'

'I can't remember exactly. A while ago. I was hoping to be able to give him some good news, but to be honest, Rosa, the work just didn't come up to scratch.'

'What's the problem?'

'You name it – poor choice of subject-matter, can't decide what he's trying to convey, technically very weak . . .'

'I get the picture.'

'If there were the slightest possibility of including him in the show, I'd have been only too delighted. But I've had so many excellent submissions from other young artists that I couldn't in all fairness let Joshua's work through.'

'Absolutely not.'

'I'm so sorry.'

'Please don't be. Joshua has to take his chances like everybody else. And by the way, I think it's great that a gallery of your standing should try to do something for young unknowns.'

I'm trying to hide my disappointment. In spite of Joshua's increasingly weird behaviour I still badly wanted him to get his show.

Zander waves away my praise. 'The young are our future. We ignore their talent at our peril. About Joshua – I hope he's not too downhearted?'

'He's fine.' I have a quick image of the weird diary and the photos of the deceased Reverend Gayle in his coffin. 'As far as I can tell.'

'I'm so relieved. I hope that the job will go some way to make it up to him.'

'Job?'

'Yes. Hasn't he told you? I'm employing him in the gallery. Not full-time – just as required. Emil needs an extra pair of hands now and again, particularly in the lead-up to a new show.'

Thanks for keeping me in the loop, Joshua.

'You're very kind,' I say.

Why hasn't Joshua told me about the job? More odd behaviour.

By now we're back at *Cedars*. Zander grasps my hands in both of his. 'Enjoy the rest of your weekend. I'm so sorry about Joshua.'

'Thanks for seeing me safely back.'

Then Zander's forgotten as I look up at the house and see a figure at one of the windows, staring balefully down.

Mike. In a tracksuit, looking sweaty. Just back from a run in the woods?

* * *

Zander Zinovieff watched Rosa Thorn walk into *Cedars*. Escorting her back had been the perfect opportunity to do what he had to do. He'd been wondering all day how to get her on her own in order to talk about Joshua Gayle and his portfolio. It was important for her to hear his side of the story as well as Joshua's. It was important that she heard from his own lips how much he'd really wanted to take the boy on. And as it turned out, he'd got his side in first. The boy hadn't had the guts to tell her anything. It had been quite a shock, he could tell. She'd put on a brave face, but she hadn't been able to hide her disappointment.

He caught sight of Mike Mason glaring down at her from an upstairs window. What an ego. He still hadn't recovered from the blatant rudeness Mason had demonstrated to his friendly enquiries about the man's British dealer. He'd become far too big for his boots. Zander would be interested to know what Rosa Thorn had done to make her old friend Mason look so murderously at her.

The spray blew into Joshua Gayle's face. He licked his lips and tasted the salt. The little waves lapped over his bare feet. Even on this bright day the sea was grey. So different in every way from the deep tropical blue of Trinidad. He felt a sudden longing for home. Things over here were too complicated, and nothing was as it seemed. He'd thought that this trip would lay some ghosts. It had taken a lot of courage to come. He'd feared that the sight of the pebble beach and the onion domes of the Pavilion might tip him over the edge, take him too far back into memory. But he felt nothing. He conjured his last sight of the place, a blood-red apocalyptic sunset that had mirrored his own torment.

He felt nothing.

He was another person now.

In another life.

TWENTY-EIGHT

When I've showered and changed I make my way to the terrace. Far from ruining Borodino's precious dining arrangements by being late, I'm the first to arrive.

Almost.

Ms Dung's beaten me to it.

I nearly turn round and retreat. I've nothing to say to her. Nothing printable, that is. And earlier she did a great job of ignoring me. But now, it seems, she's changed her mind.

'I thought everyone had died or something. Have a drink.'

I'm stuck with her. And as usual I can't keep my mouth shut.

'Enjoying your new job?'

Leni looks at me through lowered lids. Or maybe her eyes are weighed down by the five tons of mascara on her long lashes. She's wearing a minute tunic in bright green with gold trim, and shoes with enormously high spiked heels.

'Yes, I am,' she says.

'The interview you did with me about Rob must have been one of your last articles for *Dame*.'

'Yes.'

'Didn't stay with them long, did you?'

'Well, you've got to go with the flow in this life.'

'That's certainly what Gillian Gerard's having to do at the moment.'

Leni blushes. 'Whatever you think, I didn't ask for Gillian Gerard's job. It was offered to me fair and square. So I wouldn't keep making those nasty insinuations if I were you. Particularly within David's hearing. He's quite moody. It doesn't do to cross him.'

As if to illustrate her words, Borodino appears, looking like thunder. Our suave and smiling host has gone. He can hardly bring himself to say two words to either of us. What's happened between lunch-time and now to provoke such a change? I tell him again how wonderful *Shed Door Outside* looks in his new gallery.

'I'm so glad it pleases you,' he says with a tight smile.

I try a few more conversational sallies. His replies are minimally polite and nothing more. It's like being back in Sylvia Zinovieff's sparkling company. Leni's no help. She lounges in her chair smoking and saying nothing.

Mike appears. He pours himself a drink and starts talking about local history to Borodino. He doesn't get much of a response so he switches his attention to Leni, turning on the charm, flattering her, making her laugh in his inimitable way.

Me, he ignores.

I've never been more pleased to see Larry and Flavia. While

Larry's fixing drinks, I seize on Flavia like a drowning man clinging to the last piece of flotsam in the ocean. I tell her about getting lost in the wood, turning it into a comic tale.

'How well do you know Sylvia Zinovieff?' I ask.

'Last night was the first time I'd clapped eyes on her. Of course I don't get out much, so I may be reading things wrongly, but I suspect Zander purposely keeps her hidden away.'

'I wonder why . . .'

Flavia's turquoise eyes twinkle. 'Come on, darling. She's not exactly Kate Moss, is she? All that dowdy East-European gloom. God knows what a star-fucker like him saw in her in the first place.'

'Opposites attract? Or perhaps underneath Zander's sociable exterior there's a depressive Russian who's deeply attracted to Sylvia's terminal melancholy.'

Flavia laughs. 'Now you're being silly.'

'Actually according to her, there's more to him than meets the eye. Did you know that he's a fan of classical literature and grand opera – Wagner in particular?'

'Never!'

'Sylvia says so.'

'Who would have thought it. People never fail to amaze. It's what makes life such fun, isn't it? Personally, I reckon it's a marriage of convenience: she wanted a British passport and he wanted a housekeeper.'

'He sends her a dozen red roses every week.'

Flavia's finely plucked eyebrows nearly fly off her forehead. 'You astonish me!'

'And if he wanted a homemaker, he got a very bad bargain.'

I tell Flavia about the Zinovieffs' bleak living arrangements, so startlingly different from the image Zander's created with *Nature Morte*.

'It's a mystery to me why that gallery of his is so successful,' she says.

The fragrant Flavia turning nasty? Maybe she thinks of Zander as the competition even though the artists he shows are from a different universe to Larry's.

'How does Larry like being his next-door neighbour?' I ask at this point.

'He sees himself and Zander as God and Satan, competing for the aesthetic souls of the ignorant rich.' She laughs. 'Enough about Zander. A little goes a long way. How's poor Caro? I felt dreadful turning down your kind invitation to lunch after the funeral, but you know how Larry was about Steve. I had to throw the most almighty wobbly to get him to take me to the service at all.'

'Devastated, but coping.' I give her chapter and verse, then say, 'It was so good of Theo to organise everything. Caro was very grateful.'

Flavia's face lights up. 'He is a dear man. I couldn't wish for a better brother, although . . .' The animation drains away, leaving her looking worn and ill.

'What is it?'

'Nothing really.' She falls silent, but after a moment or two she says, 'I'm worried about him. It's those wretched manuscripts. They play far too big a part in his life. They've taken the place of friends, lovers, everything. It's not good. When Larry gave him an illuminated page from a medieval hymnal one Christmas, I was delighted because I felt he needed a hobby – something unconnected with death and decay. But they've taken over. He's no time for anything else nowadays.'

'Surely to have such a passion for something is good.'

'With him it's more than a passion. It's not healthy.'

'What do you mean?'

'Theo's a very shy person. Very solitary. It's always been tempting for him to give up on people altogether, and this hobby of his gives him the perfect excuse to do just that.'

'Have you told him how you feel?'

'I've tried, but he just tells me not to be an old spoilsport. He won't admit that what he's doing borders on the batty.'

'It could be worse. He could be trainspotting, or surfing the net twenty-four seven. His collection's wonderful. I'm not surprised he's preoccupied with it.'

Flavia seizes my hand. 'Theo likes you. I've never seen him open up so quickly to somebody as he did to you that night at our house.'

What is she suggesting?

'I don't suppose you'd consider going out with him? If he could get involved with a real live human being instead of old books, maybe he'd join the real world again. I know if I gave him a nudge in the right direction . . .'

Her beautiful face is full of hope.

Which I have to dash.

'Theo's terrific, but at the moment I'm really not looking for anyone else. I'd feel I was sailing under false colours, and I'd hate to lead him on. And to be honest, Flavia, I don't get any kind of vibe that he's interested in me as a potential girlfriend.'

'Oh, don't worry about that. He isn't. Theo's always been curiously asexual. I once thought that perhaps he was gay, but he isn't. No, I just sense that he's comfortable in your company. I feel he might open up to you. And after all, there are worse things than friendship as a basis for a relationship.' She sees from my face that this doesn't exactly appeal. 'I quite understand. It was unfair of me to ask. Will you forgive me?' But she can't hide her disappointment.

I'm tempted to relent, but it wouldn't be fair.

Then I have a brilliant idea, which I'll keep to myself for the time being. *Theo and Gillian*. Both rather retiring. Both crazy about art – they might just be the match of the century. I'll follow it up when I get back to London.

Then the housekeeper announces dinner.

Which is a strange affair, full of undercurrents. David Borodino maintains his sulk throughout the evening. It's an astonishing display of temperament. Why invite guests, if all he wants is to be alone with his moods? I'm relieved when I realise it's late enough for me to make a graceful exit. I'm saying my goodnights when my weekend away officially becomes the weekend to forget.

'Rosa,' says Larry. 'Any decisions yet on the Consort Park sculpture?'

I should have been expecting it. Of course Larry was going to ask me this question at some point this weekend. But I've been so preoccupied with other things that it hasn't even crossed my mind.

Do I say I haven't decided yet, or do I tell him the truth?

If I say I haven't decided, then I can go to bed now without any further hassle. But it means that tomorrow he'll start pushing his artists again, and then what do I do? Lie by omission? If he speaks to Caro on Monday he'll know I've opted for Steve Pyne. How embarrassing.

What the hell – I'm useless at prevarication.

'Actually, Larry, I've chosen a piece by Steve Pyne. It'll be a kind of memorial to him. It's carved in marble and—'

I'm babbling.

If looks could kill, I'd be well on my way to joining Rob.

'How interesting,' says Larry. His voice is permafrost. 'Your choice of course, my dear. We only hope you'll be happy with it.'

This weekend is supposed to conclude around tea-time tomorrow, but I won't last out till then. Borodino's brooding for Britain, neither Mike nor Larry is speaking to me, and I don't want to be within spitting distance of Leni. I can't spend all tomorrow with Flavia – if, indeed, she's still talking to me after my repudiation first of Theo and later of her husband's artists. The only other possibility is a visit to the farmhouse and I can imagine the welcome I'd receive from Sylvia. I'd probably end up in Marcel's dog bowl.

How to extricate myself without being rude?

I lie awake trying to concoct some excuse for leaving first thing in the morning. I'm starting to feel sleepy when I'm roused by the sound of voices. Laughing, intimate voices.

Mike and Leni.

It doesn't sound like they're exchanging shopping tips. They must be chatting on the landing outside my door. Has Leni had a bust-up with Borodino – is that what the big sulk was all about? And as for Mike, is this his way of rubbing my nose in it – making the point that Jess means nothing to him, and that he's free to screw whomever he wants? Whatever he's doing, it only serves to make my opinion of him sink even further. The voices move off along the corridor. Finally the house is silent again, and I sink into sleep.

Then I'm suddenly awake. What was that? A laugh? A shout? I can't tell if it's in my dream, or in the house. But everything's quiet now. I turn over and go back to sleep.

I wake early and slip down to breakfast hoping to avoid everyone. But David Borodino is there before me. Sleep has chased away his demons, or at least made him remember his manners. He asks me courteously how I slept. Now's the time for me to come up with an excuse to leave, but my mind's still blank.

Mike appears, pours himself coffee and vanishes behind a newspaper. Then Larry arrives. He doesn't say anything to me other than, 'Good morning,' but at least he's civil. Maybe Flavia's had a word.

David proposes a walk by the river.

'The towpath's very smooth – ideal for Flavia's wheelchair – and there's that rather interesting Bronze Age burial cairn along the route that I mentioned yesterday. I suggest we all meet here at about ten thirty. Then we'll have time for a good long stretch before lunch. It's rack of lamb with garlic and rosemary, Rosa. I asked Cook to prepare it specially, since you said yesterday that it was your favourite Sunday treat.'

No way can I announce an early departure and disappoint Cook.

At ten thirty we're all assembled.

'Where's Leni?' asks Flavia.

'Migraine, poor love,' says Borodino. 'She's spending the morning in bed sleeping it off.'

I think not, David. On my way to breakfast earlier, I'd glanced out of the landing window in time to see a taxi speeding off down the drive.

And Leni Dang's face peeping through the back window.

Trouble in Paradise? I remember the late-night laughter outside my room.

As our party makes for the river, Mike falls into step beside me.

'Can we talk?'

'What do you want?'

'To say sorry. I was a shit yesterday.'

'Can't argue with that.'

'Am I forgiven?' He's looking at his most appealing, hang-dog eyes moist with sincerity. It's hard to resist.

'It's not me you need to say sorry to.'

'You're absolutely right. I've been a complete bastard. As soon as I get back to London I'll go and see her, and sort things. Including telling her that I wouldn't touch you if you were the last woman on earth.'

In spite of myself I giggle. That's the trouble with Mike. Always has been. It's very hard to stay angry with him.

'Watch it. No need to go overboard. Why not?'

'Too tall, too skinny, too mouthy.'

'Bastard.'

'And I'm really sorry for saying that stuff about Rob. You know I didn't mean it.'

It's so tempting to get back to normal. Back to the way we were. But what he's done can't just be made right with a few penitent phrases. It's too easy.

'Mike, do you realise how devastating this is for Jess?'

A spasm of annoyance passes across the handsome face. 'Sure. I said so, didn't I?'

'She thought this was it, you know. You and her for keeps.'

He doesn't want to hear it. 'I said I'll apologise.'

'You can't mess with people's emotions like this, especially not Jess. It's true what you said about her being one of the few who sees behind the Mason Magic. Well, that's something to treasure. Don't treat it lightly. And don't take it for granted.'

'Oh, for God's sake, Rosa. You're at it again. I wanted to say sorry. I don't need another fucking sermon. Maybe you'd let me know when you've come down off that high horse of yours.' He storms off to join the others.

Then my mobile rings.

It's Caro. Sobbing.

'Can you come, Rosa?'

TWENTY-NINE

Within minutes I've explained about a friend in crisis, packed my bag, expressed heartfelt apologies to my host, and I'm driving back to London at warp speed. I don't mention to anyone that the friend is Caro. It's none of their business.

When I arrive at her flat, she hustles me out of the door.

'I don't want Mummy to hear. She hated Steve so much and she'd only say I told you so. Can we go to your house?'

Her face is puffy and swollen, eyes red and scarcely visible. She cries all the way to Consort Park. I don't ask her what's going on until we're home. I'm very relieved that Joshua's out, since I haven't decided what to do about his diary.

'Yesterday I had an anonymous letter. It said Steve was sleeping with Leni Dang.'

Her again.

'You don't know it's true, Caro. Sending anonymous letters is very suss. This could be someone with a grudge against you.'

'Like who?'

She has a point. Everybody likes Caro. Everybody's desperately sorry for her.

'It's not just that. This morning I went to Steve's studio to see what I could find out. There was nothing, except a DVD film dated quite recently. I wanted to play it through, but I couldn't get his machine to work. I realised there was a lead missing so I went to ask Kevin from the garage if he had one that I could borrow. He said he hadn't, but that there was something he'd been meaning to give me. It was a red chiffon scarf. He said that Steve's friend, Leni, had dropped it one day getting on to his Harley. He thought maybe I could return it.'

I make a mental note that if I ever run into Kevin again, I'll suggest that he do a crash course in tact and diplomacy.

This is not good.

'Doesn't mean a thing. Leni's a critic. Visiting artists' studios is part of a critic's job.'

'Maybe, but it doesn't explain the bike. He never let anyone else ride on it. Not even me. He always said girls on bikes were a disaster – they panicked too easily.'

I swear I'll kill Steve Pyne.

Too late, Rosa, he's dead already.

'How did Kevin know it was Leni?'

Caro's voice quavers. 'He said he'd seen her there several times, and he'd heard Steve using her name. When he saw her at the funeral he assumed she was a friend of us both, which is why he was returning the scarf to me. What was that woman doing in his studio, Rosa?'

'Let's ask her.'

She stops crying. 'No. I can't.'

'But I can. If she confirms that he was sleeping with her, then you're upset with good reason. But if she's able to give us an innocent explanation, then you can stop beating yourself up.'

I call Leni's mobile number, which I've had since she interviewed me. The husky, butter-wouldn't-melt little voice answers. I want to smash the phone against the wall.

'This is Leni. I'm not available to take your call right now, but if you'd like to leave a message, I'll get back to you as soon as possible.'

'It's on message.'

Caro's looking as if she's had a sudden revelation. 'Maybe it was her!'

'What?'

'Maybe it was Leni who killed Steve.'

I was hoping she'd worked through this idea that Steve had been murdered.

'Let's just wait and see what she says. What you need right now is some food.'

It won't do Caro any good at all to start accusing innocent people of murder. Even if they are conniving little witches.

Over lunch, in a bid to divert her from her problems, I tell her mine.

'It's Joshua.'

I explain about the photos and the diary.

'Rosa, that's seriously odd. You should go to the police.'

'And say what? He hasn't done anything criminal.'

'What about the money you lent him? It was for creating a

portfolio of photographs, not one of which you've seen. That's gaining money under false pretences.'

'The money's not the issue. As Rob's brother, he had a right to it. Anyway, the work does exist. Zander's seen it.'

'Really?'

'That was the good news. The bad news is that he says it's rubbish.'

'Rosa, apart from the fact that he's Rob's brother, what do you really know about Joshua?'

My diversion has certainly worked. Thinking about my problems instead of hers has had a miraculous effect.

'We should search his room. See what we can find out.'

How would Rob feel to see me rifling through his brother's things?

'Let's do it.' I lead the way upstairs before I can change my mind.

There isn't much to find. Joshua has pitifully few possessions. The diary and the folder of photos are still in the bedside table. I show Caro.

'This is so freaky. I'm not surprised you were scared.'

Apart from his passport, also in the bedside table, there's not much else. The clothes in his wardrobe are Rob's. All that seems to belong to Joshua are socks, underwear, contact lenses and his watch – the one that's identical to Rob's. I turn it over. No inscription. That's something at least.

'He was travelling light when he arrived,' I say. 'Only had a small rucksack.'

Rucksack. Where is it? Nowhere.

'Maybe it's in the shed,' I say.

'Let's go and look.'

'Can't. It'll be locked.'

'Locked?'

'Joshua had a lock fitted. He wanted all his equipment to be safe.'

'Don't you have a key?'

'No.'

'Surely he gave you one? As the owner of the property?'

'No.'

Caro doesn't comment on this, but she doesn't have to.

I haven't seen Joshua since before I went to *Cedars*. Where is he?

Caro still thinks I ought to go to the police, but then she's in a melodramatic frame of mind. She thinks someone murdered Steve Pyne.

'If he comes back, you mustn't be alone with him.'

She's starting to fade again. The haunted look is back. I try Leni's number once more, but her phone's still on message, and remains so for the rest of the afternoon.

I invite Caro to stay the night, but she declines. 'Mummy will worry.'

I then offer to drive her home, but she says she fancies a bus ride.

'Sitting on the top deck at the front always helps me think,' she says. 'And I have to work out what it means to me if Steve's been with someone else.' She opens her bag and fishes out a tissue. With it comes something else.

The anonymous letter.

She hands it over. 'See for yourself,' she says.

I'm sorry to cause you more grief, but you ought to know that your boyfriend was seeing another woman before he died. Her name is Leni Dang, the art critic of the Correspondent.

'You've no proof that this is true. Let's wait and see what Leni says. No more weeping – promise?'

Caroline gives a tremulous smile. 'I'll promise you,' she says, stuffing the letter in her bag, 'if you promise me that you won't let Joshua back into the house.'

What I didn't tell her is that I recognise the writing.

THIRTY

I scrabble through a pile of correspondence until I find what I'm looking for:

Lamb's Conduit Street
Friday

My dear Rosa,
   It's been such a pleasure, writing the essay for Rob's show. Interpreting the work of such a fine artist has been both illuminating and inspiring. And the added bonus, of course, has been working with you to create something that I'm sure will be a huge success. Let's not lose touch now the show's open. I'm going away for a few days, but when I get back, I'll give you a ring and we'll have lunch.
   Warmest wishes,
   Gill

The writing is identical to that of Caro's anonymous letter.

I think about how well Gillian and I got on during the lead up to the show. Same sense of the ridiculous. Same collusion against the combined efforts of Larry and Julian to make us take everything more seriously. Same take on life generally. I feel awful. I've been so wrapped up in my own concerns that I've taken her assurances at face value. She said she was fine, then pushed me away, and I let her. Granted, I've made a few phone calls, but I haven't bothered to actually visit again, or find out if she is indeed an alcoholic. And it's all because of my guilt about selling a painting to Borodino.

I must see her. Today. Now.

The weather's hot and sticky and I need a shower before I go anywhere. Since arriving home from *Cedars*, I've been so preoccupied with Caro that I haven't even taken my case up to my bedroom. So it comes as a shock when I finally make it, to see a black portfolio lying on my bed with a note attached.

Dear Rosa,

Thank you for believing in me and lending me the money to make my dreams come true. Unfortunately life doesn't always work out the way we want, and Zander Zinovieff doesn't think I have the talent to be a successful artist. I think he's right. I've never had much belief in my own ability. Solomon Gayle saw to that. He'd always said my work was rubbish and when I told him I wanted to go to art school he laughed in my face. He said I was to enter the Church after studying theology over here in England. But my mother told me to follow my dreams, so once I arrived in England, I changed courses and got a place studying art. I knew Father would find out, but I thought once I was away I'd find the courage to defy him. I'd been here a year before it all caught up with me. Things were going well, and I'd also fallen madly in love. Then my girlfriend told me she was pregnant. I was thrilled even though I knew it would be difficult as we were both students. The very next day, out of the blue, Father arrived. I was working in the studio at college when he stormed in and physically dragged me out. The humiliation was total. We flew home the same day. I didn't even have a chance to say goodbye to my girlfriend. I wrote to her but she never replied. I heard much later that she'd had an abortion and eventually married someone else. I've never forgiven myself for my cowardice in not standing up to him, and for abandoning her and my baby. The memories of that time are still so painful that I find it almost impossible to think let alone speak of them. That's why I haven't told you until now. After returning home I never painted again, but the urge to make pictures wouldn't go away, and eventually I found that photography had taken the place of painting in my heart. But I've never really believed it was any good. Not deep down. That's why I couldn't bring myself to show you my pathetic portfolio. I realise now that this is wrong, and that you have the right to see exactly how I have wasted your money. So here it is. Don't laugh. It was my best shot.

I swear I will pay back every penny I owe you. Zander's given me a job in his gallery, which will help me discharge the debt. That's why I haven't been around much. I'm doing as much overtime as I can.

And there's something else that I must apologise for. I'm sorry for trying to be someone that I'm not. For trying to be Rob. I know you've found it scary – I've seen your face. I've felt your fear. But until now I haven't felt able to explain.

It started off because I wanted to know my brother. I mean really know him. I thought talking about him to you would be enough. But it wasn't. And I couldn't bear it. So I decided to climb inside him – put myself in his place. I know how awful it must have been for you. Like seeing a dead man walking . . . and not just any dead man. I'm so sorry.

In parts of the Caribbean, the country people think that after a person's died, if you pretend to be him for a certain period of time, you'll take on his talents. I wanted to make art, like my brother, and I thought that if I could be him for a while, then maybe some of his genius would rub off on me. According to the superstition, this appropriation of another person must never be stated openly, or the spell won't work. I knew it was stupid, ignorant rubbish, and I wanted to tell you but I couldn't bring myself to, just in case there was some truth in it. And as long as you didn't say anything I could pretend you hadn't noticed. Deep down I knew you had, but I wilfully closed my eyes to your distress. I feel ashamed to have treated you so badly. I never wanted to frighten you, and I'm sorry I didn't make you proud of me.

Your loving brother
Joshua Gayle

Not only has he not run off with my money, he's working all hours to pay it back.

Another guilt trip for Ms Thorn.

And his explanation for why he's been behaving so oddly makes heartbreaking sense.

I look at the portfolio. So here it is, this thing that I've been itching to see, lying on the bed, staring up at me. Waiting.

I don't want to confront the end of Joshua's dreams.

I open the portfolio. The top sheet says *Summer Heat: Consort Park*. I lift it up and examine the photographic studies underneath.

They are beautiful.

They have truly encapsulated the crazy spirit of Consort Park in all its glory, in all its moods, in all its eccentricity. It's as if Joshua has climbed into my head, seen what I love about the place, and somehow perfectly captured it with his lens.

This work is brilliant.

To hell with Zander, and his poxy gallery. He wouldn't know talent if it hit him in the eye. I wish I hadn't encouraged Joshua to follow up his offer. Tomorrow, I'll do a ring round and persuade some decent galleries to look at the portfolio.

I write him a note which I leave on the portfolio in case he returns while I'm out.

Dear Joshua, Your work is brilliant. Zander Zinovieff's an idiot. And I do understand about the Rob thing. Let's talk. Back soon. Love, Rosa. xxx

I ring to check whether Gillian's in before making a wasted journey. She picks up straight away.

'Hi, Gill. It's Rosa.'

'Hello.'

Silence.

'How are you? I've been a bit worried.'

'I would have thought your life was far too full at present to concern yourself with me.'

She sounds distant. Or pissed off. Or both. Has she found out about my treacherous sale to Borodino?

But I don't want to get into that over the phone. What I want is to know why she's writing anonymous letters accusing Steve Pyne of being unfaithful to poor Caro.

'Can I come and have a chat later today?'

'Impossible, I'm afraid.'

'When would be a good time?'

'There isn't a good time. I'm involved in an extremely important project at the moment.'

'Sounds interesting. What's it about?'

Another short silence, then a torrent of words. 'If I've learned anything at all during the past few weeks, it's to keep my plans to myself. I know people like you. You worm your way into a person's confidence, and then you take everything. Well, I'm on to you. Keep away from me.'

She's lost it.

'Gill—'

She's slammed the phone down.

I feel like I've been slapped in the face. For a while I just stare at the handset. Gradually my heart quietens its jack-hammer beating and commonsense takes over. This is not the real Gillian. Unless . . . Maybe she's drunk. If so, perhaps I should give her time to sober up before descending on her.

But there's my promise to Caro.

And Gill needs help, even if she doesn't want it. I can't undo my recent neglect, but I can try not to perpetuate it. In spite of being allergic to drunks I can't just leave her wallowing. I must go round right now.

There's no response when I ring the bell. Is she ignoring me, or has she gone out? I ring again several times. Nothing. That's that, then. The hat shop's all shut up since it's late Sunday afternoon, so I can't ask Madame about Gillian's movements.

Then I see that the front door's slightly open. In London, no one leaves their door open. Not even Gillian at her scattiest. Something isn't right.

I venture into the cool dark hall and creep up the stairs. 'Gill? It's Rosa!'

Not a squeak.

I go into the living room. Has she taken on the job of wardrobe mistress for an amateur production of *Cavalleria Rusticana*?

Swathes of material in silks and velvets are draped over the sofa. Long skirts in deep, vibrant colours and an embroidered peasant-style blouse lie crumpled on a chair. On the floor is an Oriental tray along with two urns, and a couple of brass candlesticks . . . And scattered across the table is a heap of costume jewellery – strings of glittering beads, brooches and bracelets.

There's no sign of Gillian. But no sign of any booze either.

I see a school exercise book lying alongside the jewellery on the coffee table. On the front cover, in Gillian's writing, it says: *Leni Dang: A Study in Treachery*.

I open the book. More snuffling through people's private papers? This is becoming a habit.

But my notes to self are silenced as I read the contents.

Leni Dang's life is documented in meticulous detail with dates, times and places all clearly displayed. There are comments on dress, behaviour, activities, and earnest speculations, perorations and suppositions about the whys and wherefores of every encounter, all written in the scholarly objective voice of the professional academic. There are even footnotes at the bottom of some of the pages.

I was right to be worried about Gill's state of mind.

Then my heart sinks. Gillian may be going loopy, but there's no reason to doubt the accuracy of the events she's documented. The detail may be obsessive, but it has the ring of truth.

Therefore why disbelieve her account of two separate meetings between Leni and Steve Pyne shortly before his death?

One, an intimate drink in a bar off Leicester Square, the other on the morning he died when Gillian observes that they meet in Southampton Row and ride off on Steve's bike. A footnote after this complains that the day's observations had to cease, because she couldn't follow.

Poor Caro.

Poor me. I'm the one who'll have to break it to her.

I read Gillian's final entry. The first bit's a list, mainly of the kind of objects and materials I see scattered around her living room. But there's a last paragraph under today's date:

No more prevarication. I feel a tremendous sense of exhilaration. I am ready. To quote the Bard, 'If it were done when 'tis done, then 'twere well it were done quickly.'

Macbeth's dithering soliloquy before he tops Duncan.

Not a good sign.

Gillian hadn't decided what to do if the brother was at home. She'd chosen a time when, judging by her previous observations, he was normally out. But nothing was certain in this life, as she'd discovered to her cost. So she was very relieved that it was Leni who answered the door.

The girl looked really rough without the heavy make-up. She lounged in her doorway, mouth hanging open. Gillian's arms ached. Carrying all her bits and bobs up the steep flight of stairs hadn't been easy, but she couldn't let a rundown council stairway ruin the grand plan.

'I was just passing,' she said, 'so I thought I'd pop in.'

Unspoken between them flashed the knowledge that nobody from Gillian's world would ever be *just passing* Paul Robeson Buildings.

'How did you know where I lived?' Leni attempted a certain nonchalance. It didn't work.

'Do you know, I'm not exactly sure.' Gillian was at her most vague. 'Someone must have mentioned it, and for some reason it stuck in my mind. I'm like that, you know. I remember the most trivial things. Mostly they just clutter up my silly old brain, but occasionally they come good. Like now,' she said, beaming. 'Any chance of a coffee?'

She observed the different emotions flit across Leni's face: the unwelcome realisation that someone in the art world had discovered her slummy secret, superseded by the knowledge that the someone was the woman whose job she'd stolen.

'I'm rather busy . . .'

'I won't take up much of your time.'

'Actually the place is in a bit of a mess.'

Gillian gave a jolly laugh. 'You should see my flat when I'm in the middle of writing a piece. Everything gets neglected when the muse strikes, eh?'

Leni smiled uneasily. 'Yeah, but . . .'

Gillian staggered a little. 'Oh dear.'

'Are you OK?'

'I suddenly feel a little odd. Must be carrying all these heavy bags up the stairs.'

'Well . . .'

'If I could sit down for five minutes, I'm sure I'd be as right as ninepence.'

Leni knew when she was beaten. 'Come in.'

Gillian followed the girl into the sitting room. She was astonished at the discrepancy between the usually immaculate Leni, and this dingy hovel. The furniture was disgusting: a tatty sofa in sludgy green chenille, a dirty orange and brown beanbag, polystyrene granules spilling from a gaping seam, a glass and bamboo coffee-table sticky with dried-on food stains, and a G-Plan sideboard with a row of ancient cigarette burns along its edge. The only other object in the room, in spectacular contrast to its miserable companions, was a spanking new flatscreen TV, and even that was covered in layers of dust.

'I'll put the kettle on.' Leni trooped off to her no doubt equally squalid kitchen leaving Gillian to size up the room. It would do. Just about. She caught sight of a photo on the windowsill. A young Vietnamese couple stared solemnly out at her. The parents, she supposed.

Eventually Leni reappeared with two chipped cups of instant coffee.

'Lovely,' said Gillian. 'May I trouble you for some sugar?'

When the girl returned with the sugar, she said, 'I didn't think you were speaking to me.'

'That's one reason I'm here,' Gillian said smoothly. 'To apologise for my appalling behaviour the day you phoned.'

'Oh.'

'It was the shock, you see – losing my job like that. I'm deeply sorry for being so unpleasant. To you, of all people.'

Leni's heavy face relaxed. 'You seemed so angry.'

'That's just it!' exclaimed Gillian. 'I never gave you a chance to explain.'

'No,' said Leni.

'And that's what would help me more than anything. An explanation. An explanation for why a young woman I'd come to think of as a kind of daughter could betray me in such a cruel way.'

A blush spread over Leni's face.

'Why did you hurt me like that?'

Leni hid behind a curtain of hair.

'I'm listening now.'

But the girl remained mute.

Finally Gillian nodded. 'It's as I thought. You can't explain or justify what you've done. That's why I've had to deal with it in my own way.'

Leni's face jerked up. 'What do you mean?'

'To make sense of it.'

'What?'

316

'Every scholar knows that in order to understand his material, the subject must be studied in depth, from every angle. Only then can interpretations and deductions be made.'

'What are you on about?'

Gillian smiles. '*By their deeds ye shall know them*. I abandoned poor Elena Dias and elected to research you instead.'

'I don't understand.'

'I've been conducting an investigation. On you. How you live – what makes you tick. What makes you think it's OK to trample so thoughtlessly over the life of such a good friend. Because we were good friends, Leni. At least, I thought so. Anyway, I decided that studying you on the outside might tell me who you were inside, and why you did this thing to me.'

'I'm sorry, I still don't understand.'

Gillian leaned over and took her hand. 'I've been following you, my dear. I know everything you've done over the past few weeks. Everywhere you've been. Everyone you've spoken to.' She smiled modestly. 'If I say so myself, I've done a very good job. You didn't suspect a thing, did you?'

Leni snatched her hand away, her face a study in confusion and panic. 'You've been spying on me?'

'Yes. In a way, I suppose I have.'

'I don't believe this.'

'You've been my real live little mystery. Ripe for the solving.'

The hectic flush drained from Leni's face leaving it pale and clammy. 'You're crazy.'

'Quite possibly.'

'I'd like you to leave.'

'Aren't you interested in the results of my research? Wouldn't you like me to tell you about yourself? I've studied you more closely than probably anyone else ever has – even your own mother. Don't you want my feedback? Don't you want me to tell you about you?'

'Get out.'

'Not many people have the chance to experience that kind of validation. On the whole we don't look too closely at the people around us, do we? Not even our loved ones. And we don't reflect them back to themselves. Not really. We're more inclined to interpret their behaviour in terms of our own preoccupations. We don't see them objectively. But I could tell you things about yourself that no one ever could, or would.'

'Just go.'

Gillian settled herself as comfortably as she could on the lumpy sofa. 'You're a mass of contradictions, you know. It's what's made you such an interesting study.'

'Please go.'

Gillian sighed. 'That's not going to be possible. Not yet, anyway.'

Leni lunged towards her before collapsing back onto the beanbag.

Gillian stretched out a steadying hand. 'Are you all right, dear?'

'Don't touch me.'

'You stood up too quickly. Finish your coffee. The caffeine will soon perk you up.' She watched as the girl drained every drop.

The caffeine might well perk her up, but the crushed sleeping pill Gillian had slipped into her cup when she went off to find the sugar had done the exact opposite.

THIRTY-ONE

'What's wrong with me?' Leni's speech had become slurred, and she struggled to keep her eyes open. Once more she tried to stand, but Gillian gently pushed her down.

'I've given you something to make you drowsy.'

'You're mad,' Leni mumbled.

Gillian emptied the contents of her various plastic bags onto the floor. 'I'm just going to slip off your dress. Hold your arms up, there's a good girl.'

Leni started to cry, but she didn't resist. The giddiness seemed to have induced in her a terminal passivity. She allowed Gillian to remove her dress and replace it with a long, very plain black tunic.

'You can relax now, while I arrange everything else.'

For the first time in ages, Gillian felt truly happy as she bustled about. The main lighting in the room consisted of three small spotlights. Gillian, standing on the coffee-table, readjusted them so the lights shone onto the sofa, which she'd draped in crimson and gold material. Then she turned her attention to the table itself. On it she arranged some leather-bound books, a globe of the world, two small curved daggers with jewelled handles, and a crimson ostrich feather.

She smiled at the recumbent girl. 'I need you on the sofa now. Can you stand?'

Leni's eyes remained closed. Gillian, wheezing with effort, hauled her off the beanbag and on to the sofa, propping her upright at one end. Then she rummaged in a black binbag and produced a tall, ornately-worked candlestick, which she placed on the floor beside Leni, and a long narrow wooden box, which with a bit of fiddling about she arranged under Leni's left arm.

She surveyed it through narrowed eyes. It didn't look much like a coffin but it would have to do.

'Wake up, dear. It's show and tell time.'

But no matter how much Gillian shouted and pinched her cheeks, the girl didn't stir. Gillian could have kicked herself. The sleeping pills were Peter's, and had remained untouched in a drawer since his death. They used to make him nicely drowsy, not instantaneously poleaxed. But then Peter had been a big man. Leni was less than half his body weight. She should only have given her half a pill.

Gillian wanted to scream in frustration. It was imperative that the girl knew what was happening.

That was the whole point.

She went to the kitchen and made some very strong coffee. Then she soaked a towel in cold water and applied it to Leni's face. The girl twisted away from her, which Gillian thought was a good sign. She forced her mouth open and tried to pour some coffee down her throat, hoping it wouldn't choke her. Leni spluttered but her eyes remained firmly shut. Maybe she's playing possum, thought Gillian. Not quite so comatose as she's making out. She persevered, giving Leni no chance to pull away, and eventually most of the liquid disappeared down the girl's throat. Then she waited, absentmindedly fiddling with one of the ornamental daggers from the table.

Eventually her patience was rewarded. Leni's eyes opened.

'What do you want?'

Gillian smiled. 'What do any of us want?'

'I'm gonna report you to the police, you know.'

'I expect you are,' said Gillian. 'But it'll be worth it.'

Leni whimpered as she registered the dagger in Gillian's hands.

'First things first,' said Gillian. 'The conclusions I've reached in my research about your character and motivation.' She noted with satisfaction how still Leni had become. Good. It made everything that bit more authentic. 'My hypothesis was that by studying the outside, I'd discover the inside. Remember?'

Leni's eyes remained fixed on the dagger.

'Well, that hypothesis proved to be correct. You live a shallow, superficial life, doing shallow, superficial things. You have no real friends and most of your interactions seem concerned with benefiting yourself and furthering your own ambitions. You use your looks and charm to get what you want. In all the time I've watched you I haven't observed you doing one truly kind or thoughtful thing for anyone. You took my job because it was there to take. You wanted it. You took it. Simple as that. My distress was an unfortunate unavoidable by-product. The fact that I was your mentor and friend was neither here nor there – not worth your consideration.' She stared at Leni. 'Do you know what I've discovered about your inner life?'

Leni's dark eyes were huge in her sallow face.

'There isn't one.'

Leni struggled up.

'Be still.' Gillian thrust out a hand. Light bounced off the dagger.

Leni froze again.

'I see my role as not only that of a critic and historian, but also as a teacher. Putting youngsters on the right track. Helping them see. Art's all about seeing, isn't it? What is the picture telling us, et cetera, et cetera? And one of the things I've found to be of great value is the old adage "show, not tell". So . . .' Her gesture encompasses table, sofa, Leni herself. 'What does all this mean to you?'

The girl's bewilderment seemed absolute. The only thing registering in her eyes was fear.

'Look around you. Look at yourself. Look and learn.'

But Leni was beyond learning. Big tears now rolled down her cheeks. Gillian felt a mounting irritation. Why couldn't the girl see? It was all there. Was she going to have to spell it out? She drummed the dagger against her open palm, assessing the distraught figure in front of her. She should have known. Leni had always needed explanations. She was incapable of making her own interpretation. And today, the combination of fear and stupidity meant there wasn't a cat in hell's chance that she'd get the point on her own.

So be it.

'I've done something very special for you. I've recreated your very own living Vanitas painting. It explains more clearly than I ever could what you've done to me, and also something even more fundamental—'

'Please, Gillian.'

'Elena Días passed as Salvator Vera for years – until she died, in fact. The painter Juan de Valdes Leal, with whom she'd worked for years, was devastated, and some people think his most famous work was painted in response to her death. *In Ictu Oculi – In the Blink of an Eye.*'

'Please, Gillian!'

'In the blink of an eye, Death snuffs out the Candle of Life while trampling on the symbols of earthly vanity.' She frowns. 'Your left foot's wrong. It should be resting on the globe but it keeps flopping off.' She leaned forward, lifted Leni's foot up, and placed it on top of the globe. But as soon as she removed her hand, the foot fell to the floor again.

'Do try to hold it still.' Gillian repositioned the recalcitrant foot on top of the world, then fluttered round her creation, adjusting a fold of material, rearranging the pile of books, before standing back and reviewing her handiwork.

From her bag she produced a digital camera, bought specially for the occasion, and took several shots of the tableau from different angles. When she'd finished she allowed herself a frisson of approval. 'Perfect,' she murmured. She rummaged in her bag once more and pulled out a reproduction she'd regretfully torn from one of her favourite books.

She handed it to Leni. 'Look.'

Looming up from a penumbral background was a skeleton. One foot rested on a globe, the other was lost under a collection of objects – a sword, a feather, swatches of cloth. A coffin was wedged under one arm while the hand on the end of the arm clutched a scythe. The other arm extended towards a candle in a tall black candlestick. The skeletal claw had extinguished the flame, which explained why the picture was so dark. Above the candlestick the words *In Ictu Oculi* floated in space. A jumble of old books, a crown and a silver and gold helmet, all arranged on white, pink and crimson silk, completed the picture.

Hand trembling, Leni laid it down on the table.

Gillian passed her the camera. 'Aren't these digital things wonderful? Instant images.' She indicated the discarded reproduction. 'Compare and contrast.'

Leni flung the camera down.

'Careful, that's my new toy. Look again – at the illustration, and the picture in the camera, and then spot the difference.'

Leni stood up. Gillian pushed her gently back down again.

'What's the difference? Come on – you can do it.'

'In one there's a skeleton. In the other there's me. Is that what you want me to say?'

'Bravo. And what does that tell you?'

'That you've completely lost it.'

'What does that tell you?'

Leni huddled into the sofa, her eyes devouring Gillian.

'Come on.'

Leni burst into tears. 'That everyone dies.'

'Everyone?'

'Yes.'

'Including?'

Leni shook her head, screwing her eyes tight shut.

'Including who, Leni? Come on, tell me. I need to know you've understood the lesson.'

'Me. Including me. One day even I will die.'

'Even you. In spite of all your scheming and betrayals you too, just like the rest of us, will die. We all know it in our heads as a cold fact, but today I've given you the opportunity to experience the reality of it. I've pulled back the veil which normally protects you from that dreadful knowledge. You have become Death. After this, nothing will be the same. You will live your life quite differently.'

Leni's terrified eyes alternated between the two images and the motley collection of objects surrounding her.

'*In Ictu Oculi* . . . In the blink of an eye my life was destroyed. And in the blink of an eye so will yours be. Your superficial, heartless life.'

Then something inside Gillian snapped. She felt the energy being sucked out of her, to be replaced by a vacuum where thought and feeling should have been.

Had she made the girl understand? Perhaps. Did she care? No. Suddenly it didn't seem to matter any more.

What exactly had she achieved? Nothing had changed.

She wanted to leave now. Leni's petty treachery suddenly seemed meaningless in the face of her ultimate loss. Peter.

Then she became aware of a noise. Behind her.

Before she could turn, she was tossed aside like a twig in a tornado as someone grabbed her and wrenched something from her hand. A dagger. She was surprised to find it there. It was supposed to be on the table with the other things.

The first blow was so hard she heard her jaw crack. Then she was on the floor, kicks and blows raining down. A final punch in the stomach knocked the wind out of her. As she fought for breath she saw Leni in the arms of a young man. Close up she recognised him.

Kenny Dang.

THIRTY-TWO

Although not one of Leni Dang's biggest fans, I wouldn't want anything seriously bad to happen to her. I ring her number. Voicemail, yet again.

Where does she live? I turn back to Gill's magnum opus. Bingo. One of the first entries – Leni's address.

I run out onto Theobald's Road and hail a cab. When I give the driver the address, he says, 'You must be joking. There ain't no cabbie'll take you there.'

'Why not?'

''Cos we ain't stupid. It's yer no-go area, innit. Full of villains, junkies, muggers, tea leaves – you name it.'

'I'll pay you extra.'

'Last time I went there I ended up with no hubcaps and I only stopped for half a minute to let my fare out. I tell you they'll have your handbag, your watch and your mobile before you can turn round.'

'So that's a no, is it?'

''Fraid so, love.' He pulls away.

I waste more precious time hailing other cabs and getting the same response before giving up and going by tube.

Halfway between Holborn and Russell Square we stop in a tunnel. And stay stopped.

Twenty minutes later we're informed that an incident on the line is responsible for the hold-up. After that we hear nothing.

Time ticks by. The train becomes hotter and hotter, and so do I as I wonder what Gillian's doing to Leni Dang.

She was the personification of pain. At first it was undifferentiated and then as she regained full consciousness, she became aware of the various bits of her body competing for her attention. Her face, her stomach, her back – all were throbbing, stabbing, aching, all shrieking, 'I hurt the most – deal with me!' She opened her eyes to find she was lying face down, nose pressed against a filthy mud-coloured carpet.

'Wake up, bitch.'

Leni's hair and make-up were restored to their customary perfection, and she was wearing a halter-neck top and a miniskirt, both of which accentuated her slim figure.

Gillian's brain was a jumble of mismatched thoughts. Had she really been lecturing this girl on morality and mortality? Was it true that she'd reduced the child to a quivering wreck? In spite of the evidence leaning against the doorframe, she feared it was. Images flickered in and out of focus of things she'd done – haranguing the girl, dressing her up, lecturing her on Juan de Valdes Leal's painting – *turning her into Juan de Valdes Leal's painting, for God's sake*. And then the whirlwind. Battering the frenzy out of her. Cleansing and clarifying.

'Leni, I'm so, so sorry.'

'Save it for someone who cares.'

Leni strolled over to Gillian. She was wearing a pair of five-inch stilettos, which came to a halt inches from Gillian's nose.

'Like my shoes?' she said. 'You should, they're just your thing – named after a type of dagger.' She pressed down on Gillian's stomach with one pointed heel. 'This could pierce flesh as easily as butter.'

Gillian's memory stirred once more. She saw herself holding a knife. Which had been knocked out of her hand, by Leni's brother. The reason she was one throbbing mass of pain.

'Your brother,' she whispered. 'Don't let him hurt me again.'

Leni giggled. 'Scary, isn't he?' She sank the heel even further into Gillian's soft belly. 'There's nothing he wouldn't do to protect me, you know. Nothing.'

'I don't feel well.'

'You're not listening. I said there's nothing he wouldn't do for me. I'm his little sister, see. There's no way he'd let anyone harm me. 'Specially a manky old dog like you.'

The girl's eyes were black with fury.

'How dare you involve her in your sick games! How dare you defile my precious lotus flower!'

Through the pain Gillian was conscious of a certain confusion. Had Leni just referred to herself in the third person? Wasn't there a psychiatric term for that? Dissociation?

But then like a razor blade being drawn up her spine came the knowledge that dissociation had nothing to do with it.

'What are you staring at?' The girl grabbed Gillian's hair,

jerked her head back and peered into her eyes. She smiled at what she saw there. 'Congratulations, Ms Gerard. You've figured it out.'

'I don't understand.'

'Oh, I think you do.' Her fingers had relinquished the hair and found their way to Gillian's throat. 'You understand perfectly. Which is why I'll have to terminate your pathetic bout of amateur dramatics with some unacceptable violence.'

Gillian felt the fingers squeezing her windpipe. She couldn't breathe. She tried to pull the hands away, but she had no strength. She was floating, floating, floating up and away.

But as blackness crept over her field of vision, something incredible happened. Something that even in the middle of all the pain, filled her with astonishment and a perverse joy. She, who had spent the last five years smiling on the outside, but dying on the inside, who had only kept herself going with an addiction to work and ever-increasing doses of Prozac, was now consumed with the urge to live.

She summoned up the last of her strength to try and weaken the iron grip round her throat, but the hands were immovable. She felt her life ebbing away. An urge to live was not enough, it seemed.

Then, inexplicably, the pressure had gone. She could breathe.

She gulped great mouthfuls of air. The blackness receded, and the room swam back into focus. But something had happened to her vision. She was seeing double.

Two Lenis. Grappling with each other.

Two Lenis?

One said, 'Don't do it. Please.'

'Watch me,' replied the other.

'This is wrong.'

'She knows too much.'

'Not really.'

'She knows there are two of us.'

'She's unconscious. If you go now, she won't remember anything.'

'Don't be stupid. She'll know she's been beaten.'

'I'll deal with that.'

Two Lenis.

Impossible. Gillian knew it was impossible, but her head was so fuzzy she couldn't work out why.

'If she guesses the truth, we've had it. We'll go to prison. Is that what you want?'

'Gillian was my friend. She was very good to me.'

'Turning you into some sick art event is good?'

'She's not well. And that's our fault too. I hate what we've done to her.'

'It wasn't personal. You know that.'

'Anyway, blackmail's one thing – killing someone's quite another. You can't do that – you just can't.'

'So what do you suggest?'

'If you kill her you've crossed the line. Like Father. There's no going back.'

'Father was a coward. He couldn't live with what he'd done. I can. Life's cheap, Leni. Screw or be screwed. You know that.'

The two girls stood, locked together in a kind of embrace, neither of them moving. Then the impasse was broken by the sharp ring of a mobile phone.

Bad Leni picked up. She disappeared from Gillian's field of vision. Good Leni stood very still, deep anxiety clouding her face. Gillian wondered whether to speak, but then decided not.

A good decision, since Bad Leni returned almost immediately, her voice fizzing with excitement. 'We're on again,' she said.

'What?'

'I thought you'd blown it, but everything's cool. I'll deal with it. I've got to go.'

'Please don't—'

'We'll never get another chance like this. You know we won't. When Gerard comes round, you're not to let her go. Keep her here. I'll be back as soon as I can.'

Gillian heard the front door slam. Was she now alone with Good Leni, or was the brother still in the flat too? She couldn't hear noise in any other room. Everything else was silent. She had to persuade Good Leni to let her go. Kenny was a vicious brute and Bad Leni not much better. Good Leni was her only chance. But there was something else, something important that she knew, nagging away at the edge of her consciousness. But the throbbing pain in her belly was preventing her from thinking clearly about anything.

'Leni?' she whispered. 'Why does your sister want to kill me?'

'You're awake?'

'And your brother? Does he want me dead, too?'

Leni shrugs.

'Is he still here?'

'He's gone.'

Relief washed over Gillian. 'I know you don't really wish me harm, in spite of what I did earlier. My stomach's really hurting . . .'

332

But Leni was looking at her strangely. 'And I thought you were so clever.'

'Please, Leni.'

'You make a living from looking, yet you can't see what's staring you in the face.'

'Call an ambulance.'

But Leni was shaking her head. 'All that shit you were peddling earlier – teaching me to face the reality of my own death – you don't have a clue. You've spent your cosy little existence in complete safety, swanning around London like the Queen Bee, and you think you know about real life because your bloody husband went and died on you? My parents watched their whole village massacred by the Viet Cong. Try living with that.'

'I'm sorry—'

'We found them, you know – our parents. After Dad had killed Mum and then himself. When we came home from school we thought they'd be at work. But they were in bed with their heads blown off.'

'I'm so sorry. I can't begin to imagine what that must have been like.'

'No. You can't.'

'Leni—'

'Kenny knows life sucks. He knows you have to fight for what you want – fight dirty if that's what's needed. I've never been able to do that, so he's done it for me.'

'I realise that now.'

'Do you?'

'I needed to understand why you betrayed me. I've always prided myself on being a pretty good judge of character. What you did didn't square with what I knew about you. Now I understand.'

'What do you understand?'

'It wasn't you who did this thing to me. It was your sister. She pretended to be you and seduced the editor of *Dame* into giving you a job. Then she did the same to David Borodino. I was just collateral damage.'

Leni remained silent.

'I can see how it would work. Your sister's much tougher—'

'Shut up!'

'Why did you never tell me you had a twin sister?'

'Just listen!' Leni was shouting.

'OK.'

'Kenny's always looked after me,' Leni's face softened, 'even though I'm older than him. I have the degree but he's the clever one. Clever in the ways of the world. I don't have much self-belief. Kenny gets cross about that, but I can't help it. Anyway, after uni, the only thing I wanted to do was write about art. I don't know why – I didn't know much about it. I like beautiful things, I suppose. But it's a hard world to break into and a Media Studies degree from a glorified poly wasn't worth the paper it was written on. I used to read your column every week and ache for a job like yours. It's true what I said about you being my role model. I'd kill to write like you . . . Anyway, I got the occasional freelance assignment, but I wasn't really progressing. Didn't have the confidence to push myself forward, you see. It was Kenny who made me apply for the job on *Dame*. When I got it I was really surprised. Then I found out why. It was nothing to do with my journalistic skills. Don Groom, the editor, asked me to stay behind one night. He grabbed me and started slobbering all over me. It was horrible! I pushed him away and ran out. When I told Kenny he went ballistic. I had to beg him not to go and beat Groom to a pulp. But when he calmed down he had another idea.' She looked at Gillian. 'Kenny's different from other men.'

'I won't argue with that,' said Gillian grimly.

'Have you heard of Khatoeys?'

'No.'

'Ladyboys. They originated in Thailand, but nowadays they come from all over south-east Asia.'

'Drag queens?'

'Ladyboys are not drag queens. They prefer to be known as Women of the Second Category – men who've wanted to be female since early childhood. In Thailand they're an accepted part of society.'

An image, bright and clear, flashed up in Gillian's head: Mrs Prewitt gobbling chocolate on the park bench.

That was what she'd been struggling to remember. Ethel Prewitt never mentioned a sister. She only talked about Leni and Kenny.

'So . . . there is no sister?'

'No.'

'Only Kenny.'

'Yes.'

'But . . . he looks like your identical twin.'

'We've always looked very similar. Kenny's very slight and his skin's smooth and hairless. His hair's the same length as mine when he doesn't have it tied back. With the right clothes and make-up, our own mother wouldn't have been able to tell the

335

difference. That's the whole thing about ladyboys. They're more female than most ordinary females, but not in an over-the-top way like drag queens. A ladyboy looks like the real thing – an incredibly beautiful young woman.'

'But I've watched him coming in and out of your flat, always as a male.'

'Actually you wouldn't have been able to tell the difference. For all you know, you could have been following him, not me. But in fact he keeps his two lives strictly separate. He doesn't normally dress here. Tonight's an exception. His other job when he isn't being a waiter at *Zizz* is at a club called *Lilou*. When he's there, he's female – known as Kiki.'

'What kind of job?'

'He's a hostess.'

'Hostess?'

Leni stared defiantly at Gillian. 'I know what you're thinking, and you're right. Yes, he caters for the patrons' every need. Including going home with them.'

'I'm not thinking anything,' lied Gillian.

'He's saving up for surgery. One day, he'll really be my sister.'

'So why are you telling me this?'

'Why do you think I didn't lose my job at *Dame*?'

'Kenny pretended to be you?'

'Not exactly.'

'But Groom's a raging hetero. He's got a reputation as a randy old goat.'

Leni laughs. 'As I said, ladyboys are not drag queens. Even the straightest of guys finds it hard to resist. I asked Groom out for a drink, introduced him to Kiki and suggested that he might like to try something a little more exotic.' She smiled. 'He couldn't wait.'

'He was happy to sleep with Kenny?'

'He was gagging for it. And afterwards he said it was the sexiest thing he'd ever done. Anyway, it secured my job at *Dame*. And even though I've moved on it's still providing us with a few little luxuries. Groom's acquired a taste for Kiki.'

'He's still seeing her?'

'They have a regular arrangement.'

'So why steal my job if you were so well in at *Dame*?'

'It just happened. Kenny was doing his other job – as a waiter at *Zizz* – the night of Rob Thorn's opening. He noticed David Borodino flirting with me at the dinner, and saw an opportunity.'

'Chat up Borodino and get him to give you my job?'

Leni's face is as sulky as a schoolgirl's.

'Kenny's plans were on a much grander scale. He wanted me to be the next Mrs Borodino. But when part of David's courtship involved giving me your job, I couldn't very well refuse, could I?'

'Yes,' said Gillian. 'If you had an ounce of integrity, that's exactly what you could have done.'

'Actually, I felt awful. I was very grateful for everything you'd done for me. But David has to have his own way. You know that.'

'Are you in love with him?'

'No. And you can probably have your job back. Unless a miracle happens tonight, it's all over with me and him.'

'What do you mean?'

'Men like David scare me. They want to eat you up. Gobble you whole.' She hesitates. 'Can I tell you something?'

'Go ahead.'

'Promise you won't laugh?'

'Promise.'

'I'm still a virgin.'

'Oh. Well, there's no shame in that. You're still very young. I'm surprised, though. From what I know you don't seem short of offers.'

'I don't like that sort of thing.'

'What sort of thing?'

'Sex. I don't mind kissing and cuddling, but that's as far as it goes. I can't stand it if they want to get too close.'

'But if your plan was to become the next Mrs Borodino, surely you knew you'd have to have sex with him?'

'Of course I did. And I tried, I really did, but I just couldn't do it. At first it excited him – being kept at arm's length. That doesn't normally happen to him. But it's become more and more difficult to keep him off. This weekend he invited me down to his house in the country, and I knew he wouldn't wait any longer. But when it came to the point, I couldn't. I just couldn't.' She shuddered.

'So what happened?'

'I refused. He threw me out.'

Gillian was conscious of a feeling she never thought she'd experience again towards Leni.

Protective pity.

But then it faded as Leni said brightly, 'But it might still work out. That call earlier – it was him. He wants to see me again. And this time it'll be OK.'

'How?'

'Kenny's gone in my place.'

'But Borodino will soon find out Kenny isn't you.'

'It won't matter.'

'Why not?'

'Kenny reckons he'll pay a massive amount not to have his face splashed all over his rival newspapers: "Macho Magnate and the Ladyboy".'

'Blackmail.'

'I suppose so.'

'I can't see a man like Borodino submitting to blackmail.'

'Let's wait and see.' There was no shame in her voice.

'Let me go, Leni. Call me a cab – anything. I won't tell anyone what's been going on. How could I, after what I did to you earlier?'

Leni looked at her sadly. 'Sorry. We have to wait for Kenny.'

THIRTY-THREE

When I finally make my way into the estate I see what the taxi driver means. It's a dreadful place – *Clockwork Orange* territory. Not at all where I would have pictured Leni. I locate Paul Robeson Buildings, climb up to the right walkway and ring the bell at number twenty-three. No one answers, but inside I hear music: Mozart's *Requiem*.

A mass for the dead.

I ring the bell again. Still no response. The curtains are drawn across the front window, but they don't meet in the middle. I peer through the small gap. The room's in semi-darkness, it's impossible to see much. But someone's in there, moving about. I bang on the window. The curtains part and a face stares out at me.

Leni.

Still intact, thank God.

'Is Gillian with you?'

'Why should she be?'

I'm now in a bit of a bind. How to warn Leni that I think Gillian might want to harm her, without squealing on my friend?

'Can we talk?'

'It's not a good time. Sorry.'

'I need to tell you something.'

'Go ahead.'

'I don't want to shout it through the window. Can I come in?'

'Sorry.'

Just then my eye is caught by a movement on the floor behind Leni, on the far side of the room. I see a hand, the outline of a face, and, very faintly, I hear my name.

It's Gillian.

'Let me in. I know Gillian's there.'

'No, she isn't.'

'I've just seen her.'

'She's not here.'

'I'm calling the police.' I produce my mobile.

'Wait.'

A second later the front door opens. I brush past Leni into the sitting room. Gillian's on the floor, half-propped against a sofa which is covered incongruously in silk material. Her breathing is shallow, and her face putty-pale apart from an area around her jaw which is red and swollen.

'Gillian?' Her skin is clammy and cold.

'It hurts, Rosa.' Her voice is little more than a whisper.

'Help me get her up, Leni.'

Leni's rooted to the spot.

'*Now*, Leni.' I put as much authority into my voice as I can muster.

It works. Together we haul Gillian's not inconsiderable bulk on to the sofa. She's groaning and clutching her stomach.

'Fetch a blanket.' I pull out my mobile and dial 999.

'What are you doing?'

'She needs a doctor.'

'No!' Leni's eyes dart towards the door.

'You don't have a choice.'

'Wait, Rosa.' It's Gillian. 'It's complicated. Let Leni explain.'

Is life stranger than fiction? Discuss.

I listen, incredulous, as Leni recounts how gentle Gillian, having drugged her with one of Peter's pills, tried to turn her into Living Death, and how her brother, Kenny, aside from beating up Gillian, has devised a nice little earner for the pair of them by impersonating his sister.

I see why we can't involve the police. If I tell them what Kenny's been doing, then the Dastardly Dungs will retaliate by accusing Gillian of all sorts of things, and if it gets out, even if she doesn't go to court, her reputation will be ruined. She doesn't need that.

What she does need is medical attention.

'Leni, I have to call an ambulance. She's very sick.'

Leni's continually glancing at the door.

'You're scared of your brother, aren't you?'

'No. Kenny loves me.'

'So why are you staring at that door as if all the foul fiends of hell are about to come flying through it?'

'I'm not.' She won't meet my eye.

There's a sharp intake of breath from Gillian.

'Gill?'

'It hurts.'

I turn back to Leni. 'She has to be checked over.'

Leni's jaw remains stubbornly set. 'Kenny said he'd deal with things when he gets back.'

'She could be bleeding internally.' I dial 999. 'Ambulance, please.'

Leni starts to cry.

'You took her job. You don't want to be responsible for taking her life too.'

Gillian's eyes are closed.

'Gill, wake up.'

She mutters and sighs.

'Hold on. The ambulance is on its way.'

Leni is sobbing. 'You'll tell on Kenny.'

'No, I won't. Gillian's committed a serious assault on you. You could report it to the police. I don't want that to happen, so if you keep quiet about her, I'll keep quiet about Kenny.'

Leni's still glancing at the door every few seconds.

'Are you scared of him?'

'No.'

'Then what's the problem?'

Gillian starts choking.

'Leni, help me. She's on her back. We have to move her.'

Leni doesn't move.

'If she dies I don't have a reason to protect her any more, and then who knows what I'd feel obliged to tell the police.'

This does the trick. Leni helps me put Gillian into the recovery position.

'When the ambulance comes, what should we say?'

'We'll think of something.'

When the paramedics arrive we say that Gill fell down the stairs leading up to Leni's flat. The story's a good one, embellished by lots of little details to enhance its veracity. I'm quite proud of its inventiveness.

We needn't have bothered. The paramedics, at the end of a hard night's shift, are keen to quit the hell that is Paul Robeson Buildings as soon as possible, and barely listen to our finely crafted tale. The implausibility of elderly Gill visiting her friend in the middle of the night passes them by completely. As does the bizarre collection of objects scattered round the living room. Gill's soon driven off, blue lights flashing, sirens wailing, leaving Leni and me staring at each other across the chaos of her living room.

'You'd better go before Kenny gets back.'

'Will you be all right?'

'Once he's here everything will be OK.'

As I cross the courtyard, shivering in the grey dawn, I look up at her window. She's gazing down, unsmiling. I realise she's looking beyond me, squinting into the distance.

Waiting for Kenny.

The time when . . .

. . . much against his better judgement he'd gone to the party. Someone's twentieth. At a grotty student flat. They were there, of course. He'd known they would be. If he was honest that's why he'd forced himself to go. He'd watched them all night, kissing and cuddling, dancing and feeling each other up. Indivisible two. Joined at the hip. No room for anyone else. Not even the Lion and the Witch, who'd behaved in their usual loudmouthed way – making the room buzz. Making the place rock. But he'd seen the Witch looking at them. And what he saw wasn't pretty. And the Lion – hell-bent on groping everything that moved.

Then he'd seen Warlord unpeel himself and go off somewhere. The drink had made him bold. Without stopping to think, he'd fought his way to where She leaned against the wall. She'd smiled at him, and that was it. His lips were on hers and he could feel her body through his thin shirt.

Next thing he was face down on the floor being kicked along the corridor towards the front door, and Warlord's voice was pounding in his ears. 'Don't you touch her, you fucking freak. Don't you ever touch her. Or I'll do you.'

And everyone was laughing and cheering.

She shouldn't have smiled.

That's how they operate. They string you along till you don't know what you're doing, then when you make your move they back off and before you know it you're destroyed.

People who behave like that should pay.

No question of it.

He had every sympathy with all those who'd ever been tricked and bamboozled by crazy love.

Every sympathy.

THIRTY-FOUR

When I reach home I collapse into bed and fall into a dreamless sleep, from which I don't emerge until early afternoon.

In the clear light of day, last night seems utterly surreal. Did Gillian really try to turn her usurper into a living painting, only to be beaten up by Leni's transvestite brother? Is it the right decision not to involve the police? Kenny Dang is clearly a dangerous man. Who knows what he might do next? On the other hand, the last thing Gillian needs is for Leni to press charges against her for assault.

Poor Gillian.

If only I'd been more supportive, maybe I could have prevented her from losing it in such a spectacular way. I phone the hospital and enquire after her. I'm told she's sleeping and won't be fit for visitors until later.

Joshua still hasn't returned. His portfolio, and my note, lay undisturbed on my bed when I staggered upstairs in the grey dawn, blind with fatigue. I had to push them aside in order to lie down.

Where could he be?

The phone rings.

'Rosa, I know I'm being a pain, but I simply couldn't wait any longer. When you didn't phone back last night I assumed you hadn't been able to contact Leni. Any luck today?'

Caro.

In the midst of the night's high drama, I'd completely forgotten to ask Leni about Steve Pyne. Although after what I'd seen in Gillian's notebook, there didn't seem to be much doubt.

Time to shatter Caro's illusions once and for all.

'I don't know anything for certain . . .'

'But?'

'But it isn't looking good.'

'Oh no.' She starts to sob.

'Steve was seen with Leni, or rather . . .'

I realise I don't know whether he was seen with Leni. It could equally well have been Kenny. And if it was Kenny, what new light might that throw on Steve's death? Particularly as the last sighting was on the day he died.

And Kenny Dang is clearly no Boy Scout.

Do I tell Caro about the Kenny/Leni double act?

I think not. Firstly because it would break the secrecy pact I'd made with Leni, and thus dump Gillian in it, and secondly because it would only encourage Caro in her belief that Steve's death was a result of something shady.

But what if it was? What if Kenny for some reason had killed Steve? Then the police would have found some evidence. Wouldn't they?

Meanwhile Caro's still speaking. 'Who saw them? Where?'

'They were spotted twice, once having a drink in a bar off Leicester Square, and once on the morning he died outside a pub in Southampton Row. On his bike . . .'

Silence.

'Caro?'

'You say he was seen with Leni. That means the information didn't come from her. Have you not spoken to her?'

'Well . . .'

'Rosa, I won't believe he was sleeping with that woman unless she confirms it.'

'She's not exactly reliable. How will you know she's telling the truth?'

'I'll know.'

'Why don't I give you her number? Then you can ask her yourself.'

'No!' She's distraught. 'She won't tell *me* she's screwed my dead boyfriend, but she might tell you. Try again, Rosa. Please. I'm going mad here. I don't know whether to mourn him or curse him.'

Was Steve Pyne mentioned during Leni's nocturnal revelations? Caro interrupts my struggle to remember. Her voice is sharp with suspicion.

'Did you say they were seen on the morning he died?'

'Yes.'

'It simply doesn't make sense. He was so keen to show you his stuff. I know him. He wouldn't let any woman, whoever she was, interfere with promoting his work. There's more to this than meets the eye.'

'What do you mean?'

349

'I've told you. Steve's death isn't as straightforward as it seems. Someone else is involved. Someone who has a grudge against him.'

'Like who?'

'Larry.'

'*Larry?*'

'All those threats he'd been making against Steve. He loathed him. If he thought Steve was in the running for the Consort Park project . . .'

'What are you saying? That Larry somehow engineered Steve's death in order to stop one of his sculptures being bought for a minor London park? Come on, Caro. This is real life. Real people don't do things like that, particularly people in Larry's position. You've been watching too much telly.'

'But what if he wanted to stop Steve meeting you, and asked Leni to get him drunk? Steve would have been devastated when he sobered up. He was in a frightful state anyway. It could have been enough to tip him over the edge. He'd have broken his promise to me about drinking and he'd also have blown his chances of selling a piece to you. Drinking himself to death might have seemed a logical option.'

'But—'

'If Larry had any part whatsoever in it, I'll never forgive him.'

We like to think we can second-guess those we love. That we know what their reactions to any given scenario will be. But we don't. Not really. Human beings are a mass of unpredictable impulses. Unlike people in books, they don't always run true to type. Caro was convinced she knew what Steve would do in any given circumstances. But she hadn't met Kenny Dang in full drag. I wouldn't take a bet on Steve's commitment to his work, or his commitment to Caro, winning out over Kenny's persuasive charms. With Kenny on the case, Larry L'Estrange would have no need to plot Steve's downfall.

I don't say this to her. If it makes her feel better to believe in some sinister scheme to ruin Steve, then let her run with it for a while longer.

'I'll talk to Leni, Caro. I promise. I'll find out exactly what's going on.'

'And I'm going to look at the DVD film that I found in Steve's video camera. There might be something useful there. Let me know when you've spoken to Leni.'

Leni – the last person in the world I'd choose to communicate with at the moment.

Make the call, Rosa. Stop being a wuss.

Leni's voice is dull and flat. 'Oh. It's you.'

No enquiries about Gillian's health, or indeed any reference to the events of last night. Extraordinary.

'I've a question for you. I wouldn't ask, but it's very important to Caro.'

'Yeah?'

'Were you having a thing with Steve Pyne?'

'What?'

'You were seen with him on a couple of occasions recently, including the day he died.'

Silence.

'You can see how it might look to Caro . . .'

Silence.

'She badly needs to know.'

Silence.

I take a deep breath. 'It wasn't you, was it? It was Kenny.'

Silence.

'Leni, you're different from your brother. You don't like hurting people. You feel bad about Gillian, I know you do. And if Kenny was messing with Steve, I know you'd feel bad about that too. Because Kenny might think it's acceptable to cheat and lie, but you don't. Is that why you went to Steve's funeral? To make up for what Kenny'd done to ruin Caroline's relationship?'

Silence.

'Kenny wants the best for you. You and he have a special bond, don't you? That's why you went along with all his plans. You couldn't bear to disappoint him. But if you've any sympathy for Caro, please tell the truth about him and Steve Pyne.'

Then I'm holding the phone away from my ear because Leni's shouting.

'Stuff you and your cod psychology, thinking I'm too stupid to notice your bullshit. Kenny had nothing to do with Steve Pyne. It was me. I was interviewing him for the *Correspondent*, the weekend review.'

Could this be true?

'Kenny didn't want me to go anywhere near the guy after what he did to me at Rob's private view. But I told him it was my job, and I could handle it.'

'Steve was supposed to be meeting me on the morning he died. To sell some work. It was very important to him,' I tell her. 'So why would he miss that appointment just to see you? Surely you could have arranged another time.'

'I had a deadline. I needed half an hour more with him, and

it had to be that morning. He dropped me off here with loads of time to make your meeting.'

'So what happened?'

'How should I know? He said he was going straight back to his studio.'

She sounds convincing enough. I feel a fool. I'd been so convinced that Kenny was involved. Time for the big climb down.

'Thanks for telling me. It will mean everything to Caro that Steve wasn't two-timing her.'

'If you don't mind, I'm expecting an urgent call.'

She cuts the connection. I don't care. Steve was not dallying with the Dungs.

I call Caro. It feels great to be delivering good news for once. After I've finished there's another of those silences I'm becoming so familiar with today.

'Caro?'

'So where is it?' she asks.

'Where's what?'

'The article in the *Correspondent*. I haven't seen any interview with Steve Pyne by Leni Dang, have you?'

She's right.

'Maybe they spiked it when they heard he'd committed suicide. They probably thought it was inappropriate to run it.'

'Why didn't Steve tell me he was being interviewed by one of our biggest national dailies? It's the kind of exposure he longed for. A dream opportunity to set his career back on track.'

'Perhaps he wanted it to be a surprise.'

'Steve didn't do surprises.'

'He probably just forgot.'

'Hardly. I'm going to phone the *Correspondent* and find out.'

The only good thing about this conversation is that Caro is sounding strong and purposeful. A massive improvement on yesterday. She obviously needs to absorb herself in making a mystery out of Steve's death. It's her way of stopping herself from going under.

Later, I drive to the hospital to see my poor battered Gillian. The news is good; there's no internal bleeding, just extensive bruising. Gill's propped up in bed wearing a hospital nightgown and looking desperately forlorn. What must she have been through in the last few weeks? And what will it mean for her reputation if it becomes common gossip that she's been following her rival like some avenging Fury?

Well, no one's going to find out.

Apart from me, only Leni and Kenny know, and the dirt I have on them will keep their lips well and truly buttoned.

'Rosa! Why are you squandering your valuable time on visits to delinquent old women?'

'How are you?'

'Bruised body, bruised ego. Shame, self-disgust. Take your pick.' She's smiling, but her normally mellifluous voice is shaky.

'Do you want to talk?'

'What's to say? I completely lost the plot.'

'No, you didn't.'

'Maybe I was taken over by aliens.'

Gill's attempt to joke her way out of despair isn't working. Her lip trembles so much as she talks that she has to put her hand up to stop it.

'It wasn't the real you.'

'Who else was it? I wasn't deluded or deranged. I knew exactly what I was doing.'

'But—'

'No buts. I know you're trying to be kind, but I have to live with myself. I knew what I was doing. Let me claim responsibility for my own folly.'

'Give yourself a break.'

'Give me one good reason why I should?'

'Gill, one of the things people love about you is your kindness. Now it's time to be kind to yourself.'

'I could die of embarrassment. And humiliation. And disgust.'

'Stop it. If you'd broken your leg, or developed cancer you wouldn't be so hard on yourself.'

'What if it happens again? How will I know that every time someone does something to upset me, I won't suddenly go cuckoo?'

'It isn't sudden though, is it? It must have been coming on for ages.'

Gillian nods.

'Ever since Peter died?'

She's too choked to speak. So am I. *There but for the grace of God.*

'Why didn't you tell someone how depressed you were?'

'No one likes a party-pooper.'

'Oh Gill . . .'

'People are great in the beginning, but after a while you can tell they think you should just pull yourself together. Nothing was going to bring him back, so I decided to take the pills and ignore the feelings.'

'You should have trusted your friends. Talked to us. Told us when you felt down.'

Now the tears really do flow.

'I've been so lonely, Rosa.'

'Why didn't you say?'

'Who wants a Moaning Minnie spoiling the fun? People die – it's a fact of life. You have to get used to it. No sense in shoving it in everyone's faces. Best to get on with things and forget what's gone.'

'But you haven't forgotten. You bottled up all that sadness inside you until it burst.'

'I thought I'd found the way to cope.'

'How?'

'Work. Twenty-four seven. My job on the *Correspondent*, and my book about Elena Dias. When I unearthed her diary it was so exciting. So absorbing. A magical quest. I could put Peter out of my mind for hours at a time when I was on Elena's trail. And since she was dead already, I knew there were no more nasty surprises in store: she couldn't be taken away from me.' She grimaces. 'Except that now she has.'

'What do you mean?'

'Elena's as dead to me now as Peter.'

'Don't be daft. When you're better, you can go back to your research and finish the book.'

Gillian shakes her head. 'It's all bound up with Leni Dang now. I don't think I can get past that. Every time I look at one of her paintings I'll think of Leni and how I tried to . . .'

'Leni's OK. You didn't harm her, just gave her a fright. Do her good, if you ask me.'

'Leni – Elena. Almost the same.'

It wasn't the only strange parallel: Elena Dias, Kenny Dang – gender benders both. I don't point this out to Gill. The less she remembers about Creepy Kenny, the better.

'How's Caro?'

I tell her about Caro's suspicion that Larry's involved in Steve's death.

'I can't believe I sent her that letter about Steve and Leni. In my own mind I'd convinced myself I was doing her a favour. But if I'm honest I know that I was so hell-bent on damaging Leni that I didn't care how it would make Caro feel.'

'Leni says she was interviewing Steve for the *Correspondent*. She seemed to be telling the truth, but . . .'

Gillian's looking agitated. This isn't the time to upset her with more mysteries.

'When are they letting you out of here?'

'In a day or so.'

'I want you to come and stay with us.'

She squeezes my hand. 'Bless you, Rosa, but I've already made a decision on that one.'

'What?'

'If I'm to pull myself out of this, I need professional help. I'm going to check into a clinic for a few weeks – get myself sorted.'

'But—'

'No buts. That's what's happening.'

A bit of me seizes on her words with enormous relief. Although Gill seems remarkably sane today, these situations can be three steps forward, two back. I don't know whether I'm strong enough to be the rock that Gillian needs.

But then I feel ashamed. I've just told her I'd be there for her, and here I am rejoicing that she's made other plans. I've let her down once by not being there; I'm not going to do it again.

'Please come – I'd love to have you. Surely it'd be better for you to get well in the company of friends rather than a pack of strangers?'

Gillian takes my hand. 'You're a dear old thing, but it wouldn't work. I need to fall apart and be in pieces for a while. If I came to you, I'd be on my best behaviour. I'd want to protect you from my misery.'

'But—'

'You were the one who made the comparison between physical and mental illness. When you're physically ill you sometimes need to be hospitalised so that the professionals can take over. It's the same with mental illness. Right now I need the professionals. I need to misbehave in controlled circumstances.'

She's smiling, but I know she's deadly serious. And she's right. But before I give in, there's one last thing I have to be sure of: that the real reason she won't stay is because she wants to hide her drinking – something she hasn't yet admitted. Depression, yes. Alcoholism – never mentioned. It's difficult, however, even in the context of our increased intimacy, for me to accuse her of being a lush. But I must give her the opportunity to speak up. How to phrase it, without blundering in feet-first in my usual way?

'OK, I understand. But if you're worried about having to cope with people drinking in front of you, I promise that it wouldn't be a problem. I don't keep much alcohol in the house. I can go for weeks without a drop of anything passing my lips . . .' I stop.

And feel the blush creeping across my face. I've done it again. It sounds as if I'm crowing over the fact that, unlike her, I don't remotely have an alcohol problem.

But Gill doesn't rise to the bait. 'I'm not supposed to drink anyway, not when I'm taking these anti-depressants.'

Is this being in denial? Or plain old-fashioned fibbing?

'But that day I came round to your flat . . .'

She laughs. 'Oh, that. I was experimenting. Thought a couple of bottles of whisky might take the edge off things. They didn't. Just made me sick. My body wasn't used to that amount of booze and it couldn't cope, particularly on top of the pills. But getting back to what I said just now, I've no intention of burdening you with my batty presence. I'm off to let someone else take the strain. They charge a king's ransom, so I shall give them hell – make sure I get my money's worth.'

'Well, whenever you're ready, whenever *you* feel like it, I want you to promise me you'll come.'

'I promise. Although you don't know what you're taking on. As a house-guest I have the reputation of Typhoon Mary. You'll need a whole team of contract cleaners to fix things after I've gone.' She laughs. 'Fancy you thinking I was a drunk.'

I look into her eyes. I have to believe her.

I do believe her.

I think.

Gillian stared at Rosa Thorn's retreating back. The afternoon sun shone through the window in a broad ray, transforming Rosa's dark red hair into a flaming halo, and turning her into shimmering insubstantial ectoplasm, floating down the endless hospital corridor back to her own distant world of happenings and interactions. Gillian wanted to shout after her, beg her to come back, to stay for a while – ask her, even, just to turn round and smile. If only I could catch a last glimpse of her smile, she thought. That wide gash of a smile that lit up Rosa's whole face and everything else within a five-metre radius.

But she kept silent. Her bed was at the end of the ward so she had a view of the corridor which stretched away to vanishing point, and she watched until Rosa's tall, rangy figure became a tiny speck, and then vanished. How she longed to eat her own pride-riddled words. *I shan't stay with you. I'm going to a clinic. I need the professionals. I need to fall apart on my own – my friends would only be in the way.*

What had possessed her? Why couldn't she accept Rosa's offer, grab it with both hands? It was what she wanted, more than anything. What she ached for, to heal and mend in Rosa's cosy house. Be part of that chaotic, casual family life. Dear old Aunt Gill.

But that was just it. She wasn't part of Rosa's family, however welcoming they might be. She wasn't their blood. She wasn't tied to them for better or worse, unconditionally tolerated whatever. She was disposable. Rosa's Charity of the Month. Poor old Gillian, needs a bit of TLC, so be nice, kids . . .

Until they all became tired of her moods, her depressions, her eccentricities, her large intrusive presence cluttering up their space, always there, always in the way. She didn't want to stick around to hear the whispered voices in the kitchen. *How long is she planning to stay? When is she going, Mum?* She wasn't their granny, or a well-loved aunt who'd known them since birth, slipping them illicit sweeties and fifty-pence pieces when Mummy wasn't looking, and listening to their childish concerns. She was just boring old Gillian, a recently acquired friend of their mother's, who'd gone bonkers and to whom they had to be kind and polite.

She knew she was doing the right thing. She'd glimpsed the infinitesimal moment of panic in Rosa's eyes after she'd made her offer. It was gone almost before it happened, but Gillian saw it. And now she couldn't unsee it. It was there, like a speck of dirt, blurring her field of vision, preventing her from viewing a stay with the Thorns as a wonderful, beguiling possibility.

No, thought Gillian, I have to learn to love my loneliness, make it my best friend. I'm not ready to die, it seems. Not yet. Therefore I have to devise a way of living that draws me away from the void squatting in the middle of my existence, making me mad. I have to find a way of being that's not dependent on other people for its joys and delights. Elena managed it. She loved her life – lived the way she wanted to, was solitary but never lonely, and kept her secrets until death.

I can do that, she thought. Can't I?

A little voice in her head whispered, *How do you know Elena wasn't lonely?*

Because she said so in her diary.

The little voice spoke again, heavy with irony. *You think a person tells their diary the truth? Do me a favour, Gillian.*

He liked to feel that he'd built up a special relationship with each and every corpse he worked on. It was part of doing the job properly. Part of the magic.

But last night's body had been different, for reasons that he couldn't acknowledge. Even to himself.

He stood in the antiquarian shop off Charing Cross Road, waiting for news of whether he'd been successful in his bid for the Tuscan breviary he'd been coveting for so long. To divert himself he thumbed through a Victorian edition of one of his favourite plays: Marlowe's *Faustus*.

'Why, this is hell, nor am I out of it.'

He spoke Mephistopheles' words aloud into the dusty air and truly understood them for the first time.

'Why, this is hell, nor am I out of it.'

He longed to off-load onto someone. Usually he talked to Flavia, but in the circumstances she was the last person he could tell.

This was probably where a wife would come in useful.

He imagined what it would be like to unburden yourself to someone who loved you unconditionally. The way Rosa Thorn seemed to love her husband, even though he was dead and gone. Rosa was a very understanding woman. Maybe she'd understand what he'd done.

If he explained things properly.

She would understand.

He'd make her.

One way or the other.

THIRTY-FIVE

When I leave the hospital the heat slams into me in a great thick slab. I lean against a lamp-post, a hot prickly sweat breaking out all over my body.

Then I realise it's not the heat that's making me feel strange, but something I thought I'd put behind me.

Unless I'm much mistaken it's the beginning of a panic attack.

After Rob died I'd had them for months, particularly during the unfolding horrors of last winter. At my lowest point I couldn't set foot in Consort Park without feeling I was going to die.

But time and a short course of cognitive therapy had put paid to all that.

Until now.

I take deep breaths, long and slow, and focus on what could be responsible for this sudden regression. I allow my mind to free-associate and trawl for clues: Gillian's solitary figure in the severe hospital bed, haunted eyes belying her feisty words of dismissal; Joshua in Rob's clothes with Rob's face and hair, scribbling fictitious diary entries in Rob's handwriting; Mike, selfish insensitive shit, and Jess, my Jess, metamorphosing into a stranger. Once again I'm in a familiar place, a place I never wanted to revisit. A place of menace, deceit and violence.

For a moment the tectonic plates shift and I'm slipping between the cracks.

The people in my life – now I see them. Now I don't.

Even my children – untouchable, unseeable, unknowable on the other side of the world. Not needing me any more.

I am alone.

A passing stranger jostles me, and the spell is broken. I lean against the lamp-post, rivulets of sweat trickling down between my breasts.

Rosa the Drama Queen. Indulging in a bout of histrionics in the middle of a crowded London street.

But the roaring in my ears is subsiding and the darkness lurking around my peripheral vision is fast fading. Reality once more bites. Thank God.

And what could be more real than Jess? Hers is the image that remains. Her mouth, twisted and distorted. *Some things never change.* What did she mean? She's my dearest friend. If I've hurt her unknowingly, if there's something festering between us that needs to see the light, then the sooner it's dredged up, the better. Mike's triggered this hostility, but he's not the root cause. There's something else. Something going right back to the beginning. Something she touched on the last time we spoke. It needs to be sorted.

I'll go to her house right now, I think. I won't tell her I'm coming. I'll catch her on the hop.

THE ART OF DYING

As I travel back to Consort Park, weakly grateful that the attack has passed, I wonder whether this is a good idea. But the imperative to see Jess is strong so I brush aside my misgivings.

She's in. But hardly welcoming.

She opens the door and glares at me. She looks really rough. Blotchy face, tangled, matted curls and a moth-eaten T-shirt and tracksuit bottoms fit only for the recycling bin.

'Can I come in?'

For a moment I think she's about to shut the door in my face. Eventually she turns and walks back down the hall to the kitchen, leaving the door open for me to follow. She sits down heavily at the table, picks up a half-smoked cigarette from a brimming ashtray and takes a gulp of wine from a grubby glass.

She doesn't offer me anything.

'Where's Lozz?' I ask.

'At my mum's.'

'We have to talk.'

She won't look at me.

'I can't believe that you'd think for even one second that I'd do the dirty on you with Mike.'

No response.

'He's been a bastard, and I'm really sorry, but it was nothing to do with me. You must know that.'

Jess downs another mouthful of wine. I wait for her to say something, but she doesn't.

'Watch my lips,' I say desperately. 'Mike and I do not have, never have had, and never will have any kind of sexual relationship. Mike's an egotistical shit – always was, always will be. You know that. He's messed you about, and deserves to be shot.

365

I've seen him this weekend and given him a piece of my mind. He says he's sorry, but I don't think he fully appreciates the damage he's done. Love's just a bit of a game as far as he's concerned, and the fact that you're one of his best friends is neither here nor there. Jess, you really need to get over him, and let go of this, or it'll make your life a misery.'

'Shut the fuck up!' Jess throws her glass, still half-full of wine, at the wall. The sound of glass shards hitting the floor reverberates into the astonished silence.

'Don't sodding tell me what I need,' she hisses. 'I'll tell you what I don't need. You coming here rubbing my nose in it.'

'What do you mean?'

'Can't you see how it diminishes me, for you to dismiss him as a piece of shit?'

'But the way he's treated you—'

'I'd like to keep just a little self-respect if it's OK with you. Stop lecturing me on Mike like I don't know him at all and you're the fount of all wisdom.'

'I only—'

'And stop insinuating that I'm fucking stupid to have been taken in by him in the first place.'

'I'm not—'

'If you thought he was such a bastard, why've you stayed friends with him all these years? Oh, guess what – you must be just as gullible as thick old me.'

My heart is pounding. In all our years of friendship Jess has never been like this. We've had the odd row, but never anything like this. It's as if she hates me. I want to rush home and bawl like a baby. But I came to get to the bottom of whatever's bothering her, which quite clearly isn't just to do with Mike.

'The other day – all that stuff about college. What did you mean?'

'Forget it.'

Don't you just hate it when people say that?

'No, I won't. I don't understand what you were on about – all that piffle about my fan club et cetera.'

'Just fuck off.'

'We've been friends for ever. I thought nothing could change that. I thought in a shifting world there was always you . . .'

'Listen to yourself.' Mimicking my voice: '"In a shifting world there was always you". Always *your* fucking shifting world – never mine. I've just been the all-singing, all-dancing support system.'

'Well, excuse me.' I'm getting angry too now. 'There was I thinking we supported each other. Like a see-saw – you bouncing me up when I was down, and me doing the same for you. My mistake.'

Jess looks at me again, and this time it's not hatred I see, but a dreadful resignation.

'What are you saying?' I go on. 'That all these years I've been the take take take to your give give give?'

Her voice is hardly audible. 'No.'

'Then what do you mean?'

'It's hard to explain.'

'Try.'

She lights another cigarette, pours herself more wine into an empty cup and spends some time rearranging the ashtray and the bottle on the table. Finally, she speaks.

'I've always felt like the supporting act to your main event,' she tells me, sighing. 'The pretty girl's ugly best friend – good for comic relief, a real laugh, court jester in the court of Queen Rosa. I'd kind of got used to the feeling – buried it away, really. Put it in a separate compartment to all the things I love about you. Until this thing with Mike.'

More of the same. Like the other day. Why is she saying these things?

I know why. She's hurting badly and lashing out in pain. But why trash our friendship with these ludicrous misrepresentations of the past?

'This thing with Mike, which has absolutely nothing to do with me.'

'Whatever.'

'Why are you doing this?'

'I used to sit at that corner table in the bar, at college, doing my cap and bells routine, making the blokes laugh, and all the time I'd watch them watching you. I'd take the piss out of them something rotten, if you remember. At least it got me noticed. It got my leg over as well. All those sad little men who wanted to screw you were so frustrated they settled quite happily for the fat lady as consolation prize. And while I was conducting various half-arsed affairs with fucking morons, and getting the constant benefit of your profound insights whenever things went tits-up, you fell for Rob and became one half of the fucking Golden Couple – the bright flame to all us dowdy little moths.'

'This is ridiculous.'

'Everything's always gone right for you, hasn't it? Perfect

marriage. Perfect family. And when Rob's painting took off, then it was the perfect celebrity couple—'

'And then he died.'

For a split second Jess looks embarrassed.

'All this Golden Couple outshining poor mousey little Jess shit – it's crap,' I say loudly. 'You were always the fun one. If anyone hung around us at college, it was because of you – Miss Life and Soul of the Party.'

'I had to do something to keep my end up.'

'Oh, please!'

She's rewriting the past. Turning it into something I don't recognise. Turning my life into something I don't recognise.

'As for relationships, you've always said that sharing your life with a man on a permanent basis was your idea of the seven circles of hell. Variety, you said, was the spice of life.'

'Front. Pure front.'

'I don't believe you.'

'Suit yourself.'

'What about Lozz? You're conveniently missing him out of the equation. You've always said he's the best thing that ever happened to you.'

'He is . . . but he's not Danny and Anna. He won't be going out joyfully into the world to make his way. All he has to look forward to when I die is an institution.'

'And this is my fault?'

'I didn't say that.'

'You talk as if I'm some sort of egocentric diva who only ever views life from her own selfish perspective, and who's treated you as a poor little also-ran.'

'An also-ran. You got it. It feels like your life events have been the only ones that really counted. Even from my viewpoint. Pathetic, isn't it?'

I'm stunned into silence.

People. Now you see them, now you don't.

I'm looking at Jess as if through a kaleidoscope. I watch, helpless as the pattern shifts and changes into something completely unrecognisable.

'I'm sorry,' she whispers. 'I did tell you not to go there.'

'You got that right,' I say, and blunder towards the door, my eyes blinded by tears.

Words can destroy faster than a guided missile. They're twice as deadly, and much more accurate. Was any part of what she said true? If so, what can I do to repair the damage?

Do I *want* to repair the damage?

Was my twenty-year-old friendship, one of the bedrocks of my life, now completely destroyed?

The time when . . .
> *. . . time itself folds back and everything becomes as it once was.*
> *As it once should have been . . .*
> *Cosmic string.*
> *That time is now . . .*
> *Thine hour has come, the great wind blows . . .*

THIRTY-SIX

What are the ties that bind?

Fewer than you think.

Blood. That's what it comes down to in the end.

Families are always there. They may let you down. You may let them down. They may show their love in all sorts of unsatisfactory ways that you don't begin to understand. You may do things which appal them, but ultimately they are the ones who'll be there. In the end. At the end. Because that viscous substance running through your veins and arteries runs through theirs too, and you can't change it or deny it. It's what binds us together in spite of rows and estrangements and sometimes sheer bloody dislike. Friends may come and friends may go, but family is the only certainty.

At least that's my jaundiced take on the subject today.

Today I feel that friendship is a gaudy charade, a painted pantomime, full of promises and declarations for the duration of the show, then disintegrating once the curtain falls and the lights are dimmed. It's easy to walk away from a friend. The imperative of blood isn't there. There's no reason to cling on. No obligation. You decide you want out, and off you go. What's to keep you?

Nothing.

But doesn't the same thing apply to family? I think of my own parents who cut me off twenty years ago for marrying a black man, and even knowing that Rob is now dead, don't want any contact with their mixed-race grandchildren. Surely that disproves everything I've just said.

No. Because my mum and dad are still in my head. Rooted deep in my psyche, shoving themselves into my face whenever I look at my fingers and see my father's ridged nails, whenever I watch Anna toss her head in exactly the same way as my mother. They might not be any help or comfort, stewing as they still are after all these years, in their bigoted juices, but I can't obliterate them from my mind. A part of me's still hoping. A tiny bit of me still aches to fly into my mother's arms and let her make everything better. It won't happen, but I can't let them go, because they're part of me, blood and bone.

I used to say that my friends were the family I'd chosen for myself. Now I don't know.

What is it that binds me to Jess?

Our shared past. Which turns out to be a myth.

So what am I left with? Memories. False memories.

It's blood that binds. Mothers, fathers, brothers, sisters, sons, daughters. Brothers-in-law?

As I walk into my house, I think of Joshua. What ties bind me to him? He's not my blood.

373

But he's the next best thing: Rob's blood. And Danny's and Anna's.

I go to his room. His pitifully few things are scattered around on the chairs and on the floor. I look at the photo of the Thorn family, sitting on his bedside table in its shiny new frame. For some reason the newness of the frame brings a lump to my throat.

Joshua is Rob's brother.

There's my blood and bone imperative, lodged in the cheap chrome frame. The ache to belong to his dead brother's family vibrates off it like some psychic tuning-fork.

I open the drawer. The notebook's still there. A fantasy for a lonely boy. What's the harm in it?

I can't wait for Joshua to return so that we can really talk, but where is he? The portfolio of his beautiful photographs still lies on my bed, undisturbed since I moved it in order to sleep last night. My stomach starts to churn.

Where is he? Why has he not returned home for so long? It's not like him.

I no longer feel frightened *of* Joshua. I feel frightened *for* him.

This time I won't ignore my gut feelings. But what to do?

What do I know of Joshua's comings and goings? Precious little. My only lead is Zander Zinovieff. If Joshua's working for him, then he might be at the gallery.

I'm searching for the number of *Nature Morte* when the phone rings. Maybe it's Jess saying she's been playing a stupid joke on me. Maybe not.

The answering machine picks up.

'It's Leni. Please ring me . . . I need to tell you someth—' The message ends mid-sentence.

THE ART OF DYING

I continue my trawl of the directory and have just located the number of *Nature Morte* when the phone rings. It's Leni again.

'Rosa, I lied earlier. It wasn't me with Steve Pyne on the day he died so it must have been Kenny. Rosa, I think Kenny may have killed him. That's why I came to the funeral – to see if I could find out any more about what had happened. I know it sounds far-fetched, but the way Kenny feels about me isn't normal . . . It's too extreme. He was obsessed by the way Steve treated me at Rob's opening. He felt I'd somehow been dishonoured. I told him he was overreacting, but he said Steve needed a taste of his own medicine. I found out he was seeing him – as Kiki. I'm so scared. I haven't seen him since he attacked Gillian. It's how he behaves when he's really angry about something. He knows I worry and that's how he punishes me. He must have come back while I was asleep, realised Gillian wasn't there, and gone off in a strop. I'm frightened that he's gone after her . . . The thing about Kenny is, he won't let things go. He said she had to pay and he'll make sure she does. If she's with you, you must be careful.'

At this point I hear another voice, and the line goes dead. But almost immediately the phone rings again. This voice has a strong London accent, and enunciates very carefully in the way old people do who aren't used to modern technology.

'Hello? . . . Hello? . . . This is Mrs Ethel Prewitt with a message for . . .' (at this point I hear her hiss, 'What's 'er name?' and Leni muttering in the background) '. . . Mrs Thorn. Please disregard what Leni just said. She's a very highly-strung girl and she's talking a load of piffle. This business about her brother killin' some bloke's just so much nonsense. He's a little so-and-so but that don't make him no killer. Leni's got 'erself into a state, that's all. She's like that sometimes – says all sorts of daft things. She don't look like she's eaten for a week, so I'm going to cook 'er a nice meal, make sure she has a good sleep and by tomorrow she'll be as right as rain. She's very sorry for botherin' you and hopes you'll forget everything she said.' (Long pause, laboured breathing.) 'Thank you.'

Mrs Ethel Prewitt sounds reassuringly down-to-earth. And Leni was completely over the top. Suspecting her brother of killing Steve? Please.

On the other hand, Kenny may not be a killer, but he did beat up Gillian. I lock all the windows and put the chain on the front door. Should I call the police? But if they start harassing him, he'll spill the beans about Gill's little escapade with Leni.

But what if he *is* a murderer?

Is it really likely that he'd kill someone just for slobbering over his sister? Leni probably loves a drama and I get the feeling that part of her revels in her brother's over-protective posturings. Kenny sounds like a bully, but that doesn't make him a murderer, particularly over something so trivial. Added to which the police found absolutely nothing suspicious about Steve's death.

The phone rings again. Fresh revelations from Leni and Mrs Prewitt?

It's neither of them. It's the man I most want to talk to: Zander Zinovieff. Is he psychic or something?

'Rosa?'

'Zander! I was just about to phone you.'

'It's Joshua.'

'What's wrong? What's the matter with him?'

The trouble with having someone major in your life die on you unexpectedly is that for ever after, at the drop of a hat, you jump to the worst conclusions. Your nearest and dearest are always, in your eyes, teetering on the edge of extinction.

'He's just taken a little tumble, that's all. He was up a ladder hanging a painting, and he leaned over too far and lost his balance.'

'He fell off a ladder! Is he all right?'

'Nothing's broken, but he did take a bit of a bump to the head.'

'Concussion? Have you called an ambulance?'

'Not necessary. Really. He just feels a bit woozy, that's all. He wondered whether you'd be able to come and collect him.'

'I'm on my way.'

The time when . . .
  . . . base metal turns to gold.
  The transforming power of Art. Himself the catalyst.
  Farewell, Willie Wanka.

THIRTY-SEVEN

When I arrive at *Nature Morte*, Zander's peering through the window, waiting for me.

'Is he all right?'

'He's fine. He's fast asleep.'

'Asleep! You shouldn't let him sleep, not with concussion.'

'He isn't concussed. Some shut-eye's exactly what he needs. He was working till all hours.'

'Can I see him?'

'Sure.'

He leads me to a tiny room behind his office, which contains a narrow bed and little else except a chair on which Joshua's glasses sit, and under which his shoes are neatly aligned.

'When I'm hanging a show I sometimes kip here instead of going home. It's very basic, but it serves my simple needs.'

Zander, if only you knew how uninterested I am at this particular moment in your simple needs.

Then I feel guilty. What a bitch I am. This man has at least shown an interest in Joshua's work, even if he ultimately turned it down, and he tried to soften the blow by giving him a job. And he's taken care of him after his fall, tucking him up neatly in his very own little bed.

Joshua is breathing evenly, and looking like Rob.

'See? He's fine.'

'Yes.' I'm limp with relief. 'Thanks for contacting me.'

'No probs.'

'I'd better take him home.'

'Leave it for a while. Sleep really is the best medicine. Let me tempt you to a drink. I mix a lethal Sunset Boulevard. The sun's over the yardarm, so what do you say? Come into the office.'

No quick escape then. This is my penance for thinking bitchy thoughts: a yawning expanse of time sipping lurid cocktails and listening to Zander's tales of life among the great and the good. I try to focus on the glass-half-full aspect of the situation: while I'm in here being entertained, I'm not out there being dumped on by my best friend, or dodging a homicidal transvestite.

I trail obediently after him to his office with its deeply cushioned crimson sofas and heavily laden Art-Deco drinks trolley, and watch him outshine Tom Cruise in his deft manipulation of a silver cocktail shaker.

And he's certainly up to date with all the goss.

'I was at the Hurlingham Club the other day, playing doubles with Tim and Lucy, when one of the Saudi princes landed his heli on the next-door court . . .'

Or: 'Guy tells me that Madge is deeply into herring oil night cream at the moment. He says she smells like Grimsby when the boats come in.'

Or: 'Apparently Harry's secretly engaged to a Swedish masseuse. Wills and Charles are furious, but he won't give her up. Says he's damned if he'll do a Princess Margaret.'

He knows everything about everybody and despite myself I egg him on to greater and greater indiscretion. But eventually, I catch sight of the clock above the huge wall-sized mirror opposite his desk, and realise that over an hour has passed.

'I must wake Joshua.'

'Actually, there's something I'd like to show you.'

My heart sinks. In spite of the fact that I've spent the past hour enjoying his repertoire of colourful stories, there's something about Zander that I find hard to take. And the pleading tone he's just adopted sets my teeth on edge.

'You've taken such a keen interest in the work I do here.'

I have? The time I spent going round his gallery with him the other week being polite has somehow mistakenly given him the impression that I think *Nature Morte* is the best thing since sliced bread.

Why did I never learn how to extricate myself gracefully from tedious social situations?

'I think I ought to—'

'You'll find it interesting.'

'Well . . .'

'Pretty please?'

What can I say?

'I must check on Joshua first.'

'Sure.'

He's still fast asleep.

'He ought not to be left alone.'

381

'Emil's here. He'll keep an eye on him.'

He crosses to the huge wall mirror and presses a button. The mirror glides to one side, revealing a steel door. At a casual glance there's no way of opening it – no handle, no obvious entry system, just a small disc on the right-hand side sunk into the smooth, shiny surface. It's so small that unless you were looking hard, you'd probably miss it. Zander removes a steel pin from the inside of his lapel. He presses it into the disc and the door immediately slides back. He ushers me into the dark space beyond, replacing the pin behind his lapel, saying, with more than a hint of pride, 'Micro-chip in this little chappie contains all the data needed to admit me. Clever stuff, eh?'

'Alice through the Looking Glass,' I murmur.

Zander laughs. 'Open Sesame,' he counters. 'Come, let me show you my treasure.'

THIRTY-EIGHT

The mirror slides shut behind us and we're in total darkness.

Was this wise, Rosa?

He switches on a very dim light. We're standing in a narrow corridor. I don't like it.

'I think I'll give this a miss if you don't mind,' I say. 'I feel a bit claustrophobic.'

'You'll soon get used to it. Claustrophobia's all in the mind, anyway.'

'I know. That's the whole point.'

'Please, Rosa. It means a lot to me.' His eyes plead.

'Five minutes.'

His relief is excessive. 'You're such a lovely person.'

Steady, Zander.

'What is this place?'

'Before I show you, I need you to know something.' He glares fiercely at me through the gloom. 'I don't *just* run a gallery.'

'Sorry?'

'You may think I'm just a businessman.' He takes a deep breath. 'But I'm not. I'm also an artist.'

'Oh.' I don't quite know how to react. Zander seems to think it's a revelation of monumental significance.

'And I want to show you my Work.'

So that's it.

Art.

I'm vastly relieved. I was beginning to feel slightly spooked. Art I can cope with. I've been coping with art in one way or another for the whole of my adult life. Particularly recently, in my new role researching for Skinny Minnie's legacy.

Maybe that's what Zander's after – a spot in Consort Park.

'Bring it on,' I say. The sooner I've praised his efforts, the sooner I'll be able to leave.

He leads me to a peephole set into the wall. 'This was my very first piece,' Zander whispers.

I'm transfixed. 'What is it?'

In the small room beyond the peephole an old man sits weeping. Tears of desolation. I can tell they've been shed many times before, and will be many times again. An endless cycle of grief.

I want to stop watching, but I can't.

A mural of a very grand room, filled with people, covers the walls. Some of the faces are sketchy, others obviously reproduced from life. The sound of applause fills the space. On a dais in front of the mural is a life-size figure in mortar board and gown, holding a rolled diploma.

A young man. A boy, really. He can't be much more than twenty. He's beautifully modelled, every detail meticulously observed.

Then something happens.

The boy moves.

Not in a clockwork, jerky way like I remember the figures at Disneyland Paris when we took the children there once as a birthday treat.

He moves like real people move.

As the applause increases, the boy gives a slight bow and says, 'Double First, Dad. I said I'd make you proud.'

The old man leaps up and embraces him. For about twenty seconds the two figures remain locked together. Then, abruptly, the applause ceases, the boy's arms drop and he is still and silent. The man stumbles back to his chair, plucks a tissue from a box on a small table beside him and scrubs angrily at his face.

The box isn't the only thing on the table. There's also a remote control. After a few moments the man picks it up and aims it towards the figure. The sound of applause once more fills the air. The whole process begins again.

'One of our senior judges,' whispers Zander. 'Married late in life. Only son. Apple of his eye. Brilliant mind. Shortly after taking a Double First at Cambridge, the boy was found dead. Heroin overdose. Verdict of Accidental Death, but the father blamed himself. Not around enough when the lad was growing up – something like that. Do you like the way I've captured the architectural stonework? Senate House, Cambridge – completely authentic in every detail.'

'What is this?' I feel deeply uncomfortable to have witnessed such private and personal torment.

'Come.'

Not that uncomfortable.

Ashamed, but unable to stop myself, I peer through the next peephole.

The room is similar in shape and size to the last, but the ambience couldn't be more different. Again there's a magnificent *trompe l'oeil* mural covering the walls. This time it depicts a restaurant, with tables, diners, waiters – the works. It looks so real, I feel I could reach through the window and steal a bread roll from a basket on one of the painted damask tablecloths. The lighting bathes the place in a soft pink glow, and in the centre of the room is a table, laid for two people. Fine china, silver cutlery and sparkling crystal glitter as they catch the light. The meal is almost at an end. Two small cups of coffee sit, untouched. One chair is empty, but on the other sits a woman. She's middle-aged, but still beautiful, the rare beauty that speaks of inner goodness. Her clothes are period, from the mid-1960s, and her hair is cut in the dolly-bird style that I dimly remember women wearing in my early childhood. It strikes a false note – too young for her.

A door on the far wall opens and a man appears.

'That's the client's entrance. We're in the back corridor here.' Zander is like a small boy showing off his things.

The man is also middle-aged. His expression is that of someone who's come home. He sits at the table and presses a remote control. The woman's hands start moving. They fiddle with the coffee cup, and stroke the tablecloth. Occasionally she touches her throat with long, delicate fingers. She gazes at her companion.

'Do you sculpt the models as well as painting the murals?'

'All my own work.'

'How do you make them move like that?'

Zander smirks, taps his forehead, then puts a finger to his lips.

The man is speaking. 'Marry me, Gina. I can't wait any longer. We won't have much money, but we'll manage, and one day I'll be the best heart surgeon in the country. I'll make you so proud of me, my darling. No one will ever love you like I do. Please say yes.'

The woman leans forward and strokes his face. 'What took you so long?'

The man kneels down beside her. She looks around, laughing. 'You're embarrassing me. Everyone's watching.'

He produces a ring and slips it onto the third finger of her left hand. 'You're mine now. I'll never let you go.'

He kisses her, his lips lingering on hers as if he can't bear to separate.

Then there's a subtle change. Life makes a quick exit. The woman sits, lifeless on her chair. The man slumps to the floor in a foetal position, only the rise and fall of his chest distinguishing him from his lover.

He did become a great heart surgeon too. Even I recognise him. But as a confident professional, exuding power in various medical documentaries and news items on the TV, not this broken figure crumpled on the floor like a down-and-out in a shop doorway.

'Serial adulterer,' breathed Zander. 'When his wife couldn't take it any more, she slit her wrists. He never got over it. Knows it was his fault, you see. Likes to revisit the time when his intentions were pure as the driven snow.'

He's moved on to another window. 'This is a painful one.'

The other two were the comedy warm-up?

It's a nursery. The detail on the mural is so specific that again I know it's from life. There's a bed along one wall, and in it lies a tiny child, eyes closed. Beside him sits an expensively dressed woman, holding his hand. After a moment she gets up and paces the room, muttering to herself. 'I can't do this any more. It's killing me,' before eventually returning to the bed.

'Oh Jackie,' she murmurs. 'My little baby. My little love.' She presses the ubiquitous remote control.

The little figure starts to toss and turn, moaning and muttering. His words are unintelligible. His mother strokes his forehead. 'It's OK, Jack, Mummy's here. You'll be better soon, I promise.'

Then there's a sudden expiration of breath, and the boy is still.

'Jackie? Jackie!' The woman calls again and again, her face a mask of despair.

She leaves him and comes towards the back wall. Her face is inches from mine. The expression on her face is extraordinary: anticipation and dread mingling together.

Then I hear a very small voice. 'Mummy!'

The woman's face lights up. 'Jack?'

She turns. The boy is sitting up in bed holding out his arms.

'You're alive?' She rushes across to him.

'Silly Mummy. I want a cuddle.'

She crushes the small body against hers, tears streaming down her face. 'Silly Mummy. Silly Mummy.'

Eventually she lays him back down in the bed. He's motion-less now. She sits, head bowed. Then she wipes her tears and extracts a make-up case from her handbag. After repairing the ravages to her face, she kisses the boy and leaves the room.

Zander speaks. 'Meningitis.'

The tears are streaming down my face, too. 'Can we go now?'

He frowns. 'You're upset.' His face clears. 'Silly me. I've only shown you tragic pieces.'

'I don't want to see anything else.'

'But I haven't finished—'

'You're a very talented artist. I've never seen anything like it before, but—'

'What do you think of the interactive thing? Does it work?'

'I'm sorry, Zander, but isn't this really exploitative – leeching off people's grief?'

I'm too repelled by what I've seen to be tactful. But he doesn't seem to mind.

'Absolutely not,' he says. 'The clients' feelings are at the very heart of the installations. They are the *raison d'être* behind the whole thing. Let me show you—'

'No, thanks. I want to leave now.'

But he's dragged me to another peephole. 'One of my most recent works.'

I really want out, but he's gripping my arm.

'You'll get the point when you've seen this.'

As I look into yet another room, I have to lean against the wall to stop my knees giving way.

I feel like I've had an electric shock.

THIRTY-NINE

It's the frighteningly lifelike facsimile of a man I last glimpsed in Theo Grey's funeral home.

The late lamented Haz Kem.

He's dripping with bling and dressed to impress in his best rapper gear. His room is completely bare.

'I haven't got around to the mural yet, but his wife was so keen she wanted to visit even though the piece is still unfinished.'

Strutting round Haz Kem is Shamila, the grieving widow, last seen by me in the garden at *Grey's*. She's wearing a fantastic sprayed-on creation of sequins and glitter.

Not sprayed-on. Because she's now stepping out of it.

Underneath, she's naked.

'Ain't no sense in wasting good threads on you, homeboy,' she says, and wraps herself in a grubby dressing-gown that she's taken from a small sports bag.

''Member what happened last time you caught me wearing this old thing?' She laughs. 'You broke my arm. Well listen up, baby. Now you goin' look at it for as long as I say so.'

She flicks her remote control. The air's filled with cursing. It's coming from Haz Kem's mouth and is aimed at his wife, as are the fists which now endeavour to make contact with her body. She dodges the blows with practised ease.

'Bitch ho',' roars the star. 'When I've done finished with you, there ain't no two-bit promoter'll touch you.'

'You think?' shouts his wife. 'You think? I do as I please, shit-head.'

He grabs her hair. 'You my ho' and you do as I please.'

Shamila flicks the remote. Haz Kem's arms drop.

'No, I don't,' she says. 'Not any more I don't, numb nuts. Not now. Not ever.'

She throws off the dressing-gown and climbs back into the dress. 'You'll have to excuse me now, sugar. There's a sweet young thing waiting at home to screw my brains out. Catch you later.' She blows him a kiss and sashays out.

Zander's laughing.

'What's so funny?'

'I told you it wasn't all grim. When Haz died, Shamila regained her freedom after years of abuse. This is her revenge. I'm laughing with her. Laughing in joyful sympathy.'

Joyful sympathy?

'No tragedy here. Shamila's having a great time.'

'What's this all about, Zander?'

'It's about me making something which touches people's lives in ways that they didn't think possible. That's what great art does. My work is for people who can't let go.'

'People who can't let go?'

391

'It's a brilliantly simple concept. It came to me one day as I was thinking about my widowed sister and the way she's still obsessing over her husband's death. She can't seem to put it behind her. He died on their twentieth anniversary after a big row. Ever since then she's been punishing herself by going over what she wishes she'd said instead of what she did say. She can't leave it alone. It's ruining her life because her family and friends are so bored by the whole thing that we tend to avoid her as much as we can.'

'I don't see the connection to this place?'

'You must have come across the kind of people who compulsively rerun the past. You wish they'd move on and face the fact that what's done is done.'

'Maybe.'

'But sometimes they can't because the people involved are dead.'

Wait for me . . .

Three little words.

'Well, I had this idea. Through my art I could give people the opportunity to re-enact those moments. And if they were able to repeat the experience often enough, then maybe the compulsion would be satisfied.' He smiles modestly. 'And at the same time, I could demonstrate how great art transcends life and death.'

'Great art? I don't think so.'

Zander's face tightens. 'My collectors wouldn't agree,' he says stiffly. 'For them it's been a life-changing experience – providing comfort where none existed.' He stares at me intently. 'You can't tell me that there isn't a moment in *your* life that you don't take out and re-examine constantly, either because you wish you'd

392

done it differently, or because it's like some precious jewel you just want to keep looking at.'

Wait for me . . .

'Sure, but—'

'And that if you were offered a chance to actually revisit it and change the outcome, or re-experience the delight . . . ?'

'Not like this.'

'Think about it. The moment you return to more than any other, waiting for you to re-experience it whenever you like.'

Wait for me . . .

And then I think of something else – the day I first met Rob. The party in the Student Union bar. The table under which Jess and I were hiding to escape some hairy freak who was coming on to us in a big way – the uncontrollable fit of giggling, the voice, like molasses, 'I spy with my little eye, something beginning with?' And this lean mean man with melting brown eyes squatting down and staring into my eyes and Jess saying, 'I'll be off then, shall I?' And neither of us noticing her slip away. To relive that moment . . .

I have a blinding insight into what Zander's on about. But it fades almost immediately.

Because I wouldn't be reliving anything. Not with some sculptural lookalike.

'That woman with her dead child needs grief counselling, not this. What she's doing is like scratching a scab and stopping it from healing.'

'She wouldn't agree.'

'And what's with the voyeurism?'

'What do you mean?'

'I shouldn't think your clients pay to be spied on. Do they know that when they're reliving their most intimate moments, you're snooping on them through a hole in the wall? And bringing others to gawp too?'

'I haven't shown my work to anyone who isn't directly involved,' he says. 'You're the first. And I don't spy. I just do the odd check to make sure things are in proper working order. My collectors expect everything to be perfect.'

'It's not right, Zander. You must see that.'

'It's radical, I agree. Shocking even. But great art always starts by shocking people – pushing the boundaries.'

'Great art's universal. Your installations only mean something to the people personally involved. None of them would want to share it with anyone else. This'll never be shown at Tate Modern or any other gallery. Don't you want your work to be seen?'

'It is being seen. By those that matter. Some of the world's most dedicated collectors never show their collections. They like to keep them very private. You don't know what you're talking about, Rosa.'

'I know it's wrong.'

But he won't give up. He's hell-bent on justifying himself to me.

'It's all my concept – the murals, the installations, everything.'

'And it's an extraordinary achievement, but—'

'I was trained as an artist, you know.'

'Yes, you said.'

'Things didn't work out, but I always knew that one day I'd have the big idea.'

I've just had my big idea: to get out of here double quick.

'And what a revolutionary idea it turned out to be.'

I finally snap. 'It's horrible.'

He stares at me, aghast. 'Horrible?' His voice trembles. 'You really think that what I've shown you here is horrible?'

'Yes. I do.'

'I thought you'd understand.'

'Why?'

'I thought you'd get the point.'

'I'm sorry.'

He grabs me. 'You have to understand.'

'What are you doing?' I can't breathe. He's crushing me. Even my hands are trapped, rammed up against his jacket, which feels damp to the touch and makes me heave.

'Listen to me!'

I feel a sharp pain in my finger. A pinprick. It's the lapel pin that opened the steel door. My passport out of this hell-hole.

I bring my right knee up smack in the muddle of his puny bits, while at the same time grabbing the pin from his jacket and jabbing it into his chest. He bellows and releases me. I run back up the corridor towards the gallery. My hand's trembling as I try the pin in the door. What if it's only programmed for Zander? But no – it slides open. I'm back in the land of the living. I rush through to Zander's back room to wake Joshua.

But the room is empty.

Except for his glasses, which lie crushed on the floor, and his shoes, flung separately to the far corners of the room.

FORTY

I run into the main gallery.

Empty.

Any second now, Zander the Zombie will erupt from his kingdom of the living dead.

Where could Joshua possibly be? I call his name. Still no response. Maybe he woke up with an uncontrollable urge to see his brother's exhibition again. I run out into the street and go next door to *L'Estrange East*.

But the gallery's completely Joshless. There are, however, loud voices coming from Larry's office.

'Larry, I'm begging you.'

'You continually disparage the work I show here, yet it doesn't stop you asking me for money. Where do you think that money comes from, Theo?'

'For Flavia's sake—'

'Do not bring Flavia into this. You've bled her dry – taken every spare penny she has. You didn't think I knew about that, did you? Well, Flavia tells me everything. You'd do well to remember that.'

Larry's reverted to the singular. Always a sign he's out of control. But it's none of my business.

Joshua is.

Perhaps he woke up, thought I didn't want to collect him, and made his own way home. More guilt, Rosa. He hasn't exactly been made to feel welcome in the house lately. Even though I haven't said anything, he's probably picked up the vibes. Added to which he thinks he's failed with his photographs and let me down.

He's clearly not here and the last thing I want to do is interrupt a family row so I decide to head off. Just as I reach the gallery entrance the office door opens and I hear Theo Grey's voice.

'Rosa?'

I feign deafness and carry on going. Round the corner, I find a bar full of office workers letting rip after a hard day's work and huddle over an orange juice trying to get my head together.

Zander completely lost it back there. It really scared me. Does he actually believe that the creepy little rooms with their pitiful replicas of what were once living, loving human beings are genuine art installations, or is it just a very lucrative way for him to exploit the vulnerable rich?

And how has he got such a project up and running? He'd need someone with a brilliant scientific mind to install the technology that makes the figures move and speak so naturally.

Emil Barbu, his brother-in-law! Who told me that in Romania he'd been a micro-electronics engineer.

Who was supposed to be keeping an eye on Joshua.

Joshua: where is he?

I phone home. No reply.

Then the blindingly obvious hits me. Joshua hasn't gone anywhere, because he couldn't walk without his shoes, and he couldn't see without his glasses.

Both of which are still in *Nature Morte*. Smashed and scattered.

Something's happened to him, and Zander and Emil Barbu are both involved. But why should either of them want to harm Joshua? They hardly know him.

Am I making much ado about nothing?

There must be another explanation of why he should have vanished, leaving behind his specs and shoes. There must be. If only I could think of it.

Vanished.

There I go again, employing a highly loaded word where someone less melodramatic would have said *left*, or *gone*.

Maybe Joshua's fall was worse than Zander thought. Maybe he took a turn for the worse and had to be rushed to hospital.

In that case, why didn't Emil leave a note? Or come and tell me?

I have to return to the gallery. Joshua's somewhere in that building.

Darkness has fallen when I emerge from the bar. Good. Easier for me to snoop unseen. I walk back to Navarre Street and lurk in the doorway of a derelict shop with a flyblown window full of yellowing newspapers and ancient surgical trusses, staring at *Nature Morte*. I've positioned myself as near as I dare to the entrance. I also have a good view of the side of the building. I'm gathering my courage when a black van draws up and Emil Barbu emerges. He barks something into his mobile, after which I see a shaft of light appear, streaming up from the pavement. It's from a cellar, the kind you see on the pavement next to pubs, with barrels of beer being rolled down into them by burly brewers.

With practised efficiency, Emil unfolds two screens, which shield the space between the cellar hatch and the doors of the van. I can't see what's happening, but after a few minutes, he chucks them back into the van, disappears into the cellar, and a moment later the shaft of light disappears.

I cross over the road. The hatch is very cleverly hidden. It looks like pavement. No one would spot the thin strip of metal which is its edge. How do I get in without alerting Zander and Emil? I clearly can't go through the gallery.

Then I remember something: Zander said there was a clients' entrance.

I walk round the building. Bingo! Tucked away unobtrusively, right at the back, hidden by a wall, is another steel door identical to the one behind Zander's mirror. I sidle up to it and use Zander's pin. Will it work?

Yes.

I'm in. What now?

This part of the old factory hasn't been renovated. Either that or it's bare-brick chic. I'm in a dimly lit lobby with a corridor leading off it. There are several doors along the corridor. They are all in stainless steel and in marked contrast to the dereliction around them. There's a staircase at the end. Be methodical, Rosa. Start at the top and work down.

I walk up to the top floor. No high-tech doors here, just the original rickety wooden ones. I try all the rooms. Some are locked, some are open but empty – pared back to bare brick, dirty and rubble-strewn. No sign of Joshua.

I do the middle floor. Nothing. Back down to ground level.

Then I hear a noise behind me.

FORTY-ONE

Zander.

In the gloom it's impossible to interpret his expression.

'Why did you run away?'

'I'm sorry . . .'

He walks towards me. I try not to look nervous.

'It wasn't a very nice thing to do.'

I've got myself into what's known as a situation. I'm alone in a dark, semi-derelict building with a man who's becoming increasingly strange.

And no one knows I'm here.

'How did you get in? You didn't come through the gallery.'

Don't mention his entry pin. I may need it later.

'I found the back entrance.'

'And got in with the pin you stole from me. May I have it, please?'

I toy with the idea of saying I've lost it, but something in his face tells me it's better not to mess him about. I hand it over.

'Why come back at all?'

'To find Joshua. He wasn't in the gallery so I thought maybe he was here.'

Stick as close to the truth as possible. But don't mention the shoes and specs.

Why not?

Just don't.

'Why not come and ask me?'

'I didn't want to bother you again.'

'Why not?'

Why not? Think. Think.

'I was embarrassed.'

'Embarrassed?'

'For running out on you like some silly schoolgirl. I wanted to find Joshua without having to face you.'

'Why *did* you run away?'

'I don't know. It was just . . .'

'Just what?'

'It . . . it was your installations. I'd never seen anything like them before. I found them overwhelming. And you suddenly went all heavy on me. I didn't like it.'

'And now?'

Now I want to find Joshua and get the hell out of here.

'I've been trying to imagine what it would be like to have my own installation.'

'And what conclusion have you come to?'

'I've changed my mind.'

'About what?'

'About it being exploitative. Actually, I think it would be wonderful.'

He's looking at me so intently it feels like he's sucking out my soul.

'Maybe we could have a drink sometime and you could tell me more about your ideas,' I venture.

Finally his face softens. 'I'd like that.'

Cracked it.

'Great, so . . . I would just like to see that Joshua's properly recovered. Do you know where he is?'

'Let's think.' After a moment his face brightens. 'I remember. Yesterday he was clearing out one of the storerooms on the east side of the building. It's a private area for an extremely important client. I'm creating a special installation for him which takes the process one stage further – you might be interested in seeing it. Anyway, that's where we'll find Joshua, I expect.' He opens a heavy wooden door into another shadowy corridor.

'In here.'

I feel his hand in the centre of my back, moving me forward. At the same time his other hand grabs my bag from my shoulder.

FORTY-TWO

I hear a door closing behind me. I'm in pitch darkness.

'Zander!'

'Rosa?'

The disembodied voice nearly gives me a coronary. I fumble about on the wall near the doorframe trying to locate the light switch. I'm in luck.

And I've found Joshua – in what looks like one of Zander's installations. Except this one's very incomplete: there's no sculpture and the mural's only a sketch, of some sort of bar.

Joshua's slumped over a table. When he sees me he leaps up, winces, then sinks down again clutching his head. As he bends forward I see a gash on the back of his skull, encrusted with dried blood.

'What happened to you?' I ask, shocked but relieved.

'I don't know,' he says, and groans. 'I was in Zander's office, by the filing cabinet, when I heard a noise. Then there was this awful pain in my head. Next thing I know, I'm being dragged in here by Zander and Emil.'

'You don't remember being put to bed in Zander's back room?'

'No.'

So when I saw him earlier, he was either unconscious or sedated. Why would Zander do this to Joshua?

'How do you feel now?'

'Pretty grim. What's going on?'

Good question, Joshua.

I try the door. Locked.

We're trapped.

The room presses in on me. I go hot, cold and then hot again. I can't catch my breath. All the air seems to have been sucked out of the tiny space. I'm suffocating.

Panic attack.

'I can't breathe!' I gasp.

'Easy, Rosa, easy. You're hyperventilating. Hold your breath. Hold . . . Hold . . .'

Gradually my hammering heart subsides.

'Now take a long, slow, deep breath. Long . . . slow . . . deep. That's it. Better?'

I nod. But when I look up, it seems the room is contracting around me. Once again I'm gasping for air.

'Steady! Hold your breath. Look at me . . . That's it . . .' Joshua holds my face in his hands. 'Keep looking at me, Rosa. Now, tell me exactly what all this is about. Look at me, and tell me slowly and clearly . . .'

So, forcing myself to focus on my words, I fill him in on what's been happening. Gradually my control over my wayward body reasserts itself. But I'm boiling with a mixture of rage and fear.

'What is he up to?' I leap up and I hammer on the door with my fists. 'Zander! Come here!'

Joshua takes my hands. His voice is gentle. 'You're hurting yourself.'

I collapse onto a chair.

And experience an intense moment of *déjà-vu*.

When I turn to Joshua it passes. 'We can't even call anyone. He's taken my bag with my phone in it, and you don't have one, do you?'

He tries to reassure me with a smile, but a wrinkle of worry creases his forehead. Pure Rob.

'When he comes back, I'll go for him. Don't worry, Rosa. I won't let him hurt you.'

My fear is momentarily superseded by guilt. I've been so mean-minded and suspicious of him over the past couple of weeks.

'Oh, Josh.'

A smile of ineffable sweetness lights up his face. 'You called me Josh,' he says. 'You've never done that before. It makes me feel like part of the family.'

The guilt intensifies. 'You're Rob's brother. How could you not be part of the family?'

'It's so good to hear you say that. I've felt recently . . .' His voice drops and he won't look at me. 'I've felt that you didn't want me around any more.'

'I've treated you very badly.'

He breaks in. 'Have you read my letter?'

'Yes.'

'I'm so sorry for my behaviour.'

'Don't – I understand.'

'You've seen my portfolio now?'

'Yes.'

'I've wasted all your money.'

'Josh—'

'I will pay you back, I swear – every penny. That's why I took this job. Zander said he'd give me cash since I don't have a work permit.' His face falls. 'Except it looks like the job's history now, but I'll find another one. Don't worry, you'll get it all back.'

'Josh – stop!'

I've startled him.

'Your work is sensational. I love it.'

'But Zander said—'

'I don't know what game Zander's been playing with you, but what he said about your photographs is completely untrue, and as soon as we get out of here, I'm going to find you a proper dealer. Believe me, your work will be snapped up. They'll all be fighting over it.'

Josh's face is a picture of bewilderment. 'You think it's good?'

'More than good. Brilliant. Rob would have been so proud of you.'

As I look at his face I experience one of those seismic shifts that sometimes happen: I've finally accepted him for who he is. Not just in my head, but in my heart. He feels as much part of the family as if he'd been with us from day one. And I'm overtaken by a wave of tenderness. Not because he's Rob's brother, but because he's who he is. And I want so much to get to know him properly.

I cup his anxious young face in my hands and lightly kiss his furrowed forehead, just as I do to my children when they're feeling crushed by life.

And something momentous passes between us: the forging of a bond.

I look around the claustrophobic little space. We can't just sit here and wait. I bang on the door again. No one comes, but I realise something.

'This is an old door, not reinforced stainless steel,' I say. 'Maybe it's not that strong. In TV dramas the police are always breaking down doors. It can't be that difficult. Let's give it a go.'

We're both pretty feeble, me because I just am, and Josh because he's recovering from a blow to the head, but we more than make up for our lack of strength by our determination to escape.

And after a few goes, there's a splintering sound and the door gives way.

I look at Josh. 'Let's go.'

But nothing is simple. When we emerge from the room we find that the thick wooden door at the end of the corridor is locked. And it's far too sturdy to be battered down. We turn the other way.

Another steel door. But this one's open.

Behind it is blackness. Complete and absolute.

Joshua switches on the light.

It's not a way out. It's another room.

One of Zander's installations.

FORTY-THREE

It's *L'Estrange East*, right down to Rob's paintings hanging on the walls. The effect created by the rows of Art Nouveau pillars receding into the distance makes the tiny room seem vast. It's also very populated. I pick out not only the gallery staff, Caroline, Larry and Julian, but also countless art world luminaries. They're all there. Plus Mike, Jess, me and the kids.

The people who attended Rob's private view.

But that's not what's turning my legs into rubber sausages.

In the centre of the room, wearing tatty combats and a short-sleeved Arsenal sweatshirt, hair dangling over the face which is frozen into a rictus grin, is a brilliantly lifelike sculpture of Steve Pyne.

My feet feel like lead weights as I walk up to it.

I touch the face. It's soft, with that faint, bristly texture that men's skin always has, even after a shave.

And it's icy cold.

In fact, the whole room is icy cold. It's like standing in a fridge.

409

The eyes stare past me, expressionless, as I examine the intricate whirls and convolutions of the ear. Such detail.

I touch the torso.

And feel ribs beneath the skin . . .

Then, deep inside it I hear a faint humming.

And there's a smell that certainly isn't aftershave. It's chemical. Sharp yet sickly.

Formaldehyde.

Oh God, no! The room starts to spin.

'Josh. I don't think it's a sculpture.'

'What?' Josh touches the forearm which is covered with millions of hairs. He leaves his hand there for several seconds, and then turns to me, eyes wide with shock. 'It's real skin.'

We stare at each other.

Robo-corpse.

I'm aware of Josh's breath, loud and ragged, echoing round the room. Then I notice something else. There's another figure in this installation. Propped against the wall, legs splayed.

It's Leni Dang. Dressed in a skintight top that reveals a bare midriff, and a mini-skirt that reveals everything else.

The penis, for example.

Not Leni.

Kenny.

No more blackmail scams now. No more punching old women in the gut.

And his death, unlike the others in this latterday Hell Fire Club, is certainly nothing to do with nature taking its course, or the careless finger of fate accidentally squashing a life half-lived. The long hair can't hide the ugly purple marks round the neck.

THE ART OF DYING

Someone's organised for Kenny Dang to meet his Maker way before time.

'Kenny's been strangled.'

Steve Pyne throws back his head and laughs.

FORTY-FOUR

Then he shouts, very loudly, '*Filthy capitalist leech!*'

There's a short pause, after which he starts again. And again, on a ghastly, never-ending loop. '*Ha ha ha! Filthy capitalist leech!*' Over and over. Like the clown in the glass box on Blackpool promenade that frightened me so much one year on a childhood trip to the seaside.

'Like it?' Zander stands in the doorway. He's holding a remote control.

'Please . . . Switch it off.' My mouth's so dry I can hardly form the words.

He flicks the remote. 'This is my favourite piece,' he says. 'Apart from its personal significance for my client, I like to think it has a special meaning for those of us who make art. It's an *homage*, really. Anyone looking at it in fifty years' time will be able to see exactly who was who and what was what in the British art world at the beginning of the twenty-first century. And it's Rob's show. Quite a memorial, wouldn't you say?' He gives a modest smile. 'It took me less than two weeks from start to finish. You'd have to go back to the Renaissance to find an artist who could work so quickly and yet still capture the verisimilitude and the spirit of the thing.'

'The figures . . . they're not sculptures at all.'

The smile's even broader. 'No, they're not.'

'How could you?'

'Oh, it's quite legal. With proper permissions from next-of-kin, naturally. People donate bodies to medical research all the time. And what about Gunther von Hagens? He uses preserved corpses in his *Bodyworks* exhibition. He's even done public post-mortems.'

'The legality's one thing. The morality of what goes on here is something else.' Josh can't hide his revulsion.

Keep Zander talking and hope that some sort of plan occurs.

'Why use real bodies? It's very extreme.'

'It's not a new idea. In the eighteenth century the sculptor Agostino Carlini acquired the corpse of a criminal who'd been hanged for smuggling. He placed it in the attitude of a dying gladiator and took a cast of it. It was in the Royal Academy Schools for years.' He laughs. 'The students called it *Smugglerius*.'

'A cast of a corpse isn't the same thing at all.'

'True. But real people are central to my concept.'

I see the gleam of the fanatic in his eye.

'Can't you see the beauty in it?' he goes on. 'It's the mystery – the dark secret we long to penetrate.'

'Make me understand.'

As he talks I'm mesmerised by his moist brown eyes and the translucent flesh stretched so thinly over his bones that I fancy I can see the skull beneath. It's like listening to Death itself.

'I was surfing the net and I hit on a site for taxidermists. You'd be amazed how many different sorts of stuffed animals it's possible to buy . . . Anyway, there was a chatroom, too – folk wittering on about how having their pets preserved had helped the grief process. And it came to me that this fitted with my ideas about people reliving the most intense moments in their lives. It was my chance to finally prove myself as an artist. I could create a cathartic environment . . .'

'Using real corpses?'

'That was the whole point. The people blubbering over their dead dogs would no way have been comforted by giving house-room to someone else's stuffed Fido, would they?'

'How could you even think of doing such a thing, man?'

Zander interprets Josh's words as a question about practicalities.

'I know. It seemed a scientific impossibility. To preserve a corpse was easy, but to make it permanently malleable enough to use in an installation, well that was something else again. So for a while my great idea remained just that – a great idea. The breakthrough was Sylvia.'

'Who's Sylvia?'

I haven't told Josh about sulky Sylvia.

'My wife. A chemist. First-class mind. She told me that with modern advances in the science of preservation, it might be possible to preserve a corpse while retaining its elasticity.' His face clouds over. 'But it still wasn't right.'

'That's because it isn't. It's—'

I shoot Josh a warning glance. *Don't antagonise him.*

'A static, silent image wasn't enough. It needed speech and

movement. Significant speech. Significant movement. Triggers for the memory. Guess how I solved that one?'

There's only one answer. The family electronics wizard.

'Emil.'

He beams. 'Aren't I lucky? Not only a super-brilliant wife, but also a super-brilliant brother-in-law. He's quite something. How he does it, I'll never fathom, but my goodness they're realistic, aren't they?'

'I can honestly say I've never seen anything like it before. Have you, Josh?'

'No,' says Josh, who's finally cottoned on to my strategy of placating Zander. 'What you've done here's very dark. Very dark. No wonder you weren't impressed by my crap photographs. Not when you're such a genius.'

Zander inclines his head graciously.

Now I know why the place is so dimly lit. Clients would hardly want to advertise their presence, even to each other. It also explains why no hint of its existence has ever hit the headlines. The owners of these installations are pathologically desperate to hold on to their deceased darlings. If the thing were ever exposed to public scrutiny, they not only face a mega-scandal, they might also lose what they've gone to such way-out extremes to keep.

But what about staff? A clever cleaner could clean up more than a dirty lavatory by taking this to the tabloids. I think about it. There probably are no staff – just the Zinovieffs and Emil. This place isn't the Ritz. Apart from the installations themselves, the place is dirty and derelict.

It's time to talk us both out of here.

'Look, Zander, Josh and I both realise that this has to be kept secret. It's far too ahead of its time to be generally accepted. I just want you to know that no one's going to hear anything from us. As far as we're concerned, these installations don't exist, do they, Josh?'

'What installations?'

We both laugh nervously.

'I'm glad you understand.'

'Now, I really think we should push off . . .'

A look of pure astonishment passes across Zander's face. 'Push off?'

'Yes. We won't say a word—'

'But you haven't asked about Pyne and his little friend.'

I don't want to know.

'You aren't curious about them?'

'Please, Zander—'

'You've probably guessed that the buyer of this piece hasn't commissioned it in the spirit of loving remembrance.'

'Let us out of here!' Josh has finally lost it.

'You may also have noticed that Mr Dang had a helping hand into oblivion.'

'Yes.'

'Next question?'

'Zander, I just—'

'The next question you want to ask is, was it me who helped him?'

'No.'

'Well, it wasn't.'

'Of course not. You're a creator, not a destroyer.' I try to speak with conviction.

'Mr Pyne, on the other hand . . .'

No.

'Mr Pyne was a naughty boy. He somehow found his way in here one day – we think Emil must have inadvertently left the door open for a moment – and did some illicit filming. Thought he could blackmail me with footage of my installations. Anyway, I agreed to meet him on the Heath, for the pay-off, and I made him an offer he couldn't refuse.'

What is he saying? As if I didn't know. Caro was right all along.

There's more: 'And as for Mr Dang, it's absolutely appropriate that my client wants him in the installation.'

I'm clutching Josh's hand so tightly I'm in danger of crushing the bones.

'Aren't you going to ask why?'

We're both beyond speech.

'Because they were screwing each other.' He smiles. 'I saw them at it when I followed Pyne up to the Heath. Nasty. But it made my task easier. By the time Dang left, Pyne was so drunk it was easy to persuade him to swallow the extra booze and the pills.'

Poor Caro.

Poor Caro? Maybe it's her installation.

'Did Caro tell you to dig up his body?'

'Don't stress about that. My client followed all the proper procedures.'

'What client?'

'Sorry. Strict anonymity's the name of the game. Not that it matters now.'

Why doesn't it matter?

He's walking into the corridor and opening another steel door. 'Come on.'

I look at Josh. He shrugs. What choice do we have? The wooden door at the end of the corridor is locked: we checked. This seems the only alternative.

But as we follow Zander I see it's not a room he's led us into. It's a lift.

The door closes.

We're now travelling downwards. Into the bowels of the building. Away from the exit.

FORTY-FIVE

The door opens. We're in a large space that's a cross between a recording studio and an electronics workshop. Voices fill the air. They're coming from speakers positioned in the corners of the room. A workbench littered with bits of wire and metal runs along one wall. Against another stands a computer and a mixing desk.

As the identity of the voices sinks in, I look at Josh and see my own bewilderment reflected back.

Four people are speaking:

1st MAN: *I'd know that smell anywhere – old socks and rancid cheese. What do you want, man?*

1st WOMAN: *We all know what Willie Wanka wants. Fuck off perv.*

Then there's a gap of several seconds until a third voice cuts in.

2nd WOMAN: *Thanks, but I've already got it.*
2nd MAN: *Push off. She's with me.*

Josh is shaking his head. 'It's impossible,' he says.

I would agree with him, had I not, earlier in the day, heard the dead speak.

The voices belong to Mike, Jess, me and Rob. Except that Rob's voice isn't quite right.

Because it's not him.

It's Josh.

'What's going on?' Josh's arm trembles against mine.

'Time to jog your memory.'

There's now an air of suppressed excitement about Zander. He's a man on a mission. The energy he's giving off could light up the whole of East London.

He taps a keyboard. The same conversation booms out.

With one difference.

Jess has told Willie Wanka to fuck off, when another voice cuts in. This voice isn't recorded. It's here in the room.

I heard you say you liked 'I Wanna Dance with Somebody'.
I've got two copies. You can have one if you like.

Zander.

The recording continues:

ME: *Thanks, but I've already got it.*
ROB: *Push off. She's with me.*

Zander switches it off.

'Get it?' His eyes convey challenge, anticipation.

Josh and I speak together. 'No.'

'Amazing,' says Zander. 'Amazing how people forget.' He turns to Josh. 'Not you, mate. You weren't there, of course. You're just Rob's sub. I couldn't believe it when you turned up. Talk about the cherry on the cake. Mind you, it didn't half give me a shock. First time was in the street. I clocked you following Rosa, but I thought I'd made a mistake. Second time was when you came into the gallery. Remember – I dropped the vase I was carrying?'

'We have to go now.' As I say it I know I'm on a hiding to nowhere.

'Next clue.' He taps on the keyboard, the monitor comes to life, and the past leaps out to greet me.

A series of photos flash up. There's several of me aged about nineteen, looking like a wild woman, with curly red hair down to my waist, held back by a sweatband. I'm wearing leggings, leg-warmers and a baggy T-shirt: 1980s fashion victim or what? Then there are a couple of me and Jess at some college charity event dressed as Tweedledum and Tweedledee, and others of Mike Mason and Rob in football kit, covered in mud, and finally some group photos of the four of us: sprawled on the lawn outside college on a hot summer's day; at the annual ball looking wasted; and sitting in the college canteen, at our favourite table in the corner. We're laughing at something. Or someone.

'Getting there?'

'Photos of me and my friends. Where did you get them?'

Zander sighs. 'Here's your final clue.'

Another photo flashes up. Rob and Mike's Diploma show. Rob's standing beside a painting. It's a portrait of me, done in a completely abstract style – I'm unrecognisable as a person – just a collection of shapes and patterns.

I feel like I've been punched in the gut.

Rob did countless studies and sketches, and then three versions of that painting before he was satisfied. I posed for more hours than I care to remember. I haven't seen it since the day he gradu-ated. Along with a couple of other works, it was lost in transit during the move to our first flat as a couple.

I tear my eyes away from the lost painting and my lost love. On the edge of the photograph is someone else. He's fat – at least twenty stone – and his face is obscured by black-framed, thick-rimmed spectacles, long, tangled greasy hair and a bushy beard.

Zander zooms in on the face.

Recognition comes and goes, flickering through my conscious-ness like a faulty light-fitting. Now I see him. Now I don't. Now I see him . . .

I look from the photo to Zander, and back again.

The mountainous oaf who stares at Rob and Mike with such an unfathomable expression is one and the same as the dapper, elegant man in front of me, whose smooth white fingers with their manicured nails flutter over the keyboard.

'It's you . . .'

I struggle to pull back the curtains of time. He was a student on Rob's course. A memory surfaces – an olfactory one. Bad breath and body odour . . . I'm standing in a hallway. Loud music and lots of people. A party. There's a scarf draped over the light which turns people purple. Someone's crushed against me. I'm pushing him away. Rob arrives – there's a scuffle. A large body on the floor, Rob kicking the great fat bottom, and people pulling him off . . .

'Alex Williams.'

'Got it in one.'

Alex Williams. *Willie Wanka*.

It's coming back. He was always hanging around. I think he fancied me, although that party was the only time he ever attempted anything. I remember feeling a bit sorry for him, but Jess and Mike were merciless in their teasing. And Rob? Well, Rob was very territorial. Didn't like another bloke sniffing around his woman, even a pitiful loser like Alex Williams. Rob did not like Alex Williams. I remember now.

I wish he'd been a bit nicer to him. I wish we'd all been a bit nicer to him.

Joshua's glancing warily from me back to Zander.

'Zander was at Goldsmiths with me and Rob,' I say. 'Except he was called Alex Williams in those days.'

'Oh,' says Josh in a nervous attempt at levity. 'Friends Reunited.'

Zander bursts out laughing. 'Spot on, Joshua, mate,' he says. 'Spot on.' His laughter is devoid of warmth.

My insides turn to liquid.

Then something else hits me. The room where Zander imprisoned me and Josh earlier, with the sketchy mural of some kind of bar, and the table and chairs in chrome, leatherette and Formica . . .

Déjà-vu? No wonder. It's the college bar, complete with our favourite table.

The shrill tones of an entryphone suddenly pierce the loaded atmosphere.

Zander picks up. 'Sorted?' he says. 'Cool.'

He presses a button. At the far end of the room a panel on the ceiling slides back. Night air floods the room. Zander activates a ramp. It rises up, obscuring the gap created by the sliding panel. In less than a minute it descends again, and the panel slides back. It must be the entrance to the cellar that I spotted earlier.

A way out.

On the ramp are two people: Emil Barbu and Sylvia Zinovieff.

Correction: three people.

Lying immobile on a stretcher is my best friend. Jess.

In all the years of our friendship I've never seen her so quiet.

FORTY-SIX

'Full house,' says Emil in his thick Romanian accent.

'Four of a kind,' counters Zander.

Sylvia says nothing. She's looking me and Joshua up and down. Measuring us for a shroud, perhaps. Except that in this awful place, corpses don't go to their final rest under the ground, where shrouds are *de rigueur*. Here they have to sing for their supper in a whole different variety of outfits.

What did Zander mean – *four of a kind?*

He hustles me and Joshua into another room. I've never been inside a mortuary, but this is how I imagine one to be: cabinets of chemicals, trays of surgical instruments, containers with long plastic tubes snaking out of them, and sinister oblong tables with troughs at the edges, for examining bodies.

On one of the tables there is indeed a body.

Mike. Larger than life, Golden Boy Mike with the beguiling charm that's got him into so much trouble, and his warmth and sense of fun. Now silent and still.

'What have you done?' I'm shouting.

I have one of those flashbacks they say you experience just before you die: a replay of all the good times, all the intimacies of our long friendship. Our recent fallings-out can't negate all that. The thought of losing Jess and Mike is intolerable.

Sylvia helps Emil transfer Jess from stretcher to slab. My Jess. I start to cry. Sylvia casts a withering look in my direction.

'Tell her to shut up,' she says to Zander.

Zander looks at me and smiles. Such a cold smile. 'They're only sedated. We have to keep them like this for a while if Sylvia's procedures are to work.'

Procedures?

Don't go there, Rosa.

They're alive. My relief is so profound that for a split second I almost thank him.

But only for a second.

Because Sylvia's preparing a syringe. Emil seizes Josh. In an instant the needle is plunged into his arm and I watch, helpless, as the contents disappear into his body.

'Josh!'

His eyes flash panic, but the drug acts instantaneously, and even as I watch they blank over and his lids close. Please God what they've given him has merely sent him to sleep like the others and not . . . I stare at his prone body. I can't lose him now. Or Jess and Mike. And it's completely up to me. Unless I do something, they'll all die.

Sylvia's talking to Zander. 'This is Gayle's second shot. He must have a very strong constitution. He shouldn't have come round so quickly after the first one. Either that or I gave him less than I thought.' She picks up a second syringe. 'Now for Madam.'

'No!' Zander's voice is tight and hard. 'I need more time to explain to Rosa exactly what's happening here. It's vital that she understands.'

Understands why he's going to turn us into one of his art installations?

Because that, it's clear, is what he's planning to do.

Understanding only goes so far.

Sylvia exchanges a look with Emil, then raises her hands in a gesture of submission. 'Your call.' She glances at me. If looks could kill, she'd have no need of her lethal syringe.

Zander hustles me into yet another room: an artist's studio. Full of the usual stuff.

And something else.

Rob's lost Diploma Show painting of me.

Not lost after all, but certainly changed from how I remember it.

It's been slashed at with a knife. Deep furrows are gouged out in several places. Predominantly my face.

Arranged around the room are four circular tables. On the chairs perch four sets of life-size mannequins. No prizes for guessing who they represent. Each set is arranged differently: different postures, different positions within the group. Each mannequin is dressed differently too. Except for me. I'm always in the leggings and T-shirt I saw in the photos earlier.

'This is how I finalise the design,' says Zander. 'It's a way of manipulating four ideas at the same time.'

I'm right. Jess, Mike, Josh and I are about to become Zander's latest home entertainment package.

He pulls up two chairs to one of the tables and motions me to sit.

I try to control my mounting hysteria.

Here we all are – him, 1980s me, Jess, Rob and Mike, all cosying up together round the blue Formica table.

'Zander, I'm really frightened.' It's not a lie. 'Why do you want to hurt me? Or my friends and family?'

'Family? Oh yes – the brother-in-law. I can't tell you how cool it's been for me, giving orders to Rob Thorn's brother. I wonder what he'd make of it, seeing his baby brother fetching and carrying for me, clearing up my mess, watching the poor guy struggling to put a brave face on it when I told him his portfolio was a pile of poo.'

'Why do you hate me so much?'

'I used to love you. All those years ago. Back then I worshipped you.'

'You never said.'

He shrugs. 'What was the point? I knew you'd never love me back.'

'I fell for Rob. People can't control who they love.'

'I know that. Don't get me wrong – I understood. No one could have loved such a fat slob.'

A clear image of Alex Williams fills my head, and for a moment my heart bleeds for that ugly, lonely boy of long ago. 'I was young and selfish – caught up in my own concerns. I'm really sorry.'

'I didn't mind you ignoring me, just so long as I could be near you. But your mates wouldn't let me. They made my life a living hell with their cheap cracks . . .'

'Stupid teasing. They didn't mean anything by it.'

'Didn't they?'

'Zander, they *didn't* mean it. Rob, for one, would be horrified if he realised what he'd done. He hated bullies.'

Zander frowns. 'Anyway, it wasn't just about you.'

'What do you mean?'

'It was my work.'

He's rubbing the back of his hand over and over again in a circular motion. When he speaks, it's with great effort. 'It was different.'

'Different?'

'From everybody else's.'

'In what way?'

'Remember my portrait of you?'

I cast my mind back. Nothing.

'You could have kept it. It hardly took up any room. You could have, if you'd wanted to.' His voice is a dull monotone.

I scrabble frantically through what remains of my brain. I'm making things worse instead of better. Not only did I spurn his adolescent passion, I've now compounded it by totally forgetting some mythical portrait that he supposedly gave me.

Think, Rosa.

Then an image comes to mind: a piece of paper in my college pigeonhole. A tiny painting, no more than three inches square. The subject? Me. Painted in astonishing and meticulous detail.

'Like an Elizabethan miniature?'

'That's it.'

'It was *you* who did that?'

'Do you still have it?'

I hesitate. 'Of course.'

'Don't lie.'

I can't look at him.

'Back then people laughed at my work. It wasn't cool. Too realistic. Realistic painting? Nobody wanted to know. Not students, not staff, and certainly not Rob and Mike. Realism was a dirty word at Goldsmiths. I was a laughing stock. A hideous fat joke. A throwback to a different age . . . I never graduated, you know. I had a breakdown that last term, and dropped out.' He looks at me. 'I don't suppose you even noticed.'

What can I say? I was barely aware of him when he was there. How was I supposed to realise he'd gone?

He smiles sourly. 'I thought not. Anyway, I stopped painting. Couldn't do anything for years – had various crap jobs, nothing to do with art. Have you any idea what that's like? To be incapable of doing the thing you love best?'

'Awful.'

'It was. So imagine how I felt, watching first Mason, then Rob, hitting the big time with guess what? Yes, you've got it – work that's come to epitomise the return to painting – the New Realism!' He sounds unutterably grim. 'Where did they get their ideas from? Any clues, Rosa?'

I can't answer for Mike, but I sure as hell know about Rob, and Zander's early daubings had absolutely no influence on what made him tick artistically. But how to put it without further antagonising Zander?

'Rob's door paintings were all to do with his childhood . . . But let's talk about you.'

He laughs. 'Don't pretend you're suddenly interested.'

'You've just made me and my friends responsible for your

ruined life. I need to know how you got back on your feet again and became the roaring success that you are today.'

'Did I ever mention Leon Goldman?'

'You said you inherited his gallery when he died.'

'Leon saved my life – literally. At that time I had a job stacking shelves in Safeways. Life was shit. I couldn't hack it any more so I bought a ton of paracetamol. I was sitting on a bench in Heath Street counting them when Leon sat down next to me and started chatting. He was the sort of guy people couldn't help opening up to. I dumped my problems all over him, and he ended up offering me a job in his gallery, restoring pictures. He said that maybe repairing other people's work might repair me – make me want to paint again. I started the following day. He was right. I stopped wanting to die and slowly began to heal. For years I couldn't allow myself to fall in love with anyone else, but eventually I met Sylvia and I realised what real love was. That what I'd felt for you was just an adolescent fantasy.'

'I'm so glad it worked out for you. Sylvia's a wonderful woman.'

Steady, Rosa, don't overdo it.

But my friends' lives depend on how I manage this conversation.

I can see in his eyes that he knows exactly what I'm at.

'She loves me more than life itself, you know.'

'I'm sure she does.'

'She'll do anything for me.'

I give an involuntary shudder. Zander sees it and smiles.

'I genuinely thought I was over you, and all the rest of the shit. Even when Mason became a household name. Even when Rob's career took off. I was still able to keep everything firmly in the past where it belonged. I thought I'd conquered my demons. I had a great marriage, a successful business, loads of friends. I'd even started to make art again, and the success of the installations in certain influential quarters meant that my greatest ambitions were well on the way to being realised.'

He sighs and his face darkens. 'Then Larry opened up next door and invited me to Rob's private view. I knew you'd all be there. I also knew that I should steer clear, but I couldn't resist. It would be the perfect opportunity to show you all how far I'd come. What a success I'd made of my life.' He stops.

'But you made no attempt to tell us who you were.'

'I was shocked by the way I felt when I found myself sitting next to you at dinner. I'm surprised you didn't see how much I was shaking. I realised to my intense shame that the last thing I wanted to do was associate myself in your mind with Willie Wanka, pathetic loser.'

'Oh Zander . . .'

'Far from shoving my great life in your face, I dreaded you recognising me. But you didn't. Actually you didn't seem interested in me at all. Suddenly it was as if twenty years had vanished and once again, there I was – desperate to impress. I really tried to shine. I boasted about the gallery, about how popular I was, how I knew everyone who was anyone. But you made polite small talk, and I could tell you were quite bored. It was humiliating.'

'I'm so sorry.'

He stares down at the table-top.

'It wasn't just you. I'd found it much more painful than I thought at the private view, looking at Rob's paintings, knowing that in college he produced crap like that,' he indicates the slashed painting on the wall behind him, 'whereas by the time he died he was doing things that were a direct rip-off of my stuff.'

'Rob never—'

'Listening to everyone at the opening raving about him was like swallowing tacks. And then, to cap it all, over dinner there was Mason, the arrogant thieving shit who's made a superstar career out of ideas he'd nicked from me, and that witch Mackenzie with her forked tongue and acid comments. When they started playing that stupid name game, everything flooded back. Everything.'

'They were just having a laugh. It didn't mean anything. They weren't picking on you. They were doing it to everybody.'

But I'm wasting my breath.

'My life had been poisoned for the second time by you and your friends. I felt like a worthless piece of shit. Worst of all, I thought I loved you again. That my marriage was a sham. I didn't know where to put myself, what to do. All I wanted was to make you love me. To show you how successful and popular I'd become. Remember that day you came to see my show? I pulled out all the stops, but although you were nice enough, I knew you couldn't really give a damn. It was terrible, like a physical pain. An all-consuming pain raging through me and gobbling me up. I couldn't eat, or sleep. I cried all the time.'

'Zander—'

'Sylvia was wonderful. It was impossible to pretend I wasn't going through some major crisis. Eventually I told her everything. And it was she who pulled me through.'

'How?'

'Well, for starters she made me see it wasn't you that I was in love with, but an old and redundant idea of you.'

'Good for her. What a sensible person—'

'Don't be so fucking patronising. Sylvia's worth a million of you with your facile phrases and glib responses. I saw you whispering about her at *Cedars* with Flavia L'Estrange. Laughing at her dress sense, her awkward manners . . .'

'No!'

'Well, let me tell you, that woman is solid gold. In my darkest hour she was there for me. When I was beside myself with pain and grief, unable to function at all, she washed me, fed me, cradled me in her arms and loved me. She didn't care that I was crying over another woman. She loved me so much that all she wanted was for me to be better.'

Where is all this leading?

'Then it came to me one day as I lay in her arms: I was where I wanted to be. Nowhere else. Certainly not with you.'

'Well, that was good, wasn't it?'

'Shut up. I also realised that the strength of feeling for you that I'd mistaken for love was actually the exact opposite. I didn't love you. I hated you. I loathed and detested you.'

The force of this hatred hits me like a smack in the face.

'The feeling was so overwhelming that it frightened me. But Sylvia was there for me yet again. She said it was good to hate. To hate meant to live. She said the hatred could be used in a way that would make me feel good again.'

Now we're getting to the meat of the matter.

'She said there was only one way forward.' He looks at me, waiting for my response.

'What's that?' I can't manage more than a whisper.

'Revenge.'

'Revenge?'

'*Get mad*, she said. *Then get even.*'

I look into his eyes, searching for signs of mercy or compassion. I'm wasting my time.

'Yes, it was my Sylvia, bless her, who came up with the solution.'

'Solution?' I can't stop myself mentally adding the adjective *final*.

'An installation, of course. As she said, I'd helped others come to terms with trauma, why shouldn't I work the same magic on myself? Recreate the moment of my greatest humiliation, and turn it into my greatest triumph?'

'Zander, please—'

'But there was a problem. Rob was dead, and for the piece to be effective, it needed all four of you. Then Joshua put in an appearance and all of a sudden it was possible.'

'Zander, I never meant to hurt you – not back then, and not now. I certainly wasn't bored by your show. It was fascinating—'

'Lying really doesn't suit you.' He flicks a switch.

Those voices again, mouthing the by now familiar words. Zander's face is contorted as he listens.

I force myself to speak, even though the inside of my mouth is like the Gobi Desert.

'Turn it off. I can see how much it hurts.'

He strokes my face. I try not to flinch.

'Yes, it still hurts. A lot. But soon . . .' He moves closer. His bad breath threatens to knock me out all on its own without any help from Sylvia's concoctions. Some things haven't changed then.

'Soon you'll all be engaged in the ultimate futile exercise, mouthing your shit to someone who's in an infinitely better position than you'll ever be, ever again. Someone who's alive while you're dead. Me. I'll visit my installation whenever I want, and say whatever I want – do whatever I want. And none of you will be able to do a damn thing about it. I'll be the puppet-master. You'll be my capering puppets. Who'll have the last laugh then?'

He glances at his watch again.

'Zander, you can't do this.'

'Watch me.'

'What about Sylvia? Would she love you so much if you were a murderer?'

'The things she saw in Ceausescu's Romania mean she doesn't have the same respect for the sanctity of human life as the rest of us. Besides, she knows I've killed already. In fact, the way I killed Steve Pyne was her idea.' He smiles. 'Added to which she loathes you with a passion. She can't forgive you for all the grief you've caused me.' He leans over conspiratorially. 'Also she's a bit jealous, though you'd never get her to admit it. You've been a thorn in her side for a while now.' He giggles. 'Thorn in her side – geddit?'

Pardon me, Zander, if I don't share the joke.

'That day you came to our house, she wanted to set the dog on you. She saw me in the trees and realised I'd been trailing you. She thought I'd reverted to lovestruck idiot mode. She was devastated, until I told her that I was following you and fantasising about the power I'd have over you when you were part of my latest installation.'

Zander's body language tells me he's getting ready to move on to the next stage of his plan.

436

'Well,' he says.

Stall him somehow.

'This conversation that you keep playing – if it happened, it was twenty years ago. You didn't record it at the time, surely?'

'God, no.'

'Then how did you reproduce it?'

'That's Emil's department. He's a genius. Once he's got a recording of someone's voice he can manipulate it any way he wants.'

'But how did he get the recordings of us?'

'Joshua was easy – he worked here. The rest of you, I don't know – he followed you around. I really don't concern myself with the nitty gritty. My job is to conceive the piece. Emil and Sylvia make it viable,' he smirks, 'as it were. Now, Rosa—'

'How do the bodies move?'

'Micro-electronics – robotics. Emil and Sylvia are magic. They work out all the fine detail in the country, then come up here to do the business. Now, I have to press on. Back to the lab, if you don't mind. Sylvia has a fairly short window of time to do her thing.'

FORTY-SEVEN

Josh lies between Jess and Mike. Three stone effigies on a medieval tomb. Not one of them shows any sign of movement.

There's one more empty slab on the end of the row.

Zander gestures towards it. 'Your carriage awaits, milady,' he intones, then grins. 'Your carriage to the next world. Be a good girl and hop up there, would you?'

If I don't do something right now, it's curtains. I size up the opposition. Sylvia, with her syringe, is the one who poses the most immediate threat.

I take a surreptitious glance around the room, looking for something to use as a weapon, but there's nothing. Just shelves full of laboratory equipment – Bunsen burners, Petri dishes, test tubes and stands, and numerous glass containers of different shapes and sizes.

Glass.

Glass is good.

There's a shelf crammed with glass things behind the row of mortuary slabs.

'Chop chop, Rosa,' says Zander. 'We don't have all night.'

I make one last appeal to reason. 'Stop now before it goes too far. You've had your revenge. After this, we'll never be able to forget how much we hurt you. You've won. Isn't it time to forgive and forget? To move on? You don't want this on your conscience for the rest of your life.'

'Are you getting on to the table, or do I have to make you?'

It's Sylvia. She and Emil move towards me.

'I'm going.' I cross to the slab. Is this the last thing I'll ever see?

It's quite high off the ground. I lean back against the shelf, ostensibly to use it as a way of levering myself on to the slab. But shielded by my body, my right hand closes around a thin cylindrical jar on the shelf behind me, and as Sylvia, needle poised, gets within plunging distance I smash the end of the jar against the shelf and jab the jagged remains towards her face.

'Back off,' I shout, and see the fear flash across her face. Keeping my back to the wall, I make for the cellar exit in the next room. They all follow. I can't take on three of them but I'm hoping the thought of having their faces slashed to ribbons will stop them making a move on me.

I'm almost there, when Sylvia strikes. I take my eye off her for one second in order to locate the ramp. That's all it takes. She knocks the broken glass jar out of my hand.

Then we're on the floor. With my first blow I kick the syringe out of her hand. It rolls under a chair. At least now it's an equal playing field. I've occasionally wondered what it would be like to be in a real rumble, but I didn't expect my Fight Club debut to be a fight for my life. Sylvia's face is contorted with rage, and she's snarling unintelligible words in Romanian. But I have the advantage: I'm bigger than she is. And defending my very existence. The amount of adrenaline pumping round my body must far exceed hers. I seize her shoulders and bang her head against the floor. Suddenly she goes limp.

I've KO'd her.

But there's no countdown.

Zander and Emil are nearly on me. I grab the syringe from under the chair and wave it at them.

'One step nearer and you'll get this!'

Emil keeps on coming. I don't hesitate. I jab the needle into him with as much force as I can, and push the plunger.

The effect is gratifyingly instantaneous. His mountainous bulk sways, then topples, hitting the floor with a resounding crash that sets all the glass jars tinkling on their shelves.

Two down, one to go. Not bad for a lifelong pacifist.

But then Zander's on me, foul breath making me gag.

'Want to ruin my life all over again? I don't think so. I'm going to do you and do your mates, and when you're dancing to my tune I'm going to laugh myself stupid.'

He's far too heavy. I can't budge him. His fingers close round my throat. I try to prise them off but it's hopeless. This is it.

'Steady on, old boy.'

FORTY-EIGHT

Theo Grey.

Theo's in it with them. He's part of it.

Shy, gentle Theo with his passionate love of his manuscript collection. Theo, highly respected director of *Grey & Son*. Theo, loving brother of Flavia.

This can't be true.

There's no time for reflection. Zander's rolled off me. I make my move, but he's got me before I'm even on my feet.

'What's going on?'

Zander's hand grips my arm. 'It's personal.'

Theo looks at Emil and Sylvia, both still out cold, and then at my friends on the mortuary tables.

'Why don't we go into your studio and sit down? Then you can tell me all about it.'

'It's not really your concern.'

'Oh? I think it is.'

Is that a threat?

Zander hesitates, then crosses to his wife.

'Sweetheart, wake up.' Gently he strokes her face.

'Leave me alone,' she mutters.

He takes his jacket off, folds it up and places it tenderly beneath her head. 'Sleep for now, my angel.' Then he looks at me and Theo.

'I suppose we can't progress till Sylvia comes round, anyway.'

He marches me through to his studio. Theo follows. He flashes me a glance. It's cold – no recognition.

Zander says, 'You really needn't concern yourself with this, Theo. All I'm prepared to say is that in the long run it could be of great benefit to the business.'

'How?'

'Can I trust you?'

'I think I've proved myself by now, don't you?'

Zander sizes him up. 'OK, then. I reckon some of our clients would be prepared to pay for an extension of our services.'

'What do you mean?'

'They think they're special, that the normal rules don't apply to them. Their expectations of what they can and can't do is different from those of ordinary people. I suspect they'd pay hand-somely for the major irritants in their lives to be transformed through art. For those irritants, from being the grit in the oyster, to become the pearl beyond price.'

Theo frowns. 'By being immortalised in one of your instal-lations?'

'Precisely.'

'Is that why those people are laid out next door like fish on a slab?'

'My way of discovering if my theory's valid. By trying it out on myself.'

'And Rosa?'

'Let's just say she's the largest piece of grit in my oyster.'

'So let me get this straight. Rosa and her friends have done something that's upset you, and to make yourself feel better you're planning to kill them and turn them into installations?'

'Put crudely, yes.'

'Furthermore, you're proposing that this is a service you could offer your clients? To cater for people's desire to revenge themselves on those they feel have wronged them in some way?'

'Revenge is the wrong word. I see it more as a purging – to enable the people who run things to function at optimum capacity. Which, in its turn, would benefit the rest of us. What do you think?'

Theo stares at Zander for a long time.

'I think you're barking,' he says eventually. 'A rabid dog. You need to be put out of your misery.'

From his pocket he produces a gun. He leans over and presses it against Zander's head. There's a loud noise, and Zander slumps forward over the table, half his head blown off.

FORTY-NINE

It takes a split second, that's all. One moment Zander's explaining his wondrous scheme to Theo, the next he's dead. My ears ringing from the noise of the gunshot, I sit, paralysed, for what seems like for ever.

Eventually I regain the use of my faculties. Theo sits as if carved out of stone, seemingly unaware of my presence. Dare I risk moving, or will he shoot me too? I rise to my feet, trying to attract as little attention as possible. He seems oblivious, but as I reach the door, his head shoots up. His voice booming into the dreadful silence makes me jump.

'Greed and obsession,' he says. 'Banal, isn't it?'

The gun is pointing roughly in the direction of my stomach. 'Please, Theo . . .'

'The day Larry gave me that first manuscript was the day I stopped being in charge of my life. They're so beautiful. So desirable. Aren't they, Rosa?'

I manage a nod.

'The more I had, the more I wanted. I spent all my own money, borrowed from Flavia – even started dipping into the firm's coffers. Then I met Zander at my club. Of course, it was a set-up. He deliberately targeted me. We had a few drinks and I ended up telling him all about my collection. When I mentioned I was after a particularly fine piece, but that I didn't know how to finance it, he said I might be interested in a little venture he was launching.'

'His installations?'

'He made it sound like a philanthropic service – easing people's pain and grief.'

'What did he want from you?'

'Can't you guess?' He gestures towards Sylvia's room, still clutching the gun. Fear closes my throat.

'The people who use *Grey*'s are the elite, the ones who think the normal rules don't apply to them. This is the market that Zander wanted to tap into. He proposed that I give him a regular rundown of our bereaved clients. He'd do a background check, and if he thought they'd be susceptible to his scheme, he'd make an approach, couching it in such a way that if the idea appeared to horrify them, he'd be able to backtrack and claim they'd misunderstood what he was saying. But if they wanted in, my job would be to remove the bodies before burial or cremation, do the basic embalming and then transfer them here.'

He's glaring at me. He wants input.

'And you agreed?' I say, for want of something else.

'I never thought it would happen – after all, it's pretty bloody far-fetched, isn't it? But to my amazement a couple of people fell for it. They paid an absolute fortune. When I saw how much money I could make, I was hooked.'

'Surely you knew how wrong it was.' The words tumble out before I can stop them.

He gestures dismissively, with the gun. I don't know how much longer I can exist at this level of fear.

'The persuasive power of all that loot was too strong to resist. I blanked out on the ghastly reality. I told myself we were performing a worthwhile service. Lord knows, people were grateful enough. I felt like Jesus Christ raising Lazarus from the dead.'

'So what changed?'

He rubs his forehead wearily. 'Sickness.'

'You're sick?'

'Sickness of the spirit. It crept up on me until finally I felt my inner self was decaying more rapidly than the corpses who came through our doors. But I couldn't stop buying more and more items for my collection. I was corrupted. In the true sense of the word.' His eyes are full of despair. 'I've taken the fine reputation of a two-hundred-year-old firm and destroyed it – *Grey's* won't survive the year – and I've deceived my sister, whom I love more than anything in the world.'

'But it's over now – you killed him.'

Theo's laugh is bleak. 'Confirmation, if I needed it, of the person I've become. Only the truly corrupt can terminate the life of another human being. I'm a murderer – same as him.'

'You killed him to save me. I'd be dead by now if you hadn't arrived.'

'I kidded myself that I wasn't doing anything wrong. It wasn't illegal, after all. People have the right to say what should become of their dear departed. If they want them turned into art instead of being buried or cremated, then that's their business. And I tried to believe that I was helping people to come to terms with their grief . . .' His mouth is working, but he can hardly form the words. 'Then yesterday Zander brought a body to *Grey's* . . . but this time there were no grieving relatives.'

'Kenny Dang?'

'I could see he'd been strangled, but did I demand an explanation? No, I just kept quiet and did my job. I'd passed a point of no return. I'd turned a blind eye to murder.'

'Oh Theo . . .'

'I saw what I'd become, and I detested myself. But I couldn't face going to the police and plunging *Grey's* into a public scandal. I didn't sleep at all last night, wondering what to do. I thought maybe I could implicate the others, but somehow keep my name out of it. Not for my own sake, but for Flavia and the firm.' He sighs. 'But in my heart I knew the game was up. Then I remembered a particularly fine breviary that I'd been lusting after.' His face darkens. 'God help me, in spite of everything, I couldn't bear to lose it. I thought if I could acquire this one last thing . . .' His eyes burn fiercely.

'Put the gun down, Theo. It frightens me.'

'But I just couldn't bring myself to buy it with money from Zander, not knowing what I did about Kenny Dang's death. So I went to *L'Estrange East* and asked Larry for a loan. He turned me down, as I knew he would, but it was while I was there that you came in shouting for Joshua. I realised that before going to the police, I desperately needed to talk, and that the someone I wanted to talk to was you.'

'Why me?'

'Because you were there: A good listener. I felt that if I could make you understand, then I'd be able to cope with whatever happened. So I followed you to that bar. But I couldn't bring myself to speak. I was too ashamed. I followed you back to the gallery. When I saw you go in the back entrance, I knew something was badly wrong. The only people who know about that door are clients, and they're bound by total secrecy. It's one of the unbreakable rules. If anything leaked out it would be the scandal of the century. In fact, clients know that Zander has a safe deposit box somewhere containing incriminating tapes of them in their installations. It's his insurance policy. Anyone tempted to blab knows that if Zander was exposed, they'd be exposed with him.'

'You let me go in there and take my chances?'

'I got cold feet. I wasn't sure what you'd do once you'd seen the installations. I chickened out. I couldn't face the scandal after all . . . So I drove home.'

'Nice one.'

'But I couldn't leave you. I had to make sure you were all right, so I came back. But by the time I arrived there was no sign of you. I searched the building from top to bottom, and ended up down here. I heard what Zander was planning and knew I had to stop him. I remembered Emil once showing me a gun which he kept in a drawer in his lab – a souvenir from his unsavoury past in Romania – so while you were all busy scrapping, I helped myself.'

'Are you going to kill me too?'

Before he can answer, the studio door opens.

Sylvia Zinovieff registers Theo with his gun and Zander's body. That it's a body, and not her living breathing husband any more is obvious, since he no longer possesses a face.

It's all over in an instant.

One moment she's attacking Theo, fists flying. The next there's a shot, she slides to the ground and Theo's looking at the gun as if it's an alien life-form.

He's committed two murders. I'm witness to both.

Slowly he raises both his eyes and the gun, and looks at me.

'I'm so sorry, Rosa,' he says.

For a moment it seems that time really does stop.

Then I dive into Sylvia's lab, slamming the door behind me. There's another shot.

I listen to the thudding of my heart. I look at Jess, Mike and Josh, oblivious on their stone slabs, and Emil, equally comatose on the floor. Seconds seem like hours before I reopen the door to the studio.

Theo Grey's body lies beside his two victims, gun still clutched in his hand. His turquoise eyes gaze sightlessly up at me above the red gash where his mouth used to be.

FIFTY

There have been many times in my life when I've heard the phrase 'establishment cover-up' bandied around in the wake of some particular scandal. I've always nodded sagely, as if fully cognisant of the depths to which those with power and influence will sink in order to keep from the world the knowledge of their imperfections. But a part of me has never truly believed in such carefully orchestrated and wide-ranging conspiracies.

Until now.

The two constables who responded to my 999 call were quickly joined by a Commander of the Metropolitan Police Force and his colleagues, once they realised the ramifications of what they were dealing with. And from that moment onwards a blanket of silence has descended over the whole affair. It was put about that *Nature Morte* had gone bankrupt and that the Zinovieffs had fled the country. Their deaths never hit the papers. Nor did the swift and furtive deportation of Emil Barbu to Romania where he was apparently wanted in connection with crimes against humanity committed under the Ceausescu regime.

As far as the general public is concerned, Zander's installations never existed. The world remains in blissful ignorance of what went on behind the mirror in the chic office at the back of *Nature Morte*.

While still at the police station, filling them in about the horrific events of the night, I was visited by a discreet gentleman in a well-cut suit who asked in the nicest possible way that I keep quiet about what's happened. His justification was that a couple of the people who'd purchased items from Zander's special collection were Very Important Indeed and had to be protected in the interests of national security. Jess, Mike and Josh have also encountered this man of the shadows.

The three of them made a pretty swift recovery. They were kept in hospital for twenty-four hours, and as soon as the police had finished with me, I hurried over there.

My first stop was Josh. When he saw me, his face lit up and he held out his arms. We were still entwined when there was a discreet cough. In the doorway stood Jess, looking pale but otherwise fine. I disentangled myself from Josh and rushed over to her. More hugs. Big ones. Then an awkward pause, the events of the night still not enough, in all their horror, to blot out the knowledge of our last disastrous conversation.

She spoke first.

'Do you mind if I borrow her for a few minutes, Joshua?'

We went to her room and she filled me in on what had happened to her. She'd just dropped Lozz off at his grandmother's for a couple of days, and was walking back to her car when she was seized from behind and hustled into the back of a van. That's the last thing she remembered until waking up in hospital. She was astonished about the true identity of Zander Zinovieff.

'Willie Wanka,' she murmured. 'I didn't have a clue when I met him at Rob's dinner, although I did say he reminded me of someone. No wonder he looked so defensive, waiting for me to realise he was that slob who was always hovering around you with his fucking tongue hanging out.' She grimaced. 'I must have been pretty vile for him to want to turn me into his stuffed pet.' She looked at me properly for the first time. 'What goes around comes around, eh?'

I couldn't think of any response, but there was no need. She was struggling to make sense of it for herself. 'I wonder if it's the same for everybody, that time – the student time. Life was so heightened – so vivid. Everything seemed magnified – work, friendship, love – everything. Me, Rob, Mike and you. Always you at the still centre, with everyone else swirling round you.'

It wasn't sorted yet. This thing between her and me.

She was still talking. 'When real life kicked in, we thought we'd lost it – that intensity. But it was still there, wasn't it? Burned into our brains. Rob's private view was the catalyst that caused it all to kick off again.'

All the aggression had gone from her voice. I wanted to say that if I'd made her feel bad about herself, I was sorry. Really sorry. That I wouldn't have hurt her for the world. Then I pulled back. Why should I apologise? She was the one who'd blown a gaping hole through our friendship with her wild accusations.

She watched the progression of thoughts across the ever-open

452

book commonly known as my face. 'I've been a little crazy over the past few weeks.'

'Yes.'

'I've said some fucking awful things.'

'Yes.'

'If I could take them all back, I would.'

'So that stuff you said – your feelings about our friendship – was it all lies?'

She couldn't look at me.

'See, that's the problem, Jess. You meant it, didn't you?'

'No!' The word burst out of her. 'Not like that.'

'Like what, then?'

She chewed on her lip, trying to formulate the right words. 'You're my best friend. I can't imagine life without you. Which is why I've always been deeply ashamed of this stupid jealousy shit.'

'I really don't understand. Jealousy about what?'

'Just . . . things . . .'

'What things?'

She allowed herself a small smile. 'Looks.'

'Come on!'

'You're thin. I'm fat. Sometimes that really pisses me off.'

'Oh please!'

'And you manage life so well while I just seem to lurch from crisis to crisis.'

'Last winter was me managing life well, was it? I don't know how I'd have coped without you then.'

'Yes, but none of that was your fault. I, on the other hand, seem to be constantly shooting myself in the foot. I just can't get things right.'

'How can you say that? What about your job? Everyone knows what a brilliant teacher you are. And Lozz. Wonderful though he is, he's not easy. I can't think of many single parents who'd have coped so well with all the problems a Down's syndrome child can bring.'

'I mean emotional stuff really. I always seem to be weeping on your shoulder about some shit bloke. And you always seem to be dishing out the sensible advice. It kind of grates. Sometimes I really resent it.'

'You've hidden it well.'

'I'm the world expert at keeping it separate from all the good things I feel about you. It's like caging a wild animal in a dungeon and pretending the distant roaring is the wind. I've always tried my best to ignore it. I thought I'd succeeded. Then I fell for Mike and all hell broke loose. I'm so fucking sorry.' She started to cry.

She was my friend, my oldest friend, who'd just escaped a truly horrible death. And my relief that she was alive was overwhelming.

'Tell you what, Jess, let's forget that these last few weeks ever happened.'

She looked at me. 'Do you really mean it?'

I tried to smile. 'Yes.'

It was my turn to avoid her gaze, because it wasn't quite true. The brain was willing, but the spirit was still too bruised to forget the pain her words had caused. And the trust had gone – that unconditional assumption that whatever else happened, Jess was always 100 per cent on my side, always there for me.

What she had told me couldn't be unsaid, however much I wanted things to get back to the place where we once were. And that place, I now knew, had always been different for her than it had been for me. The friendship I thought I had was an illusion.

Nothing would ever be the same, and only time would reveal where we really stood in relation to each other. Jess knew it and so did I. When, once again, we hugged each other in the bleak hospital room I, for one, was aware that the close embrace was the easy option.

It avoided eye-contact.

As for Mike, he couldn't wait to vacate the premises. The country as well as the hospital. A car arrived before the end of the day to whisk him to Heathrow where he'd booked the first flight he could back to LA. As he said himself, his mural was finished, what was there for him to stay for? He'd given his statement to the police: Zander had press-ganged him into *Nature Morte* to give an opinion on a new artist he was thinking of signing on. He remembered nothing after sitting down in the office.

His reaction on finding out that Zander was Alex Williams, the man whose life he'd trashed all those years ago, was pure Mike. He said that he hoped the police wouldn't dwell too much on Zander's student days in any future statements to the media. He felt there was no sense in tarnishing his global reputation with silly and inaccurate tales of misspent youth. At this point in his tale he paused, waiting for our response.

'No sense at all, Mike,' I said eventually.

Jess just sucked her teeth.

We waited for him to make some reference to the games he'd been playing with Jess. A proper apology, perhaps. We should have known better. Proper apologies aren't Mike's style. When in doubt, take the easy way out.

And right on cue, when the silence became unbearable, he spoke. 'Well, girls, I gotta split. Take care now, Rosy Posy. Love ya, Jess.' He swept us both up in one of his massive embraces.

And then he was gone.

I looked at Jess. She smiled, ruefully, but with a certain weary affection. 'Arsehole,' she said.

At least she and I could agree on that bit of our mutual past.

FIFTY-ONE

When Josh and I finally arrived home, it felt as if I'd been away for years and experienced several lifetimes in the intervening period. After we'd properly acclimatised ourselves to normality, I brought Josh's portfolio downstairs. I needed to look at something beautiful and good, and enjoying the photographs together went some way towards distracting us from our recent experiences. The sheer vitality and exuberance of the work was a wonderful corrective to the death-drenched mausoleum behind *Nature Morte*.

Josh couldn't quite believe my unqualified enthusiasm. 'All I can see are the faults and the shots that I didn't get.'

'All I can see is that your brother would have been incredibly proud of you.'

'Really?'

'You'd better believe it. And tomorrow we start the big search,' I said. 'Only the best dealer in town's going to be good enough for my brother-in-law.'

Think positive. Think of the good things. Only in that way can you blot out the darkness, forget the horror. I found that out last winter.

Later we turned on the news. No mention of Zander Zinovieff, or his activities. But two items stood out. The death of Theo Grey, Funeral Director to the stars, was briefly announced. Mr Grey had been found dead the previous night. There were no suspicious circumstances.

'Yeah right,' I said.

However, it was the lead item that made us really sit up and take notice. David Borodino, multimillionaire property tycoon and owner of the *Correspondent*, was retiring, effective immediately. He was selling all his holdings including the newspaper, and embarking that very evening on an extended solo trip around the world on his yacht.

'To every man there comes a moment when he feels the need to commune with the spirit. I have reached such a moment,' he was quoted as saying. 'I intend to retreat from the world and contemplate the absolute.'

'Pretentious git.'

'Isn't that a bit sudden?' said Josh.

'Very.'

Sudden didn't quite cover it. My brain went into overdrive as I ran through the events of the past few weeks. Within seconds everything fell into place.

'It's the last piece of the puzzle.'

'What do you mean?'

'Where did Zinovieff get the funding for his installations? No way would he have sufficient capital, not with all the technology

458

involved. And anyone prepared to invest the mega-bucks needed for such a dodgy enterprise would have to be in on the plan.'

David Borodino.

'I reckon he bankrolled the whole caboodle,' I told Josh. 'Even provided Zander with a place at *Cedars* where Sylvia and Emil could perfect their experiments. Zander actually told me how good Borodino had been to him. When he mentioned the important client with his own private space, I was very stupid not to have guessed who it was. He said he was preparing something for this client – a special installation that took the process one stage further . . .' I stopped, as the full implications of what I was saying sank in. 'An installation whose central figures didn't die from illness or accident . . .'

'What are you saying?'

'Zander said he didn't kill Kenny Dang. So who did?'

Josh's eyes widened. 'Borodino?'

I remembered the man's quickly concealed rage at the dinner in *Zizz* when Zander had called him Shirley Temple. I also remembered Larry's remark about David's machismo. What would his reaction have been when he discovered he'd been trying to bed a bloke?

'Think of the disgust and humiliation he would have felt when he discovered that Leni was Kenny. I reckon he went ballistic and strangled him in a fit of rage.'

'It makes sense.' Josh frowns. 'But why add Kenny to the installation?'

'To regain power and control over the scum who'd had the bare-faced audacity to trick him in such a way – to humiliate Kenny in death as Kenny had humiliated him in life.'

'Another thing. Although Zander confessed to killing Steve Pyne, it was still Borodino's installation.'

'Yes. Steve badly dented his pride.'

'How?' Josh wanted to know.

'By humiliating him in front of the entire art world. He insulted him, threw drink down him, laughed at him. *Filthy capitalist leech*. That's what he said immediately after he did it. And that's what he was made to say in the piece. As soon as Borodino heard about Steve's death, he must have commissioned Zander to turn him into an installation.'

'I'm glad the man didn't have a grudge against me,' Josh shuddered.

'Quite.'

'Do you think the police have worked out Borodino's involvement?'

'I don't know, but sooner or later they will. That must be the reason for his sudden departure.'

'But wherever he goes they'll catch up with him.'

'Maybe.'

'What do you mean?' Josh looked at me.

'Maybe they won't even try.'

'They can't just ignore what he's done.'

'Did you see a news item about the discovery of a triple shooting in a place frequented by some of the most important and influential people in the country, where the latest advances in taxidermy and robo-technology have been employed on the corpses of their loved ones in order for them to act out some of their private hang-ups?' How cynical I sound.

'No, but—'

'We already know there's a big cover-up going on.'

'Legally speaking, Zander's collectors probably haven't done anything wrong, so on that score I can't see much harm in the authorities keeping quiet. But we're talking about murder here. If all the killers were dead, then there'd be no harm in letting things drop. But only two of them are – Zander and Theo. Not Borodino. They can't let him blatantly get away with killing people. Whoever he is.'

'I think they just have.'

But Josh was right. To let David Borodino get away with murder was a step too far. I spent the rest of the day wondering what to do. If I went to the police I'd just be making a whole heap of trouble for myself. Maybe I should just let it go. But then I had a brainwave: if I threatened to tell the media, it would make it extremely difficult for the authorities to bury things. They'd have to pursue Borodino. I couldn't live with myself if I did nothing. If I stayed silent I'd be colluding in letting a murderer get off scot free.

The following morning I knocked on Josh's bedroom door to tell him that I was going to the police station.

'Josh—'

'Shh!' He was listening to the *Today* programme.

David Borodino was gone.

Like Robert Maxwell, he'd apparently fallen over the side of his yacht as it reached the open sea on the first leg of his spiritual voyage. The boat had been found in the early hours of the morning, drifting unmanned off the coast of the Scilly Isles. Unlike Maxwell, Borodino's body hadn't been recovered. The incident was being viewed by the authorities as a tragic accident.

A tragic accident – or suicide? Or a Lord Lucan scenario?

From my limited knowledge of Borodino I very much doubted he'd take his own life. He was a gambler. He'd play things out to the end.

How very fortuitous for the authorities. With Borodino's death, Kenny Dang's murder could be quietly forgotten.

If he *was* dead.

I was pondering the implications of this when the doorbell rang. Two men stood outside, propping up a vast package.

'Mrs Thorn?'

'Yes?'

'Special Delivery.' They manoeuvred the thing into the hall and propped it against the wall.

'Cheers, love.'

I signed for it and off they went, leaving me staring mystified at the huge thing.

'Josh! Can you come down here!' I finally called.

Together we ripped off the packaging.

It was *Shed Door Outside* – Rob's painting. The one I sold to David Borodino.

There was a note. *This belongs with you. Be happy. Live well.* *D.*

My eyes were so blurred with tears that I could hardly see the painting.

We were both deep in contemplation of Rob's last work, when the front door opened and I received my second shock of the morning.

'Yo, Mum!'

Danny.

The colour drained from his face as he caught sight of Josh.

'Welcome home, Dan,' I said. 'Meet your Uncle Josh.'

EPILOGUE

At the end of September, when the trees are just beginning to turn, Consort Park holds its annual celebrations. There are competitions and stalls and jazz bands and a bouncy castle and international food displays and lots more. This year, in a corner of the flower garden, the newly installed sculpture *Andromeda* is about to be inauguarated by one of our local councillors. A small crowd has gathered to witness the event. It's mainly older people – those with young families are off indulging in the many activities which Consort Park lays on for its day of fun. I'm with Anna and Danny, both safe and sound after their summer adventures. They are whingeing because they want to join the long queue waiting for a ride in the tethered hot-air balloon which floats above the park, and Josh is doing his best to persuade them that they owe it to me to stay and give moral support, since *Andromeda* is my project. I suspect he's on to a losing wicket, but just to watch him interacting with his niece and nephew makes my heart sing. After the pair of them had got over the shock of seeing their

463

father's stunt double, they were ecstatic to have a new uncle, and Josh has filled a gap in their lives that I thought would remain forever empty. They are trying to persuade him to settle in England for good – preferably with us in Consort Park. Since he's been taken on by a major London dealer, they might get their wish.

I turn to Caro, who's gazing at *Andromeda*. 'Any regrets?'

She smiles. 'Only little ones.'

Caro deserves all the happiness she can get. She's had to face the fact not only that Steve was murdered, but that he'd betrayed her with Kenny Dang in their special and private place.

I told her what had happened after she imagined Steve safely in the ground for all eternity. She deserved the truth. But she won't visit his new grave.

'I can't grieve for him any more,' she told me. 'A bit of me still loves him, and always will. But not in that way. What I feel for him now is pity more than anything else. What happened to him was ghastly – far worse than he deserved.'

Soon after this conversation she asked me whether, instead of *Marble One*, I would prefer *Andromeda* for Consort Park.

'But that was Steve's last present to you,' I said. 'You said you'd never part with it.'

'I don't want it,' she told me. 'Not any more. I won't take money for it, either. It's tainted.'

This was shooting herself in the foot.

'You've always wanted your own gallery. This money could be your start-up fund. If you feel it's too much, fair enough. I've another idea. You take some of the money, and with the rest, Consort Park Residents' Association could set up a trust fund for young sculptors fresh from art school and just starting out. There could be a rolling programme which changes year on year, showing their work in another corner of the flower garden.'

So Caro is to open a gallery in Clerkenwell. In fact, it is she who is now Joshua's dealer. The moment she saw his work she was desperate to represent him. Larry can't believe she doesn't work for him any more and is constantly on the phone plaguing her with questions about his business. He and Flavia are here today, though I'm not quite sure why – I assumed his major hissy fit over me not choosing one of his artists for the park would last for several more weeks. Probably Flavia persuaded him to bring her. Either that or he sees a business opportunity to promote work by his younger artists for the Consort Park Sculpture Trust.

Flavia's looking frailer than ever after the death of her brother and the subsequent closure of *Grey & Son*. I don't know whether she's been told the truth about Theo's activities and the manner of his death. I hope not. He wouldn't have wanted her to live with that knowledge, and neither do I.

'Doesn't she look wonderful?' It's Gillian, now on the path to full recovery, in mind as well as in body. She gazes at *Andromeda* with real passion, her dislike of Steve Pyne swept aside. A lesser person would be more circumspect about broadcasting such a change of heart, but she doesn't give a damn what people think. It's great art and that's all that matters to her in the end. She's decided to start a new art magazine, and has thrown herself into the project with all her old enthusiasm and skill. Maybe one day she'll return to her biography of Elena Dias, but that day's still a long way off. At the moment the thought of Elena conjures madness and pain, and she's determined to put all that behind her. She told me recently about her moment of epiphany. She'd returned alone to Lamb's Conduit Street after her stay in the private clinic, having refused to let me accompany her. She was glad to be home, but dreading the shades of Peter, which lurked in every corner of the little flat, ready to leap out and ensnare her with their beguiling sweetness. But as she stepped through the front door into her pretty living room, cleared of all the detritus of her illness, and glowing warm and welcoming in afternoon sunlight, to her surprise what she felt was a great sense of peace. She unpacked and then made her first cup of tea, going through all the familiar rituals as if she'd never been away. It was only after she'd sat down in her usual armchair that she realised what she'd just done.

She'd taken the photo of Peter from the table beside her chair and placed it on the mantelpiece on the far side of the room.

He stared out at her, solemn and loving as ever. But the expression in his eyes seemed different. As if he viewed her from a long way off. From a place where she could not follow. Didn't want to follow. Not yet. And then she realised something else: *she had no wish to speak to him.* Not to a photographic image which couldn't hear her.

Gillian and I meet a couple of times a week. We increasingly enjoy each other's company. After all my doom and gloom about the nature of friendship, my capacity for involvement doesn't seem to have diminished too much. However, if I've learned anything over the past months, it's to take affection where you find it, in a fairly existential way. Enjoy the moment, but don't build your life round it.

Leni came to my house the other day. She was the last person I expected to see. She stood, hunched on the doorstep, her hair dull and tangled and her face gaunt and grey without its usual heavy layer of make-up.

She didn't bother with any of the social niceties. 'They said you saw him.'

I knew immediately who she was talking about.

'Yes,' I said. What did she want from me?

'Did he – did he look at peace?'

I thought of the horrific parody of a person sprawling lifeless in Zinovieff's vile excuse for a work of art.

'He looked as if he were sleeping.'

If she wanted to hear more, it wouldn't be from me.

'Thank you,' she said.

An awkward silence followed. I didn't want to invite her in, but I couldn't very well shut the door in her face.

'I thought you'd like to know, I'm going away.'

I had to stop myself from saying, 'Good riddance.' I was ashamed at the amount of animosity I still felt towards her. The civilised part of my brain looked on in disapproval at my lack of compassion towards this poor girl who'd lost her beloved brother in such dreadful circumstances. But I couldn't help it. Her loss didn't negate what she'd done. Leni and Kenny were two sides of the same coin. By allowing his protective obsession with her to develop unchecked, she'd made it possible for him to embark on his trail of destruction and deceit. And even now, underneath her apologies and protestations, I sensed in her a smug pride that he'd do such things for her sake.

'I'm going to Vietnam,' she said. 'I need to find my roots – deal with that lost part of me. I thought maybe Gillian could ask for her old job back.'

It was said in such a casual way that I couldn't contain my hostility.

'I'm sure she'd be thrilled to pick over your leftovers,' I said.

This little outburst effectively killed any further attempts at communication, and after a muttered farewell, Leni slunk off.

I told Gillian what Leni had said. She shook her head. 'You can't go back. The past has gone. The present and what you do with it to make your future – that's the only reality.'

I'm trying to apply this principle to my relationship with Jess. She and Lozz are here today. At the moment she's clutching his arm in a desperate and unsuccessful bid to stop him stroking Andromeda's left breast. I catch her eye. She smiles at me. We've a way to go yet, she and I, but we're both still hanging in there.

At last I spot Pru Gibb, mistress of ceremonies. She's bustling along, hand firmly on the elbow of a scrawny scrap of a man who looks scared stiff.

She mounts a specially prepared dais and calls everybody to attention. 'Ladies and gentlemen, I'd like to welcome Councillor Crosby, who has very kindly agreed to inaugurate the Minnie Brady Memorial Sculpture for us here today.'

As Councillor Crosby embarks on what turns out to be a very long and tedious speech, I hear Larry mutter, 'We can't help feeling a Raymond Banks carving would have been so much more suitable in this context.'

'Shut up, Larry,' says Gillian and winks at me.

Thorn

Vena Cork

In the city's open spaces, there is time to kill . . .

A tragedy has changed Rosa Thorn's life for ever. Now she has to start again with a new job, a new school for her children and some empty space in her life. But strange things start to happen . . .

When a growing sense of unease turns into sudden violence, Rosa fears for her safety and even more so for the wellbeing of her children. For her daughter is the subject of someone's demented infatuation. But like a diseased town fox, the real threat stalks the shadows, in the night-black recesses of the under-growth, not just of the city, but of the human mind . . .

Vena Cork's astonishing, thrilling debut novel is as shocking as it is unputdownable – a brilliant, menacing, psychological thriller that takes you to the edge of darkness.

'One of those rare and energetic books you can't put down yet don't want to end' *The Times*

'An outstanding debut' *Time Out*

0 7553 2394 7

headline

Jacquot
and the Waterman

Martin O'Brien

The Waterman is no ordinary killer, but then Daniel Jacquot is no ordinary detective.

An ex-rugby player, still remembered for the winning try he scored for France in a Five Nations final against the English at Twickenham, Daniel Jacquot is now a chief inspector, working homicide with the Marseilles *Judiciaire*.

It's here, in this city by the sea, that a shadowy, elusive killer steps on to the field of play, drugging, raping and drowning three young women in as many months. With a new partner, a rising body count and only a three-word tattoo to work with, Jacquot tracks his quarry, gradually closing on a ruthless, yet sometimes eccentric murderer the press have christened *The Waterman*.

Jacquot and the Waterman is a dazzlingly accomplished page-turner and the debut of a brilliant new voice in crime fiction.

0 7553 2286 X

headline

The Graft

Martina Cole

Looking back, Nick Leary couldn't say exactly what kept him awake that night. He'd had a lot on his mind; perhaps he'd been thinking about the 'respectable' business that he ran, or about his two sons sleeping in the room next door. Or was it simply the sound of his beautiful wife's steady breathing beside him . . .

Whatever it was, he was awake when he heard someone's footsteps downstairs, and Nick's instinct was to fight. It had always been that way, to protect the things he treasured most: his family, his privacy, his reputation. He'd grafted for these things all his life and no one was going to jeopardise them now.

But Nick's instinct was wrong, and what happened that night was the start of something even he could not stop . . .

Praise for Martina Cole's previous bestsellers:

'A blinding good read' Ray Winstone

'Cole pulls no punches, writes as she sees it, refuses to patronise or condescend to either her characters or fans' *Independent on Sunday*

'The stuff of legend . . . vicious, nasty and utterly compelling' *Mirror*

'A real page turner' *More!* magazine

'Violent and edgy . . . powerfully written' *Eve*

'The strength of Cole's novels is their dark underworld setting . . . It's gripping stuff' *She*

0 7472 6766 9

headline

Now you can buy any of these other bestselling books from your bookshop or *direct from the publisher.*

FREE P&P AND UK DELIVERY
(Overseas and Ireland £3.50 per book)

Thorn	Vena Cork	£6.99
Deadly Web	Barbara Nadel	£6.99
Mandrake	Paul Eddy	£6.99
Flint	Paul Eddy	£6.99
Trans Am	Robert Ryan	£7.99
Underdogs	Robert Ryan	£7.99
Nine Mil	Robert Ryan	£7.99
No Good Deed	Manda Scott	£5.99
Night Mares	Manda Scott	£5.99
Stronger than Death	Manda Scott	£5.99
A Place of Safety	Caroline Graham	£6.99
Missing	Mary Stanley	£6.99
Alarm Call	Quintin Jardine	£6.99
Lethal Intent	Quintin Jardine	£6.99
Atlantis	David Gibbins	£6.99
Shattered Icon	Bill Napier	£6.99

TO ORDER SIMPLY CALL THIS NUMBER

01235 400 414

or visit our website: www.madaboutbooks.com

Prices and availability subject to change without notice.